Where the Sun Don't Shine

By

Scott R. Baillie

This book is a work of fiction. Places, events, and situations in this story are purely fictional. Any resemblance to actual persons, living or dead, is coincidental.

ISBN: 1-4107-1183-8 (e-book)
ISBN: 1-4107-1184-6 (Paperback)
ISBN: 1-4107-4281-4 (Dust Jacket)

This book is printed on acid free paper.

1stBooks - rev. 04/05/03

Dedication

To my mother, Evie Baillie, in loving memory.

Your life shines in my heart.

PREFACE

Life in a small American town is often painted with images of unlocked doors, quaint houses, neighbors knowing everybody's business and having a true sense of community and patriotism. Real Norman Rockwell stuff. Perhaps that exists somewhere, but rarely within the city limits of the many mining towns dotting the Rocky Mountains and her foothills, where disaster, pollution, wild west values and violence are the rule.

Yet mining towns and their functions, good and bad, are at the root of everything that has made this country remarkable. Gold rushes, mother lodes and silver strikes drove our westward expansion and turned the resources of the most isolated areas into the riches of the cities. Without the dreams and hardships of miners, without their sweat, their broken bodies and bloody sacrifices, we as a nation would have withered and never prospered. Or so it went for most of our national history.

By the mid seventies, the federal government, liberal politicians, various labor organizations and selfish corporate boards were extinguishing the mining concerns throughout the greater West. The miner became extinct along with his family and community. A country built on smelted ore, refined steel and human sweat was changed, in the span of a decade, to a nation backed by burger franchises and microchip factories.

Both my grandfathers were miners. My father was a miner and a mining engineer. His brothers were miners as were both of mine at various times. My cousins mined and so did my nephew. I financed my undergraduate degree by working summers and weekends a mile beneath a mountain, drilling, blasting and digging ore. I learned more about mankind while underground than in any of my subsequent wanderings.

I have met, worked with or befriended rock stars, writers, military generals, television celebrities, millionaires, a billionaire and even a rocket scientist or two, but it's the hard rock miner that fascinated me the most. The miner's view of life, economies, people, relationships and the world as a whole was usually simple and always right.

This novel was born over coffee with my friend Grant. Our ruminations about life, God, politics, Hollywood, kids and careers would always weave back to my days growing up in a small Northwest mining town, its texture of life, and the spirited substance of the people there. This book, while a work of fiction, reflects those people's attitudes and perceptions as witnessed by a teenage boy. The story is tragic and hopeful. It is a fabrication, a story, drawn from the passion of miners, their families and the imagination of a miner's son.

December 2002   Scott R. Baillie
Seattle, Washington

Acknowledgments

Thanks to: God for the gift; my father, J. Melvin Baillie, the miner's heart, you are my hero; my daughter Stephanie and son-in-law Daniel Richard, I love you; to their son Logan, Papa's Boy, you brought light to my darkest moment; my brothers Ron and Mel and my sisters Doreen, Patti, Cindy and Carol, you shaped who I am; Grant Goodeve, my trusted friend, for listening, laughing and believing long before the others; my Hollywood stars, Pam Wallace, Kamran Pasha, Kathy Yoneda, Matthew Papish, Lee Ruttenberg and Ken Lee, you proved that goodness thrives in show business; my critics, Julie Thomas, Susan Hedrick, and Polly Bickel, for letting me be the male voice; Gloria Kempton, my first writing coach, for the push; Rick Robertson and Tess Thompson, for helping me hang on; Jason Probst, your writing amazes me; the Baillies - John, Teresa, Steph and Janelle, for keeping the family ties; my in-laws, Buddy and Jerry Mallory, you made wonderful children; the Hawkeswoods - Cliff, Teriann, Tiffany and Tamara, you brighten every moment; the Mallorys – Patrick, Paula, Sam, Laura, Jacob and Hannah, what a delightful surprise you've been; Mike and Bob Santi, Wendy and Tammy Lindroos, you were more like siblings; Charles Farmer, always my champion; Randy Conrads, your simple idea changed my life; the friends of my youth, Blaine Richardson, Mike Barrett, Arnold Kurt, David Brandt and Dean Kulju, see you at the end of the road; my Army buddies, Bob Coates and John Papendorp, always remember Indiana; Jeff Tauge and John Faulkner, I still believe in the music; the Doobie Brothers, Heart, and Bob Hope, for sharing your stage with a star struck kid; Phil Grabmiller, the greatest guitarist I've ever known; my friends from Amazon.com, John Vlastelica, Sri Rao, Paul Kotas, Paul Bock, John Mevissen and Renata Sadunas, you made my time there remarkable; Scott and Deb Grover, Adam Finklein, Bart and Wanda Bartel, Stephanie and Ryan Schell, Eddie Chastain, Titus Richard, having you in my life has made it richer.

A very special thanks and appreciation to the Idaho and Montana miners and their families for their love, hope, optimism, sacrifices and life lessons. You are the real beauty in those magnificent mountains.

And finally, to my sweet wife, Kathleen – I will love you beyond my last tomorrow. You awakened this heart to a new life. You inspire me more than you'll ever know. I thank God for you every day.

"…and they will look to the earth, but behold, distress and darkness, the gloom of anguish; and they will be thrust into thick darkness."

Isaiah 8:22 KJV

PROLOGUE

The nipper whistled as he rinsed toilet buckets, his fetid work highlighted by a solitary miner's lamp. An airtight bulkhead of wood and sawdust stood a dozen yards ahead of him, sealing the old mine from the new. One mile deep and one mile back in the mountain there were no flickering flames, just angry coals, the only light, seeping forward, consuming oxygen to continue living. Five hundred degrees of heat twisted iron train tracks and melted metal ladders as the slow burn inched forward. Dank air was replaced with deadly gas, filling the miles of voided rock. A shallow breath of the toxic mixture will kill a man, bursting his lungs, drowning him in his own blood. There was now enough poison in these tunnels to create a tomb for a thousand men. The fire crept like a cobra, unnoticed, eating posts and train ties, ladders and chutes, filling the forgotten tunnel with its vaporous venom. Slithering slowly towards the bulkhead, the serpent would soon strike.

CHAPTER 1

October 1974 – Sunnyside, Montana

Sulfur stench burned at Lucas Kaari's nose as he drove his pickup truck north to the high school parking lot. The Bull Run Mining Company was pumping poison into the air again from its smelter plant. The aroma was unnoticed by most people in Sunnyside. They had grown immune after a generation of breathing the stuff. Today Lucas could actually taste it.

Scabby Cipher sat in the passenger seat fumbling with some last minute homework as he juggled the warm Pepsi he was drinking for breakfast. His paper, pen and notebook kept slipping from his lap. Lucas leaned forward and looked up at the sky. The October morning sun was desperately trying to shine through the man made clouds.

Lucas adjusted the volume of his eight-track stereo, filling the cab with *Bachman-Turner Overdrive's* latest hit. Scabby began singing along in perfect pitch and harmony. His voice had always amazed Lucas. It was the only thing about the boy that could be called beautiful. Music was the common ground of their friendship. Lucas wrote lyrics, Scabby composed and sang. He envied Scabby's singing as much as Scabby praised his use of words. They talked of a putting a band together someday and leaving Sunnyside far behind. Lucas knew it wouldn't happen but enjoyed the dream anyway.

A bright red blur flashed past them and swerved directly into the pickup's path. Lucas slammed on the brakes. His truck skidded slightly and stopped, barely missing the '54 Chevy that had pulled in front of them. Scabby dropped his soda onto the carpet. Brown foam rose up and quickly settled into the nap. Lucas stared ahead and cursed, his eyes closing slightly. Mickey Whitehead climbed out of the Chevy, baseball bat in hand and glared at Lucas. Two other boys, Lucas recognized them as wrestlers, exited the car as well. He ejected the tape from his player and placed it carefully into the tape case on the floor, never taking his eyes off of Mickey. Scabby picked up the half full soda can and hurriedly locked his door. His stumpy fingers were nimble and sticky.

"Oh man, what's this about?" Scabby asked. He pushed his dark-framed glasses back up the ridge of his nose with his thumb.

"Heather McKenzie, I believe," Lucas answered slowly and knowingly.

Mickey was tall, lean and muscular. Much larger than either Lucas or Scabby. He was also a well-known and respected athlete. At Sunnyside High School Mickey ruled the hallways with his charm, looks and wit. Teachers respected him because of his record setting feats. Students feared him for the same reason.

Lucas watched as Mickey positioned his bat. The big boy's perfect smile hid a hint of evil, his eyes betrayed any semblance of goodness. Lucas could hear him laughing, joined by a jock chorus from either side of his truck. Briskly, Mickey swung his baseball bat, shattering the driver's side headlamp. Lucas saw a spray of broken glass jump into the air. Several pieces dropped and danced on the hood before sliding to the ground. Again Mickey laughed. He was now tapping the bat on

1

the hood and glaring at Lucas. His smile was twisted into a snarl. Lucas could see the boy's chest rise and fall as his nostrils flared with each breath. He was a bull readying a charge.

"Come on Kaari, crank out a couple of tears for the boys here," Mickey shouted. He swung his sidearm again, breaking the other lamp. The impact shook the truck. The jocks chuckled. Mickey placed his foot on the front bumper of the truck and leaned on his elbow. Staring down his prey, he looked like a carrion buzzard hovering over a dying animal.

"Come on out. Bring that little greasy four-eyed maggot in there with you. Believe me, I'll bust every piece of glass on this fly trap until you get out here."

Mickey was in his element. A tough guy in a tough crowd, only this time playing to a small audience instead of a stadium of fans. He began to bounce the truck with his foot, then started pacing back and forth. Lucas considered his options. They were extremely limited. He ruled out killing Mickey, at least for the time being.

Lucas watched as Mickey moved, his baseball bat popping into the palm of his left hand. The veins in this forearms were bulging, testament to his physical condition.

"Kaari, come on. I want to have a chat with you," Mickey said, his voice very soft and pleading. "We have a problem we need to solve. Pull up your panties and get out here." Mickey's buddies stood to either side of the pickup blocking any quick exit. Scabby was whispering under his breath. Lucas thought he heard the Lord's Prayer.

"I've got nothing to discuss. Just move your car. You're blocking traffic," Lucas shouted loud enough to be heard, but not enough to be threatening.

Cars were backing up behind them. Several students had pulled to the shoulder of the road and watched from a distance. Mickey swung his bat and blasted out the turn signal lens cover. Yellow glass colored the air. Lucas jumped at the impact, mentally calculating the cost of new headlamps and turn signals. Mickey took off his letterman's jacket and tossed it to one of his buddies.

"You idiot!" Lucas screamed, "Get out of my way or I'll run this truck over you." He was shaking as he gunned the engine. He let the clutch slip a little, inching the truck forward.

Scabby sat rock still, staring straight ahead, acting as if the scene before him wasn't happening.

"What are you goin' to do Luke?" Scabby whispered, his lips remaining almost as still as his body.

Lucas glanced towards his friend, *The dummy is a ventriloquist,* he thought.

"What are you gonna do?" Scabby whispered again. His voice hissed over his clenched teeth.

Lucas realized that Scabby was sweating, adding to the already fetid air. Mickey stepped onto the bumper and began bouncing.

"I guess I'll run him over, I don't know…", Lucas paused as he spoke. He let the clutch out again and depressed the accelerator. Mickey's friends moved away from the sides of the pickup.

Mickey tapped the bat on the center of the windshield. Lucas revved the engine. Mickey grinned his hideous grin and raised the bat. For a moment he looked like some carnival jerk trying to ring a bell with a mallet.

Lucas lifted his arm to cover his face, expecting the worst. Scabby was already leaning over in the seat, his head between his knees. The sound of shattering glass filled the air. Lucas pulled his face from his sleeve. The windshield was untouched. Mickey was still standing on the bumper with the bat over his head. Only the expression on his face had changed. It was now etched in shock and horror.

A large silhouette stood behind Mickey on the hood of his red Chevy. Lucas couldn't tell who it was, but the person had brought fear into those outside his truck. He was also kicking in the windshield of Mickey's car with his cowboy boots. Lucas pressed his face towards the windshield, covering his eyebrows with his hand.

"Who in the hell is that....?"

CHAPTER 2

Lucas leaned further forward and squinted. His brother Russell had jumped from the hood of Mickey's car and was standing behind the boy. Mickey turned just as Russell grabbed his shoulder. At six foot four with almost two hundred and twenty pounds of chiseled muscle, forged ten hour days in the mine, he loomed over Mickey.

Russell whispered in the boy's ear. Mickey handed him his baseball bat and stepped away from the pickup. Russell walked towards the driver's door. The other boys moved away quickly and joined Mickey.

"Roll your window down you little jerk," Russell was grinning at his little brother as he spoke. Lucas quickly complied and dropped the driver's side window, anxious for the fresh air and thankful to speak to his brother.

"Now what on earth have you done to tick this little boy off anyway, baby brother?" Mickey glared at Lucas. Lucas smiled back. Scabby was squirming in his seat, elated at his rescue.

"I think because Heather and I are going to the game together tonight. I'm not sure. Maybe you should take it up with him," Lucas said with sarcasm.

By now more students had stopped and were watching the commotion. Russell placed the baseball bat on his shoulder and turned towards Mickey. He stomped his foot as if scaring away a stray dog. Mickey returned quickly to his car, opened the door and climbed behind the wheel. He brushed fragments of the broken window off of his car seat and onto the ground. His two friends joined him. In an instant, the Chevy sped off toward the school.

"What did you say to him?" Lucas asked.

"I just told him that I was going to come over here and talk to you and when I was done, I was going to come back and cram this bat between his beef sheets. Guess he believed me?

"Thanks." Lucas said sincerely. "You didn't have to bust his windshield though. Now he's gonna try to kill me for sure."

"Listen boy, stay away from that guy. Do you want me to follow him and straighten out his thinking ahead of time?"

"No, I'll be fine. I guess he's just bored and wanted to have some fun. I can take care of myself. Besides, I've got Scabby for protection," Lucas said, trying to change the subject. He didn't want to elaborate to his brother about Heather for fear of later ridicule.

"Yeah right. Hey, Scabby, did you get the crap scared out of you? It sure smells like it." Russell began to laugh. He then became serious as he spoke, "Heather's knees are bolted together. Ain't you or Whitehead ever going to pry them apart. Don't get your hopes up or your butt kicked over it."

Lucas became slightly annoyed with his brother. Was it that obvious how he felt about the girl?

"It's not like that," he said a bit exasperated.

"Yeah. Right," Russell said sharply, raising both eyebrows as he spoke. "Anyway, listen, I'll be at a party tonight with Lori. I'm going into work Saturday and Sunday afternoons. I need to stockpile some overtime cash in case the union strikes this week. There is a lot of grumbling at the union hall and I don't need to be caught short."

Lucas nodded his head as Russell talked. "Anyway, leave the basement door unlocked. Mom is giving me a lot of heat about getting drunk and keeps locking me out."

Russell still lived at home. A concession his parents had made in the hopes of encouraging him to save money to attend college. He had been underground at the Bull Run mine for over two years and made more money than his father.

Russell was smiling. He reached into the window and grabbed his brother's ear. "Look, I'm late for work. Be careful tonight, ok? Just don't forget to leave the door unlocked."

"Sure. No problem. I'll make sure you get in."

It really was a problem, but Lucas would do it anyway, accepting in advance the reprimand from his parents.

Five years ago Russell was the best athlete that ever stepped onto Miner's Field. He was an All-State pitcher and the son every man dreamed of raising. Mr. Kaari never missed a game and was at one time president of the high school's booster club. For years, Lucas had to live in his brother's shadow. College scouts had come around and offered the world to Russell just to have him play for them. He had chosen to play other games instead, usually with Lori Murphy. He was well known and well liked by everybody in Sunnyside. Lucas was afraid his brother was a 'lifer', somebody content to exist by working their life away in the mine. He shuddered at the thought.

Russell tossed the baseball bat into the back of Lucas' truck and strolled through the crowd that had gathered. Lucas watched as he walked away. A Cadillac plastered with political placards rumbled by, parting the gathering kids even further, a small American flag wind snapping from its radio antenna.

For the moment Lucas admired Russell, almost wishing he had his brother's careless attitude and confidence. Glancing at his watch, he cursed, he would be late for first period. Scanning the crowd once more, he could no longer see his brother. It reminded him of a movie where the unsung hero fades into a mass of on-lookers. Russell disappeared just as casually as he had arrived.

CHAPTER 3

"In this county there are five whorehouses, and I haven't been to one of them," Ernie Shaggal said proudly to the bored students. As a campaigning Commissioner for Silver Bow County, Montana, Shaggal always addressed high school kids ready to cast their first ballots. Sunnyside High School would bring him no less than eighty affirming votes. Lucas was transfixed with the way Shaggal's chins quivered each time he moved his mouth.

His trance broke as a hand next to him thrust into the air. Lucas turned his head towards the raised hand. Ernie stopped mid-sentence and fixed a serious look at the eager student.

"Yes, young man, you have a question?" the Commissioner said as he adjusted his shoulders and shirt collar.

"Which one?" Scabby asked.

"Which one what?" replied Ernie, surprised at the question.

"Which whorehouse haven't you been to?"

Ernie stood frozen and puzzled for a moment. The shocked look on his face melted into a pinched scowl. His dual chins became one jowl as he thrust his head slightly forward.

The classroom awoke with laughter. Lucas grinned to himself, marveling at a politician caught speechless. Nobody was paying any noticeable attention to Shaggal until the mention of whores. Like every one else in the room, Lucas knew that whorehouses were as much a part of a mining town as bars, unions, and street fights. In Sunnyside, Montana town folk knew the prostitutes but pretended they didn't. It was expected that any male over the age of sixteen visited the houses at least once. Had they not, their manhood would be questioned. Scabby hadn't visited them yet even though he was already eighteen. Lucas had window shopped the prostitutes once with his brother, but saved his ten dollars and his virginity, choosing to fib in the locker room about an interlude instead.

"Scabby", Lucas said, "Perhaps you should rethink Mr. Shaggal's statement. I don't believe he meant that he frequented the local prostitutes." He tried to sound adult and serious, but his eyes betrayed his own admonition. It was apparent that he thought Scabby's statement was funny, too.

"Sorry Ernie. I didn't mean no disrespect," Scabby said quietly. Lucas knew that Scabby didn't understand why everybody was laughing. He was famous for both good and bad timing, but probably better known for not realizing it.

"Quite alright, son." Ernie's red cheeks turned pink as he spoke. He ignored the question and continued his speech.

Round, tall and fifty, Ernie was also an entrepreneur who owned two bars, a grocery store, a pizza joint, a pawn shop and the first self-service gas station in Sunnyside, Montana. If a kid could see over the counter in any of his taverns, he would serve him beer. For this gracious gesture alone Ernie would collect the eighteen-year-old vote. It was the fall of 1974. When he won in November, this would be his twentieth year in office. He was running unchallenged.

The oppressing monotone of Shaggal's voice had a hypnotic effect on the classroom, pushing each student into eyes-wide-open sleep. Several students, including Heather McKenzie, were actually taking notes on Ernie's lecture. Lucas watched as her pen made fluid movements across the lined paper. Her long auburn hair touched the top of her pen. With her free hand she pulled the hair back, revealing an intent look on her face. For a moment he felt guilty for not taking or at least faking notes himself.

Heather laid her pen down, leaned back in her chair and stared curiously at Ernie. The Commissioner would glance towards Scabby, who was pretending to take notes. Lucas could tell Heather was becoming bored too. He was also certain that Scabby would not be able to purchase any alcohol this weekend.

The Commissioner droned on. His sports coat was at least twenty-five years old. Its faded tweed design reminded Lucas of the couch in his parent's basement, maybe just as lumpy, too. From the back of the room, he could see that the jacket was straining at its solitary button each time the honorable Ernie inhaled.

Lucas turned his head and stared out of the classroom window. He squinted his green eyes slightly as he looked towards the snow-touched western mountains and the foothills of the Continental Divide. At seventeen, an interest in local political affairs wasn't on his list of priorities. He ran his fingers through his hair, pushing some of the longer locks behind his ears, making a mental note to get a haircut before his father started lecturing him again.

Across the football practice field behind the school he watched the autumn leaves weave gracefully to the ground, severed from their branches by a brisk breeze. In the narrow part of the valley he could see the Junior Army ROTC rappelling down the short cliffs near the creek. He and Scabby had joined ROTC last year just for the thrill of swinging off the mountain on ropes. They both quit after the first semester.

Lucas glanced back at Scabby, who had put aside his notes and was reading a comic book tucked inside his textbook.

Unfortunately, Lucas thought, *Scabby Cipher is my best friend and worst nightmare.*

Class broke promptly at 3:00. The teacher had given final instructions for a term paper due on Monday about the rumored miner's wildcat strike and its potential effect on the community, then bid his students a good weekend.

Scabby shadowed Lucas as they walked from the classroom, momentarily blinded by the sun flooding the all glass hallway. At six feet tall, Lucas towered over his friend by almost a half a foot. He found himself often looking at the dandruff flakes nested in the parting line of Scabby's black hair.

"For the love of God, Scabby, you need to think before you talk. Doesn't your brain ever engage before your mouth?" Lucas felt angry and embarrassed at and for his friend. Scabby seemed unfazed by Lucas' words, and continued trudging through the cacophony of classmates milling towards the school's exits. Lucas glanced up and looked for Heather. She had disappeared into the moving mass of students.

"Think about what, Luke?" Scabby's eyebrows raised slightly, causing his forehead to crease. His eyes looked a bit bug-like to Lucas, exaggerated by thick black rimmed glasses. Scabby crinkled his face, forcing his glasses to move up his nose, rather than pushing them up with his finger.

"Never mind, and don't call me Luke." Lucas only liked to be called Luke by his family and Heather. Scabby knew this, but always slipped.

At the top of the third floor stairway, Lucas stopped for a moment and read a hand painted poster hanging on the wall. The massive white butcher paper had been taped together to form a ten foot by ten foot banner. Orange and black letters had been carefully brush stroked with powdered paints, promoting the homecoming football battle between the cross county rival team, the Bobcats, and the Sunnyside High School Prospectors. He recognized, even at this tremendous size, that the handwriting belonged to Heather McKenzie. He smiled to himself and ran down the stairs.

Lucas made his way up the hall to his locker on the first floor. He watched as students scrambled towards the main entrance of the school, racing to buses and parked cars. Several long-haired senior boys, *stoners,* Lucas thought to himself, were lighting cigarettes as they walked towards their vehicles, silently and willfully defying the teachers and bus monitor's rules against tobacco on school grounds. Several of the adults glanced at the stoners, but none took any action, probably out of fear or disdain. Either way, Lucas knew they were disliked by the adults and by the majority of the student body as well.

Most of the other students were babbling about the impending football game and the possible beer and petting parties afterwards.

Friday had arrived and forty-eight hours of freedom loomed ahead. Lucas had to work for three hours after school then he, too, was free.

As a senior he was lucky to have his own book locker without the burden of a locker partner. He wove along an invisible path down the hall, dodging students dashing on their own transparent trails. Just as he had since they were ten years old, Scabby strode a half a step behind Lucas, often bumping into him or stepping on the back of his shoes.

"Hey Kaari, you better hide. Mickey Whitehead is looking for you. He wants to finish what he started this morning." Randy Peeper was speaking. Lucas tried to ignore him. Peeper's locker was next to Lucas'. Randy was suspected of liking other boys. Although nobody ever claimed proof, lots of stories circulated around school concerning a keg party incident last spring and Randy's attempted seduction of other males. Even speaking to him was not good for one's reputation, and here he was talking to Lucas and Scabby.

Scabby was smiling at Peeper and looking over his shoulder into his locker. Lucas glanced up and down the hallway, praying silently that nobody important saw him with Peeper.

"I'm not afraid of Mickey." Lucas looked around again. In reality he was terrified of him. The boy was an all around jock and jerk who chose to hate fellow students from time to time, especially if he thought they had an interest in his girlfriend. And Lucas certainly did.

"Last period he said he was going to break your arm off and beat you with it. Said he didn't like the idea of you making moves on Heather." Randy seemed thrilled at delivering Lucas' death sentence to him. Raking his right hand through his thick brown hair, Randy turned his back to Lucas and put his notebook into his locker. Lucas noticed how perfectly arranged Randy kept his books. He reached into his own locker, catching books and papers as they slipped off the top shelf. Picking his jacket off its hook, he slipped his arms into the sleeves.

"Hey, she asked me to take her to tonight's game," Lucas said, emphasizing the words 'me' and 'her'. "The dumb ox knows she broke up with him, right?" Zipping his coat, he slam-kicked the locker's door shut, its noise lost in the shuffling crowd sounds.

"He doesn't care. He is going to take it out on you, not her." Randy's smugness showed through his feigned sincerity, each word carefully accented. Lucas wanted to insult Peeper and make some bravado remark that kids close-by could hear. Instead, he smirked back, snorted and shook his head from side to side.

Heather McKenzie had known Lucas since the day he was born. Their mothers, themselves childhood friends, gave birth within two days of one another, Heather arriving first. The McKenzies had lived next door to the Kaaris for over twenty years. Heather and Lucas were closer than most siblings. Mrs. McKenzie used to call Lucas Heather's twin brother. Until he was five years old Lucas thought he was.

Lucas knew Heather was miffed at Mickey, just as she had been a dozen times in the past month. Even Lucas didn't consider this evening's game's attendance a date, though his desire for her was always with him. He often wondered what it would be like to romance her. The dynamics of that kind of change in their relationship scared him so he forced himself not to think of her in those terms. They were intimate intellectually and had a shared history, but openly desiring her in any other capacity or hoping for an emotional tie made him uncomfortable. Lucas was her diversion until she smoothed things out with Mickey. At this point in his life, he had come to accept this as his lot.

"Thanks for the warning Randy," Lucas said, carefully choosing his words, "I'll think of you as my arm is being mangled and my colon engorged."

Randy grinned in disgust, gently closed his locker door and spun the combination lock several times.

"Luke, did you see the picture of *The Osmonds* that Randy had taped up in his locker?" Scabby said.

"God, Scabby, just shut up." Lucas smiled as he tilted his head back and stared at the ceiling. His dimples deepened as his eyes slowly blinked shut, "Just shut the hell up."

The two friends exited the front of the building and walked towards Kaari's metallic blue Toyota pickup truck. The scent of fall was hanging low in the valley. The sulfur clouds had dissipated. This was a rare clear afternoon. Most of them never allowed the sun to appear as anything other than a hazy bright dot. Smelling leaves was unusual, too.

"The mine smelter must be shut down," Lucas said, "There's no more stench in the air. At least if Bull Run goes on strike the air will be clear for awhile."

"Yeah, if there's a strike the air will be clear," Scabby said, parroting his friend. Lucas looked at Scabby. He hated when Scabby echoed him. Over the years Scabby had adopted this language mirroring as a way of affirming their friendship.

"God sure put this place where the sun don't shine much," Scabby added.

Lucas grinned and laughed as he unlocked the driver's door and climbed in behind the steering wheel. Reaching across the seat he unlatched the passenger side. Scabby climbed in and retrieved a warm soda can from a sack under the seat.

"Roll your window down Scabby. You're stinking up the truck." Lucas was used to this exercise with his friend. Most days the smell inside the truck overpowered the sulfur scent outside. Although he was blunt he knew that it wouldn't hurt his friend's feelings. Scabby had poor hygiene. Like his six brothers and sisters, he had never been totally schooled in taking care of his personal appearance. His clothes were always wrinkled and unwashed. It was discovered in gym class in the seventh grade that he didn't wear underwear either.

Last Christmas Lucas had given Scabby an *Alice Cooper* tee shirt as a gift, only to watch it literally wrinkle moments after Scabby pulled it over his head.

"Sorry Luke, I don't smell nothing." Scabby's nostrils wiggled slightly as he tilted his head like a mutt checking the wind.

"You never do Scabby. That's part of the problem." Lucas spoke quickly, his voice a bit distant and nasally as he tried not to breathe through his nose. Turning on the radio he cranked the volume so he wouldn't have to talk to or listen to Scabby. From the corner of his eye he watched as his friend dug in his ear with the eraser on a pencil, Lucas' mind began to wander as he drove.

Scabby's real name was Gabriel. Lucas' friendship with him had come with a social price. Scabby stank the same rancid way ten years ago when they first met at Sunnyside Elementary.

Lucas had been riding his bicycle across the school playground on his way home when he saw a group of sixth grade boys beating up a much smaller kid. Curious more than anything, but afraid of the older boys, he rode closer to see what was causing such fury. Other children were running or riding closer as well. Swings stopped swinging as kids raced to see the fight. From a distance he could hear loud laughter, cursing and crying.

He recognized several of the older boys. Most of them were sixth graders and the kind of kids you stayed away from; Dale Murphy especially. Though he was only two years older than Lucas, he was built like a teenager, even sporting a small amount of facial hair on his lip. He was a known truant who seemed to gain power from his peer group by picking on smaller boys. His trademark was pulling the fire alarm during rainstorms or taking a leak on the radiator in the boy's bathroom in the winter, causing the most horrific odor to fill the hallways, which ultimately would cause the cancellation of classes. Dale was leading the assault on a diminutive child laying on the ground in the fetal position, clutching his groin, encircled by the male pack. The crumpled boy was Gabriel Cipher.

"You little piece of trash," Murphy raged as he pumped his sneaker into Cipher's stomach, "You and your scab family tried to starve us, you little worm." His foot thudded dully on the boy's head. Blood spewed from just above Gabriel's eyebrow and out of his mouth and nose. The other boys moved in closer and started striking Gabriel with their boots and shoes.

The watching crowd grew bigger as the sixth graders and Murphy began to randomly chant the word, "Scab" over and over again. Their laughter at the helpless victim was unlike anything Lucas had heard before. Each boy was beginning to try and outdo the others in their cruelty. It reminded him of the time his family cat cornered a mouse in the backyard, only to be joined by other neighborhood cats. The felines hesitated taking a chance on latching their teeth into the rodent, but just as one did the others pounced as well. Eventually the cats fought over their prey, only to leave it bleeding and dying as they journeyed off into the alley. Lucas had buried the mouse in his mother's flowerbed. He remembered saying a prayer over it and asking for the cat's forgiveness. These adolescent boys were far more aggressive and less humane than the cats.

"Scab, scab, scab," the heckling grew louder and the footfalls more severe. Gabriel was crying loudly, almost screaming. Each kick to his chest or stomach stopped his wailing and forced him to shriek, the air driven from him and the cry cut short. His little hands held firmly to his privates as the pack targeted this area especially. He clutched them so hard that Lucas thought Gabriel might actually be hurting himself worse in some ways than his attackers.

Lucas' heart skipped several beats. He was only eight years old, far smaller than any of the boys breaking Gabriel's body. The pathetic cries coming from the fallen child rose a rage inside of him. Pulling back on the handlebars of his bike, he lifted the front tire off the ground at the same time pedaling forward. His bicycle lurched on its rear wheel and drove toward the attacking mass. Spinning faster and faster he rammed full force into Dale Murphy's lower back, the front tire slamming down just above the belt and hard into Dale's right kidney. The impact toppled Dale over face-first onto Gabriel causing some misplaced kicks from the other boys to hit Dale's face instead.

Murphy, startled at the unexpected blow, let out an anger-filled scream and rolled onto his back. Gabriel squirmed under Murphy, instinctively protecting himself even further. Lucas lifted the front tire of his bike up into the air and slammed it down hard at Dale's trunk, crushing his genitals. The sound of Murphy's voice reminded Kaari of some vixen in a horror show just as she was being confronted by a werewolf's appearance. It was at once sharp, hysterical and long.

Dale Murphy continued to cry and curse. His vicious minion, surprised by this interruption stopped for a moment and looked at their fallen friend, writhing like a snake, whimpering like a newborn baby. Lucas backed up his bicycle, unsure of his next move. His chest was pounding with fear. The crowd turned towards him. One of the fourth grade boys took a tentative step in his direction. It was Mickey Whitehead.

"You stupid moron! I'm going to crack your head open and spit in your skull." Mickey moved quickly toward the youngster and his bike. From four feet away, Lucas spit in Mickey's face. He stopped, fully enraged, wiped his face and lunged toward Lucas. Pulling his bicycle wheel upward again, the front tire struck Mickey on the chin, clamping his bottom and top teeth onto his tongue, severing the tip. Blood immediately filled the corners of his mouth. He too began to cry.

The younger kids who had gathered to watch the slaughter began to laugh. Seeing an eight-year-old stand up to the playground bullies was a fantasy being played out before them.

"I'm going to kill you. You better watch yourself. I'm going to break your neck you little jerk." Mickey's taunts were difficult to understand as they slurred around the blood and spittle flying from his mouth. A teacher began running and yelling across the playground. Children scattered. The bully boys retreated, cursing Lucas and the other children, condemning them to years more of their hell and brutality. The laughter continued as the thugs stalked off the playground with the teacher in frenzied pursuit.

Lucas got off of his bike and walked over to Gabriel, who was still shaking and crying on the ground. He knelt next to him. Gabriel's face was covered with dirt and fresh blood. His discolored yellow teeth were tinged in red. His eye was already becoming swollen and shutting. His hands still clutched his crotch.

"Come on," Lucas said helping Gabriel to his feet, "let me help you home."

Gabriel struggled to stand. Steadying himself on Lucas' arm, his legs crumpled like a colt finding its gravity. For a moment all Lucas could see was a trembling, bloody mouse. Gabriel continued crying. Lucas was unsure whether he was simpering from the shock of what happened or from the terror and pain of the attack.

They walked their bikes instead of riding them, Gabriel's groin too tender to sit. The smoke-choked skies blotted the sunlight for the most part, creating a dismal pall over the two children. Lucas tried to talk to Gabriel, but didn't really know what to say. They had known of each other most of their lives, but had always been relegated to different teachers, mostly because Lucas was a bit brighter, not just intellectually, but in spirit and demeanor. Children like Gabriel always seemed to be passed on to lesser or older teachers.

As Lucas walked with Gabriel he observed the boy's clothes. They were tattered from the fight, but now he could see that the threads at the knees were well worn and his once colorful shirt was tinted with gray and seemed a bit too small. The sound of their bicycle tires crackled on the gravel.

Gabriel himself was a bit stocky in build. His oily black hair seemed to always hang over his smudgy glasses. Flakes of dandruff clung to the inside of the lenses. Gabriel would often squint to lift the glasses back onto his face. The lenses were very scratched as well. Now, after the beating, the left one had a crack in it.

After a long silence of walking, Gabriel finally spoke, though his words were almost unintelligible. His voice was so hoarse from screaming he sounded like an old woman who had chain-smoked most of her life.

"Do you think it will stick?", he asked. His expression was blank, except for a slightly raised eyebrow. Lucas thought maybe the eyebrow was bruised.

"Do what?" Lucas' said. His expression was mixed with surprise at not just the raspy sound, but the oddness of the question. The boys stopped walking and faced each other. The sky had begun to darken as the sun set behind the western mountain. A cool breeze moved train track dust into small spirals.

"Do you think the name will stick. Scab, I mean. Seems everybody has a nickname. Last year everybody called me Grease, because my mom put some of my dad's tonic or something in my hair before school. I hated that name." His voice began to gain energy as he spoke.

"I don't know. Maybe they'll call you Fighter or Punchy or something like that." Lucas knew that would never happen. He was simply trying to assuage Gabriel.

"No. They'll call me Scabs or something." Gabriel turned his shoulder toward Lucas and looked downward. He began pushing his bike forward again. The boys were moving parallel to the train tracks that wound past Gabriel's house.

"Why were they calling you that? Scab, I mean." Lucas had heard the term before, used in anger by adults, but didn't see the fit in this circumstance. He remembered his own father using the word once.

"Daddy crossed the picket line during the last strike. Had to. Our house got flooded again and he needed to fix it. We didn't have no furniture, no nothing. It all got ruined. He even had to tear out the carpet. There is still a big hole in the kitchen floor." Gabriel stopped and slowly knelt to tie his shoe. Lucas looked down at the dirty boy again. The toes of his sneakers were well worn. A soiled sock poked out of the end of one.

Lucas remembered the flood. The Cipher's house, a shack really, stood on the edge of town in an area called Logan's Pond. The Silver Bow train track ran behind their house and the Greenwood River ran in front of it. The pond was some backwash from the Greenwood, a mosquito spawning ground, which flooded every couple of years. The other houses in Logan's Pond were just as run down. Old cars littered the driveways to the houses. Broken appliances adorned the front porches. Tarpaper covered the outside walls instead of paint. Lucas remembered seeing a pile of old shag carpet heaped up in front of the Ciphers.

"So what if he crossed the line?" Lucas said.

"Guess you don't do that. I dunno. We had no groceries and we had no place to sit. No couches or nothing like that. So he went to work instead of going on strike. They beat him pretty bad because of that though." Gabriel's voice grew even weaker. "They busted his arm and Momma had to get a job in Warm Springs at the mental hospital. She had to drive forever to work and back."

Lucas knew that the Cipher's station wagon was a disaster on four bald tires. It was one of the ugliest cars in town. He was surprised Mrs. Cipher made it to work at all. Gabriel's mother was only fifteen years older than Gabriel himself. Given her circumstances, most people thought she was a handsome woman.

"Why'd they call you a scab then? Those boys I mean." Lucas climbed onto his bicycle. Tired of walking, he rode slow circles around Gabriel.

"I was playing on the monkey bars after school. Minding my business you know. Murphy and his buddies came up and told me I was the closest thing to a baboon we had at the school. I told them to shut up." Gabriel's tongue was swollen. His effort to speak was making Lucas ill.

"Anyway, they pushed me off the bars. That's how I got this." Gabriel pointed at the wound above his eyebrow. "I started to cry and that's when they started making fun of Daddy. So I threw a handful of dirt at them and started running. Next thing they are kicking me and calling me a scab. Murphy's father is the one Daddy says busted his arm."

The boys were now walking down the middle of the railroad tracks near Logan's Pond. Lucas knew that his mother would be worried about him, especially when she found out that he had gone all the way down to the Cipher's house, an area she didn't necessarily want her boys to venture.

The Greenwood River was running slightly high, filled with the gray and brown silt and stale sewage pumped into it by the upstream mining concerns and mountain communities. Rounding the last corner, Lucas could see a small column of smoke floating from the Cipher's house.

"Can I ask you two favors?" Gabriel's voice seemed as close to normal as it had since the fight. Lucas knew Cipher felt better just seeing his home.

"Sure. What?" Lucas replied.

"Well, first off, thanks for saving me." Gabriel's voice sounded noble. "Those guys are going to try to kill you now you know, but I want to be there to help. I want to be your friend. Ok?" He cupped his left hand and placed it on Lucas' shoulder. Lucas cringed slightly but didn't move away.

At first the thought of being Gabriel's friend appalled him. His own insecurities about himself and his own small circle of friends was already bad. Adding somebody as different as Gabriel Cipher could only make things worse.

As he stood looking at the crusty, dirty boy in front of him, he heard his own voice before he fully formed his thoughts, "Sure. We can be friends. What else?" The words were empty sounding. Gabriel smiled for the first time. His discolored and broken teeth still had some blood between them.

"I know this may sound stupid, but I know what those jerks are like. I know that tomorrow they are going to pick on me and get the other kids going, too. But if you start something first it won't be so bad," Gabriel said, each word tumbling out of his mouth faster than the previous one.

"What are you talking about?" Lucas was staring at his new 'friend' with an expression of confusion. He shifted his arm slightly again hoping Gabriel would remove his hand. It remained perched on Lucas' shoulder.

"What I mean is, those guys will start calling me names. But if you call me something first, maybe everybody else will call me that, too." He was sounding desperate.

"Well, sure. That doesn't make much sense to me, but nobody has called me anything but Lucas, except my mom. What do you want me to call you?" Lucas stared at his filthy companion.

"Scabby." Gabriel's voice was flat and matter of fact.

"Scabby?" Lucas stuttered the word. "That's horrible. I can't do that."

"It's better than Scab Butt, Scab Face, Scab Breath, Scab Eater or any of the other million filthy things they can come up with. If you call me Scabby at least it won't hurt so much." Gabriel's expression was hopeful again.

Lucas waited a long moment before he spoke. What could he lose? Tomorrow he probably wouldn't even speak to Gabriel.

"Ok. Sure. Scabby, huh?" Lucas could barely bring himself to say the nickname.

"Yup. Scabby." Gabriel was still smiling, only now he gazed directly into Lucas' eyes.

The two boys stood staring at each other for a moment. One full of pain and fear, the other filled with uncertainty and some regret, looking at his new shadow.

Almost ten years later those emotions were still very much a part of both boys. Scabby and Lucas had become so associated with each other that were one absent the teacher would ask the other where his friend was. Lucas still held back and at moments was even cruel to him, but time had shown him that Scabby had a heart and mind that were far deeper, much broader, more open and alive than most of the ruling elite of their school.

A loud commercial for logging truck tires jolted Lucas back to the present. He turned the radio volume down. Scabby was still working the crud from his ear, only now with a paper clip. Lucas shuddered.

As he steered his truck to the edge of town, Lucas thought about the word 'cipher.' He had looked the word up in the dictionary once. It meant '*nothing*'.

Scabby really was like a cipher, a zero, he thought. One of the kids that society ignored. But to Lucas, Scabby's gift of friendship was his treasure. He had learned to trust Scabby like no other friend. Scabby lived life vicariously through him. Lucas long ago realized that he needed the adoration.

The pickup bounced over the dirt road past Logan's Pond and pulled into the Cipher's muddy driveway. Scabby climbed out and leaned back through the open passenger window.

"Should I bring my guitar to your house?" Scabby asked.

"No. Let's just hook up at the game then get a pizza or something. I don't feel like playing music tonight."

Scabby looked a little bewildered then said, "Ok. I'll walk into town and find you at Miner's Field."

As Lucas backed his truck down the mud ruts, he saw Scabby's baby sister standing barefoot in a dirty dress at the top of the porch steps. Scabby scooped her into his arms, kissed her and carried her into the house.

CHAPTER 4

Lucas drove back towards town. The speakers on his eight track player crackled as he hit a pothole. He finally admitted to himself that he was scared. Each time he saw something move outside he swerved his truck slightly. He was lucky this morning. He might not be so blessed this afternoon.

Mickey had antagonized him for years. The underlying tension kept Lucas away from some social situations. When Heather started dating Mickey, Lucas tried to make her see who and what he thought Mickey was. A chill set into their friendship after that. Lucas decided to try and avoid talking about Mickey, choosing to see Heather when he could and not focus on his negative feelings. He steered his truck onto the paved street, relieved that the crunching sound of the gravel road had ceased. He adjusted the volume on his stereo and inserted a tape.

This year Mickey would have been a State star in football, but the coach had unexpectedly barred him from play. Lucas wondered why Mickey didn't fight the suspension. He acted like he didn't care. It probably didn't matter anyway, Lucas thought. Mickey was also a track star and the best shot-put in the state of Montana. He was almost an A student. These things alone guaranteed him a scholarship to the University of Montana in Missoula. Football would have only served his vanity.

Being sidelined gave Mickey his first taste of autumn freedom. Most other years he was forced to practice and play, a virtual captive of his coach and athletic abilities. He was much more visible now, causing Lucas to think twice before going to school events. Now Mickey's Fridays were spent pursing other interests, mostly Heather. Lucas ejected the tape from his player. Only the sound of the vehicle's engine could be heard.

Once or twice at Papa's Pizza Mickey had confronted Lucas, only to have Heather make him back down. Lucas would usually stay home and play music or write songs in his basement with Scabby or cruise the city streets in his pickup, listening to rock and roll and drinking cheap beer.

Lucas got to the Shop & Save grocery store a few minutes before four. Glancing around, he saw that almost every parking spot was occupied by a car or truck. He decided to not clock in early. Instead he sat in his truck and continued thinking about Mickey and Heather. He had never understood the connection. Why would Heather be interested in a person like Mickey in the first place? She had poise, intellect, charm and all the other attributes that made her the perfect woman - perfect in Lucas' eyes anyway.

Scabby told him once that he thought Heather liked Mickey because it kept other guys away and allowed her to pursue her academics.

Rumors floated throughout the past two years that Heather and Mickey were heavily involved sexually, but Lucas had comforted Heather enough times to know that these were just jealous lies from otherwise bored classmates. By making Heather imperfect it seemed to elevate the ego of those who had no lives themselves. Mickey used to allude to sexual deviations with her, but never directly claimed any. Heather had heard these stories as well. Mickey lied to her when she asked about them.

Lucas thought his job sucked. He had never intended to work through high school. On a whim, in the fall of 1972, he and Scabby had applied for jobs at Ernie Shaggal's grocery store, The Shop & Save, or S&S as the town referred to it. Lucas got the job. Scabby was turned down.

Lucas wasn't quite old enough to legally work, but Ernie's brother, Georgie, managed the store and liked Lucas. He hated Scabby's father and therefore hated Scabby. Lucas had just wanted to make some comic book money, but his father wouldn't let him quit. He insisted that Lucas learn how to earn. He also required that Lucas save half of his money for his education. On the up side, his dad matched him dollar for dollar for every thing he saved. The job paid less than two bucks an hour, but Lucas already had enough money for his first year of college.

Opening the door to his pickup, he stepped into the cool fall air. He carefully locked his door and dropped the keys into his shirt pocket. He walked slowly towards the back of the store.

The S&S was one of two grocery stores in Sunnyside. The other was an old Safeway serviced out of Missoula. Georgie was fond of telling customers, with just a hint of sexual undertone, 'There is no Safe Way'. Every time he said that, people gave a gratuitous laugh even though they thought the joke stunk. Safeway's prices were better than the S&S, but they didn't give people credit accounts and the S&S did. Just like all of Ernie's businesses. Lucas' dad told him that the town must at any one time owe Ernie over a half a million dollars.

The S&S employed about seven box boys, as the grocery sackers were called. No girls held the position. Georgie thought that girls couldn't handle the lifting and so forth, yet he hired them to work in the bakery and produce departments. Lucas' mother said that several girls used to work as carry outs at the S&S, but she couldn't remember seeing any for the past few years.

Lucas stopped briefly and chatted with an elderly couple on their way into the store. They smiled at him and asked about his parents. After a minute or two the conversation stalled and they said their good-byes. Tucking his shirt into his pants, he walked to the alley entrance and leaned against the building. In the distance he could hear the sounds of clanking shopping carts. The scent of fresh baked bread filled the air.

Heather McKenzie had applied for a job last summer at Lucas' recommendation. He had even talked to Georgie about it. Georgie did interview Heather, but told Lucas later that all of the box boys would be trying to get it on with her in the basement warehouse and he couldn't afford that kind of distraction. This angered Lucas, but he never told Heather since he probably would have tried to find time with her down there if he could.

This was payday Friday, one of two big days each month in Sunnyside. It was also the first Friday of the month, which meant the welfare mothers got their checks and food stamps. It would be hell at the check stands and Lucas hated the chaos. The shift would be short for him however. He got off at seven.

Each box boy was given a number depending on their seniority at the store. The more time in grade one had, the higher their number. Lucas was number six tonight, which meant that he would have less time at the checkout counters and more time stocking the store shelves.

As he opened the metal door to the shipping dock he could hear his least favorite cashier, Maureen Stuckey, causing all kinds of grief for the box boys. She had worked at the S&S since the first day it opened in the 1950s. When Ernie bought it, part of the deal was that he had to keep Maureen employed. She was a generally nasty woman with a bad temper and prone to giving dirty looks. Lucas did the best he could to keep her happy, but that didn't ever seem to make much of a difference. With the frenetic activity and long lines at the check out, she would be at her peak.

As Lucas clocked in and tied his apron around his waist, he could hear muffled background music and shuffling shoppers. The smells from the bakery were much stronger in the store than they were outside. On occasion, Georgie would announce some momentary special over the store's loudspeaker. Every minute or so one of the cashiers would call for a box boy by number. The last call Lucas heard was for 'Carry out number four please.' He knew his number would be up very soon.

"Hey, Kaari, you puke, what the hell are you doing?" Lucas turned around quickly at the voice interrupting his wandering thoughts. It was Adam Shaggal, Georgie's son and the lead clerk for the floor crew, which included the box boys. Adam was macho, cocky and full of himself. The younger boys admired him and tried to copy his attitude.

Adam was beyond harm and dominated the box boys. He was about five foot ten and had the physical cut of a body builder. At twenty-three years old, he had been already married and divorced. He seemed to enjoy the single life and preying on much younger girls. Adam was rarely seen without a fifteen or sixteen year old on his lap, in his truck or at his side.

Adam spent much of his free time at the local YMCA working out and generally making a spectacle of himself with his mouth and attitude. Lucas' brother Russell had warned him several times to watch out for Adam. He said that Adam was a dangerous drunk. There was a story a couple of summers ago that Adam had persuaded one of the girls who worked part-time in the bakery to party with him after work. The girl later claimed that Adam tried to get her to sleep with him. When she wouldn't, the story goes, Adam supposedly tried to force her into it. The ensuing struggle blackened the girl's eye. She also had apparently bitten Adam on the inside part of his leg near the groin, leaving significant teeth marks.

The incident was hushed up rather quickly by Georgie. The girl quit her job, but mysteriously had a brand new car a week later. Shortly after that she was working at Ernie's pizza restaurant. Adam disappeared for the rest of that summer, spending time at Flat Head Lake with his cousins.

"Get out on the floor, Kaari. Restock the coolers and get some paper bags up to the front counters. Move it." Adam smiled at Lucas and knuckle-hit him in the arm as he walked past him. Adam was strong and physically aggressive. The pop hurt his arm. Lucas rubbed at it as he headed to the milk cooler to restock the dairy products. Adam was whistling as he disappeared around a canned vegetable display.

"Carry out number six please!!!". The exasperated voice of Ms. Stuckey rang through the store. The intercom distorted as the woman nearly screamed her request, her mouth too close to the microphone. Adam could be heard laughing a couple of aisles over. The tone of Stuckey's voice was rank with a lack of patience and loaded with a mix of control and frustration. Lucas dropped his price marker into his apron pocket and jogged to the front of the store.

The lines of customers snaked back from each of the seven check out stands into the store aisles. Shopping carts were overloaded. Lucas could see the usual miner's staples on the bottom of each cart; cases of beer and bags of pretzels and other snack chips. He realized that the rest of his afternoon would be spent sacking groceries.

The line of people at Maureen's checkout stand was noticeably shorter. Several customers were slowly moving away from her, preferring instead to wait in longer lines. Maureen was oblivious to the obvious. She was focused on the welfare mother who had braved her line and was now grilling her.

"You know that cigarettes aren't allowed by the food stamp people. You know that, right?" Maureen was condescending to the young woman. Lucas' skin crawled into goose bumps at the tone of Maureen's voice. Two young children clung to their mother's dirty skirt, a third slept in her arms, cradled to her breasts, unaware of the bitter woman belittling its mom. Lucas dropped his head and placed groceries as quickly into the bag as he could, hoping to spare the young lady any further torture.

"Yes, I know. I have money for the tobacco." The young woman was becoming embarrassed. Lucas glanced up at her. She was juggling her purse and baby, trying to find her wallet. He reached forward and grabbed a large can of peaches, almost dropping them. Other items slowly worked their way towards him on the conveyance line.

"Show me the money first. I don't want to have to re-ring this." Maureen was being evil, Lucas thought. The young woman produced a wadded twenty from her purse. Lucas stood up straight, waiting for more groceries. The lines at the other check out points were growing shorter. Other box boys pretended not to notice what was happening at Maureen's counter.

"And the douche. You *know* we don't accept food stamps for douche. Right?" Maureen spoke loud enough for people at the neighboring check stands to hear. She was glancing around, hoping that people would notice she was protecting their tax dollars by preventing a welfare cheat. The young woman's face was dark red and her bottom lip quivered slightly. Lucas felt a lump in his throat.

"Yes, ma'am. I know. I think I have enough cash." She spoke softly as she fumbled with her baby's blankets. The child began to fuss, awakened by the confusion.

"You think? You don't know? I hope that you don't have any other forbidden products in there." Maureen was slinging items onto the conveyer belt and ringing them into the cash register.

"What do we have here?!" Maureen raised her voice yet again in mysterious triumph. "Tampons! Not allowed. Not allowed! And they don't have a damn price on them either."

Maureen grabbed her microphone. Pressing the communicate button she blew into it checking for a connection. Her breath could be heard throughout the store.

"Adam, I need a price check on super absorbent tampons, please..." Some customers began laughing as Maureen grinned.

"That's enough, Ms. Stuckey." The voice came from behind the young mother. It was a bit frail, a bit soft, but full of power. Maureen's eyes flew open wide. Who dared confront her? "Leave her alone Maureen. Ring up her order and leave her alone."

Nellie Montgomery stepped around the young woman. Lucas grinned. He loved Nellie. She was in her late eighties, had snow-white hair, and knew everybody in town. Her skin was tan and deeply wrinkled from years of working outdoors in her yard. She always wore a broad rimmed straw bonnet, tied under her chin by a big yellow bow. At five foot two, her head came up to the mother's shoulder and put her eye to eye with the wide-awake baby. The child smiled as Nellie tickled its lips with her bony index finger. It cooed as Nellie clicked her tongue.

"Mrs. Montgomery, perhaps you should mind your own business." Maureen was confrontational. All eyes were on her. The other check out clerks had stopped ringing orders. Lucas folded his arms indignantly and glared at Maureen.

"Perhaps this is my business," Nellie had moved again and was standing directly in front of Maureen.

"This young lady doesn't need your wrath. Just because you make your life hell, doesn't mean hers has to be. Remember, Ms. Stuckey, we are sometimes visited by angels and we don't even know it. Maybe she is an angel…"

Nellie pulled three twenty dollars bills from her clasp purse and handed them to the young woman. "Here, love, take this and pay for whatever you need. Buy these babies some treats, too." Nellie moved back behind her cart, never taking her eyes off of Maureen.

"Would you please hurry? I need to get home to my gardens before it gets too dark." Nellie's voice was very calm. The young woman had regained her composure and was also staring harshly at the cashier. Huffing, Maureen rang up the rest of the woman's order, not speaking another word. Her finger nails clicked loudly on the cash register keys.

Lucas helped the woman to the car with her groceries and hurried back into the store, hoping he could wait on Nellie. Maureen had rushed Nellie's order through as fast as she could, not once making eye contact with her. Lucas wanted to laugh, but thought better of it. He did, after all, have to work with Maureen. Nellie was just beginning to balance two large grocery bags in her arms when Lucas returned.

"Mrs. Nellie, let me take those for you." Lucas said. He'd called her Mrs. Nellie for years.

"Lucas, love, I've got them ok. You have work to do." Nellie shifted the bags under each arm. Her purse slung over her shoulder.

"No. I'll take them." He snatched the bags from her hands.

"If you insist." She smiled at him and patted his elbow. She began to totter towards the exit. Lucas took short steps besides her. He watched as she shuffled and walked at the same time. As long as he could remember she had moved this way.

As they strolled, Lucas thought about the stories the old woman had told him through the years. She had worked at the Sunnyside Hospital, retiring over twenty years ago. She began her job there in 1920. She said it was the only job she ever had. She had been a mid-wife and had delivered hundreds of babies throughout the Depression and war years. Her husband, Gene, had retired before her after a career as a schoolteacher and principal at Sunnyside elementary. He died of a heart attack while working one of their small mining claims with Nellie one sunny summer afternoon ten years ago over on the Little Clark Fork River. They had no children. Nellie use to say that between them they had two thousand kids. Lucas thought how lucky he was to be one of them.

"Why do you think Maureen is such a crazy bitch, Mrs. Nellie?" Lucas said.

"Watch that mouth, Lucas. I can't believe you kiss your mother with that dirty thing." Nellie was actually angry when she spoke. "Maureen is an adult and you need to respect her, no matter what she is like."

"Sorry. It's just that I can't stand her. She is awful to everybody, including you. I don't care if she is an adult. She doesn't deserve any respect." Lucas was defying Nellie as he spoke. He clutched her elbow as they crossed the street behind the store. A car slowed almost to a stop to let them pass safely.

Nellie always walked to the S&S. She lived four blocks away, up against the north mountain. Lucas had never seen her drive, although she had a beautiful old '51 Woody in her garage.

"Maureen is a troubled little girl, love." Nellie spoke with a hint of sadness in her voice.

"Little girl? She's an old bat." Lucas was still pushing a bit with Nellie.

"Lucas, I was her age when she was in my husband's second grade class. She used to watch her Daddy beat her Momma. He took a belt to her plenty of times, also. That was a long time ago, love, but some scars don't ever heal right."

Nellie was now holding onto Lucas' elbow as they walked. She was a little short of breath as she spoke. "Just remember child, you want to be the face in the mirror when it comes to Maureen. What you want to see from her, she needs to see from you."

Crossing the last street, Lucas could see her home. Nellie's house was huge. It looked like a colonial mansion to Lucas. Always painted white, the house was a landmark of sorts. It was one of the first built in Sunnyside.

Lucas listened to Nellie talk. She told the same story each time he carried her groceries home for her. Her father had the house constructed in 1885 when he was a superintendent at the Bull Run mine. He had homesteaded what was now the northeast quarter of the town. Over the years he sold off most of the land as the town grew.

Nellie was born in the house. Her parents had one other child, a son, who died during a polio epidemic around the turn of the century. Nellie had lived on the property all of her life. She and her husband had lived in a smaller house on the backside of the land until her parents passed away. She tended the one and half acres of grass and gardens every day. When all of the other yards and trees were barren, Nellie still seemed to coax green from her grass. Even now some of her flowers stood tall and colorful amidst the dead yellow and brown leaves of fall.

Lucas walked through the kitchen door just as he had many times over the past few years and placed the groceries on the table. The room was big, bright and warm. It always smelled of fresh soups or breads. Nellie usually made him take two cookies from a jar on the counter.

He remembered the first time he met Nellie. He was five or six years old and walking home from kindergarten. He had reached his hand through the pickets of her fence to pick a flower for his mother. Nellie had spotted him from her kitchen window and came dashing out of the house. He remembered how scared he was as he dropped the flower and started to run. She quickly caught him by his shirt collar. Instead of yelling at him, she knelt down and hugged him, saying, "You should always cut flowers, love, never pick them. If you cut them, they'll grow back." She led him by the hand back to her garden and let him clip a bouquet for his mother. She had him prune each flower himself. Together they wrapped them in bright tissue paper. His mother had cried when he presented them to her. She called Nellie and asked to pay for the flowers. Nellie had refused, asking only that the child be allowed to come visit and help her in the garden. He had loved his Mrs. Nellie ever since.

The phone rang as Nellie untied her straw bonnet. "Just put the bags down, love. I'll take care of them." She picked up the phone and spoke for a brief moment. "You had better get back to the S&S. That was Georgie. He is threatening to take your job away again." Nellie was smiling as she spoke. Lucas ran down her kitchen steps and out of her yard. He turned and waved at her. She was looking out of the kitchen window. Her tiny fingers waved back.

CHAPTER 5

Maureen didn't speak to Lucas the rest of the evening. She was still in a slow burn over the scene she had created with Nellie. Lucas laughed to himself several times during the next couple hours of his shift, thankful that the cashier had left him alone most of the evening.

"Shop & Save. May I help you?" Lucas spoke with as much adult authority as he could. The phone in the stock room had rung just as he was retrieving a handcart. The time was going rather quickly. A few more tasks and Adam had promised Lucas he could leave.

"So you're not in the hospital?" the caller asked. Lucas recognized the voice as quickly as the caller seemed to recognize his.

"No, but I am around a lot of sick people anyway." He smiled as he spoke into the mouthpiece.

"Then you are at least with your own kind." The sarcasm was light, intended to invoke a laugh.

"Thanks, Heather," Lucas said. He took a pencil from behind his ear and placed it into the pocket of his grocery apron.

"Not a problem. I heard Mickey gave you some trouble. I'm so sorry," Heather said. The sincerity in her voice caused him to grin.

"When are you coming to get me?" She sounded cheerful, sad and expectant all in the same breath.

"Thirty minutes tops. I need to replenish the beer cooler and I'm out the door. Where are you?" He spoke quickly. He could see Georgie talking to a customer a couple of aisles away and didn't want to face his wrath over taking a personal phone call. Lucas poured purple ink onto his price marker as he talked, cradling the phone with his chin.

"Working on a paste up of the school paper," she said.

Lucas exacted a commitment from Heather to be ready when he got there, then bade her goodbye. He hated waiting for anybody, even her. The football game would have already started and he didn't want to miss much of it.

The walk-in beer cooler was on the far side of the store. It usually needed to be refilled twice on a payday Friday. Lucas wrapped himself in his coat and entered the cooler from its back door. Adam was already inside filling the near empty shelves. Occasional beer buyers would open the cooler access doors, unaware that clerks were stocking from behind.

"Lucas mucus, welcome to my office." Adam said, "Care to join me for a cold one?" Adam flashed an open can of Coors from the bottom shelf and tipped it towards him in salute. Lucas looked at the floor near Adam's feet and saw a stack of empty cardboard boxes. He could see two other empty crushed cans discreetly hidden among the trash.

"You're gonna get fired. Georgie is just right outside." Lucas stooped slightly and look out from behind the shelves and into the store. Georgie had disappeared.

"My old man isn't going to see. Here have one." Adam tossed a can to Lucas. "Open it and drink it fast. Get a quick buzz before leaving. I'll dump the empties."

Lucas caught the Coors and said, "I better not. I'm off in twenty minutes."

"Great, it'll jump-start your evening."

"No. I can't."

"Yes. You can."

"Punk."

"Moron."

The two young men stared at each other for a long second, both grinning. Adam tipped back his beer, finished it and shoved it into his stash.

"What the heck…," Lucas mumbled and pulled the ring top off of the can. A blast of beer foam sprayed from the opening. He covered the can top with his lips and started to drink as quickly as he could, catching most of the erupting alcohol.

"Neat mouth trick. Who you been practicing on?" Adam slapped Lucas in the stomach.

"Shut up pin head," Lucas said, beer foam spilling from the corners of his mouth. "If I get canned for this I will hunt you down and kill you."

"That would be a favor to both of us. Drink up Shriner or you'll lose your fez." Adam patted himself on the head as he spoke.

Lucas began quickly filling the empty shelves in front of him with six packs and half cases of beer. The cold air in the cooler reddened his face. His hands were becoming numb. He finished the beer Adam had given him, accepted another, committed to himself this was the final one.

"Why are you working here again? Why'd you quit Bull Run? You could earn more money, have your weekends free." Lucas was making small talk hoping that Adam would not tempt him with another round.

"Simple. They wouldn't serve me free beer underground." Adam belched loud and long moving his jaw back and forth to change the sound and tempo. Both broke into laughter. Lucas downed his second can. They finished packing the racks and grabbed a bundle of torn cardboard. Adam carefully tucked the empty cans deep inside his trash. Adjusting the back of his belt with his free hand, he walked past Lucas and opened the cooler door.

The two exited the back of the store and carried their refuse toward the trash compactor. It was dark and cold in the alley. The street lamp had burned out several days before and not yet been replaced by the city. Lucas threw his armload into the bin and turned around. He stopped suddenly and dropped his arms to his side.

"Oh, man! I can't believe this!" Lucas almost shouted. He was angry. Adam tossed his garbage aside.

"What's wrong? You wet your pants? Too much beer?" Adam never missed a chance to verbally abuse Lucas.

"No, you jerk. I can't believe it. Mickey Whitehead broke my damn headlights and I didn't get them fixed. There's no way I can drive in the dark" Lucas was exasperated and anxious. "I've gotta pick up Heather McKenzie in five minutes and I've got no way to get there. Damn."

Adam started laughing. Lucas turned to him and scowled. "Hey, you could show some sympathy here. See if I ever try to make you feel any better."

Adam was holding his sides. The alcohol in his system was having an apparent effect on him. Lucas looked at him and started laughing too.

24

"Here, loser," Adam said reaching into his jeans and extracting his key ring. "Take my truck. Bring it back tomorrow. I'm out of here in two hours with my girlfriend. She can come and get me. Her parents are gone. I won't need my wheels." He kept laughing as he spoke.

"Are you sure? I mean, thanks." Lucas accepted the keys. "I won't wreck. I promise."

"Yeah, well just don't stain the seats with your little girlie either."

"That's enough, wise guy. We're just friends."

"Right. Real tight friends. What do you do, talk about boys and clothes and stuff?" He began laughing again. Lucas had had enough.

"Thanks, you moron. I'll bring it back tomorrow." Lucas ran into the store and clocked out his time card. For a three-hour shift he had earned about six bucks.

Lucas climbed into the cab of Adam's vehicle. *This is a real truck,* he thought. A four-wheel-drive Chevy with massive tires, a massive engine and a massive eight track stereo system. A Cobra CB radio was mounted into the dashboard, monitoring trucker traffic. Two huge whip antennas were bolted to the back bumper. A chrome roll-bar with four halogen fog lights curled over the back of the cab. The vehicle was also immaculate inside and out. In Sunnyside a man was not judged by his character as much as he was by his choice of trucks. This one was well known and attracted a lot of attention, especially from high school girls. *He is still dating these young girls,* Lucas jealously thought, *All because he has a beautiful 4 X 4.*

Firing up the engine, Lucas felt the floorboard vibrate under his feet. The motor grumbled, muffled just right to ensure maximum horse power and attention. The scent of spice moved through the cab air, wafting from the small cardboard tree hanging from the rear view mirror. The stereo jumped to life as *Creedence Clearwater Revival* rocked in full force, almost deafening Lucas. He loved it. He enjoyed the feeling of power, the sense of strength, the joy of being seen behind the wheel. The alcohol from the two beers made him feel extremely confident as well.

On the passenger floorboard Lucas saw a paper bag. Inside were six more Coors. Obviously a key element in Adam's evening plans. Lucas thought for a moment that he should ask him if he wanted them, but decided instead that he would have one and let Adam fend for himself. The Shaggal family owned most of the beer in town. Adam won't go dry tonight. Lucas opened one of the beers. It felt almost as cold as those in the store. *One more for the road,* he thought. He turned up the stereo volume.

Sunnyside High School stood at the west end of town, nestled slightly up the side of a mountain. It could be seen from most anywhere in the city. Lucas drove slowly through the uptown business district on the way to the school. Passing the bank parking lot, Lucas saw several groups of guys standing by their parked cars. Most of them were either dropouts or recent graduates who opted for a job in the mine and a night life in the bars. Near Miner's Field Lucas saw the grandstands packed with Prospector supporters cheering the team. The scoreboard showed no points for either school.

Even in this small town, cruising was the favored pass time. Scabby and Lucas would often drive for hours. Looking for girls, looking at cars, watching for fights.

Usually nothing ever happened, just a continuous loop around the town, listening to rock and roll, talking about the future or lack of it.

The majority of the stores were closed. The only activities on the streets were in front of the half dozen or so bars and in the alleyway entrances to the whorehouses. When Lucas was younger, he and Scabby would sneak uptown and watch as miners came and went into the brothels. It was always funny how the patrons acted like they were walking down to one of the clubs and suddenly sidestep quickly into the alley.

Lucas drove slowly, sitting high off of the ground. His own truck rode so low that he now hated it. He imagined that his peers made fun of it's size. Scabby seemed to be the only one that truly appreciated the effort Lucas made with his pickup. Most of the union members called his truck a rice burner. Some of the drunken miners would come into the store and question his patriotism for purchasing an imported vehicle and not a union made American automobile. He tried to ignore them, biting his tongue instead of asking them about their Honda or Yamaha motorcycles. It was better to feign ignorance. Lucas' dad refused to let him buy a bigger or newer vehicle, even threatening to withhold college funds if he didn't show financial prudence.

He drove past the last bar and turned onto High School Road. There were only two cars in the school parking lot. Lucas pulled up to the front doors, parked in the principal's reserved spot and turned off the engine. The school hallways were lit and he could see a custodian on the second floor mopping. Near the gymnasium a light was emanating from the journalism room.

He stepped out of the truck. His bladder was full and his head was light from the beer. He drank the remainder of the third beer and tossed the can into the pickup bed. In the distance he could see the blinking lights of the smelter smokestack. The mine yard just below it was bathed in an eerie pale orange light. The cold air stimulated him a bit. He walked towards the school doors and stopped half way. Turning, he strode across the damp grass and stood just beyond the light hitting the lawn. In the classroom he could see several students, including Heather, seated around a long table.

Moving closer he leaned his shoulder against the brick wall of the building and watched the internal scene for a moment. Heather was kneeling on a chair, leaning over a large sheet of paper. Her shoes casually dropped beneath her seat. She held a rubber cement coated brush in her left hand and dabbed the back of a smaller slip of paper. Lucas watched as she gently applied the cutout to the larger paper, taking her time and making the placement perfect.

She was wearing flared jeans with no back pockets. Lucas followed the seam of her pants from her ankle to her hips. He noticed how the material made almost a perfect S shape. Her waist was accented by a green knit sweater cinching just above her navel. A small line of bare skin showed between the two garments. *No man's land,* he thought.

Lucas moved closer to the window. He could see Randy Peeper sitting on the edge of the long table talking with his hands to a sophomore boy. The younger student appeared uneasy and was pushing back in his chair. Ms. Ingram, the senior

English teacher, sat at a typewriter in the corner of the room, pecking out some last minute tidbit for the newspaper, ignoring the students who chattered around her.

Heather finished her pasting and leaned back in her seat. She was now sitting on the heels of her stocking feet, admiring the appearance of the news article. Lucas felt his face warm slightly as he watched her move. The full form under her sweater drew the rapt attention of two girls seated at the table, jealous Lucas supposed, because of their inadequate chests.

The urge to urinate was painful. Lucas consider voiding his bladder into the hedge next to him, but reneged on the thought and decided to use the boy's room just inside the front door. Being caught with his pants down outside of a window looking at girls was not how he wished to be remembered.

Entering the school building at night made him nervous. He looked at the row of lockers, including his own. He thought how ironic it was that all the knowledge of the world was locked away at night. Darkness creates ignorance and ignorance bliss, he supposed. He laughed lightly to himself at the idea and ventured into the bathroom.

He flushed the urinal and stepped towards the restroom mirror. His eyes were becoming bloodshot. The alcohol and cold temperature had caused red splotches on his face. The tip of his nose was red as well.

Damn, give me floppy shoes and a polka dotted shirt and I could be a circus clown, he thought.

Splashing water on his face, he patted it dry with a paper towel, hoping to even out the color. His dark hair was messed from the wind and he had not had a chance to fix it. Searching his back pocket he found his comb and raked it over his head. The hair was full and tugged at the comb teeth. He checked to be sure he had zipped his pants, then exited the washroom.

He walked down the hallway towards the journalism room. His sneakers quieted his footsteps, squeaking sharply once or twice on the shiny tile. Just outside the classroom, he could hear Heather's voice. She was very animated in her speech, apparently lecturing one of the other girls. He tried to listen but could only hear fragments, the words lost in the echoes of the hallway and Ms. Ingram's rapid typing.

"Time and tides wait for no man... or woman," Lucas shouted as he stepped into the classroom. All heads turned towards the door. The typing stopped, then resumed. He realized he was partially drunk. His words felt slurred as he said them. Heather jumped and slapped her right hand to her chest. She smiled broadly.

"Lucas Aaron, you scared me. Not funny." Heather acted mad as she spoke.

The other two girls looked at Lucas and giggled. One leaned over to the other and whispered. Lucas nodded at them, uneasy at their conspiratorial look.

"I thought it was very funny," he said.

"Not everything you say and do is funny." Heather began gathering her books as she spoke.

Lucas stared at her and smiled back. She knew all of his jokes and all of his stories. Most of the time she pretended she hadn't heard them. Some he wished she didn't know. *She must be tired tonight,* he thought.

Heather slipped her shoes on and began looking for her coat. Randy Peeper pretended Lucas wasn't in the room and continued talking to his younger friend.

"Shall we?" Lucas said as Heather walked up to him. He gestured broadly at the open classroom door and bowed slightly. Heather looked at him and lost her smile. *Damn, she smells the alcohol,* he thought.

Heather bid goodnight to her fellow journalists and thanked Ms. Ingram who simply waved, not bothering to look up. Heather walked out of the classroom ahead of Lucas. Her gait was quicker than usual. She didn't speak.

"Mr. Kaari. Stop please." Lucas froze. Ms. Ingram was speaking to him. She stopped typing and stood up, turning towards him. He held his breath.

"Ma'am?"

"Is there something you want to tell me?" Her hands were on her hips. Her normally happy face wore a slight scowl.

"Um, I'm not sure. I don't think so…" He was confused and prayed she hadn't smelled the beer.

"You didn't turn in your project notes. Every senior was to turn them in. You won't get a grade if I don't see those notes on Monday." She turned around and sat back down at her typewriter. In a flash her fingers resumed their rhythm. Lucas exhaled. Heather was already down the hallway, almost to the door. He ran to catch up with her.

"Problem, miss?" Lucas asked as they stepped into the night air.

"You smell like you've been drinking." Her tone was even and serious.

"Yeah, strange how beer will do that." Lucas tried to joke, but saw the words were having no lifting effect.

"Where is your Toyota?" Heather asked.

"Your boyfriend blinded it earlier today and I didn't get a chance to get it fixed. I'm driving Adam's truck." He pointed towards the huge Chevy parked at the curb.

"I'll make Mickey fix your truck for you tomorrow." Heather spoke with an apologetic tone and a touch of sadness.

"I thought you weren't speaking to him."

"I'm not, but he had no reason to abuse you like that."

"Why do you even bother? He treats you like garbage, too."

"That's between him and me."

"Excuse me for caring."

"Excused." Heather was mad and Lucas knew that she would stay that way for awhile.

"If we hurry we can get to the game before half-time." He tried to get the evening back on track.

"I don't feel like going to the game. Can you just take me home? My dad is working late. I should be with the kids." Heather had assumed the care and responsibility for her younger sister and brother since her mother's death three years earlier. Lucas thought she often used the caregiver excuse instead of speaking her true feelings.

"They'll be fine. Let's just go and have fun. Seriously, I'm not drunk." Lucas tried to enunciate each word as clearly as he could and began yielding to her anger.

He opened the passenger door for Heather. As she climbed in, her feet tangled with the paper sack of beer. She looked straight at Lucas and closed the door herself.

"That's just great..." Lucas muttered to himself as he walked around the front of the truck. Climbing in, he noticed Heather had turned her back slightly towards him and was looking out of the window.

"Look, I'm sorry, ok? I'll take you home if that's what you want. I'm a little drunk, ok, but that's it." Lucas sounded sincere as he spoke.

Heather continued staring out of the window for a moment, then turned towards him.

"Luke, I don't care if you want to drink. I don't care if you get drunk. I just know that you are better than that. You don't need to be like the rest of them."

Lucas felt like he was being lectured by his mother.

"I'm not like the 'rest' of them."

"Then act like it and stop pretending you are."

The truck didn't feel that great any more. Lucas started the engine and drove down the road towards town. To the northeast he could see the lights of Miner's Field. He turned the stereo on and found an easy listening station from Missoula. Heather had relaxed a bit after venting at him. She was now looking out of the windshield at the lights of the city. Her brown eyes looked like black buttons.

"Let's skip the game," she said.

"But it's Homecoming. Our last one."

"Then let's remember something else. Lets make a memory for ourselves," Heather said, grinning suddenly. Lucas looked at her smile and became uncertain as to her meaning. He had spent thousands of hours with her over the years and knew her moods well. This was a new look.

"Like what?"

"Like that!" Heather was pointing out of the windshield. Lucas traced her finger and looked in the indicated direction.

"No way! Not me!" He was half laughing half shouting. "I'm not going up there. Not even with you." Heather was pointing towards Cemetery Hill. Three enormous crosses stood over the cemetery. Lit at night, they could be seen for miles, a solemn reminder of the dead and a beacon to the living.

"I want to turn them off," Heather said, "I want to be the first girl to climb the hill at night and shut them down."

Lucas debated arguing with her. The thought of climbing the thousand feet up the hillside on a frozen night in October was not that appealing to him. Having Heather as a side kick was enough to sway him. He turned the steering wheel and headed towards the crosses.

Cemetery Hill was actually a plateau of a much larger mountain. Ever since Lucas could remember he had seen the three crosses shining each night. His mother had taught him the story of Jesus' death and the thieves on the cross. He used to think that the bodies of the three were still hanging there. The image had frightened him tremendously. As a child he could see the hill from his bedroom. For a long time he would pray that God would protect him from the crosses. As he matured and began to understand their meaning, the fear left him, but it still reminded him of death and unpleasantness, not life and goodness. Going to the cemetery at night would certainly revive some of those old feelings.

Driving through town they passed the union hall. The parking lot was overflowing with station wagons, trucks and dirty cars. He saw Ernie Shaggal's Cadillac plastered with bumper stickers and posters. The car was illegally parked at the hall entrance, next to a fire hydrant. There was even an old logging truck butting up against the building. Lucas knew that the timber industry was married to the mining concerns. Without a buyer for their logs and custom wood, the forest workers would ultimately suffer from any strike or work stoppage. During the last strike some of the sawmills had shut down, firing back up only when the miners returned to work.

There were a dozen men standing outside the hall drinking beer. Lucas could hear them swearing loudly, even over the music playing and through the rolled up window. It appeared as if a fight were going to erupt. He slowed down to absorb an extra second or two of the impending battle. He recognized many of the faces, most of them had come into the S&S at some point.

"That doesn't look good," Lucas said, pointing to two men standing nose to nose. They were making the most noise. Lucas heard the word 'scab' used several times.

"It's what wild animals do when you stir them up." Heather spoke in a nonplussed manner. "Let's go and let them fight in peace." The irony of her statement was not lost on Lucas. He turned towards Heather. She was looking at the milling miners. Her face was a bit sullen; sad and mad at the same time.

Driving through town, several young girls waved at the pickup, assuming, Lucas thought, that Adam was driving. Girls never waved at him. He honked the horn to pacify them. Heather hand slapped his chest saying, "Don't flatter them Lucas. Besides, they'll think I'm with Adam." Lucas laughed and honked again. Heather punched at him with her elbow.

The gate at the bottom of Cemetery Hill road was chain-locked as always. Lucas pulled the pickup truck onto the side of the road, its right side tires riding up higher than the driver's side. "You'll have to slide out through my side," Lucas said. He opened the door and reached his hand back in towards Heather. She met his fingers with hers and scooted across the seat.

"It's cold. Do you want to wear my coat? Yours is too thin," he said. Heather was wearing her sweater and a jacket that was designed more for fashion than function. As bright as she was, Lucas was constantly reminding her to dress warmly when they went somewhere. Heather would always get cold before him and ultimately ask to leave early.

"No. I'll be fine. This won't take long." She buttoned her jacket as she spoke. She pulled her dark hair into a ponytail and secured it with a band. Lucas felt flush again as he looked at her oval face, its small nose slightly turned up. The dimple in her chin was almost invisible. He turned away from her, hoping she hadn't noticed his stare.

The cemetery loomed about nine hundred feet above them. The hillside was fairly open, the vegetation stripped by the smelter's acid rain. Hearty leafless bushes held onto barren dirt. Lucas glanced up the hill. A well-worn trail snaked through the brush. Kids had ridden their bikes along the path so often over the years that the ground was hard packed. Lucas and Russell used to take their sleds down the trail during the heavy snows. The light from the crosses gave the scenery a washed out look. Shadows mixed with brush everywhere, creating a black and white jigsaw puzzle.

"Do you want to hold my hand while we walk?" Lucas asked, trying to sound strong.

"Why, are you scared the boogey man will get you?" Heather giggled as she questioned his question.

"Fine. I hope you fall and break your neck."

"That'll only happen if you run over me on your way down the mountain, screaming for your mommy," Heather teased. Lucas felt himself getting a bit mad and embarrassed.

"Great. Then I'll lead the way. You try to keep up." Lucas ran up the trailhead. Heather was eight inches shorter, but seemed to move just as fast as he did.

The alcohol was wearing off. The exertion of the climb helped. Lucas could feel his back and chest getting warm. Half-way up the hill, at the first turn in the trail, they stopped and rested.

"This is really stupid, Heather. Your dad is going to kill you and me," Lucas said as he glanced around nervously, unsure what, if any, danger lurked near them.

"Still scared are you?" Heather was out of breath. Her chest rose and fell in quick tempo. Lucas found himself staring at her in the dim light again.

"I'm not scared, just worried. Why are we doing this, I guess, is the question?" Lucas sat down on the side of the trail and pulled his knees to his chest.

"Because I'm expected to do everything normal. Everybody thinks I can't do something spontaneous. Even you think that. Do you know how boring that can get?" Heather was standing in front of him, forcing Lucas to look up, or else stare directly at her chest.

"There is nothing boring about you," he said. He continued to watch the rise and fall of her ribs.

"It feels that way from here." She touched her fingers to her breastbone as she spoke. "I never get to do anything exciting." Her breathing had slowed.

Lucas stared at her in slight disbelief. Everything about her seemed exciting to him. She was beautiful, smart, talented. Nobody ever argued that. The entire county knew her and seemed to love her.

"Is that why you go out with Mickey, because it's exciting and dangerous?" Lucas trod close to the subject of her boyfriend again.

"I date Mickey because he's good, he's handsome, and he's athletic. Isn't that what girls are supposed to want?" Heather spoke fast, in a tone that told him he had entered dangerous ground.

"I don't know. You tell me. You always have the right answers." Lucas was intentionally antagonizing her. His jealously and disgust with Mickey wasn't too well hidden. He jumped to his feet and brushed his hands across the back of his pants.

"Mickey is a moron, ok? There. Is that what you wanted me to say?" Heather said, barely moving her jaw. Lucas was surprised at her use of the word moron. He couldn't recall her ever saying anything bad.

"Maniac is more like it." He began to grin as he spoke.

"Call him what you wish. At least I know what he wants. He's consistent. He doesn't pretend. Like some people." Heather was staring hard at him.

"Oh, I see. So you play with him, is that it? So you don't have to deal with anybody else that might come your way and try to make you happy?" Lucas straightened his back and tilted his head forward. A strong wind gust pushed his hair into his eyes.

"Shut up Lucas. You've got no business talking to me that way."

"Give me a break, Heather. Come on. I've known you longer than anybody. You think you have me all figured out too, but you really don't. It's so obvious that you are the one using Mickey and not the other way around. That has to be a thrill for you, controlling somebody. That's it, isn't it?" Lucas began to pace.

Heather faced Lucas squarely and glared. He knew he had stepped over whatever invisible line she had drawn between them. "Maybe I love him. Did you ever think of that?" Her phrases were sharp and well paced.

The words froze in the air. Lucas' heart stopped for a moment. Tremendous sadness and anger filled him at the same time. He suddenly hated Heather and wanted to verbally hurt her.

"You loved your dog, too," he said, "He crapped on your rug and peed on your porch, but you still loved him. He tried to screw anything that moved. I guess I can see how you can love Mickey." Heather's look turned to shock. Lucas thought she was going to slap him.

"You're repulsive, Lucas Aaron." She turned and started to run up the trail, heading towards the summit. Lucas ran behind her. He grabbed her shoulder, stopped her and turned her around. Heather pulled away from his grip. She had tears on her cheeks.

"So tell me again that you love him. Tell me enough times and you might convince me and yourself." As Lucas spoke, his heart started to soften. Heather turned away from him and tucked her arms under themselves. Her head hung down, her face partially hidden by her ponytail. Lucas extended his hand palm up and placed his fingers under her chin. He gently lifted her head and directed her eyes towards his. "It's not fair to you. Don't lie to yourself. You don't have to lie to me. If nothing else, you can trust that I only want you to be happy. To be safe. That's all."

Heather brushed her tears with her coat sleeve and looked at Lucas. She dabbed her nose with the other sleeve. "I do trust you. Maybe you're the only one I've ever trusted except my mom. I don't know." She stopped speaking for a moment and stared at the dark ground again.

"Remember when we were five years old and you convinced me to walk to the grocery store with you?" Lucas nodded his head as she spoke. "I was so scared. I knew my mom wouldn't have let me go, but I wanted you to think I was brave. It was important to me, I think."

"I remember. I remember your mom finding us at the candy display and dragging us home by our wrists. She was so mad," Lucas said, smiling. "My dad started yelling as soon as your mom handed me over to him. That was the first real whipping I ever remember. My dad came unglued. God, I cried hard."

"I was crying too, when I got home. I was crying because I heard you screaming when your dad hit you. If I hadn't agreed to go, you wouldn't have been punished. I thought you were going to hate me forever." Heather's voice trailed off as she spoke. She stepped towards Lucas and hugged his neck. Her face was hot as she placed her cheek against his face.

"I miss my mom," Heather said, choking on her words.

"I miss her, too," he whispered to her, "I miss her, too."

Lucas wrapped one arm around her waist and caressed her hair with his free hand. Heather dropped her arms behind his lower back and squeezed him, the right side of her face resting against his coat. He couldn't tell if she was still crying.

Several moments passed before Lucas spoke. "I thought we were going to make a memory, not relive one." He tried to sound cheerful and encouraging. Heather released her grip on him and smiled. She wiped her eyes again with her bare fingers. Lucas took the lead and headed up the hill.

The cemetery covered several dozen acres. Dead miners, dead families, dead war heroes and the lesser known mortals were all buried here. The cemetery was owned by the city of Sunnyside. A caretaker shack sat in the far back of the property. It was indistinguishable at night and generally obscured during the daytime by bushes. An unfortunate groundskeeper lived there on and off during the spring and summer when lawn maintenance was essential. Every effort was made to keep the gravesites green and fresh from Memorial to Labor Day. The cemetery usually looked nicer than the city park. Some families would actually hold picnics at the edge of the grounds. Lucas and Scabby used to ride their bikes up the cemetery road and would wander throughout the graveyard, looking at old tombstones and making up life stories about the people buried there. They even had a fort near the mouth of a steel-grated cavern on the backside of the hill. They called it the Suck Tunnel because of the strong air currents that were continually drawn into it. During all those years Lucas had never been to the hill at night.

It was a high school ritual to climb the cemetery hill at least once and turn the crosses off. Throughout his childhood Lucas would see the lights extinguish as he lay in bed staring at the hill. He never desired to make the journey, although he had been invited a couple of times. His brother Russell had turned the crosses off in his senior year and claimed to have seen ghosts when he did it. This didn't entice Lucas to make the trip either.

Frosted air touched the ground, leaving diamond shards of ice glinting in the light of the trio crosses. Lucas' footfalls broke brittle grass blades already brown from the smelter smoke and finished off by the passing fall season. Heather held onto the back of his jacket as they climbed the hill to the cemetery. Her hands knotted on the coattail cloth, her knuckles pronounced as they reflected back the washed out light. Below them they could hear the slurping of the Greenwood River pushing sludge and dead water south. The empty chilled air carried the sounds of cars passing through the barren city streets. Down near the mine yard, train wheels slowly squealed. Lucas looked at the full moon hazily floating behind the tainted clouds as breath vapors swirled around his head.

Reaching the summit, they turned and looked back down on the village. Thirty nine hundred people were hidden away in their homes, driven there by the early darkness and frigid wind, content in their conversations and television programs, waiting for winter to exhale.

Heather ran around Lucas and reached the crosses first. Over the years the city had tried to prevent kids from shutting them off. They built a fence around them, moving the switches higher on the poles, locking the switch boxes. With each effort, some wise teen would figure out a way to disconnect them anyway. The city stopped their attempts when someone took a rifle and shot out the florescent tubes. Lucas guessed it was finally not worth the bureaucratic effort to suppress the children's challenge. Besides, this rite had been going on for decades. Most of the city fathers had probably shut down the lights themselves in their youth. But Lucas had never heard of a girl making the trip. Heather was the first. Lucas stood about thirty feet away and watched Heather as she stood at the foot of the cross, the switch just out of her reach. She leaned her head back and was staring straight up.

"This thing must be three stories tall," she said turning her face towards Lucas.

"At least," he said.

"Come on up and help me figure this out." Heather stepped forward and placed her hands on either side of the pole holding the cross.

Lucas ran to her side. She was shivering. He pulled open his coat and invited her to step in. She moved under his arm and towards the warmth of his chest.

They stood wrapped in one another's arms beneath the middle of the three crosses. Their shadows dripped down the mountain and dissolved into the blackness. To the west the smelter smokestack, the tallest man made structure in Montana, blinked its aircraft warning lights in steady monotone rhythms; a safety beacon spewing sulfur poison over the sleeping valley. Street lamps and porch lights traced random lines around and through the town. The stadium lights of Miner's Field stood out brightly, creating a perfect square. Referee whistles and football fan cheers broke through the night, providing the only signs that life existed.

As Lucas looked at his hometown he began to see the shape of a heart emerge from the blended light points. The polluted Greenwood River sliced the heart of the city in half, rendering it into two distinct sides. It reminded him of the people in the town itself. Their hearts and lives were divided over simple issues that spanned three generations. He wound his arms around Heather a little tighter, pulling her close, burying her beneath half his coat. With his free hand, he reached behind himself and pulled the power switch into the off position. The light of the cross disappeared as their silhouettes melted into the dark.

For a moment silence filled Lucas' ears. He realized both he and Heather were holding their breath. Turning his head, he looked at the rows of headstones behind them, their polished marble shapes slowly emerging from the blackness as his eyes accustomed themselves to the half-light of the moon and remaining crosses. Long shadows ran from the base of each marker. Heather moved closer beneath his coat, seeking more warmth from his chest. The measured beats of his heart quicken as he felt her squeeze his waist. He knew she could hear each pulse. She shivered slightly then spoke.

"I don't know which is more frightening, the dead behind us, or the dead below us." Her voice was muffled a bit as she spoke into his shirt. Her index finger peeked out from her cuff and pointed toward the city. Lucas looked down at her. In the pale light she was like a black and white photograph. All semblance of color was gone, replaced by shades of blacks and grays.

She continued speaking, "People in this town don't even know how to live, so how can they think that dying means anything?"

"Dying means everything, Heather. It's why we are so afraid. Being afraid of death every moment of every day, it guides decisions, it changes motives, it inhibits everything. It distracts us mostly, I think, from really living." Lucas spoke with strength and certainty, vaguely aware of the carnal thoughts that seeped into his mind each time she moved.

"That's the point. This town lives in the shadows of the world, the real world anyway. Dreams and hopes and ambition are the things that make me feel alive. It's the stuff that gives purpose. It's the thought of not having those three things that makes me fear being dead. This town has none of that. Nobody hopes for a better life, nobody dreams of bigger things. The only ambition is to make it through to payday. People have nothing to hold on to. Somehow they have themselves convinced that they are living, when the truth is that they are already dead and I feel like I'm dying with them." Heather stared at her feet. Her voice was empty and small. She slipped out from his grip, pulled her sweater sleeves down over her hands and tucked them under her arms.

Lucas stood for a long moment before he spoke again. "What about you? You've got everybody believing in you. The school, our friends, your family, me." Lucas moved behind Heather and stretched his arms around her shoulders, intertwining his fingers just above her breasts. Heather lifted her hands and gripped Lucas' forearm.

Resting his chin on the top of her head, he continued, "Yeah, maybe they don't have these great ideas about changing the world, but they seem to think that you will. Your life makes people around you feel alive. Maybe that's enough. Maybe that's all anybody really needs to be alive is to believe in somebody else."

The moon was gone, covered by easterly moving clouds. Lucas closed his eyes as he continued holding his friend. He believed in Heather. He believed that the only feelings that mattered were the ones that she caused. He knew that if these were his last days on earth, that this moment, this quiet embrace, would be all he would need to know that he had lived.

The other two crosses darkened without much effort. Lucas lifted Heather up by her waist so she could pull the switch on the remaining one to legitimize her claim. Fall dried leaves flew across the frosted ground behind them. A chilled breeze from the west pushed Heather back into Lucas' coat.

"Damn. We didn't bring a flashlight," Lucas said, "It's going to be tough to find our way down the trail without falling."

Heather didn't speak. The cemetery seemed to make her uncomfortable. Her arms were pulling against Lucas' rib cage a bit too hard.

"Hold my hand, this time. I don't want you to fall," he said. Without insult, Heather cupped her hand into his. Lucas felt her cold flesh. It warmed him inside. They began slowly walking toward the head of the trail.

A sharp noise sounded behind them. Lucas turned quickly. His eyes were now adjusted to the almost pitch-blackness. "Did you hear that?" he whispered.

"I think it was a limb or something dropping from the tree. The wind is blowing a bit," she said. Her voice betrayed her uncertainty. The noise crackled again, only closer. This time it sounded like a footfall or something being dragged a short distance. Lucas stared hard into the darkness. The outlines of the tombstones were fairly distinct. A shape was moving between the row of headstones closest to them, slowly heading in their direction.

"Come on! Let's get out of here!" Lucas yelled, pulling Heather so fast her first few steps were stumbles. She screamed as the shadow rushed towards them.

"Hurry, let's get to the truck!" Lucas was in a panic. The trail seemed much shorter as they rounded the first corner.

The shadow stopped, switched on a flashlight, panned the bushes, and cursed, "You damn brats."

Lucas glanced over his shoulder as he ran. He could see the cemetery caretaker turn the power switches back to their on positions. The man's vulgarities became muffled as he shuffled back towards his shed.

CHAPTER 6

Lucas had the pickup speeding down Cemetery Road before Heather had fully closed her door. They had seen the lights return on the crosses and gathered that the caretaker was still in residence on the hill.

"I think I wet my pants," Lucas said, staring at his dry crotch. Heather began to laugh.

"Told you the beer was too much, you big baby," Heather said. Any trace of sorrow or anger from their hillside conversation was gone. Lucas drove through town one more time and headed home.

The lights in his parent's driveway were dark. Lucas could see no other signs of life upstairs in the house either. He glanced at the McKenzie house. Heather's father had apparently made it home from work. His bedroom light shone through a drawn amber curtain.

"Want to sit on the back porch for a second?" Heather asked. As children they had played for hours on the back deck of the McKenzie home. Heather would willingly play with Lucas' army toys provided he would later be the voice of Ken to her busty Barbie.

The steps to the deck were slick with frost. Heather held Lucas' hand for support. Her fingers were warm and her hand dry and soft. A summer porch swing stood in the corner of the deck under the awning, protected from the destiny of early snow and waiting for another sultry summer. It's fringed canopy brushed against Lucas' head as he eased himself into the swing. Heather joined him. They were facing Cemetery Hill. The crosses were lit and shining over the valley again.

The swing long needed oil on its springs. As Lucas pushed back and forth with his feet a low squeak filled the night air. Heather was still holding his hand. An awkward silence filled the space between them.

Heather finally spoke, "You said that believing in somebody is living. What if you don't believe in yourself? Then what?"

Lucas thought for a moment, searching for an answer to a question he had never considered. "Then maybe that's hell. Maybe that lack of individual faith is a private hell. Why?"

"Are you in hell, Lucas?" Heather said. She turned to him and looked directly into his eyes. Her beauty stopped Lucas' next words. He felt he was seeing her for the first time. She looked nothing like he had remembered. Nothing like she did even minutes before. The girl next door was gone. Sitting next to him, holding his hand, was a treasure from God.

Lucas felt tears stinging his eyes. Afraid of crying, he blinked quickly. Looking at her face, the cheekbones colored from the night air, he placed his open palm on her cheek, moving it in a small circle. The skin was cool and smooth. He slid his hand to her hair, gliding the fingertips around her ear. It, too, was touched by the autumn night.

Heather leaned forward, drawing her face towards Lucas'. Her left hand found the back of his head, her fingers burying themselves in his hair's curly waves. He closed his eyes. She leaned into him. The tender touch of her lips to his drew away his breath and seized his soul. The warmth of her mouth, it's taste, the tempo of the kiss, swept through his spirit. The ecstasy of the moment, the gentle caress of her hand, blended with his hidden passion.

She smelled of springtime and wild mountain flowers.

He left the earth, his heart lifted into the night clouds, carrying away the burdens of his secret desires. His body was no longer his. He no longer felt connected to it. Light swirled before his eyes. The sound of a thousand waterfalls surged in his ears, crashing in thunderous splashes with the hammering of his heart. The kiss continued for a moment and a millennium.

Another kiss followed; this one more passionate then the first. He felt his body molding to hers as she fell slowly onto him, their bodies reclining in the swing, arms tangling as the momentum took them. Her hands found his chest and slid up his ribs to his face. His hands explored the small of her back and pulled her tight. Then it was over. The world slowly returned. He held her in a close embrace, chests together, breathing as one.

They lay quiet for several minutes, neither one speaking. Lucas stroked the long strands of her hair that fell around him. They lightly kissed several more times. He wanted to stay here, locked in this instant, immovable, with her forever.

"Believe," Heather finally said, her voice hushed and breathy, "in yourself and I think you will find heaven." She stood, taking his hands into hers.

"I've always known your heart Lucas. You think this town believes in me? Maybe. But you make it a better place. You move through life, touching those around you in a thousand different ways. You make them better people. But you need to trust yourself and believe in who you are. Just as you believe in me, I believe in you." She gently kissed his cheek.

Walking towards the door to her house she turned and said, "Thank you for being in my life and for making a memory." She opened the door and was gone.

Lucas stood on the deck in silence for several minutes. His mind played out the scene over and over again. The questions of his heart and his unspoken desires had returned. Doubt and guilt erased the freedom of the last half-hour. He was becoming angry with himself. No longer content with the kiss, his desire for Heather was wrapped in a blanket of confusion. He ran down the deck steps and into the basement of his own house. Collapsing on the couch, he buried his face in its pillows. His tears soothed him to sleep.

CHAPTER 7

He slunk unseen onto the last timber car as it entered the mine portal. Friday, midnight, no miners in the mine yard. His lamp extinguished, he rode a mile into the mountain, unnoticed, to the main shaft. Slipping behind a parked train, he had exited the timber car again without being seen.

The main station was vacant. He could see the shaft gates. Behind them stood the elevator, the main skip, that lowered men and materials in and out of the mine.

The hoistman running the skip, hidden by forty feet of solid rock, never saw his passengers, he only responded to their bells, triggered by signal cords on the skip.

From his dark place he watched the timberman load his wares onto the skip. An hour passed as the wood was hoisted from the train into shaft. Finished, the timberman drove his train motor to its charging station, where it's battery would be refreshed.

Quickly, he opened the gate to the skip and squeezed behind the bundled upright timbers. The timberman returned, entered the skip and signaled for a drop into the bowels of the mine.

The ride went quickly. The temperature rose as the skip sank past each level. The timberman whistled, unaware of his hidden companion.

At the well lit 2800 collar station the skip slowed, stopped by a signal tug from the timberman. Peering from behind his wooden shield, he saw the timberman walking down the drift toward the battery barn to retrieve another train motor.

Safe in his solitude, he stole across the station and began his walk in the opposite direction, quickly finding the dark. He moved slowly along the track, feeling his way with his boot, turning his lamp on only when he was certain the timberman couldn't see him.

After twenty minutes he came upon the first air door. Extracting a map from his backpack, he shone his lamp at its lines. He still had another half mile to walk before he began his climb downward.

The first steel door helped control the circulation of air to the mined out stopes below. By opening and closing it, the quantity and direction of fresh air would change. He opened it with the overhead hydraulic lever and closed it once he had moved through it.

Water trickled in the ditch beside the track. Mud filled the spaces between the track ties. He slipped occasionally as he continued his march. The satchel on his back was becoming heavy, its straps pulling at his collar bone. He stopped and rearranged its contents, careful to keep the flares from being crushed by the hatchet and crow bar. At least he would be empty handed on the ride out.

He looked at his watch. It was almost two a.m. He had four hours to start the fire and exit the mine before the morning shift arrived.

He walked further. The rust on the tracks was now becoming thick, evidence of the lack of traffic in this old part of the mine. Finally, the top of the old stope appeared. He surveyed the planks and timbers that had been set in place years ago. Pressure treated, they had not given to deterioration or rot. The first board was the toughest, requiring all his strength and leverage to get it to release from its spikes.

He removed enough so he could slip between them. With a dangling foot he found the old ladder and began his descent.

The air smelled of rotting wood and mildew. There was no air circulation as he eased himself down. Slowly he made his way onto each rung, checking its stability before committing his full weight.

Eight hundred feet below he found the next level. It was dry and hot. Shining his lamp up and down the old drifts, he could see the dark wood timbers and boards pressing up against the top and sides of the mile-long drift, the timbers soaked decades ago in oil to lengthen their useful life. They would burn slow, but would burn hot, creating dense smoke.

He stood still in the stifling heat for a moment and checked for air movement. There was none.

Walking a half-mile, he found the old shaft collar station. There he stopped and rested. Sealed off when this area of the mine stopped being productive, the power lines had been removed and all machinery taken out and put to use in the more mineral rich areas. The skips and cables were gone. All that remained was a three thousand foot hole in the ground.

The maps showed miles of abandoned tunnels, stopes and drifts. Every foot encased in wood. Each old level bulkheaded from the new.

Using his ax, he splintered an abandoned supply chest into kindling and piled it high into the center of the abandoned mine shaft station. Throughout the area he lay flares on the wooden floor. They would serve as extra fire triggers as the station burned, ensuring a fast blaze.

With the crowbar he pried a three foot hole into the planks that sealed off the old shaft. As the fire grew it would exhaust itself through the shaft and vent through the surface opening, creating enough fear to shut the mine down. The old workings would be flooded quickly by management, hoping to extinguish the fire before it spread to the new stopes. The shut-down would last for months. The government would get involved and so would shareholders. Because the miners were not at fault, the company would have to pay full wages until production resumed. The workers would have their revenge without the pain of a strike.

The thought made him smile. This could be the end of Bull Run's abuses. Their great profits would be paid out to the miners in full. Maybe they would even sell the mine to cut their losses. After a costly fire, it would probably go at a bargain price. His friends would thank him, if he could ever tell them.

He dropped his backpack and extracted two bottles of barbecue lighter fluid. Dousing the pile of broken wood, he soaked as many of the pieces as possible.

The flare started on the first strike. Its red flame illuminated the collar station. He looked around at the dancing shadows of pink and orange and touched the tinder. It started burning, slowly at first, the liquid fuel heating the combustible wood beneath it. He waited until the flames began touching the top of the drift. Smoke began to draw towards the opening in the shaft. The job was done. He prided himself on the good work.

He fell once running towards his exit. His lamp flickered. He cursed himself for not bringing a spare. If the bulb broke, he would die in the darkness, either from a broken neck or the deadly flames.

The opening to the stope was exactly where the map indicated it would be. If nothing else, Bull Run had great engineers in the early days, he thought.

A chill ran up his back. Staring at the boards over the stope, he had forgotten his crowbar. Terror set in. He was tired. He looked at his watch. Two and a half hours and he needed to be safely out of the mine. His only chance was to return to the station and find the crowbar or try to get around the burning station and climb back out. Either way, the fire would most likely be heading up the open shaft.

He could feel the heat and hear the roar of the fire before he saw the flames. Rounding the corner to station he stopped abruptly. The fire was not drawing up the shaft. Smoke was filling the top of the drift and moving slowly towards opening he had made.

He saw the crowbar. It was laying thirty feet from the flames. Racing towards it, he felt the heat begin blistering his rain slicker.

The crowbar burned his gloves when he touched it. Choking from the smoke, he groped along the ground and found the satchel he had discarded. Wrapping it around the crowbar, he again picked it up and crawled quickly away from the fire. The back of his pants had started to smolder.

Running again down the tunnel, he found the sealed stope. Smoke began to fill the top of the drift above him. Coughing and choking, he pried at the boards. They held firm. His eyes stung from the smoke as it lowered towards him. The fire was moving the wrong direction and much too fast.

The board gave way. He pulled up the second and squeezed between them. The crow bar slipped from his grip and fell away into the darkness below. He scrambled down the ladder. Cool air rushed up past him, feeding the fire above.

At the bottom of the stope, he found the crowbar lying in some mud. This old tunnel looked like the one above, timbered and dark. Shining his lamp up and down the drift he tried to determine which direction to pursue. He removed his gloves. Searching the pockets of his rain slicker, the maps were nowhere to be found. A noise above him broke his concentration. He glanced up. The sight terrified him. Fiery planks were falling down the stope, bouncing and lodging themselves along the wooded ladder, igniting them.

He chose left and ran blindly, falling every several steps. The air continued to draw past him. The fire was a living creature, breathing in as much air as it could find.

The drift split in two. Again he chose the left one. After a hundred yards he found an old bulkhead sealing the tunnel. His escape route blocked. His light began to flicker again. He cursed.

Returning to the last divide in the drift he traveled down the main tunnel a thousand feet. It too was sealed. The panic began to overwhelm him. His hands were bloody and blistered. He dropped to the ground, his back pinned against the bulkhead. His lungs ached. His heart was bursting. He resigned himself to death.

His trip in and out of the mine had been carefully planned. The maps were easily stolen and would never be missed. The worker's schedules were no problem either. He had enjoyed the thrill of the planning. The execution of the plan and its glorious outcome were his joy and his reward. He thought of his family and wondered if they would even care that he was missing. He supposed that his body would be burned so completely that no one would know for certain if anyone had started the fire.

He lifted his head slightly and shone his light down the drift. He was thirsty. The fire would not kill him for some time. He didn't want to suffer needlessly. He stood up and began searching the sides of the drift for puddles. The rail ditch had long ago been filled in by miners prepping the closure of this part of the mine, but perhaps some low spot existed where he could find a puddle. All water did seek a low point after all, he thought.

Then there it was. In his panic he had run past it. The final sealed stope in his escape route was tucked off the side of the drift, obscured by some fallen rock and timber. Climbing over the collapsed supports, he saw the opening was almost caved in itself.

These boards lifted easily. Slipping into the small opening, he pulled the loose planks back into place. The climb down was fast. He found his way quickly to the new workings.

He stole onto the ore skip and rode on top of the crushed rock to the main tunnel, unobserved. The same timberman unknowingly gave him a ride out of the main tunnel. He slipped out of the mine yard and walked the alleyways into town.

CHAPTER 8

Ernie had one last stop to make on his Friday swing through Sunnyside. As a prominent business leader and popular politician he made it a policy to stand on both sides of any issue. Throughout the years he had developed an ability to convince the voters that he had all of their best interests at heart. This year, without opposition, he didn't really care what he said and wasn't so guarded when it came to confrontations concerning his political platforms. Voters and dollars equated to the same thing in Ernie's world. A vote was bought with a drink or a lie. It didn't really matter which. Miner's spent their lives trapped in the humid darkness. If Ernie could give them the hope of a brighter tomorrow, he would do that. Bull Run wasn't the enemy of the people, Ernie often said, it was the mentality of the people in this community that was the real threat. Tapping the deadened nerve of a man married to a diamond drill half a mile inside a mountain, whose only desire is to make it through another day, week or year, without getting crushed or divorced, and turn that nerve into action, that is what Ernie thrived on. That gave him life.

Ernie looked around at the dark mountains on either side of the valley. In the western distance, he saw the illuminated smokestacks and buildings of the smelter. It was only 5:30 p.m. yet the sun had already set. The air was cold and a bit damp. Pulling his coat closed in the front, he leaned against his car for a moment. A hundred years from now, people would still remember him, he thought - The Great Ernest Shaggal. It didn't matter that the legacy would never leave these valleys and hillsides. It was only important that local history not forget that a child of the mines beat the outsiders and won. He coveted the day that he would sit in the offices of Bull Run. The East Coast corporate investors would be driven back to their skyscrapers, cursing the day they had met Ernie Shaggal. He could see himself in the office, adorned with pictures of him and the Governor. Accolades from the community and union would be hung on the walls. He would be in charge. He would rule the county, not just from his corrupt commission seat, but from the board of Bull Run. It would happen, he promised himself. Even if he had to die trying.

Ernie loved the night, especially in the fall. It blended all things, good and evil, together, making them indistinguishable from one another.

Twenty-five years ago Ernie had been a mineworker, originally running the main hoist at the Bull Run. The job required no physical activity; just sit in a chair in a huge empty cavern and pull levers, lowering and raising the ore carrier to the surface. He chose the graveyard shift. On a busy night he might run the hoist up and down the shaft three or four times. The pay wasn't bad, but the loneliness eventually got to him. To fill the vacant hours he ate non-stop and poured over the well-worn stack of pornography left by hoistmen on the other shifts. A drop-out at the age of seventeen and virtually illiterate, he eventually taught himself to read as he became bored with the pictures. He was once suspended for a week after he was caught sleeping. It was rumored that his foreman had found him aggressively fondling himself while reading a porno magazine but opted for the napping story instead, making a point to Ernie, yet saving him the embarrassment and ridicule that such a story would cause. It also went better with the union shop steward. People still asked him if the rumors were true. He always denied it with a feigned laugh.

Ernie hated the mining company after that. He became involved in union politics and eventually became one of its leaders. The highlight of his tenure was forcing the Bull Run management to transfer his old foreman to a surface desk job.

During his last four years underground he set an all time record for accruing overtime. Every penny was stashed and paid for a partnership in one of the busiest bars in Sunnyside, the Silver Barrel. He bought his partner out a year later and renamed the joint The Pour House.

Ernie proved to be an opportunistic entrepreneur. On payday Fridays he would cash miner's paychecks for them, giving them their first pitcher of beer for free. Everybody was given credit during the week, which was promptly repaid once their checks were converted to currency. Another bar soon followed; the Silver Lining. Three nights a week, Ernie would bring bands in from Missoula or as far away as Spokane to play cover tunes. He alternated country and rock bands. Business was good as long as silver prices held and the miners stayed working. During strikes, beer tabs went up, revenues went down. Ernie never turned anybody away who wanted a drink. He knew that eventually strikes would end and tabs would get paid. Before he was thirty years old he had made a fortune, at least by Silver Bow County standards. His holdings included the bars, two quick-stop gas stations, a grocery store, a pizza restaurant, a septic tank cleaning business, a pawn shop, motel and the only taxi cab in Sunnyside. The miners loved him. The mining company accepted him. A stuffed ballot box put him into office as county commissioner after his predecessor died mid-term.

The union hall parking lot was full of pick-up trucks and old cars. Ernie smiled to himself as he walked through the front door. Years ago he used to sponsor dances on Friday nights at the union hall. It was here that he found out how easy it was to get drunks to like you, especially teenaged girls. Now fat and fifty, young women still showed up at his house in the early morning hours to work off their bar bills.

Tonight, however, Ernie was here to remind union members that they should vote. He had a printed list of other politicians that he was endorsing and had the agreement from union leadership that the members would abide by the list when they went to the polls. Most miners didn't really care who was in office, except for the county sheriff. In Silver Bow County a person needed a law enforcement leader who understood the ways of the mining community. The perfect cop kept the peace, but also kept his eyes closed.

His legs were growing tired and cold. The tips of his toes were numb. He wiggled them slightly, feeling their cold clamminess rub against one another. He farted loudly, glancing side to side hoping he stood in solitude. A car load of drunken teenagers drove by, music blaring from their partially opened window. Ernie grunted as he pushed himself away from his car and moved towards the front door of the union hall.

"Never fear, Ernie is here!", Shaggal bellowed as loud as his lungs would allow. The union hall was packed with laborers chain smoking cigarettes and drinking draft keg beer, which Ernie had graciously supplied. The air was humid, smelled of sweat and appeared blue to Ernie. His eyes immediately began to sting.

The bright light bulbs looked like they had rainbows around them. Several men immediately broke from their huddles and walked towards Ernie. He quickly began to shake hands as he moved through the crowd.

"Why the hell are you even campaigning you old crook? Nobody is even running against you!" The question came from one of the older men who stood in a circle around Shaggal. His rotten teeth made Ernie momentarily turn away.

"Just so I can get out and meet vermin like you." Ernie grinned as he spoke. The old man hesitated for a moment then smiled back, slapping Shaggal's right shoulder with his left hand.

Ernie worked the room, asking each man about his wife, girlfriend or both. The union hall was one huge open room with a small suite of offices on the far end. Ernie hand-shook his way towards the office. His cheek muscles began to ache slightly as he faked a smile to each person that spoke to him.

"Where's Billy?" Shaggal asked as he poked his head into the first office. Inside sat a nasty looking redhead woman who had seen better days. She had worked as a prostitute years ago at the Powder Rooms in the old uptown part of Sunnyside. Now she was the union's only paid employee, a thank you, Ernie guessed, for her years of service to the community. Ernie had lost his virginity to her decades ago. She was very efficient he recalled. He doubted that she remembered.

"Out back taking crap, sugar." She called everybody sugar. Her name was Delores Young. Everybody called her Dolly.

"You're looking like crap yourself, Shaggal," she continued. Ernie flinched at the thought of being downgraded by her. "You need to get some sunlight or something. I'm surprised that you ever get a woman," Dolly said. She started to laugh. Her voice was phlegm-filled from too many cigarettes. She started coughing. She was obviously unimpressed by Ernie. At this point in her life, Ernie thought, she probably doesn't really care about anyone.

He watched as she placed a lip-stick smeared cigarette into the overfilled ashtray on the desk. She picked up a plastic cup of beer, stained too with a bright red smudge, and sipped. Ernie hesitated for a moment, deciding whether to sit and wait for Billy, or re-join his fans until Billy finished his constitutional.

The back door of the office opened inward. A tall, skinny man with an extremely thin hairline emerged, tucking his shirttail into his pants. His trousers were too short, displaying over half of his white socks. The sound of a gargling toilet could be heard behind him. He addressed Ernie first.

"Out stirring up the troops?" he asked.

The man's name was Billy Murphy. He was the current Mineral Worker's Union president. MWU was one of the largest independent unions in the country. All of its members lived in Silver Bow County. Most of them worked for the Bull Run mine.

Billy won his union post partially because of his hatred of the company, but mostly because of his loyalty to Ernie.

"Yeah, the best part of my job. Blending with the masses."

Both men looked at Dolly. She took the unspoken message and excused herself, "Hey, look boys, I gotta go. My date is waiting for me." Dolly grabbed her cigarette and took one last drag.

"So where's your date tonight, Dolly? The Sunnyside Rest Home?" Billy spoke with a lustful sneer to Dolly. Both he and Ernie began laughing. Dolly adjusted her bra strap and leaned her head backwards, exhausting the smoke from her lungs.

"At least the sheets are clean," Dolly said smiling. She pushed her rolling chair backwards, stood up and walked out the door into the main meeting hall. The voice sounds of miners grew louder then softened as the door slowly closed behind her.

"She still has a nice rear after all those mattress miles don't you think?" Billy had continued staring at the door as he spoke. Ernie could tell that his friend was fantasizing about the old hooker.

"Well, she probably has so many stretch marks that she looks like a road map of Montana when she's naked," Ernie said. Both men chuckled.

Ernie's face became sullen. He was here for business. Walking behind Dolly's desk he sat in her chair and moved it forward. The scent of her cheap perfume hung in the air, tainted by her beer and tobacco.

"So what's the story with the strike, Billy? I'm hearing lots of talk. Talk that doesn't make me sleep very well." Ernie's tone was flat and a bit loud.

Billy pulled a folding chair up to the desk, spun it around, straddled it, crossed his arms on its back and leaned forward. Ernie read the body language. It was a bit too familiar.

"I won't lie to you," Billy said.

He's lying to me, Ernie thought.

"These guys are getting fired up. Bull Run earned more money last year, profited more, than it has in the past three years combined. Our contract runs another year, but these guys want a part of the pie. They don't want to wait until management sits down with us in twelve months. Twelve months after they have figured out a way to spend the money and screw us over." Billy spoke fast and friendly. The speech was pretty well rehearsed, Ernie thought.

"Billy, the last strike screwed me. I almost lost everything. I'm not going to let you guys suck me dry this time. You stop this wildcat strike Billy. It'd better not happen, or this union is going to get torn to pieces. I'll see to it. I'll get the national union boys, the Steelworkers, in here and break up this little club. They've wanted in here for years, but we've kept them out. This time, I won't stand in the way. Are you following me?" Ernie stood up and leaned slightly forward as he spoke. Billy sat back in his chair. Bare skin could be seen between his pant legs and the top of his athletic socks.

"You've got nice things, Billy, real nice. Nice home, nice trucks, nice boat, nice cabin, nice kids. Folks might wonder how you paid for that on a miner's wage."

"Look, I'm doing the best I can, see. These guys trust me, but I can't get them to think straight this time. I'll keep trying but I can't promise anything." Murphy was beginning to sweat. He stood up and walked towards the door. Shaggal walked with him.

"When are they talking about walking out?"

"Monday. They're saying they'll walk on Monday."

"Listen to me, Murphy. You've got less than three days to turn this mess around." Ernie was now roaring at Billy. Billy backed up. Ernie could feel his face getting hot.

"Look," he said in a calmer voice, "Just stop them. I've been to the mine office once today to talk. I'll go again tomorrow and see if there is anything I can do."

Ernie pulled the door open. The noise was louder than before. More mine workers had shown up after hearing that the beer was free. He began to smile again, extended his hand to the closest miner and disappeared into the crowd.

Billy walked back to Dolly's desk, sat down and cradled his head in his hands. After several minutes he pulled his wallet from his pocket and retrieved a folded piece of paper. Placing it flat on the desk, he pressed on the creases to make the numbers legible. Mis-dialing twice and hanging up once, he finally stayed on the line. The phone rang and was immediately picked up.

"It's Murphy," he said, "Its done. Nobody will be working Monday. You have my word."

Murphy hung up the receiver, tore the paper into strips and burned it in Dolly's ashtray. Moving across the room, he opened a large standup locker and retrieved his hard hat and mining boots then left the union hall through the back entrance.

CHAPTER 9

The Mineral Hotel had once been the pride and joy of uptown Sunnyside. Its six stories of hand made red bricks had been brought in from the East Coast by special train almost a hundred years ago. The silver barons had pooled their wealth and created a show piece in which to entertain themselves, their mistresses and any visiting illuminati that ventured into the wilds of western Montana.

When tourists and dignitaries stopped visiting the town and the silver misers moved to the coast, The Mineral slowly fell apart, at one point hosting only a guest or two a month. Rather than close it down, the last owner turned it into a series of studio apartments and charged by the week. This move kept the building alive, but didn't improve it's appearance.

The Sunnyside police patrolled the halls several times a night, breaking up brawls or ejecting drunks who had wandered over from the whorehouses next door.

Billy Murphy stood outside the door of apartment 3B and looked at his watch. He hadn't slept since Thursday. It was half past seven, Saturday morning. He was dirty and tired.

He looked around him. The hall was stale and musty and smelled like urine. The brown carpets were showing threads. Cigarette burns and various stains covered every square inch. His daughter Lori had moved into the building two months ago after a violent fight with her mother. Billy couldn't do much to stop her. She was nineteen and a drop-out. Her waitress job at the Silver Supper kept her fed and clothed. The apartment rent was cheap. She seemed to manage without her parents. Billy had vowed not to interfere. He would rather let Lori fail and crawl home than have her back fighting with her mother. His other children were learning her habits and began making his daily life a nightmare. Lori's absence brought peace to everybody but Billy.

His wife was wounded with guilt but refused to deal with the yearnings for her eldest daughter, choosing instead to harangue Billy into doing it for her. Today he would put aside pride and offer his daughter a return home and forgiveness.

He tapped lightly on the door, not wanting to frighten Lori were she still sleeping. After a moment he rapped louder and considered speaking her name. He held back hoping not to disturb the neighboring apartments. Noise rustled behind the door. Billy could see shadows moving near the crack at the bottom of the door frame.

"Lori?", Billy spoke, "Are you awake."

The door opened an inch. The voice that answered was not hers. It was masculine.

"Who the hell wants to know?"

Reacting before thinking, Billy pushed the door inward, creating enough space for him to step into the room. He was standing face to face with a naked Russell Kaari.

"What? Billy, what the hell are you doing here?" Russell's voice was scratchy from a lack of sleep and an aggressive quantity of beer. His hair was matted and damp. Small sweat beads clung to his forehead and the hairs on his chest.

"Where's my daughter?!" Billy demanded, surveying the small room. The place was a disaster. Dishes were everywhere. Empty beer cans lay in crushed piles near the couch, coffee table and on the kitchen floor. Panties and boxer briefs lay mixed with socks and shirts near the nightstand. Sheets and blankets were twisted and dropping off the bed. The room smelled of marijuana and sweat.

"She's in the bathroom. You shouldn't be here. She doesn't want to see you." Russell wrapped himself around the waist with one of the fallen blankets.

"You're the one who shouldn't be here. It's bad enough your old man and Bull Run are screwing my family, now you gotta get your pecker into it too. I should rip the damn thing off." Murphy was angry as he spoke, debating whether he should strike the young man.

Russell seemed angry as well.

"You're the one that's driving this strike madness. Don't blame my father. He's just the mine manager. He has to deal with the problems *you* cause."

"Spoken like a company man's son." Billy's words were simple, but uttered like they were foul. He sneered as he said them.

"I'm my own man. I'm also my father's son." Russell moved towards Billy trying to intimidate him.

"You're also a dead man."

Murphy swung hard and struck Russell just below the eye. The impact lifted Russell to his toes and drove him backwards over a chair and into the wall near the bathroom door. His modesty was again betrayed as the blanket fell away.

Lori swung open the bathroom door just as Russell fell. She was wearing nothing but a short white T-shirt. Billy stepped forward, reaching for Russell, trying to strike him again.

Lori grabbed her father and screamed, "Leave him alone Daddy." She started hitting him with her fists. Billy stepped backwards. Enraged, he slapped her across with face with his open hand, toppling her to floor next to Russell.

"Stop it Daddy! Stop it! Get out of here!" Lori was hysterical. She backed herself against the wall near Russell's head.

"I'll leave, you little slut. You're a disgrace. Don't you ever come around me or your mother again. If I see you talking to your brother or sister, I'll kill you and this worthless piece of company garbage." Billy spat at Russell. "Do you understand me?" He slammed the door and pushed his way through the small crowd that had responded to the ruckus.

Russell was stunned but conscious. Pulling himself slowly to a sitting position, he cradled Lori's head in his arms, pressing her face to his chest. He began rocking her. His voice was soft and broken as he spoke to her, "I'm going to kill him. I swear, baby, I'm gonna kill him."

CHAPTER 10

Scabby let himself into the Kaari house. He knew that Amanda Kaari, Lucas' mother, wouldn't care. He had been coming over for years and she trusted him, liked his sense of humor, his manners and his good nature. Today he was mad. Mad as hell.

Last night his best friend had stood him up. Scabby had looked for Lucas at the game. He'd walked to the Prospector's victory party at Papa's Pizza. He had phoned Lucas' home. His parents hadn't seen him. He had even gone to the high school before giving in and walking the railroad tracks home. He was convinced that his best friend was dead, killed by Mickey Whitehead.

Lucas' bedroom was empty, which put Scabby into a panic. He considered waking Mr. and Mrs. Kaari. Instead, he found Lucas in the basement sleeping.

"Luke, are you asleep?" Scabby spoke in a normal voice. Lucas didn't move. Scabby shook his sleeping friend's shoulder and said louder, "Hey, are you awake?"

Lucas sat up quickly, startling Scabby, who jumped back a step.

"Hell, Scabby, you scared the piss out of me." Lucas rubbed his eyes. "What time is it anyway?"

Scabby looked at his watch and shook it, "Almost eight thirty" he said, "What are you doing down here? Where's your brother?" Russell's room was off of the basement family room. The door was open and the bed still made.

"Heck, I don't know. I'm not his keeper."

"Mrs. Nellie would say that you are."

"Mrs. Nellie says a lot of things. Some I like, some I don't."

"She'd tell you that your word is your bond, too." Scabby looked at his friend and frowned, hoping that Lucas would see his displeasure.

"What's that got to do with anything?" Lucas raked his hair with his fingers, pushing it out of his face.

"You lied to me. I've never lied to you. Why didn't you come get me?"

"I didn't forget. Something came up. Something pretty important."

"I'm not important to you?"

"No, no, you are. I just had to take care of something."

"Something? You mean Heather McKenzie?"

"Yes. Heather. We drove around. We turned off the crosses."

Scabby sat down in an overstuffed chair across from the couch. Lucas was now sitting up and scratching his chest. His clothes were as wrinkled as Scabby's.

"I thought we were going to do that together someday. Just you and me. That was our plan, right?" Scabby said.

"Well, we've talked about a lot things and never done them." Lucas was sounding defensive as he spoke. He yawned loudly and rolled his head.

"Just another lie of yours I guess," Scabby said flatly.

Lucas stood up and glared at him, "Listen, I've never lied to you. I've stuck up for you when I shouldn't have. I've given up a lot just being your friend."

The words stung as he said them. Scabby stood up and walked towards the basement door, almost tripping over Lucas' keyboard.

"I don't need no sacrifices from you. I'm just glad you're not dead." He left the door open as he walked out.

"Damn it, I didn't mean it that way. Come back here." Lucas followed him through the doorway. Scabby was already running towards the railroad tracks.

Lucas quietly walked to his room. His parents were still sleeping. It was rare to see them up on a Saturday before 9:00. He turned down the covers on his bed to make it appear that he had slept there. He had done the same to his brother's before leaving the basement. After his shower he would go look for Russell.

"Where is your truck, son?" The voice was Jonathan Kaari's.

Lucas turned and saw his father standing in the doorway of his bedroom. Mr. Kaari was tall and lean. His salt and pepper colored hair was a mess. He was wearing a T-shirt and boxer shorts, apparently just having got out of bed.

"I traded with Adam Shaggal for the evening, you know, for something different."

"You don't need to take chances with other people's vehicles. Take it back and get yours before that drunk wrecks it and ruins my insurance." His father spoke flatly and waited for Lucas' assurance.

"Sure, Dad. I won't let it happen again."

Jonathan turned and headed into the hall toward the stairwell. Lucas heard him walking down the steps.

The McKenzie and Kaari houses were only twenty feet apart. The available building space in the town was scarce, necessitating close homes and small yards. Lucas' bedroom window faced Heather's and her younger sisters. The two families had made a courtyard of sorts between the homes and would often sit together there visiting during warm summer evenings.

It was dark and overcast outside this morning. The radio said that snow might fall in the higher elevations. Lucas parted his bedroom curtains to look at the sky, investigating the need for a heavy coat. A slight motion caught his eye. Heather's room was lit, the overhead light illuminating its interior. Heather's five year old sister, Katie, was opening the shades, apparently looking for snow as well. She waved at Lucas, who quickly waved back. Katie abruptly turned from the window and ran out of the room, beckoned, he supposed, by Saturday morning cartoons.

He continued looking across the courtyard and into the room. Posters of flowers and Elvis Presley, tokens of Heather's mother, were thumb tacked on the walls. The room was sparse, only two twin beds and a dresser. Another figure entered the room. Lucas closed his curtains quickly, still peering between the two halves. Heather walked towards the dresser, her hair covered by a dark brown towel. Her body wrapped in a companion of the same hue.

She closed the bedroom door and began towel-drying her hair. Lucas watched as guilt and anxiety began building in his chest. Standing straight up again, she squeezed the ends of her hair with the towel then dropped it to the floor. Lucas stared as she combed out the hair snarls with a hand brush. In a moment her locks were smooth and straight.

Removing her lower towel, she dropped it to the floor as well. Lucas had seen Heather nude before, but at the age of six there wasn't much difference between her body and his. Things certainly had changed.

51

Scott R. Baillie

She moved to her dresser and began retrieving undergarments. Riveted, Lucas stopped breathing. The image before him burned deep into his brain, fiercely refining his vision of feminine beauty.

"You should wear a sweater today when you go to work." The voice behind him broke his concentration like a blast of thunder. Lucas snapped his head away from the curtain.

"You're right, Mom. I was just checking the sky to see if it was raining." His mother walked into his room and sat next to him on the bed. Lucas shifted his legs, hiding his arousal from her.

"Scabby was worried about you last night. Is everything ok?" His mother was frowning and looking him straight in the eye.

"It's fine, really." Lucas tried to sound confident, but knew his mother could easily read his thoughts.

"Don't forget, your father and I won't be home tonight. We are driving to Helena for a political fundraising dinner for Congressman Temple. We'll be back tomorrow after lunch."

Amanda stood up. She turned back towards her son and continued speaking, "Are you hiding something from me?"

Lucas' mouth went dry. "No. Like what?"

"Like, where is your brother? I didn't hear him leave this morning."

"He said he was going to work some overtime. I think he went in on the morning shift."

Amanda looked at him suspiciously for a brief moment then said, "I hope you're not covering up. Are you?"

"No. I'm not. I promise," Lucas lied.

His mother smiled at him, leaned forward, kissed his cheek and said, "Ok, Luke. You should see Scabby before you go to work. He was genuinely upset." She left the room.

Lucas peered back through the space in his curtains. Heather's shades were drawn. He fell back on his bed, gasped and closed his eyes. After several minutes sleep briefly overtook him. He dreamed that Heather's father and Mickey took turns beating him.

The shower was relaxing. He had to force himself to drive the visions of Heather from his mind. His emotions would alternate from joy to fear to anger. He could see her face when he closed his eyes. The taste of her kiss was still fresh, each memory making it more real. The image of her nude body quickened his heart and made him shake. He pretended she had intentionally left the shade open.

Sprays of water rushed over his head and down his back. The warmth of the water eased the tension in his neck caused from pillowless sleep on the couch. He thought of Scabby and the hurt look on his face. He thought of his senseless words to his friend.

Lucas knew the feelings he expressed to Scabby were real. He would never intentionally hurt him, but what he said was true. He had given a lot to Scabby. He had never chosen him as a friend. Throughout the years he had tried several times to make Scabby go away. He would see him walking down the sidewalk to his house and not answer the door or pretend he was sick. When Scabby invited him to spend a weekend at his house, he would fake another engagement. Despite all of the subtleties, Scabby kept coming back.

He couldn't remember whether Scabby had ever had any other friends, even in grade school. In Cub Scouts, Scabby would play with other boys, but the ultimate result was some name calling or insults. Lucas came to Scabby's side time and again, sparing him further pain or ridicule. Then they discovered music.

Lucas wrote poems and stories. They were his secret world. He wrote about his life, his dreams, his dog, anything that meant something to him. He hid them from everybody, including Scabby and Heather.

Scabby found the writing notebook one night while waiting for Lucas to finish dinner. At first Lucas was angry and embarrassed. Scabby calmed him and told him how impressed he was. They would make great songs he had told Lucas. Together they started putting them to music. Crude at first, the songs became more refined and complex. For four years they wrote and composed in Lucas' basement. It became their bond. They shared them with nobody. Not even Heather.

Heather accepted Scabby, even from the first signs of friendship with Lucas. During junior high when she started changing into a young woman, she would ask Scabby to sit with her and Lucas at lunch. As she grew in popularity her circle of friends would acquiesce to both Lucas and Scabby's presence.

Last night the balance of that relationship had tipped. Heather and Lucas were closer than before. Their actions changed the direction of all their friendships. Scabby could not follow them this time. Lucas knew he had to explain it to his friend, but he didn't know how since he wasn't even sure he could define with words what had happened. Scabby always took what Lucas said as if it were some gospel, but this morning in the basement he had pushed back. He had given Lucas a sense of his own pain and emotions.

Lucas began to feel angry at Scabby. They were both adults, or close to it. The time had come for Scabby to take the world on his own and not lean on Lucas. Standing up for oneself defined character, Lucas thought, and it was up to Scabby Cipher to determine that.

The shower water had become lukewarm. Lucas stood under it a moment or two longer allowing the cool water to invigorate him and stave off any further physical yearnings he was feeling for Heather.

Heather's father, Vernon, was sleeping late. The note left for her on the kitchen table said not to awaken him before noon. He intended on working both afternoon shifts over the weekend. She was used to her dad working odd hours. The only shift he kept open was Sunday morning. This was church time. As a practicing Catholic, he had committed to the priest and his wife that their kids would be raised in the church. When his wife died, he continued with this promise, relying heavily on Heather to maintain the order and balance in the house. Heather took care of her younger brother and sister. She had become the other guiding force in their home.

She sat on the edge of her bed preparing for another Saturday at home. Laundry faced her as well as a dozen other chores. Heather had never stopped grieving the loss of her mother. Perhaps she never would. The last words Heather had whispered to her were a promise to take care of her little sister and brother. Her mother's last words were a promise that she would dance with her children and husband when they met again in Heaven.

Heather had cared for her mother up until the last, when she couldn't even walk and relied on a wheelchair. Each day her mother gave up a little more, but not without a fight. She taught Heather what it was like to keep going despite the circumstances.

In a strange way, by assuming her mother's responsibilities, she felt very connected to the woman. Each night before she fell asleep she would tell her mother what had happened during the day with the kids, all of the events big and small that she missed. Heather believed that her mother could hear. Last night was the first time she told her about herself and how she really felt. She told her about Lucas and the crosses and the kiss and about Mickey. She told her how confused she was and how she didn't know what to do next. She told how she thought Lucas would now misunderstand her and how she had screwed up their friendship. The one way dialogue went on into the early hours until she finally fell asleep. Heather wished that her mother could have spoken back.

She stood up and slipped on a pair of jeans and an old sweatshirt with the letters U of M printed in peeling letters. Pulling her hair back, she pinched it into a ponytail. In the mirror across the room she saw herself from the top of her head to her bare feet. For a moment she stared blankly, absorbing the person staring back. Turning slightly, her curves revealed an ample young woman. She hated her hips, they are too big she thought. Her breasts needed to be subdued by sweaters and sweatshirts. Her waist was too thin. Thankfully it could be disguised by the same top garments. Even in this camouflage old men and young boys would still stare at her, some leering, others making suggestive remarks, all of them eventually smiling. This had started when she was fourteen.

Mickey Whitehead's senior picture was turned face down on her dresser. She flipped it over and looked at his face. His chin was square and his eyes dark blue. His blond hair hung in ringlets to his shirt collar. He had been one of the first to make a comment about her appearance without the underlying insinuations. Heather had known him since catechism and had taken her first communion kneeling beside him. Their father's had worked as partners together underground and were still close friends.

She thought about the friendship that had developed between them. Mickey would hang on to every word she said. She would laugh at his attempts to be funny. They enjoyed each other's company and spent time in the same social crowd at school. Mickey was generous with her, buying her little gifts and including her on ski trips or summer outings with his family. Her father trusted him and felt comfortable knowing that Mickey was very protective of her.

After several months Mickey had taken the brave step of asking her to 'go' with him. Heather remembered having her girlfriends explain the complexities of this term and all of the etiquette involved; don't talk to other boys, hold his hand whenever anybody was around, kiss him often and deeply. She had pondered this for quite some time, Mickey always pushing and asking for a decision. Finally she yielded, which started a gossip cycle that continued now into it's second year.

For a time their relationship was fun. A sense of closeness grew between them. He was gentle and concerned with her happiness. She had never slept with Mickey, though he had tried many times to convince her that she should, that he wouldn't tell, that it would show she loved him. Mickey said many of the right things. She had almost given in on one occasion late last spring, in a passionate moment, when he removed her top and raced his hands under her bra. She didn't resist initially, enjoying the sensation of his touch. The moment was broken by his aggressive attempt at something more. Heather tried to gently rebuke him, backing away from his embrace. Mickey had begged at that point, eventually becoming enraged. This precipitated the first of many break-ups. He began drinking with his friends. Shortly after that the rumors about them became even more vicious.

And there was the Lucas problem. Mickey was so filled with hatred for him. Heather had known Lucas since her first conscious moments. It was hard not to talk about him. He was like family. Mickey's jealousy toward Lucas would create argument after argument. Heather refused to agree to stop being his friend. Mickey had threatened to break Lucas' bones if Heather didn't give him up. She dropped Mickey for a time because of the threat. He came back with deep apologies and promises to leave Lucas alone. Eventually he would start again trying to extricate Lucas from her life.

Last weekend Mickey had shown up drunk at her house while her father was working the afternoon shift. The kids were in bed and Heather was watching *The Carol Burnette Show* when he came calling. Despite her father's strict warnings, she let the boy into the house alone with her. Vernon McKenzie liked Mickey but made it clear where the boundaries were concerning his daughter – hands off, period.

Mickey was sloppy and smelled awful. He confessed to consuming vodka and beer, beginning right after school. Most of his words didn't make sense. Heather had had enough and took the initiative to end her relationship with the boy that evening. He started crying. What followed was a three hour confession of his love, exploits and faults. She listened, at points crying herself, not out of sympathy, but pity. She had heard much of it before. Heather had been shocked at some of his intimate revelations and saddened at others. Finally she was determined that Mickey would not be an active part of her life.

As she escorted him to the door he began begging her to sleep with him again. Standing strong she ignored the aggression. Without warning, Mickey seized her arm in a tight grip and forcefully kissed her. Heather had pulled back and tried to free her wrist. He refused to release her, instead fumbling with his free hand at the front of the waistband of her pajamas. She slapped him hard. In shock he let go. She raged at him to leave and threatened to call the police and her father. Mickey stumbled out of the back door into the darkness. She didn't speak to him all week. He glared at her in the hallways at school. New rumors raced through the grapevine. Yesterday, he apparently terrorized Lucas.

Her thoughts returned to Lucas. Standing at the kitchen sink, she rinsed breakfast dishes and glanced out the window. There on the hillside in the distance stood the crosses. She smiled to herself. She had asked for a memory with Lucas and now had one that went beyond what she could have envisioned.

The kiss was unexpected. As children they had pretended to be married and even kissed each other on the lips to see what that was all about. At the time, nothing. Last evening though was different, she'd felt alive.

Lucas was a beautiful boy. Three years ago, his face was almost feminine, his build skinny and slight. It wasn't until he was fifteen that he grew the masculine attributes that made him attractive.

Her girlfriends asked about him often and questioned why he didn't really date, insinuating that he maybe didn't like girls. They asked her lots of other personal things about him. Heather never betrayed Lucas, choosing only to say he was shy. She knew though that Lucas' issues were deeper than that. He seemed afraid of everything, but masked the fear with his gentle laughter.

She finished the dishes and stepped onto the deck off of the kitchen. Her youngest brother, Vernon Jr., was playing on the steps with one of his friends. Heather sat on the porch swing and looked at the mountains. The clouds around them were dark gray and covering the tops of their peaks. It felt like snow. Still barefoot, she tucked her feet under thighs.

Kissing Mickey, though sometimes exciting, didn't compare to what she had experienced with Lucas last night. She began to feel shame and guilt over her involvement with Mickey.

Lucas was different. He was gentle, scared, caring, passionate, and sensuous at the same time. She had liked his tenderness the most. His demeanor, his spirit, his look, his smell, his taste, all made her want him, completely. She had never felt that way about anybody, ever. She had dropped a wall, let him in. The emptiness inside of her, the sense of loss, the anger at Mickey, the challenge of living, the expectations, if just for that moment, were gone, filled by his presence and touch. In that kiss, that single loving instant, her world had been at peace.

Lucas did love her. She had known it for a long time and blamed herself for what was apparently a troubling issue for him. But their souls touched on this swing last night. She would have yielded completely to him. Even now she wished for him, needed him, back in her arms. Heather ran her fingers over the spot where Lucas had been sitting the night before.

Their new journey took a short step last evening. It was a trip without a map, though she knew their destination. This could be their ultimate voyage.

A door slammed next door. She turned her head towards the Kaari's driveway. Looking down she saw Lucas walking towards Adam Shaggal's truck. She slouched slightly in the swing, momentarily embarrassed. He glanced toward her and stopped. A simple smile spread across his face. She lifted her head from hiding and smiled back. The cold air around her warmed slightly.

CHAPTER 11

Billy Murphy went home and beat his wife. They met at the door where she lit into him after he told her about the episode at the hotel.

He looked at her as she raged and thought about walking past her. Trying to step around her into the living room, she moved into his path. He had never before struck her, but the middle finger she thrust in his face did it. The first slap brought her right back to his face. His hand hurt. She was surprised, but now ready to fight. A quick nail scratch from her across his neck and he moved from open palms to fists. Vivian Murphy was short, a little younger than Billy and just as aggressive as he was. They fought through the kitchen and into the living room, Vivian throwing knick knacks and ashtrays as she went.

"Damn you, Billy, touch me again and I'll call the police."

"You might die trying," Billy sneered. He focused all his anger on her.

He stepped to Vivian, grabbed at her hair and flung her towards the couch. She stumbled and snatched a large picture book off of the coffee table. The spine of the book met Billy's cheek with such force the bone collapsed. He too stumbled across the floor. Vivian ran up the stairs towards the second floor. Billy followed her, the mud from his mining boots, now dry, grinding into the carpet as he followed.

At the landing Billy froze. The rage in his body switched quickly to shame. Vivian was huddled in front of their two younger children, her back towards him, protecting them, even though they were almost her size.

"I'll kill you, you bastard, I'll kill you!" Vivian was screaming and crying at the same time, her face almost purple, the veins in her neck visibly pulsing. His son and daughter stared at him, their eyes wide and unblinking. Billy dropped to his knees and tried to touch his wife. She recoiled with her elbow, striking at him, covering her face. He tried again to touch her and she refused, cursing his name. He stood up and walked down the stairs, tracking dried mud and gravel.

In the garage, Billy removed his elk rifle from the rack over his work bench. He had recently cleaned and oiled it, intending on one last hunting trip before the winter. The stock and barrel were cold. He raised the weapon to eye level and peered through the scope. The weapon was fully loaded, as he always kept it. Turning, he walked back into the house. He could hear his wife's voice and the sobs of his children.

His family was still shaking on the landing floor. Seeing the gun, Vivian again placed herself over her children who were fearfully pressed against the wall. Billy stared at them for a long moment then continued up the stairs.

He stepped into the tub of the guest bathroom, placed the barrel of his weapon under his chin and fired with his thumb. The back of his head peppered the shower walls as his body slumped. He didn't want his wife to have much of a mess to clean. The neighbors never heard the shot, only Vivian's screams.

CHAPTER 12

Lucas returned Adam's vehicle to the S&S. Adam was late to work so he left the keys with one of the cashiers.

His truck seemed so confining now as he drove to the downtown area of Sunnyside.

The new headlamps cost about six bucks. He had swapped them out in the parking lot of Kurt Arnold's auto parts store, turning down the owner's offer to help. Kurt was a huge man with drooping pants and a golden heart. Kurt refused to let Lucas pay for the lamps, instead adding their cost to Mickey Whitehead's father's account. The morning was a bit slow so he had stood and watched Lucas work, giving him directions and telling him stale jokes. Lucas obligingly laughed.

The lights weren't aimed properly, but Lucas decided he would have to tend to that later.

The screwdriver he was using had slipped several times causing him to cut his knuckles. Blood had filled in the scratches and was now dry. He stared at his hands as he steered the pickup through town. They were cold and dirty. *Just like the streets,* he thought.

He found Scabby sitting by the railroad tracks near his house tossing pebbles into Logan's Pond. The weather hadn't improved much. Lucas thought that it might actually be colder than it was earlier in the morning. The wind had started blowing a little and was scattering dust around Scabby. The pond water was murky, but clearer than the grayish mud flowing down the Greenwood River. Weeds in the pond had long died off and turned brown, remnants of them rotting on the bank.

Scabby ignored Lucas as he pulled the truck alongside the rail bed. Zipping his jacket, Lucas stepped out of the vehicle and walked tentatively towards the seated boy.

"Ok, so you're peeved at me. How long is this supposed to last?" Lucas said, trying to be light hearted, hoping to erase the tension in the air. Scabby continued pitching pebbles. Circles rolled towards the edge of the pond, starting where the rock broke the surface of the water. Lucas positioned himself on the rail next to his friend.

"Come on. Talk to me," he said, more serious this time.

"Not much to say Luke. I said it all earlier." Scabby shifted his weight slightly as he threw another stone.

"You said very little."

"Enough, though, I think. Don't you?" Scabby looked at Lucas. He placed his thumb on the bridge of his glasses and pushed them up his nose.

"Look, I'm sorry if I hurt your feelings, leaving you at the game and all. I just needed to spend some time with Heather." Scabby continued staring. Lucas paused for a moment then continued, "Never mind. You wouldn't understand."

Scabby stood and threw a fist full of pebbles into the water, creating chaotic splashes. His hair was recently washed although his glasses were still very smudged. He turned toward Lucas.

"You assume a lot, about me I mean. You pretend to be my friend. I think you always have pretended." Scabby stopped speaking and kicked loose a larger stone and threw it further out into the pond than the others. The splash sent water back towards the boys, wetting the legs of their trousers.

"I've never faked our friendship, ever." Lucas knew his words were insincere.

Scabby dropped the pebbles he had been holding in his hand.

"Friends level with each other," he said, "They don't stretch the truth. It's not the fact you promised one thing then did another. That doesn't really bother me. You just act like you care about me, us, when that isn't so." Scabby was now looking away.

"But I do care. Why would I be here if I didn't?" Lucas said defensively. His cheeks were becoming colored from the cool air and his friend's directness.

"You're here to make you feel better, not me."

Lucas thought for a moment. He realized that Scabby was making sense. It was beginning to annoy him.

"Look, I feel like a slug ok? Can't we just put this behind us and get on with our friendship. It really isn't that big of a thing," Lucas said.

"You don't really get it do you? You don't give me no more credit than the rest of the people I know. Deep down inside you believe you 'let' me be your friend. You told me you gave up a lot by being my friend…"

"I didn't mean it that way…."

"But you said it. The truth is that you have gained a lot by standin' by me." Scabby picked up a stick and began poking at the hard ground in front of him.

"Look at you," Scabby continued, "You're pretty smart, girls think you're cute, you have a job, a clean house, nice clothes. Your dad manages the mine while my daddy can barely read and has to haul miner's poop for a living. Not just take their insults, but clean up after them." Scabby's voice was strong and becoming filled with emotion. "Being with me makes you look all the better, not worse. Maybe it's time I stopped doing *you* the favor."

Lucas was speechless. He was becoming angry, not at Scabby but at himself. Down inside he realized that Scabby Cipher was right, at least about his reasons for their friendship.

"It's also about Heather, isn't it?" Lucas said, trying to offload some of the guilt he was feeling. A cool gust of air blew over the boys. Lucas could smell the smoke from the smelter.

"No. It's all about you. Heather is my friend, just like she is yours. She doesn't need me. She chooses me. I don't want her like you do."

"I don't want her, not like that," Lucas lied defensively, "All I can say is sorry, Scabby."

"Yeah, you're sorry." Scabby sneered at Lucas.

"So what do you want from me?"

"Nothing much. Just sincerity and honesty. The basics," Scabby said.

"Maybe I haven't been fair. Maybe what you say is true. But why would you continue being my friend, I mean after you came to this great revelation?" Lucas stood up and turned towards his friend. Sarcasm filled his words.

"Don't make fun of me." Scabby quickly pulled up the zipper of his jacket. His eyes were locked onto Lucas.

"I'm not. Its just hard for me to believe that you would have put so much emphasis on how I treat you or mistreat you I guess. Makes me wonder why you would have ever stuck around." Lucas said.

"Because I like you. You help me dream. I can't make up poems and songs like you. The only color in my life is what you help put there." Scabby thrust his hands into his pockets. His voice was becoming less harsh.

Emptiness filled the air between the two boys. Lucas searched for his next words.

"That's it?" he finally said, with a bit of surprise.

"Yup. That's it. I've never asked you for anything. Do you realize that you have never once come to my house without me inviting you? You have never invited me to do anything with you unless I suggest it?"

"That isn't true," Lucas said, knowing that Scabby was speaking the truth.

"Name one time."

Lucas couldn't.

"So where do we go from here?" he said, raising his eyebrows, staring at Scabby.

"That's up to you." Scabby again sounded stern. He was once more staring hard at his friend.

"Dammit Scabby." Lucas threw his hands into the air. "Ok, you're right. I've made a mockery out of this friendship and you. I guess I'm the fool after all. Fine. If you don't want to remain my friend, I won't beg you."

"I didn't say I didn't want to be your friend. I just want you to treat me like one. Respect me for me, not tolerate my existence." The boys were standing face to face.

"You know what your problem is Scabby? Do you?" Lucas was shouting and pointing his index finger at Scabby.

"Tell me!" Scabby said, gritting his yellowed teeth as he spoke. His glasses had slid to the tip of his nose.

"You are a professional victim. You won't even stand up for yourself, yet you ask me to respect you? You let everybody put you down, push you around, step on you, make fun of you. I've tried to save you from all the hurt. I've tried to help you become something or somebody."

"Somebody like you? I'd rather not."

Lucas was surprised at Scabby's words.

"Now who's lying?" Lucas said, "You've always wanted to be like me, but you don't have it in you. You're going to end up being a loser just like your father."

The words hurt both of them. Lucas could see it. Scabby tried to speak, but nothing came out of his mouth.

Lucas started to utter an apology, "Look, I didn't mean…"

"Don't talk to me no more," Scabby said. He spun around and began running down the tracks towards his house. Turning, he shouted over his shoulder, "He's a better man than you'll ever be, ever."

Lucas sat back down on the railroad tracks and put his head into his hands. He could feel the vibration of an ore train coming his way. Slowly, he stood up. Walking to his truck, he looked at the Cipher's home. Smoke drifted from chimney and blended with the gray clouds above.

CHAPTER 13

Sunnyside city streets had never really been smooth. Originally mud and gravel during the first part of the century, the lanes were eventually paved to appease the drivers who were retiring their horses and buying Fords. The same streets had been torn up and patched at least a dozen times since to make way for sewers, water mains, gas lines and the other necessities of a civilized city.

The avenues resembled inconsistent patchwork and were constantly argued about during city council meetings. Frost heaves would break open potholes in the winter. Repair work wouldn't begin until summer. The only good time to drive the city streets was in the fall, though the bumps were still very big and obvious.

Lucas drove through town looking for Russell's truck. After several loops around the main and side streets, he realized that his brother would have probably hidden the truck and walked to see Lori at the Mineral Hotel. Most likely the vehicle was in the mine parking lot and Russell was in bed with the girl.

Lucas thought about the Murphy family. They did not like the Kaaris. Throughout the past decade, especially since Jonathan Kaari became the mine manager at Bull Run, the two families had been at odds. Billy Murphy had grown up with Jonathan and at one point they had even been roommates, sharing a cheap uptown apartment before Jonathan married Amanda. Lucas remembered listening to his father's stories of Billy and his drunken escapades.

Billy had married his wife Vivian when she was sixteen and three months pregnant. Lori was the result of that youthful endeavor. Russell had been born to the Kaaris a couple of years earlier.

When Jonathan started working his way through the company ranks, his old union friends became jealous. A company job guaranteed work during a strike without the fallout that crossing the picket lines would cause a union man.

During his climb, Jonathan had taken an active part in the various negotiations with the union and had helped avert strikes and usually was in favor with the union. Jonathan had after all been a Mineral Worker's member before he went to college. Still the division of union and management became obvious to both the Murphys and Kaaris, so strong during the last strike that Billy Murphy had stopped talking to all company employees unless it was in an official capacity. Jonathan continued to address Billy in public only to receive a cursory nod or wave. Finally Jonathan stopped acknowledging him altogether.

The last strike was the toughest the community had seen in years. It seemed to drag on forever, exceeding eight months before the realities of defaulted mortgages and repossessed vehicles set in. Lucas remembered that his dad was even targeted at the picket lines a time or two.

County police sat to the sides of the picket lines while the union walked. Violence had erupted as several union workers, yielding to hunger and asset losses, broke strike and crossed the line. Regional news became national and for the first time in anyone's memory, Sunnyside made the *CBS Evening News* when the mine superintendent's garage was firebombed. Lucas was friends with the superintendent's son and even saw him on TV.

The attention brought the State's senators and congressmen to town, all vying for the visibility that a negotiated settlement would bring. Bull Run, after all, provided a significant amount of tax revenue to the State of Montana. A settlement was already in the final stages waiting for union ratification. The politicians got the credit and were re-elected. None of them had been seen in town since.

The divided feelings between union and non-union families continued to grow after the resolution. Lucas remembered sitting in church and watching an entire union family get up and move to another pew when a company family sat next to them. At school the hatred from home would appear in classroom discussions. Over time the mood became a general feeling of contempt. Words like 'company' and 'union' became parallel to the everyday swear words used in and around the mine.

Sunnyside had not seen an ethnic minority member live inside the city limits in over one hundred years. Local mining history was filled with examples of Chinese immigrants randomly killed during the latter part of the last century, when they came to provide services to the miners. Deadman Gulch on the east side of the county was named after one of the roundups where several Asians were flogged, killed and hung from the cedar trees.

Lucas hadn't seen a black man face to face until four years ago when an Army jazz band had performed at his junior high. Jonathan Kaari told his sons non-whites didn't like living in the colder climates. Lucas asked why Eskimos and Indians seemed to do so well. His father did not have an adequate answer.

Several years ago Lucas watched the activities of the Freedom Marchers in the south on television and had learned about the discrimination against blacks in school. That world seemed so far away and like most things on the news was not real to Sunnyside anyway. But during the last strike it was apparent that prejudice was real and not because of the tint of skin. Bigotry was very much a part of the heart of Sunnyside, except nobody would admit or talk about it. If you were a company man, you were a non-person. If you crossed the picket line you were a scab. If you were union you were trouble. Your thoughts and ideals, if in conflict with others over labor issues, gained you and your family a label and hostile treatment. Lucas saw it in Scabby's blood on the playground.

Driving past the mine parking lot, Lucas saw several union members leaning against the fence at the entrance. Two of them were drinking beer. One of them thrust his middle finger into the air and yelled 'company boy' as he drove by. Lucas shook his head and turned around. He wasn't afraid, at least not yet anyway.

Russell's truck was parked in the far corner of the lot, obscured by other vehicles. Apparently a sizeable crew was working overtime this weekend preparing for the wildcat strike that seemed inevitable. It was too early for Russell to be working. Lucas drove to the Mineral Hotel, stopping once to allow an ambulance to speed around him.

Lori opened the door to 3B and peered out at Lucas. Her left cheek was bruised and she had been crying. The whites of her eyes were pink and red.

"Lori, is Russell here or at work?" Lucas tried to sound impatient.

She rubbed her nose and sniffed, "Come in Lucas." The door opened and revealed the clutter. Russell was gone, but had obviously been there all night. "Russell went to work," she said.

"What happened to you? Your face looks like hell. Did Russell do that?" Lucas said, anxious and unsure of the answer.

"Daddy did. He came here earlier and beat on me and Russell. Threatened to kill both of us." Her voice cracked and tears appeared at the corner of her eyes. She walked across the room and sat on the edge of the sofa, moving an empty beer bottle.

"That jerk. Did you call the police?"

"Why? They won't do anything. Daddy is a big shot union guy. He and Ernie own the cops. They aren't going to listen to me. He's told everybody I'm a slut anyway. He'd tell them that Russell did this and get him arrested."

Lucas could see she wasn't wearing a bra and was stooping forward to hide her breasts. Her hair was still wet from a recent shower.

She continued, "Russell looks worse than I do. It's a good thing he was still a bit drunk and high or else he might have felt the pain of the punch."

"I need to work this afternoon," Lucas said. "Are you going to be ok here?"

Lori leaned further forward, pulled her kneecaps together, slanting her legs, her panties peeking out from under her oversized T-shirt. Again Lucas had to consciously draw his eyes from her.

"No. None of us will be ok. At least not for awhile," she said, staring hard at the dirty floor.

"Why?" he said.

Lucas stared at her, unblinking, worried, as he tried to make some sense of her words.

"Your parents will want to kill us too." Lori's hair was obscuring her face.

"My parents think that you aren't good for Russell, his future and all. But they won't kill you. Why would you say that?"

"Look, you know a bit about me, most everybody in this town has an opinion about who or what I am." Lucas nodded as she spoke. "A lot of what is said is true, but a lot ain't."

"That's usually how it is…around here anyway," Lucas said.

"I've been with boys, you know, since I was thirteen years old. There hasn't been as many as people think. And I never been with more than one at a time, either. That rumor still makes its way back to me. I haven't touched anybody since I've been with your brother, and that is the truth. That's almost two years." Lori was looking up at Lucas, her eyes so swollen he could no longer make out their true color. She paused for a long time before she spoke again. "I'm pregnant with Russell's baby."

The words hit him hard. Lucas stood looking at the young woman. Russell had never bragged about his exploits with Lori, but never said he loved her either. Lucas fumbled for something to say.

"Are you sure?"

"Sure of what? Is it Russell's?" Lori was suddenly angry.

"No, no. I'm sorry Lori, I didn't mean that. I'm just…. Are you certain you're pregnant?"

"Yes. Two months already. You're parents are going to kill us," she said again.

"When are you going to tell them? They aren't home this weekend. They need to know."

"I haven't even told Russell yet."

"God," Lucas said. He strolled nervously in a small circle around the living room.

"Yup. It's real. But I ain't having my baby without a father. That's no life. A child needs its parents." Her tears began again. Lucas walked to the couch and sat next to her. He ran his arm around her back and pulled her shoulder to him. Lori tilted her head into him.

"It'll be alright," he said. His reassurance sounded sincere, but he didn't feel it was honest. She continued crying.

The telephone interrupted her tears. The conversation was brief and to the point. The horror on her face stopped her sobbing. Lucas stood up, frozen, listening.

"What do you mean he's dead..." Lori's voice was hysterical, "...he was just here..."

Lori dropped the phone. Her hands began trembling.

"What is it? Is it Russell? Is he ok?" Lucas began to panic.

"No. It wasn't Russell. It was Momma. She screamed at me." The absence of life in her voice hung in the air between them. "Daddy just killed himself. She said it was my fault...," Lucas caught her as she collapsed to the floor.

CHAPTER 14

Georgie Shaggal drove to his brother Ernie's home immediately after Lucas had phoned in the news about Billy Murphy. Georgie hung up, agreeing to let Lucas have the afternoon off. Ernie was already pacing the floor with a telephone stuck to his ear when Georgie walked into kitchen.

"I don't give a damn. The idiot said you weren't striking." Ernie was raging into the mouthpiece. "For all you know his wife shot the bastard. Stay put. I'll be there in twenty minutes. Yeah, well you can kiss mine too." He slammed the phone into it's cradle.

Georgie stood next to his brother, "You already heard apparently," he said.

"What in the hell would the idiot shoot himself for? My God." Ernie was throwing his hands up and down as he spoke, standing on his toes with each motion. "This is going hurt us bad, real bad."

"You didn't have anything to do with it...did you?"

"Hell no! No! What do you think I am?" Georgie kept quiet as his brother roared. "Those bastards will go out for sure now. Damn it...." Ernie began pacing faster.

"Should we go down to his house? You know, to see what we can do?"

"Ain't nothing we can do, unless you can raise the dead...the son of a ..."

Ernie grabbed his telephone and dialed several numbers. He began cursing again into the receiver. Georgie let himself out and drove back to the S & S.

The crowd at the union hall was very small compared to the one gathering outside of the Murphy household.

"We don't need to overreact to this. Whatever Billy did, he did for a reason. But I don't think it should make our decision for us." Billy had been dead less than two hours. The voice belonged to Vernon McKenzie. "We need to hold off on this strike and wait until we find out what happened." McKenzie leaned his elbows on the pedestal in front of him.

"Lies," shouted one of the miners seated a couple of rows over from where McKenzie stood, "He'd want us out. He knew the company was going to keep screwing us. Let's set up a line right now." Several other miners agreed verbally or clapped their hands in approval.

"We need a full vote, not this wildcat nonsense," Vernon said as he moved away from the podium and stepped closer to the couple dozen men. "I am going to work and I suggest you do too. We'll all need money if this goes down..."

"There'll be a picket line waiting for you when you get out. I ain't goin' under. Not now. I'd rather starve than add another dime to those crook's pockets." The same miner spoke again. The others again applauded, this time louder.

"A few more days won't kill anybody," said Vernon.

"Not true. It's already killed Billy."

"We'll find out about Billy as soon as the sheriff has a chance to..."

"To what.... Cover up? That's lunacy Vernon and you know it...."

The crowd was becoming agitated. Vernon could tell that his words were useless. He walked to the door. Another dozen miners walked in as he left.

Vivian Murphy had to be sedated. Lucas had driven Lori to her parent's house and elbowed through the crowd. Mrs. Murphy, hysterical, had pushed her daughter away. Words and accusations were exchanged before one of the investigators asked them to leave, promising he would come see Lori later.

"I'll try to find Russell. He'll talk to your mom," Lucas said.

"She's putting this on me. Daddy told her about me and Russell. She thinks that's why he did it." Her words broke through her tears. "She blames Russell just like she blames me."

"You didn't do anything." Lucas tried to pacify her.

"We broke his heart," she said, "Daddy grew to hate your family as much as he hated the company…" Lori stopped speaking, losing her words.

"I'll find Russell. He'll know what to do."

Lucas took Lori home and put her into Russell's bed. Heather saw them from her kitchen window and ran to the Kaari's basement. She had heard the news in a phone call from her father. Letting herself in, she found Lucas closing Russell's bedroom door.

"What's going on? What's Lori doing here? Why isn't she with her family?" Heather's words came in a flurry. Lucas walked towards her and took her hands into his.

"She's pregnant. With Russell's baby," Lucas said. Heather stopped speaking. Her mouth opened slightly as she stared at the closed door.

"What? Do your parents know?"

"Not yet. They are in Helena tonight."

"God, Luke, they need to know. She can't stay here. They'll wonder why she isn't with her family."

"I think this is all the family she has left. Her mother is blaming her and my brother for Billy's…death." Lucas hung onto his last word. He realized he had trouble saying it.

"Where's Russell? Does he know?"

Lucas told Heather about the fight that Lori and Russell had with Billy at the hotel and how Russell had gone on into work.

"I'll stay here with Lori. Go to the mine office and see if you can get them to find Russell."

Lucas awkwardly hugged Heather. Neither of them had a chance to express their feelings about the previous night. They looked at each other. Lucas bent and kissed her lightly on the lips, hesitating for a moment.

"Go," she said, pushing gently on his chest. Lucas closed the basement door quietly behind him, walked out of the gate and climbed into his pickup. It had started to rain.

More men had gathered at the gate to the mine parking lot. A city police car was parked a half a block away. Lucas pulled up to the gate and drove slowly through it. Several of the miners stooped and glanced into the cab. He heard the phrase 'company boy' uttered once or twice. The men returned to their beers and conversation.

The parking lot was fuller than usual for a Saturday afternoon, but not as congested as a weekday. Lucas found a visitor's spot near the main office and parked. The rain had already stopped, but the air was cold and damp as he stepped out of his truck. He zipped his coat to his chin.

"No way of knowing where the kid is," said the fat mine guard, "I can call down to the 5600 level and see if they know where he is. I doubt that he is up in his stope running a drill. Most likely he is cleaning up the tracks or something."

"Stope?"

"Yeah, his work area. You know, ore pocket, gotta climb up or down ladders between levels to get to it, where they drill and blast the ore. Don't you know squat about mining?"

"No, sir. Not really," Lucas said, glancing nervously around the mine yard. In the distance he could hear the low pitched hum of the compressors pumping fresh air down a ventilation shaft. Above them on the hill he could see a tower with a large pulley wheel situated on top and a long black cable extending over it and dropping deep into the ground. The wheel moved occasionally, raising and lowering men or supplies through the ground.

"That's right. Your dad ain't no miner. Least not anymore. I remember when he used to drill ore in the stopes." Lucas could hear a slight disdain in the man's voice. The guard coughed hard and spat a mass of phlegm past Lucas and onto the ground. A soiled handkerchief appeared from the man's chest pocket. He placed the cloth on his nose, digging at this left nostril with it.

The guard dialed several numbers on an old black telephone. He spoke loudly to somebody on the other end. Lucas could not tell from the words used whether the guard was actually talking to somebody who could hear him or not. After several minutes of yelling he hung up and turned back to Lucas.

"The hoistman hasn't seen him. But one of the timberman thinks that Russell is up on 3700 repairing track. No way to know really. You'll just have to wait until he comes out after shift."

"When is that?"

"11:30 or so, less he works a double, then it'll be in the morning. The hoistman will give him a message if he sees him." The guard looked over at the small group of miners at the front gate. "You'd better get out of here. Them boys are keepin' a watch on you."

Lucas walked to his pickup, watching so he didn't step in the old man's spittle. He drove back through the gate. Two of the men wouldn't move out of his way, forcing him to stop. One of them tossed an empty beer bottle over the cab and into the back of his truck. The bottle shattered.

"Where's your daddy, sweety-pie?" The taller of the two miners said sarcastically.

"Probably hiding out with his old lady. Left this little boy to fend for himself," said the other. Lucas knew both of the men. They were regulars at the store. He accelerated slightly, steering around them.

"You look scared," the short man hollered. Grabbing his crotch he said, "Come back later, I got something that'll scare the life out of you." The group began to laugh. Lucas looked into the rearview mirror. Another beer bottle was tossed at him, landing in the street. The parked policeman waved at Lucas as he drove by.

"Bastards," Lucas said under his breath.

CHAPTER 15

Nellie Montgomery was shaking raindrops off of her straw hat when Lucas first saw her. A warm smile crossed her face as he walked towards the fence.

"Mrs. Nellie, can I talk to you for a minute?"

"Of course, love, you can help me start a fire in the kitchen. Come in." Nellie climbed the steps to her back porch ahead of Lucas. He could tell that she had been working in her yard despite the bad weather. Dirt and mud were clinging to her shoes. Her hands were gloved and dirty. It looked like she was wearing a pair of old khakis.

The kitchen smelled of baked bread and cinnamon. "Cookie?", she asked as he took off his coat, carefully placing it on an oak hook behind the kitchen door.

"No, ma'am. Thank you."

She took one from a jar on the counter and handed it to him.

"Try one anyway," she said.

In the far corner of her kitchen stood a round pot-bellied stove. Lucas walked over to it and sat in a wicker chair facing the glass fire door. The house had electric heat, but Nellie said she liked the radiant warmth from the iron stove better. She kept a teakettle steeping on its surface. When the fire would get too hot the kettle would boil causing it to whistle. Nellie would then adjust the air flow and bring the temperature back down.

"I didn't see you at the store earlier today. That Adam boy brought my bags home for me. He looked awful, like he'd been in a fight," Nellie said.

"He's pretty wild. Probably fell down drinking last night," Lucas replied.

Together they put paper and kindling into the stove. Lucas struck a match and held it to the newsprint. Closing the iron door, he watched through the small window as the fire crept over the pieces of wood.

"You appear far too serious for a Saturday. Are you feeling ok?" Nellie placed a hand on his forehead. Her fingers were smooth and cool.

"No, I'm ok. You heard about Billy Murphy, right?"

"I did. When I was at the store. Poor soul," Nellie said, her voice becoming soft.

"I was with his daughter when she found out. It wasn't pretty." Lucas touched the side of the stove to see if it was getting hot. The stovepipe began creaking as the metal expanded from the heat. He bit into the cookie and chewed slowly. Several small crumbs fell to his lap.

"The good Lord must have had you there for her. He knew that she would need you."

"Maybe. She needed her mother more, but she wouldn't talk to her."

Nellie looked at Lucas with a puzzled expression. He spent the next twenty minutes relating the news of Lori's run-in with her father, the pregnancy, and Russell. He told her of Mrs. Murphy's reaction.

"She has had a lot of grief over the years. They lost their son Dale to a hunting accident three years ago, remember?"

Lucas nodded his head, and said "He was with his father when it happened, wasn't he?"

The front of Lucas' pants were getting warm. He pushed his chair away from the stove and leaned back in it, stretching his shoes towards the fire. He could feel the dampness in his socks from the rain.

"Yes. They were deer hunting over in Red Ives," Nellie said.

"Dad believes that Billy blamed himself. Thinks that was why Billy became so mean," Lucas said.

"Well, love, some people deal with hurt in different ways. Billy just wanted to hate somebody for the loss. He couldn't really find anyone that could take it away."

"Then he lost his daughter," Lucas said, crossing his arms over his chest.

"He never really lost her, love. Children try to find their own way, some earlier than others. She just wanted him to notice her, even if it meant making him angry. The love of a child never dies."

"You never had any kids, did you Mrs. Nellie?"

The kitchen became still. The kindling crackling in the stove was the only sound. Nellie folded her hands in her lap and stared at the flames through the soot covered grill of the stove. Her eyes grew distant. "Get your coat on, I want to show you something," she said.

Lucas was puzzled but put on his jacket and helped Nellie with her winter coat. Slipping on her woolen gloves, she took his hand in hers and walked out of the kitchen door and down the steps into the yard. The wind was blowing lightly. A misty rain had begun falling again.

Nellie led him past her garage and walked through an enormous flower garden, barren now, but colorful in the summer. At the bottom of the mountain butting against her property stood a tall willow tree, its branches bare and hanging low to the ground. A cement bench sat facing the tree. Red bricks ringed the trunk. Nellie and Lucas sat on the wet bench together.

Nellie began to speak. Her tone was quite and thoughtful.

"My husband, Marvin, loved me very much. Too much, if you can imagine that. I was fifteen the first time I saw him. Daddy ran him off every weekend for a couple of years. He finally gave up and let me start keeping company with him, though, but only when he or Momma were around."

"Let me guess, he asked you to marry him under this tree right?" Lucas said with a sly grin on his face, trying to second guess the old woman.

"No, love, he didn't. One summer night, when it was Daddy's turn to keep his eye on us, he fell asleep on the front porch. Marvin and I sneaked off and found ourselves in this garden. The stars were so beautiful then. It was like you could see straight to heaven." She paused for awhile before she spoke again. "We lay on our backs and tried to count them. There wasn't any moon, just swirls of light. We were so nervous that Daddy would come looking for us. Every time we heard a noise, our hearts would jump. Marvin and I got swept away with the moment. Two months later we had to tell my parents that I was with child. Momma and Daddy were heartsick."

Lucas sat in silence. He looked at Nellie. Her face was serene. The corners of her eyes were moist.

"I thought you didn't have any children."

"Well, love, Marvin and I married almost immediately. It was either that or send me away. Daddy was determined one way or the other. I couldn't leave. I was too much in love by then. Anyway, we were married quietly right here, in this spot," she said, touching the concrete bench with her fingers, "Seven weeks later, I lost the baby."

Lucas was still holding her gloved hand.

"I'm so sorry...I don't know what to say..." He searched for words, but couldn't find any.

"It's ok. It was so long ago. We were the only ones, my parents, Marvin and me that knew about the child, although there were rumors."

She placed her free hand on his wrist, patting it gently.

"We had a small ceremony for the baby; it was a boy, though I never did see him. We buried him right there, in a little wooden box Daddy made. He'd lined it with the material from inside of his Sunday suit. It was so sweet and beautiful."

She pointed toward the willow.

"Marvin and I planted that tree over the grave as a marker. Every day since then I've watched it grow." She dabbed at her eyes with a tissue she had retrieved from her coat pocket.

"The love of a child is precious. It can't be lost or taken away by anyone or anything." Nellie stood up and walked toward the tree.

"Lori's Daddy loved her, he still does and so does her mother. Your parents will love her and that little baby. God doesn't make mistakes, people do." She walked back to Lucas. "Let's go back inside where it's dry, love."

The kitchen was much warmer now. The kettle was gently blowing steam. Nellie lifted it's wooden handle and moved it to the side of the stove top.

"How did you know that you loved Marvin? What made you know that he was the one?" Lucas looked at her as he spoke. Peacefulness had returned to her face.

"I didn't know for a long time. He was a new teacher at the grade school, all of twenty years old. Handsome, witty. Everybody knew him. All my girlfriends flirted with him. I pretended I didn't care." She smiled as she spoke.

"You must have been pretty then too..." Lucas said.

"Do you think I'm not anymore?" Nellie began to laugh. Lucas turned red with embarrassment.

"I didn't mean...."

"I know what you meant. It's hard to see the peach complexion through these wrinkles." Her eyes danced. "I looked a lot like my mother. She was very beautiful...."

"But how did you know?" Lucas asked.

"When I stopped lying to myself. When I saw his heart and heard it. Then I knew."

"And you felt that way all the years you were together?"

"I still feel it now, love. Just as strong..." Nellie stopped speaking in mid-sentence. "Why all of this? Are you in love?"

The question was too direct. Lucas turned away and stammered, "I'm not. I don't know. Maybe." He stood up, walked to the kitchen sink and retrieved a glass from the drain board.

"Heather McKenzie?" Nellie slowly closed her eyes as she said the name.

"How did you know?" Lucas said, turning his head back towards the old woman, surprised at her understanding.

"I've known for a very long time," Nellie said, "It's in your eyes. She must see it, too."

"I've never told her. I can't tell her," he said, drawing a glass of water from the tap.

"Why?"

"It would ruin what we have now. It might not be real. She might say no and not speak to me again. Lots of things." Lucas walked back to the stove and rubbed his hands together, extending them towards the fire. He sat down and began rocking slightly on the edge of his chair.

"There are worse things in this life than telling somebody you love them. You will never know if she is the one, if she doesn't hear it from you."

"I don't want to hurt if she rejects me." Lucas could feel his spirits sink.

"You will hurt a little forever if you don't. You are so young, so incomplete. Falling in love is the easy part, Lucas. Owning the love is sometimes very painful. If she doesn't love you the way you want, then you need to accept that. You can't make somebody love you. Love has its own terms."

Lucas remained silent and continued staring at the fire. Nellie stood up and adjusted the damper on the stovepipe, slowing the fire a bit.

"I kissed her last night," Lucas said, changing the subject slightly.

"And...?" Nellie said as she sat back down.

"She kissed back. And again this afternoon." There was a hint of energy in his voice.

"That doesn't mean its love."

"Well, what does it mean?" he said, furrowing his eyebrows. Rain pellets began tapping at the side windows. A storm was coming from the west.

"It's a beginning. You both are learning to trust yourselves and each other. Take small steps together. The rest will come."

"Is telling her I love her a small step?" Lucas said simply.

"It's the most important one."

Nellie walked over to Lucas and kissed his forehead. He stood up and hugged her, stooping to place his head on her shoulder. Her gray hair was damp.

Nellie stepped back, cradled Lucas' face in her hands and said, "Love knows all things and is very patient, my sweet boy. Don't be so anxious about what would, could and couldn't be. Speak to her with your heart. Love will do the rest."

CHAPTER 16

The portal to the Bull Run Mine reminded Russell of the entrance of an old cathedral. He had seen pictures of the old church archways, how they were held together with simple lines. Usually angels were etched somewhere on them. The opening to this tunnel was neatly framed in a concrete curve and had the company's name in stately letters at the top. Rather than the door to heaven it was a gate to hell.

The man train was fairly full for a Saturday afternoon shift. Russell figured with the impending strike that a lot of miners would try to earn an extra day or two's pay. The temperature changed immediately as the train entered the mine. The air was humid and warm and smelled like dirt and mildew. Around him miners turned on their lamps, careful not to shine their lights in one another's eyes. Across from him sat Delmer Cipher, the 'Nipper'. He usually was avoided and sat alone.

Delmer was eating a sandwich he had pulled from his lunch pail. Four men usually rode together in these coaches, but with the light crew, most coaches held only one or two workers.

"Hey, Nipper, why are you eating before lunchtime? Doesn't your wife feed you at home?" Russell said, trying to make small talk.

"Well, sometimes I lose my appetite, or worse, cleaning out the honey buckets," Delmer said between bites, "Those stools can get mightily ripe."

"What could be worse then cleaning up people's crap all day?" Russell asked.

"Accidentally sticking your hands in it," Delmer replied casually.

Russell shuddered and realized he had just lost his own appetite.

The motorman accelerated the train. Russell stared out of the open air coach and watched the walls of the tunnel rushing by less that ten inches from his face. The train operated much like a city bus, powered by overhead high voltage lines. It could travel at close to 35 miles per hour, making the trip from portal to main shaft in around ten minutes. Despite the warnings to keep hands and feet in the coaches, several miners had lost fingers or hands over the years by not being cautious. Russell moved closer to the center of the coach, holding his lunch pail and water jug closely in his lap.

Above him he could hear the sparking of the line as it touched the motor's power arm. He could smell the aftermath of the electrical discharge. The wheels of the train banged and squealed as it progressed towards its destination. Behind him he could hear other miners talking or laughing. Several men up front were involved in some horseplay with a younger man, trying to pour cold water down the front of his shirt. As the train moved deeper into the mountain, the temperature from the compressed rock grew warmer. By the time he reached his work area, the temperature was usually around 82 degrees. Russell breathed deeply and closed his eyes. He loved working here.

"Care for a pork rind?" Delmer said licking at a gap between his teeth.

"What?" Russell replied, startled from his daydream.

With his good arm Delmer thrust an open bag towards Russell. His left arm was always locked in a 45 degree angle at the elbow.

73

"Here. A pork rind. Try one. I made them myself." Delmer shook a paper bag in Russell's direction. The outside of the sack was soaked dark brown with oil.

"No thanks. I've got a hangover. That'd make me puke." Russell turned his face away from the opened sack. Delmer continued his feast. Russell turned back and looked at him. The wheels of the train coach squeaked as the train rounded a sharp corner.

"Of all the jobs in this place, why did you choose that one?" Russell asked.

"Because of this," Delmer said pointing at his crooked elbow. "Ever since it got broke, I can't really do much else. Besides, it keeps me out of the way. Most jobs need a partner, ain't nobody around here going to work side by side with me." Delmer retrieved another pork rind.

Russell looked at the twisted arm. He had heard the injury was caused years ago when Delmer broke strike.

"Would you do it again? Cross the picket line?" Russell asked cautiously.

"They'd never let me," Delmer said in a hushed voice. "If they could have, they would have killed me last time. I got seven kids to feed. It'd be hard to do that if I was dead."

Russell stared at Delmer. The man was tall and skinny. He had several missing teeth. The shape of his face and forehead looked a lot like his son's, Scabby. Russell heard the word *strike* shouted by one of the nearby miners.

"If we strike, maybe you could go to Idaho or Wyoming or the Dakotas to work. That's what a lot of these guys will do."

"Nah. They'd spread the word that I had scabbed. Its just better that I stay around here. The good Lord will take care of us." Delmer smiled as he spoke. "I started cleanin' the church last year. It don't pay much, but least we'd have food money."

Several men sitting nearby began staring hard at Russell. Speaking to Delmer was silently discouraged. Russell continued talking anyway and glared back at the men.

"Word is we're going out on the line Monday morning. Supposed be to ugly."

"Is that what you want to do?" Delmer asked.

"I don't think it's right that the company just keep all of its money and hold back from us. We've got to do something," Russell said.

"Your daddy helps make the decisions on who gets paid what don't he?" Delmer said, digging at the space between his front teeth with a dirty fingernail.

"Sort of. He tries to work deals that everyone will like." Russell heard the swoosh of an air door as the train passed through it. The change in air pressure made his ears pop.

"Nobody wins in these things. Its gonna be tough on you and your daddy if there's a strike. You're still livin' at home ain't you?" Delmer asked.

"Not for much longer," Russell said. He stopped talking and began thinking about Lori again. She hadn't said anything but he knew something was wrong with her. He felt it.

"You're a bright boy. Why'd you settle for working here? If I had your brains I'd find me a surface job or get me a life someplace else." Delmer leaned forward and removed his rain slicker.

"I love my life. I don't want to work anyplace else but underground." Russell knew that he sounded insincere.

"Nobody loves it in these tunnels. Your back will give out in a few years, then you start hatin' this place and blamin' everybody else for your bad life." Delmer paused for a moment and took a drink from his ice water jug. "You know any old retired miners?" he said, wiping his wet mouth with his sleeve.

Russell thought for a moment then answered, "No, not really."

"See, that's one of the problems. The union fights for retirement money for us members. We even strike for it. But we never get a chance to get much of it. Gotta be lots of money sittin' there somewhere, because ain't no old men drawin' any."

The train began to slow down. The clanking of the wheels dropped in pitch. Russell was thankful that this conversation was ending. The lights of the collar, the station at the top of the main shaft, came into view.

Delmer pushed another pork rind into his mouth, wadded the paper sack and placed it in his lunch pail. The rest of the miners grabbed their belongings, sat on the edges of their seats and sprang from the train when it stopped, fighting their way to the 'skip', the elevator that would lower them deeper into the mine. The skip tender pushed at the men yelling, "Get back ladies, I can't open the gate until you get back."

Russell stepped from the train. Delmer walked to a huge upright storage cabinet with the word 'Safety' painted in green on its door.

"Want one?" he asked Russell as he attached a self-rescuer to his miner's belt.

"No. Doubt I'll ever need it." Russell watched as the men in front of him kept shoving at one another.

"Yeah, probably never need it." Delmer said. They walked onto the skip together. The skip tender pulled the signal cord several times indicating to the hoistman the skip was ready to be lowered. It began moving at once, lowering forty miners down the shaft into the heat and total darkness.

CHAPTER 17

The skip would descend almost a mile, stopping at several different levels. Miners exited at each one. Russell watched Delmer climb off at the 3700 level where one of the track repairmen turned a hose on him for laughs. Delmer held his lunch pail to his face and walked past the man, trying to ignore him.

Russell tugged the signal cord at 4200 feet and stepped off. The station was well lit. He looked up and saw that the top of the drift, or tunnel as topsiders called it, was secured with a series of rock bolts and heavy gauge wire fencing. He felt safer under this than under the old fashion timber cribbing.

"What the hell are you doing here, Kaari? Thought you were partying away the weekend." The man speaking was Russell's supervisor, Freddy Whitehead.

"Should ask you the same question," Russell finally replied. He slipped off his yellow rain slicker as he approached the man.

"The old lady is busting my balls about a new refrigerator. A couple of weekends down here and she'll have her icebox, then maybe she'll let me back in the bedroom," Whitehead said as he grabbed his crotch. Both men laughed.

Russell was a couple inches taller than Freddy, but easily fifty pounds lighter. He hung his slicker on a nail above a wooden bench and sat down next to his boss. Miner's had knick-named Freddy, *Chrome*, because of his balding head. Most miner's had pet names, tagged because of some imperfection, mistake or because of their job. There was the burned out Vietnam vet called *High Guy*, the pipe fitter named *Stroke* because of the collection of pornography he carried in his lunch pail. There was *Little Squeaky,* a kid from Maine so-called because he appreticed for somebody called *Squeaky.*

Russell didn't even know some of their given names. He was called *Ditch* by many of the men. His first job underground was keeping the water discharge channel along the main track free of obstruction. He hated the name and refused to respond to it. Freddy would answer to his given name or his moniker. He didn't seem to mind.

"I think its 'cuz you love it down here so much or you're afraid this level might become productive without you," Russell said.

"Think so, Einstein? I was making this mine money before your old man had a notion to deflower your Momma."

"Come on Freddy, you got it made. What, two years to retirement? I've seen your desk above ground in the management office. You suck up to my dad and anybody else who has pull up there."

"Yeah, I've seen what your daddy pulls up there." Whitehead grabbed his groin again. Russell smiled. He liked having Freddy for a boss. Most of the crew on 4200 had bid to be a part of his team.

Freddy was the supervisor for the 4200. A tough man, he had almost twenty five years underground and was liked by most everyone. Everything that took place on this level, in these eight miles of drifts, stopes and tunnels was ultimately his responsibility. He was still a union member, but had an office above ground with the company men. His insight was valuable in determining production direction for this area of the mine.

"Your son is trying to hurt my baby brother again. I had to stop him yesterday from killing Lucas," Russell said changing the subject.

"Mickey? Heck I'm sure he's just playing. You know kids. He'd never hurt Lucas. They've known each other since grade school. 'Sides, ain't your brother a little, you know, light-in-the-loafers?"

"Is Lucas a faggot? Old man, I think I'm going kill you..." Russell grabbed Freddy's suspenders and prepared to hit the man's face.

"Nah, now listen. I was just playin' with you. Sheesh. Cool down." Freddy had a huge semi-toothless grin on his face.

"Just the same, I'll teach him a lesson if he touches him. You might let him know." Russell half-laughed as he spoke and pushed Freddy away.

"A whooping might be good for him. I've given him plenty myself," Freddy said with a bit of pride. "He's got a lot of frustration since he ain't playing ball. I've had to take him down a notch or two already this month." Freddy sat down on the bench next to Russell.

"He's got a lot of jealousy in him, too," Russell said.

"Wouldn't you? The little man is like a hound. He's following Vernon McKenzie's girl like she's in heat. Heck, can't blame him though, I would too. Wouldn't you?"

"How can you say that. She's your best friend's daughter." Russell scowled at his boss as he spoke.

"Yeah, and she's got the firmest flesh and nicest curves in two counties," Freddy said with a grin and a wink.

"How can you talk about her like that? Maybe you need your butt kicked too, old man," Russell said winking back sarcastically.

"Speaking of a beating, what the hell happened to your face?" He reached out and touched Russell's bruised cheek with his thumb. Russell recoiled.

"Billy Murphy took me down a notch, too, I guess."

"That torpedo of yours is going to get you into a boat-load of trouble with that girl, you crazy kid." Freddy was laughing as he spoke.

"It already has..."

Freddy looked curiously at Russell.

"By the way, where is Vernon?" Russell said. He stood up and tucked his T-shirt into his pants as he adjusted his miner's belt.

"He ain't here yet. He's coming in later this afternoon."

The conversation turned to work. "I don't want you in your stope since you ain't got no partner today. Just clean out the waste ditch alongside the tracks at the bottom of your stope and get the rails straightened up. It'll make it easier for you Monday." Freddy stood up and turned on his miner's lamp.

"We won't be here Monday."

"Why? 'Cause of the strike? It ain't going to happen. I saw Ernie Shaggal up talking to your old man in the office last night. Your daddy told Ernie that he had been speaking to Congressman Temple and that he was getting him to come to town tomorrow to talk to the Mineral Worker boys. He's supposed to see him tonight in Helena."

"No kidding?" said Russell optimistically.

"No kidding!"

Russell climbed onto a manchee motor, a small battery powered train engine used to pull supplies up and down the tunnels on 4200. He stepped onto the dead man's switch closing the electric circuit and engaged the motor. The manchee sped off down the tunnel towards his work area.

The temperature on this level was cooled by a series of huge air conditioners. Large ventilation pipes were strung along the side of drift and ran back towards the various tunnels and work areas. It was still very warm, but it could have been much worse.

The mining engineers who mapped and designed the various levels of the mine took air circulation into consideration. Without adequate airflow, the workers could get over heated or even suffocate.

Russell passed the main air conditioner station. The cage door protecting the cooling units was open. He slowed the manchee and stopped. An electrician was stooped over one of the fans with a wrench.

"Why no cool air today?" Russell asked.

"Routine maintenance. Should have it up and running by tomorrow evening."

"God, it's going to be hotter than hell back here by then."

"So just go home."

"Can't."

"Then don't complain. There is enough airflow going back to your stope. It'll be hot, but you can still work. We used to open the water lines and run a spray of water over us to keep us cool. You might try that. You'll be wet from sweat anyway. Here, take some salt pills, drink a lot of water, and sit down if you start getting numb." The repairman tossed Russell a packet containing two tablets of salt concentrate.

"Wonderful. Heat stroke. Can't wait," he said out loud. Russell was already sweating, mostly from the after affects of his alcohol intake.

"You're the one who wants to work, mullet head. Take it or leave it."

Russell swallowed the tablets and washed them down with water.

The manchee jumped forward when Russell pushed the throttle. He arrived at the ladder and chute to his stope five minutes later. The airflow was almost undetectable. The heat was much worse than he thought.

Stepping from the train, he looked at the tracks and drainage ditch. Neither of them was in serious need of attention, despite Freddy's conclusion. Any work expended would be non-productive Russell thought. He decided to climb to his stope and see what needed to be done there.

The ladder was made of wooden two by fours and stretched upward over 500 feet. Russell had made this climb no less than four times a day, every day that he worked the stope. He and his partner had been on this job for almost a year. Their silver ore pocket was rich and would probably last at least another six months or so before the grade began to diminish.

Once in the stope, Russell scanned the work area. It ran about forty feet in opposing directions. At one end stood the work tools; two jack leg diamond drills, several piles of timber, a case of oil for the jack legs, a saw, a couple of sledge hammers, pry bars, several large hoses and an assortment of pipes. A muddy copy of a porn magazine sat atop some stray boards.

Shining his light towards the ore face where he and his partner drilled, Russell saw a huge pile of crushed gravel, or slush as the miner's called it.

The gravel was the result of a series of timed explosions made by Russell and his partner into the face of the rock. Using six foot diamond drills, they would bore a series of twenty or thirty concentric holes into an circular pattern called a round, and fill the cavities with dynamite and prell, a highly explosive mixture of ammonia based fertilizer and diesel fuel that had been dried into small pellets. The resulting explosion, detonated from the 4200 level would leave the pile of slush and move the face six feet further into the ore vein.

Russell decided to clear the slush and prepare the face for drilling. The stope was extremely hot and humid. Russell looked at the air line dropping into the stope from the ladder above him. This ladder punched through to the 3700 foot level. A chute next to the ladder was used to raise and lower supplies and served as service entry for the air and water lines.

Russell took a ten-inch pipe wrench from his belt and opened the end of one of large hoses. A blast of air rushed from the opening, creating a tremendous rushing and whistling sound. He stepped back and searched his pockets for earplugs. Finding them, he inserted one into each ear. They deadened the noise, but only slightly. The air movement felt good. It helped evaporate his sweat, though he was still very miserable. Again using his wrench, he clamped another air hose to his slusher. Tugging the operating lever, the slusher roared. The pneumatic engine was working fine.

Connecting his slush bucket to a pulley he had mounted in the ore face, Russell began dragging and scraping the ore into a chute next to the descending ladder. This chute could hold up to three days worth of slush. A motorman on the 4200 would empty the chute during a normal shift and run the ore out to the main shaft. No motorman would be available today.

Running the slush bucket would require good hand eye coordination. His vision was still blurred from the impact of Billy's fist and the lingering effects of a belly of booze.

Russell could feel his body heat rising, but tried to exert as little energy as possible. He figured the temperature must be close to 110 degrees with 100 percent humidity. The work was mindless. He began thinking about Lori again. If she was pregnant as he suspected, there would be a heated confrontation with his parents, ending with their broken hearts. Maybe they would never speak to him again. Perhaps they would disown him. He tried to picture himself without his family. The image hurt. He thought that his brother would still come around, but even that was an unknown.

He thought back to when Lori had seduced him a little over two years ago. She was barely sixteen.

They had met at a late night summer keg party near the Dark Bridge. The trestle, a steel suspension type, served the railroad companies, spanned the east fork of the Greenwood River and had been a favored spot for teenage beer parties. Russell sat down and took a drink from his water jug.

The east fork of the river was several miles from Sunnyside. It ran from the Rockies to a merge point with the mine-polluted Greenwood fifteen miles downstream from Sunnyside. Surrounded by thick woods and a deep swimming hole, the bridge tradition had passed from generation to generation. During the day, families from the county would play and swim at the bridge; at night teenagers would unleash their urges to drink, smoke pot and conquer the opposite sex.

Lori later told Russell that she wanted to make love to him the moment he walked past her to get a beer. She was lightly intoxicated and made the first move, walking up behind him and squeezing his butt. Minutes later, in the darkness of the woods, she had fondled him through his cutoff jeans and allowed him to feel her breasts. Her intention was clear.

They made furious and urgent love on the grass upstream from the bridge, almost getting caught by several drunken ninth graders who had accepted a dare to jump from the trestle in the dark. He remembered crawling on all fours with her, pants down, hiding themselves from the boys.

Russell had committed to calling her the next day, but didn't. He still couldn't remember why. More days went by. Lori confronted him at Papa's Pizza the following Friday night. He took her outside to calm down. A half-hour later they were naked again in the back of her parent's car in the corner of the high school parking lot. They had been together ever since. Over time he had grown to love her, though he kept those words between them and categorically denied his affections for her to his friends.

Russell finally stood back up, opened the slusher's control valve and began dragging cracked ore to the mouth of the service chute.

The cable snapped on the slush bucket, shot back towards him, whipped against his shoulder, lay open his shirt and deeply cut the flesh beneath. Jumping backwards, he avoided serious injury, but hit his back hard against the rib of the stope.

"Damn it," he cursed out loud. Removing his gloves, he pulled away the torn part of his shirt. The wound was at least six inches long and bleeding.

"Damn it," he swore again. Blood began to soak through the material. He decided he needed to leave the stope and get the injury cleaned. *I should have stayed in bed,* he thought, *But hell, I almost got killed there too.*

The climb to the 3700 level was hot and exhausting. Russell figured he could find a first aid kit at the collar station and take care of the injury, then climb back down to his work area. Freddy Whitehead would never know he had been in the stope.

Midway up the ladder Russell puked. The salt tablets mixed with the remnants of last night's abuse and the underground heat turned his stomach sour. He almost fell down the ladder when his head started spinning.

As he walked the drift towards the 3700 collar, the signal lights hanging from the top of the tunnel turned red, indicating that a train or motor was coming. Russell stepped to the side of the track and stood at a curve in the tunnel. He could hear the motorman before he saw him, the wheels of the motor banging against the iron rails.

The nipper, Delmer, pulled the hand brake on the motor he was driving and slid to a stop just shy of Russell. A small flatbed rail car was coupled to the manchee, towing four plastic garbage cans of feces and lye. Each container was labeled, 'Shit. Do Not Open.' There was a troubled look on the man's face.

"What's wrong, Delmer?" Russell asked.

"I'm not sure. Something's not right back in the old K drift." Delmer's voice was strained as he talked.

"K drift? Never heard of it," said Russell.

"It's back near the old workings. It's where I dump and clean the toilet cans. The air is moving the wrong way." Delmer pulled a red handkerchief from his pocket and wiped his brow. The air in the drift was barely moving.

"The conditioners are off down below. Maybe that's what's causing it." Russell rolled his shoulder. His flesh and muscles were sore.

"They've been off before. The air doesn't ever move the opposite direction then. Something is drawing the air back into the old workings." Delmer pointed back down the tracks as he spoke. His miner's light flickered slightly.

"That's not possible. That whole area is closed off. Has been for years. It might even be flooded back there," Russell said, leaning against the side of the drift. He was still breathing hard from the climb.

"Dear Jesus, what happened to your chest?" Delmer said, staring at the blood on Russell's shirt. The stain had spread to his armpit.

"Lost a battle with a slush bucket. Give me a lift and I'll clean it up, then I'll check out this K drift problem with you." Russell ran his hand over his face, erasing beads of sweat. He climbed onto the hitch behind the motor and balanced himself. Delmer started the motor again.

The two men rode the manchee to the collar where they cleaned and dressed Russell's injury. The trip to the K drift took almost twenty minutes.

CHAPTER 18

Lori wanted to be taken back to her apartment. She expected Russell after work. Lucas offered to have her stay at his home and wait, but she wanted to be alone. He drove slowly through the streets, listening to her retell the story of her father's visit earlier that morning. His heart hurt for her. Losing somebody you love to death takes part of you with them. Lucas looked at the young girl and saw her face was half-dead, the light of life in her eyes was gone. Only when mentioning Russell's name did there seem to be a flicker, which quickly died in a flood of tears.

Lucas walked her to the apartment. The hallways were already becoming clogged with drunks and kids looking for drugs. The stale smell of cigarette smoke hung in the air. Music blared from behind each apartment door. Lucas could hear shouting as well, angry drunken voices spilling curses. A baby's cry blended into the audible mix. He couldn't imagine living in a place like this. He pitied Lori for the life she was living. Russell was fun, energetic and lacking responsibility. Lucas supposed his brother would try to persuade Lori to abort their baby and leave the families out of it. Hearing her desire to keep the baby was certain to create a major issue for both of them. Lucas wondered if the relationship would endure that struggle. Lori fumbled with her key as she unlocked the door. In her small hand, the keys looked heavy. The lights were still on in the apartment when they entered.

"Are you sure you want to stay here. Mom and Dad would understand your need to be someplace other than here. You could probably stay with Heather tonight." Lucas held her elbow as he spoke.

"It'll be ok. I need to be here when Russell gets back. We need to talk this through." She unconsciously touched her stomach as she spoke. Lucas looked at her hands again. They trembled slightly. He hugged her and waited in the hall until she locked the apartment door before him. On the floor above he could hear people stomping to the muffled sounds of *The Guess Who*.

The sun settled early behind the western hills. Sunnyside began to button itself up for the night. The only activity was at the union hall and the mine gate. Lucas drove to the S & S to get his paycheck and check in with Georgie. He knew that Georgie would have more information on Billy, and to appease his own curiosity wanted to talk to him about the suicide.

The store closed at eight o'clock, but the stock clerks would work until nine ensuring that the shelves were full for the after church crowd the next morning. With a half an hour until closing there were still quite a number of cars in the parking lot. Lucas parked in front of the main doors to the store and walked in, turning immediately into the store office. Georgie was working an adding machine, tallying the day's cash take.

"Aren't you afraid of being robbed? You got thousands of dollars sitting out there." Lucas began speaking to Georgie before his boss saw him. On the small office desk were several tall stacks of paper currency. The sound of the adding machine stopped at the sudden interruption.

"Not as long as I got this," Georgie said patting at his vest. It was rumored that Georgie carried a pistol, although nobody ever saw it.

"Besides, this damn valley is so short and narrow, the cops would block it off and we'd find whatever son-of-a-gun took the money before he could get too far." Georgie had spun his office chair to face Lucas. The springs groaned as he leaned backwards and interlaced his fingers behind his head.

"You and your brother take care of Murphy's girl?"

"Yes, sir. I did. She's hurting pretty bad. Russell still doesn't know. He's underground."

"Her mama is hurtin' bad, too. Ernie took her and the kids to his lake place. Going let them cry it out out there. Got a couple of people watching over them as well as the preacher McElroy." Georgie called every religious man a preacher. In this case the preacher was actually the Catholic priest. The lake place was about thirty miles west of town.

"Lori needs to see her mother," Lucas said, hoping that Georgie would offer some solution.

"It'll happen soon enough. Your brother needs to be with her for now." The phone rang as Georgie finished his sentence. He picked up the receiver and began speaking. Opening his desk drawer, he retrieved an envelope and handed it to Lucas. Lucas thought it a bit funny that the man could read his mind. Lucas waved the envelope at Georgie and walked towards the checkout lines. He peeked into the envelope to assure himself of its contents.

"Kaari, get over here, I'll cash that for you." Lucas had been standing in line behind four shoppers with filled carts. Adam Shaggal removed the chain blocking off the last check stand and turned the cash register key on.

"Thanks," Lucas said as he signed the back of the check and handed it to Adam.

"My oh my! Fifty one bucks," Adam said sarcastically. "Wanna hit the whorehouses for a couple of half and halves? You can buy." Lucas shook his head no, held out his hand and received the money.

"If they charged a buck a minute, I'd loan you a quarter. I'm sure that'd take care of your needs," Lucas said.

Adam grinned broadly at the insult. "They don't call me a minute man for nothing," he said. "Thirty seconds, thirty minutes, it don't matter as long as I get my pleasure." Other customers standing behind Lucas snickered at the comment. Most of them held cases of beer.

"You and Scabby goin' to the kegger at Flat Top? It's probably the last one of the year. It's getting too friggin' cold," Adam said.

"I don't know. Scabby is pissed at me. I hadn't thought about it. Why Flat Top? The road up there is too dangerous. Besides, the cops can see the fire from town can't they?" Lucas ran his sentences together. His thoughts felt jumbled as he spoke.

"Sure they can. But they're so busy with this Murphy suicide thing and the strike craziness that there aren't enough of them lard butts goin' around to worry about a bunch of kids having fun. You can ride with me, pecker head, if you're too scared of the road."

"I'm more scared of your drunk driving. You can ride with me." Lucas realized he had just committed himself to attending the kegger.

"Done. I'll get some beer for the ride." Adam closed his till and headed towards the beer cooler. "You folks will have to step into the other lines," he said to the waiting customers. One of them cursed at Adam. Adam promptly made a vulgar hand gesture at the man.

Lucas walked to the back of the store to wait for Adam. He considered calling Scabby and inviting him along. As he thought about it, he realized he was mad at Scabby and probably would just end up arguing with him. Besides, his parents were gone, Russell was busy and Heather was home watching the younger kids. He could use a beer after a day like this.

The ride to Flat Top would take about forty-five minutes. The old logging road was only used by hunters and kids. Lucas checked his gas gauge as he started his engine. Adam climbed in and closed the passenger door. Lucas inserted a tape into his eight-track player. Rock music filled the cab.

"Sure this rice burner can climb the hill?" Adam said. He placed a paper bag on the floor boards of the pickup.

"If it can't, you can walk or push," Lucas replied. The pickup pulled out of the parking lot and onto the main street. He adjusted the stereo's volume.

Driving past the mine smelter Lucas could see the smoke pumping far into the night sky. The lights on the smokestacks were barely visible. The fumes were very strong again.

"Good news, kid," Adam said as he too noticed the smell, "The cops won't be able to see Flat Top through the smelter smoke. Knew that stench was good for something." Adam smiled and opened a beer. He offered one to Lucas who refused.

"Saving yourself for the kegger, dear?" Adam said sweetly, puckering his lips.

"Knock that stuff off," Lucas said, "I might have one up there, but I'm not about to get drunk again tonight." He knew he was trying to convince himself more than he was Adam.

Adam laughed and pushed at Lucas' shoulder and said, "You better keep this pickup in low gear and drive like hell if you want to make it there." Lucas downshifted and swerved off of the pavement just past the plant and onto the gravel logging road. A yellow sign lay in a ditch. He could read the words, *Watch For Logging Trucks,* in peeling paint. The sign was peppered with bullet holes. Another vehicle pulled off behind them.

Adam kept quiet as he drank his beer and listened to the stereo. Lucas pressed the gas pedal to the floor and steered his small pickup as gracefully as possible. The engine whined loudly but pulled along faster than he thought it would. The road was deeply rutted from hunter's big trucks wheels. His tires rode the ruts virtually steering the pickup for him.

"I had her once you know," Adam said after a song ended.

"What?" Lucas replied, ejecting the tape from the player. Adam's statement came from nowhere, it seemed.

"Lori Murphy. I made it with her before your brother did. I think a couple of us got her that night." Adam had a puzzled look on his face as if mentally counting.

"That's enough Adam, I don't want to hear this. Besides I think you're full of it." Lucas pulled the tape from the stereo and dropped it into a tape case on the truck seat. An air freshener swung wildly from his rear view mirror. The car behind them was dropping a bit further back.

"Think what you want, but it's true. Right up here at a party a few summers ago. I think she was fifteen or something. She wanted me to do her ugly friend, too." Lucas could see Adam grinning in the dark. He wondered why Adam would broach the subject and if he was just making it up. Probably just lying to make him mad, he supposed. Instead of responding, Lucas let the conversation die.

The road suddenly became much steeper and circled into a switchback. Lucas shifted into first gear. His back tires spun loose on the gravel. The rear of the pickup bounced. The vehicle kept moving forward, slinging gravel and dust into the air.

"Gun this piece of imported crap!" Adam was laughing and bouncing slightly in his seat. His right hand held onto the dashboard. His left clutched a beer and rested on the seat.

Lucas could see a huge bonfire burning at the top of a nearby mountain. They were still a mile or two away. Flat Top sat directly across a little valley from them, but the road wound around in a series of switchbacks before cresting at Flat Top.

"Where's your girlfriend tonight?" Lucas hoped to redirect the conversation with his question.

"Which one? What night is this?" Adam faked a puzzled look and grin as he spoke.

Lucas smiled too. "Why do play around so much. Don't those girls get hurt?"

"Course they get hurt. That's ok though. Keeps me free from having to stay with any one of them too long. They're all young and dumb. I'm doing them a huge favor. They need to get hurt so they can appreciate whoever they get next."

"You want to live like this forever?" Lucas asked. He cringed at thought of spending a lifetime in Sunnyside.

"I'm here for a good time, not a long time, little boy." Adam tipped back the last of his beer, rolled the window down and tossed the can into the back of the pickup.

"I don't get that kind of thinking. I'm out of here as soon as I graduate." Lucas raised his eyebrows and spoke with assurance. The road straightened out and became level. He shifted into second gear. The truck increased its speed. Sunnyside had all but disappeared into the cloud below them.

"You think so? You think you'll get out of here? You ain't no different than the rest of us. Beer, broads and bud; that's what we're all here for. That's all anybody wants." Adam pulled a marijuana joint from his shirt pocket and waved it at Lucas.

"Not me," Lucas said.

"We'll see. You bed that McKenzie girl and you'll be begging to work the nastiest jobs in the mines just so you can stick around and diddle her. Your plans won't mean a thing." Adam lit the joint and drew a deep breath.

"Tell you what, if you don't get her somebody else will," Adam continued, "Probably me. Yeah, that'd be cool, me making both the Kaari boy's women." Adam began to force a chuckle as he expelled the pot smoke from his lungs.

"Go to hell, Adam," Lucas said angrily. "She'd never go for a guy like you."

"A guy like me? I've got what they all want. And I ain't talking just about my large wallet." Again the grin and a deep draw from the joint.

"Your ego is all that keeps you going. You think below the waist," Lucas said, trying to sound insulting. He rolled his window down, hoping to evacuate some of the sweet smoke.

"Hell, it got me through high school didn't it?" Adam spoke without exhaling. His voice sounded throaty. He snorted as he tried not to laugh. Lucas tried not to laugh himself.

"What makes you think you're such hot stuff?" Lucas said, holding back a smile.

"I got family," Adam said, blowing out another plume of smoke, "I got connections. In this town, I'm the prince. I don't have to work for nothing if I don't want. Just gotta be me." He flicked a small ash onto his hand.

"What? Your corrupt uncle Ernie is your connection? Give me a break. He runs your family like puppets and could give two bits about you. All he wants from this county and you is what's in it for him. My dad says Ernie is going to kill this whole town someday," Lucas said. The pot smell was beginning to get to him.

"Kill it? Son, he already owns it. He owns you too, you idiot. Who signs your paychecks?" Adam was getting irritated. Lucas looked him directly in the eye. Adam stared back, hard, as he pinched out the joint and put it back in his shirt pocket. He exhaled his last lung full of smoke at Lucas.

"I hate you, you jerk." Lucas lowered his voice as he spoke, trying to sound threatening.

"Yeah, well you're in a pretty big club. Have a beer." Adam dropped an unopened can into Lucas' lap. Lucas closed his legs before the beer injured him. The aluminum was instantly cold through his pants.

Picking up the can, he opened it and drank as much as he could. The truck bounced several times, causing foam to run down his neck. The bonfire was just ahead.

Adam burst into laugher. So did Lucas.

CHAPTER 19

Lucas had difficulty finding a place to park his truck. Adam had already jumped out and was pursuing some young girl with a hearty chest. The heat from the huge fire could be felt through his closed side window. Dozens of people were standing in small groups drinking and talking. Lucas checked his watch. It was a little past nine o'clock.

Bonfire. Lucas thought about the word as he drove slowly, weaving around already drunken teenagers. Bon, means 'good' in French he thought. 'Good fire', he mused. On a night like this, cold, windy and on the top of a barren mountain, this would certainly be a 'good fire.'

Lucas hoped that he could find some friends, have a beer and forget about the past two days. He was tired from the mental stress. His parents would be home tomorrow from Helena. Happy and festive, their mood would be destroyed by Russell's latest choices. He tried not to think about it too much.

Adam had forgotten the sack of beer again, or left it for later. Lucas took another one and opened it. He parked his truck on the roadside, two feet from the steep downhill drop. A step too far and he would tumble straight downward for hundreds of feet, breaking every body bone and most likely dying. There were no trees to stop a body once it started sliding, and barely any brush. Looking down toward Sunnyside, he could vaguely make out any light pinpoints through the smelter smoke. The only reason to party up here was for the fresher air, certainly not the view, he concluded. And of course, the cheap beer.

Lucas considered his drinking and wondered if maybe he did consume too much. Heather insinuated as much each time he talked about alcohol. He shook off the notion and drank half the can he was holding. Drink to celebrate, drink to forget, just drink, he thought.

Lucas opened his truck door and immediately smelled smoke. Not from the bonfire, but from some errant marijuana cigarette. It seemed the world was moving from grain to grass. He tried pot twice, each time becoming so fearful of being caught that he didn't enjoy its effects at all. Beer was better and more acceptable to him. His foot kicked a few stones loose. He could hear them bouncing down the mountainside for several seconds before their sounds gave way to the night

Directly in front of him, he saw no less than seven people jammed side by side in an old double cab Ford truck. The windows were rolled up halfway and smoke wisped out of them. He could only hear male laughter. *Stoners don't get the girls*, he thought. *At least not the good girls.*

The only light on the mountain was coming from the bonfire. A dozen pickups had been loaded with scrap wood from one of the lumber mills and dropped here on Flat Top. Kerosene and a strong breeze consumed the wooden fuel and shot flames twenty feet into the night sky. Lucas walked towards it. The rising orange flames flickered shadows around him. Loud music pumped from speakers perched on the hood of yet another Ford pickup.

He counted no less than forty vehicles parked on either side of the road. Most held high teens in some stage of frustrated fondling. The stories at school on

Monday would be far better than the grappling he was seeing. A touched breast would become a spectacular interlude. A groped groin, an orgy. It seemed all anybody ever wanted or talked about was sex. He believed no one really ever did it, yet the lore and bravado led the school to think that every girl was a slut and every guy a stud. If you bought into that, Lucas thought, you'd feel there was something wrong with you if you didn't get a girl every weekend. He didn't especially want to keep his virginity, but he didn't want what came with losing it either, especially now, with Lori's pregnancy. He feared hurting his parents more than being ridiculed by his friends.

He finished his beer and tossed the empty can into the back of one of the parked pickups. It clanked and tumbled as it rolled towards the closed tailgate. Lucas saw several other cans in the back, along with sandbags and an old metal ice chest. At least a hundred people were standing around the huge fire, drinking beer from plastic cups or smoking joints. Some were doing both and laughing the loudest. The more seasoned party people had beer mugs and glass bongs. They seemed to put out an air of sophistication compared to the other adolescent revelers. A couple of greasy-haired, cool-chick girls spoke to him; normal cigarettes blazed from their fingertips. He recognized them from his study hall. Usually sitting in the back, they chattered about any male that passed by. He smiled and kept walking, hoping they wouldn't follow. For an instant he felt uncomfortable being here. The drugs, alcohol and surly crowd weren't appealing. He thought about walking to his truck and driving back down the hill.

"Lucas, you're alive!" A female voice shouted from the crowd. Several people glanced at him then returned to their conversation. The cool-chicks puffed away and stared in the direction of the voice, too. He turned slightly and looked toward the unknown speaker. A hand was raised in the air holding a clear plastic cup of beer. Lucas could not see who it was, but she was making her way towards him. The beer holder was short, but seemed expert at navigating the crowd. He supposed a small person was used to zipping around people. He stooped slightly in an effort to see who was heading towards him. In an instant a body emerged attached to the uplifted hand and arm. It was Rita Dominico; beer in one hand, waving with the other.

Lucas walked towards her. Rita was just over five feet tall and had short black hair. Long hair was the current style, but she had tastes all her own. She was wearing tight, flare-bottomed jeans. Italian by heritage, her skin looked perpetually tanned. She also sported the finest feminine chest at Sunnyside High School. Rita stood on her toes and hugged his neck. Her cheeks smelled of distant lemons. Lucas felt his face flush for a moment. Rita was pretty and likeable. He was glad to see her.

"Of course I'm alive," Lucas said, unable to think of any wry comments to impress her. He saw she needed no impressing.

"We all thought you'd be dead by now, according to Randy Peeper," Rita pointed back towards the fire crowd. She used the index finger of her beer drinking hand. "All Randy can talk about is how Mickey Whitehead was going to bust you up. You'd think he was Whitehead's publicist or something."

"I haven't seen Mickey since yesterday," Lucas said, thankful at the thought.

"Well, you'll see him tonight. He's here somewhere. I talked to him twenty minutes ago. He's getting pretty hammered." Rita sipped at her beer and looked up at him with big dark eyes. Lucas looked back then glanced away nervously.

"Want a beer?" she said.

Why would I be here if I didn't want a beer, he thought. He grinned at her. She smiled back, only bigger. It felt like a smiling contest to him.

Before he could answer Rita took his wrist in her hand and pulled him towards the fire. Lucas' senses were becoming acute as he looked at every face in the crowd, expecting to see Mickey Whitehead at any moment. Moving towards the kegs, Lucas noticed that the crowd became thicker. They looked like bees in a hive protecting the queen.

As they walked, several people complimented him on his standoff the previous day. He simply smiled and nodded, knowing that the face to face with Whitehead had scared the life out of him. He knew things would have been different had his brother not intervened. Maybe Russell should have let him handle his own fight. He'd have to contend with Mickey someday by himself anyway.

The beer kegs were tapped and sitting in the back of the same truck that blared the music. A *Rolling Stones* classic filled the air. Rita pushed through a group of guys standing around the keg. Short as she was, she seemed to move people aside quite easily. Lucas noticed the keg boys were all overweight and chewing tobacco. A couple of them were trying to grow beards. He supposed they stayed closest to the kegs so they could drink more and see which girls were getting loaded. At some point in the evening one of them might be drunk and bold enough to make a pass at one of the girls. If she were drunk enough herself, the whole bunch of them might even score.

Every one of them eyed Rita's breasts as she walked past. She must be used to this, Lucas thought, though they would never succeed with a girl like her. The cool-chicks maybe, but not a bubbly ball of fire like Rita.

The beer nozzle was being manned by some part-Indian guy in his early twenties. Lucas had seen him around town a lot and at every party he had ever attended. He was unsure if the fellow even worked. Scabby thought he was employed as a bouncer at one of whorehouses. Lucas wasn't sure and really didn't care. He did know that the man could draw a foamless beer though. Lucas looked into the cup Rita handed him. Perfect pour. The Indian demanded two bucks, which Lucas handed over. No smile or no thanks from him. No big deal, Lucas thought.

"Two bucks for a beer?" Lucas asked Rita as he closed his wallet. He tried to hide Heather's picture, but Rita saw it anyway and shook her head without commenting.

"No. Two bucks for the party. He'll make money on this thing," she replied. Her smile was big, her teeth perfectly straight and white. He couldn't help but enter her grinning contest again. It was contagious like yawning.

Rita took his hand this time and pulled him back through the crowd. He had known her since kindergarten and had often played with her and her brother Tony after school. They had several classes together this year and would sometimes eat together at lunch when he couldn't find Heather.

"Let's sit on the hillside," she said tugging him up a graduated slope overlooking the bonfire. Lucas complied and followed. A dozen other kegger people were already reclining on the slope. Weaving between them, they climbed thirty feet up the hill and sat down. *Perfect*, Lucas thought, *I can watch out for Mickey.*

"Did you come up here to the party by yourself?" Lucas asked as he began sipping his beer. He had been cold, but the heat from the fire washed over him as they talked. Even from this distance he could feel that the heat could become uncomfortable. The crackling of the flames momentarily drowned out the crowd noises.

"No. I drove up here with some girlfriends. They disappeared with some geeky guys from Missoula that had found out about the keg. Don't know where they are now. Some of the jocks were trying to run them off. Those jerks are always looking for a fight." She sipped her beer then said, "Where's Heather? Is she here?" Rita scanned the gathering as she spoke. Lucas watched as sparks from the fire climbed into the night sky and disappeared.

"Right. Heather at a kegger," Lucas said indignantly. "She'd never come to one of these. Besides, if I showed up with her, Mickey would really try to kill me."

Lucas swallowed more beer and stared down at the crowd. He recognized most of the faces as classmates or local dropouts. Everybody was animated and seemed to be yelling loudly instead of talking. He saw a few boys with a funnel hose beer bong challenging one another to a drinking contest. Across the valley he could see the faint lights of the three crosses on Cemetery Hill. The smelter smoke was lifting. One of the crosses went dark. He stared into his cup.

He talked with Rita for almost an hour about Billy Murphy's suicide, the strike, Russell, school, who's doing who and a dozen other not so relevant topics. He purposefully avoided bringing up Heather again. Rita listened and consoled him when needed. She even talked him into running down the hill twice to get more beer for both of them. The crowd had almost doubled in the time they had been sitting on the hill. He still didn't see Mickey anywhere, though he was constantly looking out for him.

Rita pointed to a couple of drunken freshman just outside of the light of the fire. One of them had his buttocks hanging completely out of his pants. He was apparently too drunk to pull them up after he took a leak. They both howled, Rita spraying beer as she laughed.

Lucas felt the pressure of his own bladder and shifted his weight slightly. He looked at Rita and gritted his teeth. She was leaning back on her elbows against the hillside. He was feeling the first light-headed rushes of intoxication. His eyes fell to her blouse. He had to force himself to look away. She caught him staring anyway, but didn't seem uncomfortable.

"I didn't know a girl could drink so much beer and not pee," Lucas remarked as he looked at her half-empty beer cup. Several drained cups sat between them.

"Italian heritage," she said smiling. "Actually, I'm dying. My back molars are popping loose from the pressure." Rita crossed her legs and leaned a bit forward. "I just didn't want you to think I'm a wimp."

"Follow me. I'll keep a look out for you while you…"

Rita was on her feet shuffling quickly down the hill before Lucas finished his sentence. She again held her beer cup above her head. They jogged side by side back towards his truck. Rita disappeared into the shadows of the driver's side and relieved herself, careful not to slip and fall down the hill. Lucas turned his back and waited. He snickered out loud only to hear her curse him, which only brought on more laughing. She returned the guardian favor, giggling at the length of time it took him to finish.

"Want another beer? There's some in the truck." Lucas pointed towards the cab of his vehicle. Rita had taken a hold of the crook of his arm. She seemed a bit unsteady as they walked.

"Only if we drink it in my car." Rita's voice changed slightly from her last words. Lucas thought she sounded seductive, but concluded she was being playful with him.

"Why not here?" Lucas said, trying to downplay any notions he had of her intentions.

"Because I have better music," she replied. This time her voice came across as normal.

"Ok," was all he could say. He retrieved the beer from his pickup and walked with her back towards the bonfire, her hand firmly laced to his elbow.

Rita's car, actually her father's, was an enormous Dodge with four doors. It was parked in a large turn-out, up against the side of the hill. From the road, the car could not be seen clearly. Other vehicles were parked nearby in no apparent order. Lucas could hear stereos playing and the sound of voices and laughter.

"How in the hell did you get this up here?" Lucas said as he climbed into the passenger side. The interior was immaculate. It had recently been cleaned. A pile of schoolbooks sat in the back seat along with a small purse.

"Drove like the wild woman I am," Rita said. Her voice again taking on the seductiveness he had heard moments earlier. Lucas tried to ignore her tone this time. He placed the beer sack on the seat between them, opened it and served them two cans. Rita inserted a tape into the stereo. The group *America* began playing. Lucas would never admit to his male friends, but he really liked the band and it's mellow music. It's the kind of music he and Scabby wrote.

They sat a long time without speaking. Rita started the car's engine and warmed the interior. She removed her jacket as did he. Lucas looked at her in the dark. Her face and skin were highlighted by the dim light of the stereo, the pupils of her eyes reflecting back fragments of the light. She was mouthing the lyrics to a song about the *Wizard of Oz*. He couldn't believe that he was again drunk. Rita was showing signs of intoxication, too. Lucas continued to watch her silently sing. She rocked gently side to side with the rhythm of the music. He began quietly singing as well.

"I like you Lucas," Rita said unexpectedly as the song ended. She did not look at him as she spoke. She placed her hand on the side of her face as if in thought. Her eyes stared at the dark through the windshield. She balanced a beer can on the steering wheel and lightly tapped its side with her other fingers.

"Well," Lucas replied, "I like you, too." He was unsure what to say actually. His inhibitions were almost gone. He found himself becoming infatuated with the girl. He wanted to tell her other things, darker things, but kept his mouth quiet.

She turned and looked at him. Her face had softened into a gentle almost serene appearance. Her eyes were again very big and very black. They moved up and down slightly as if trying to read him. Another soft rock song began playing on the car stereo. She turned the volume down slightly. Lucas took a slow sip and stared back at her, making eye contact, reading her as well.

"No, I mean it, I really like you." She emphasized the last four words. Turning her body to the right she sat on her own leg and faced him. Reaching towards the stereo, she turned the volume down even more.

He understood her, clearly. His heart was racing as it had the night before with Heather, this time he felt only desire, immediate and necessary. He reasoned for an instant that he should leave, then dismissed it. He placed the remaining beers on the floor of the car. Rita slid towards him and climbed onto this lap. He didn't try to stop her. Outside, one of the partygoers tossed a bucket of gasoline onto the fire. A ball of flames rose brightly into the dark heavens. The fire became hotter and brighter. A cheer from the crowd filled the air.

They kissed aggressively. Lucas became quickly aroused. Rita shifted her weight on him, aware of his desire. Deeply again, they kissed. The interior of the car glowed from the orange light of the growing fire. His hands found her shirt and fumbled at each button. Youthful and firm, she was wearing no bra. Her stomach was soft and flat. He slid his hands down her sides and to her hips, returning slowly to her chest. He felt her shudder.

She straddled him, one knee on either side of his hips. Her assurance moved him. Lucas slouched slightly and continued exploring her as their mouths meshed. The kissing intensified as she cradled his cheek with one hand and tugged his belt with the other. They began to rock with the slow rhythm of the music. Rita arched her body as she leaned back, her mouth wide open, eyes briefly closed, face almost touching the interior ceiling of the car. Lucas increased the tempo in his fingers. Her hand found its way beneath his waist band. Lost in the moment, Lucas' eyes were closed. He opened them suddenly. In the distance drunken boys began yelling in war whoops at the enormous pile of burning rubble.

"I can't," he said, pulling his face and hands away from her. She sat back, a surprised expression crossed her flushed face. Lucas breathed in rushed breaths. He felt his chest shake and his arms tingle. Shadows of flickering light painted Rita's partially exposed flesh.

"I can't do this. Not here. Not now," he said, staring at her exposed chest. His yearning for the young woman was intense and irrational. He struggled for more words but found no strength to utter them.

She leaned into him, "It's ok, Lucas. I mean, if you haven't done it before. It'll be ok." Her voice was breathy and full. A slight look of desperation and disappointment touched her eyes.

"No. It's not like that. I just can't do this." He fought his desire to pull her back towards him and encourage her to continue exploring, but began to push himself up in the seat instead. The song ended and the eight track clicked as it found another tune.

"But, I know you want me." She moved her hips slightly and squeezed her hidden hand; her tone hopeful as she forced a sinful smile. Lucas groaned at her touch, almost losing himself.

"I do, but I don't. I don't know what I mean." His mind was screaming, his body pulsed with unspent energy. He could feel his sides begin to hurt. Her hands retreated.

Rita's face became sullen, yet she continued to gaze into his eyes. Sitting back on his knees she began slowly buttoning her blouse. Each clasp and closure quickened his heart again. The last of her secret flesh covered, Lucas placed his hand on her legs as if to steady himself.

"Then why go this far? I'm in this, too, you know," she said, anger punching each syllable.

"I'm sorry. I just can't'…." he stumbled over his words again. "Please don't be mad…."

Rita rolled off his legs and sat on the seat next to him and stared forward. Tucking her shirt into her pants, she covered herself with her coat. Her breathing was still very heavy and exaggerated. "I'm sorry too," she said flatly. She pressed her chin into her chest and crossed her arms under her jacket. In the distance, the bonfire returned to its former intensity, its fuel spent. Darkness again filled the car.

They sat in silence for several minutes. Lucas adjusted his clothes and slipped on his coat. Rita turned the car engine off, annoyed at its drubbing. The sweat scented air began to cool slightly. The interior of the windows were white with moisture from their labored breathing. With the change in temperature they fogged even more.

"What are you? Too good for me or something? I wouldn't let anybody know. I wouldn't tell. Isn't that what you guys tell girls?" Rita finally said. Lucas could hear the sarcasm. The statement stung him with its familiarity. He never considered himself better than anybody, rather he was unsure of himself and what people perceived him to be. This was the second time today that he had been asked virtually the same question by two friends. Just sitting there he could hear her loss of self-esteem.

"No. Nothing like that," Lucas said, "It's about me, not you." He cringed as he uttered the cliché. Wiping the mist off of the passenger window he pressed his ear against the cold glass. Small pellets of water rolled down the window and collected together in a sizeable drop.

"What then? You're a virgin right? Scared?" She paused and shyly looked at him. "I am too…" Her voice sounded softer with a soothing edge to it. She hesitated for a moment then said quietly, "I told you that was ok, didn't I?"

"You did say it was alright, yes," he replied, avoiding an answer to the question of his virtue. Noticing it was still open, he buckled his belt. He had lied about losing his virginity for years and was nervous about the actual act but not uncertain how to perform it. Being seduced by or seducing a pretty, intelligent girl like Rita wouldn't have been the worst thing he could imagine doing, but the ensuing complications would stand in the way of his feelings for Heather, he thought. Taking Rita would hurt him in the long term and probably both girls as well. He didn't have Heather, but the idea that she would find out that he was intimate in a car at a keg party gave him enough strength to resist.

He stared at Rita, her silhouette barely visible in the darkness. He thought for a moment and said, "You are very beautiful..." The words felt trite.

She snorted slightly under her breath, interrupting him and looked towards the driver's door and bit gently on her bottom lip. Two drunken girls bumped against the car. They tried to peer in but couldn't see through the steamed windows. He continued talking.

"You are beautiful... and being a virgin or not isn't the issue. It's something else. Believe me, my body wants you. I want you. Years from now I'll hate myself for not taking this moment. But I can't. I just love Heather, that's all."

His own words startled him. He had never said them to anybody out loud. Rita's face was turned slightly away from him. The light from the stereo was still on, illuminating her in pale green. He saw long tears rolling down her cheeks.

"We're just a bit drunk is all," Lucas said trying to explain or excuse their attraction to one other. "We're friends. We should stay that way."

Rita finally looked towards him again. In his stomach he felt a twinge of embarrassment. She was sizing him up. He could see a stir of emotions in her face.

"I *wanted* it to be you, Lucas. For a long time. Even if I wasn't drunk, I'd want you. This just made it easier is all," Rita said. She wiped her cheek tears with her bare hands. "I wanted you to be my first...." Her words seemed to confuse her. "I've loved you since junior high. Don't you get it?" More tears. "Don't you?"

Lucas turned towards her. "I didn't know," is all he said. Rita was running her eyes up and down his face again, searching for something from him. He found himself fixing his own eyes on hers. There was a mystery in them, an encouragement, a sweetness. They seemed deep and infinite.

He could hear Nellie Montgomery's words about love. Now here he sat with a gentle girl taking the risk of revealing her heart. He thought back to all the conversations he and Rita had had, all of the games they had shared, all of the times they interacted, the lunches, the walks. He could see it, pieces knitting together. He had just missed it. She had given him indication after indication, yet he was just too preoccupied or immature to know what was before him. He couldn't find the right words to tell her. Anything would be trivial and his actions had already moved her away from him. Rejection sat between them.

"Maybe I'm foolish. Maybe I'm just an idiot. I'm sorry if I hurt you. I'm sorry I went as far as I did. But I need to follow my heart not my head. Please understand. Please." He leaned his back against the passenger door.

Rita continued to stare at his face.

"Heather's the fool and doesn't know it," she finally said. She paused, still dancing her eyes over him. A knowing expression replaced her absent look. "You haven't told her, have you?"

Lucas watched her. The power of her glance, the draw of her spirit, the tenderness in her voice tugged at him. Even as the emotional intensity wore down, he could feel his lust re-emerging.

"No. I haven't told her. I think she knows though." He considered touching Rita's cheek.

"You didn't know about me," she said softly. Rita reached towards him and brushed a stray lock of hair from his eyes. He reached for, then held her hand.

"I didn't," he whispered. He felt sorry for hurting her feelings at the same time fighting the impulse to hold her, to resume the path to intimacy. He tenderly kissed the back of her fingers. She slowly withdrew her hand.

"Then tell her. You need to. Or I will." Rita sat up straight, never averting her eyes from his. She lowered her coat and adjusted her blouse again.

"Tell her what?" he said, rubbing his eyes with his fingers, hoping to break the hypnotism of the past moments.

"About this. About us. Tell her that you love her Lucas and stop torturing yourself. If she knew how you felt, she'd tell you the truth about how she feels. If you don't tell her then I will. If she rejects you, then fine. Then maybe you'll see that there is somebody who does love you. Then maybe you can start living instead of lying to yourself."

All traces of anger were gone from her voice. Lucas became frightened at the notion that Heather might learn about Rita. He knew they were friends. Rita would surely ask Heather about him.

"It isn't your place to say anything. You don't need to tell her. I will. Tonight. But right now, I need to relieve myself, again." Lucas grinned and opened the passenger door. He needed to change the subject.

"I have every reason to tell her." Rita began to laugh. She sounded devious to him. "You got me so worked up, I forgot that I need to find a bush, too."

The smell of smoke and the sound of loud music were still hanging in the air. Lucas walked twenty feet to the base of the mountain. Rita disappeared to the front of her car. In the cool air Lucas' head began to clear. He had feelings for Rita, but it wasn't love, it was a moment. The urgent desire was still inside of him, but was slowly abating. He was thankful for the darkness. In a way he felt some guilty satisfaction that such a beautiful girl would want him intimately. Most of his classmates would brag and embellish what had just happened. That wasn't him. He'd keep this to himself. Finished, he zipped his fly, and turned back towards Rita's car.

"Rita? Is it clear? Can I come back?" he shouted. She did not answer. Rock drums and voices were drifting all around him.

"Hello? Where are you?" Lucas walked back in the direction of her Dodge. Its shape emerged clearly when he was five feet away. The flames from the bonfire were higher than before. The ground a mass of dancing orange light and black shadows. A noise came from the front of the car. Lucas walked toward it, expecting Rita. He saw two figures instead, one tall, one short.

Mickey Whitehead was leaning against the car, Rita was in front of him. His right hand wrapped around her waist, his left hand over her mouth. Mickey had apparently surprised her. She squirmed, trying to break his grasp.

"Hey jerk," Mickey said with smile. His lips and chin were wet, and despite the cold night air, his forehead glistened with sweat.

Lucas charged at Mickey without thinking, the beer made him bold. Surprise your enemy he had been taught in ROTC. Rita bit Mickey's hand and pulled away from him, cursing his touch. Mickey met Lucas' face with a fist. Lucas stumbled backwards. He could taste his own blood.

"Where's your body guard?" Mickey said. Jumping toward Lucas he struck his face again. Lucas tried protecting his head, but moved too slowly. The impact of Mickey's knuckles made a meaty squishing sound. Each closed fist impact to his cheeks and eyes caused white sparks to flash in his head. The blows came fast and frenzied. Never a fighter, Lucas failed to stop most of them.

Lucas ran at Mickey again and knocked him back against the car. He pounded his right fist into Mickey's face several times before the bigger boy pushed him away. Mickey's mouth was beginning to bleed. He touched the corner with his thumb and squinted one eye. Lucas watched him spit. The firelight illuminated the entire area, though the fight sounds were drowned out by the rock music. Lucas struck at him again, laying blind punches, most missing their target. Mickey jabbed Lucas hard in the ribs causing him to buckle forward and lose his breath. A gagging noise coughed from Lucas' throat. Mickey kicked him in the face with his knee. Lucas continued swinging. More blows connected with Mickey's face. A side punch landed on his ear, enraging Mickey. Each punch seemed to give Mickey more energy. Lucas stopped, dropping his arms to his sides.

"Time to quit dancing," Mickey said, grabbing at Lucas and tackling him low and near the hips. The force of the landing cracked Lucas' lower back sending waves of bright pain up his spine. The weight of the athlete on his chest prevented him from moving. Mickey began a rhythmic beating about Lucas' face. Each fist fall brought more agony to Lucas' head. Freeing one hand, he managed to block Mickey momentarily. Rita took the opening and kicked at Mickey's face only to be deflected by his projecting elbow. Mickey tossed his head to one side, flipping his blond hair from his face.

"Not much of a fight is it?" Mickey sneered. He grabbed Lucas' arms and crossed them over his chest. Lucas tried to wiggle his arms loose, but couldn't.

"No big brother, no bicycle tires, no friends," he said, impacting Lucas' cheek and mouth with his fist to accent the phrases. Mickey's knuckles began to bleed. Lucas felt as if he would lose consciousness. Lucas was fully aware of the pounding, but there seemed to be no more pain. His eye was swelling shut. As the boy raised his fist high above his head for one more tremendous punch, Lucas winced, ready to receive the blow. It didn't come. Instead he heard a loud dull sound. Mickey slumped forward on him.

"Yeah, and no more of your crap, neither," a new voice said from somewhere in the dark.

Mickey was groaning and grasping the back of his skull as he rolled onto his back. Lucas opened his eyes and looked up. Scabby was standing over him and Mickey. He held a broken branch, the size of a small baseball bat, in his hands. He was grinning. His glasses reflecting the embers of the fire.

Scabby moved and stood over Mickey, raising the club over his head with both hands. Mickey covered himself and attempted to roll aside.

"Don't do it Scabby, please," he begged. Scabby's face was wild, no trace of fear, only rage. His lips were sneered and quivering. The sight was frightening.

"This ends here, Mickey. I don't need no reason not to smash in your head." Scabby flinched a bit, Mickey pulled his hands to his face. A crowd began to collect around the fighting boys. Lucas slowly got to his feet, helped by Rita. Mickey lay cowering below Scabby. Blood oozed from his scalp onto the ground. The music stopped. The flames from the bonfire flickered in Scabby's eyes, glazing them, making them appear on fire themselves. Lucas looked at him then down at Mickey.

"Let him go Scabby, he's not going to fight anymore tonight," Lucas said. Scabby held the limb steady with both hands. His arms trembled as he took aim.

"Look at him, Lucas. He ain't so tough now."

"He's hurt. Let him up. Give me the branch." Lucas limped towards Scabby, extending his hand. Scabby's nostrils were frothing. His glasses held to the tip of his nose, forcing him to look over them.

"No. I'm sick of this. He's got to stop tormenting us." Scabby was shouting as he raised the club higher. Lucas looked at Mickey, covered in dust. The boy was breathing heavily. Ten years ago the roles were different. Today, Scabby was the victor, pushed to this point by the senseless ire of a bully. The crowd drew closer to the fallen athlete. No one spoke.

"I'm sorry Scabby," Mickey mumbled from behind his hands, "I'm sorry."

Scabby stood still for a long while, his eyes locked on his broken prey, before he dropped the branch, spit on Mickey and stepped toward Lucas.

"Are you ok, Luke?" he finally said. There was concern in his voice, but also the wavering timbre of someone on the edge. Lucas thought he sounded like he wasn't yet connected to the present.

"Where did you come from Scabby? I thought you were angry at me," Lucas said. Scabby reached towards him and began dusting the front of Lucas' shirt, knocking loose dried grass and small bits of gravel.

"I was, but I got to thinkin'. You need me like I need you. A lot of what you said was true. I ain't goin' to be no victim no more. I only care about what I think, about my family and about you. We've been friends too long." He continued brushing Lucas, loosening debris from his elbows and back.

Lucas leaned against Rita's car. Scabby joined him. Lucas' face was sore and his lips were beginning to swell, but he wasn't seriously hurt. Mickey was helped to his feet by several stoners who cooed over his injury, suggesting a drag of pot to lessen the severity of the pain. Rita was wiping at Lucas' face, dabbing at his nose and bleeding lips. She was using a sanitary napkin. Lucas flinched but didn't say anything to her about it, hoping nobody else noticed.

"I think I should take him to the hospital. Looks like he needs stitches," Lucas said. Blood was soaking into the back of Mickey's shirt. Nobody was directly attending to his injury. Mickey clutched his scalp with a dirty hand. The sight was a bit moving to Lucas. Though he had been this boy's adversary for a decade, seeing him stagger and suffer lifted some of the harsh feelings. Mickey began walking in a slow circle. Watchers moved away from him. In this crowd, at this party, he was definitely alone.

"Are you crazy? You want to take him to the emergency room? After what he just did?" Rita said with shock. "Let him walk back, the worthless jerk."

"He isn't going to hurt anybody else tonight. I'm burned out. I'll take him to the emergency room then I'll go home. It'll be alright. Scabby can help you get home," Lucas said.

Rita touched his bruised cheek, and kissed it gently. Scabby looked at her and raised an eyebrow. Lucas averted his glance and put his arms around Rita in a slow embrace, careful not to appear too familiar. She squeezed him back.

Scabby said to Rita, "Yeah, I hitched up here. Rode in the back of a truck. I could use a ride back down the mountain. You too drunk to drive?"

Scabby walked around Lucas and stood next to Rita. He still hadn't pushed his glasses back up his nose.

"No, I'm fine," Rita said. "I'll give you a ride home. I'll check on you tomorrow, Lucas." Her voice was as tender as her touch. Lucas leaned forward and hugged her again. Scabby appeared uncomfortable and turned away. Rita lightly kissed Lucas.

"Thanks. I'd appreciate that. Don't worry about me though, ok?" Lucas said. Rita nodded her head. Lucas saw a mist of tears at the corner of her eyes. Emotions unbounded by alcohol and the adrenaline of a fight had affected her too. He tried to read her eyes and face once more, only this time she wouldn't look back. He turned to Scabby.

"Help him to my truck. You ok with that Mickey?" Lucas said.

Mickey looked over at Lucas. His eyes were glassy. He could barely speak. "Yeah, that's fine." His voice was empty and rasped.

Lucas and Scabby walked with Mickey to his Toyota pickup. Someone had finally placed a wet towel on the back of Mickey's head to stop the bleeding. Scabby closed the door behind Mickey. One of the stoners offered to ride along in case Mickey started up again. From his appearance, Lucas knew the boy was high and would probably fall from the back of the pickup on the ride down the mountain. Instead, he shook his head and refused, thanking him just the same.

Turning his truck around, he started down the hill. Mickey leaned his head forward, clutching the towel over his wound. Lucas heard him grunt as his fingers found the tender spot. Neither of them spoke for a long time, only the sound of the vehicle wheels grinding gravel and rocks together punctuated the air. Lucas turned the heater on and began to defrost the inside of his windshield. He thought about playing some music to break the tension that was still between them, but opted for the silence. He was beginning to feel sick.

As he drove he noticed that the lights of his pickup were shining off to the side of the road instead of dead center. He had forgotten to reposition the new lamps. They drove a long ways in silence.

"I'm not trying to take Heather from you, you know that right?" Lucas finally said. "It's over between you two, can't you understand that?"

Mickey didn't answer. His forehead was resting on the dashboard, bouncing occasionally as the truck hit rocks and potholes.

"Why do you hate me so much?" Lucas asked, "I've never done anything to you."

Mickey leaned backwards. His eyes were closed. Lucas could smell hard liquor on his breath. He was afraid that Scabby had done some serious damage to Mickey's skull. The towel was beginning to soak through.

"I hate what you stand for," Mickey said.

The words sounded painful and forced. Lucas wasn't sure if the words were from anger or not.

"I don't even know what I stand for, Mickey."

"You're a company man's son. A pretty boy. Teacher's pet," Mickey continued, still resting his head against the back window. His hands were resting on either side of his legs, balancing him.

"I don't even know what that means anymore. I don't have anything to do with the mines." He ignored the other points Mickey was trying to make.

"That's just how it is. That's how it'll always be," Mickey said. "Union men and company men aren't supposed to like each other. Neither are their sons."

"But that has nothing to do with me...us. And I think its twisted. Nobody needs to hate anybody just because of what they do. What a person does isn't what they are. You're not angry at me for that. I think it's about Heather."

"Heather despises me," Mickey said after a few silent moments. His eyes were now open, although he was squinting. There were scratches on his neck. His hair was dirty and matted. Bloody spit moistened his lips.

"She hates nobody. She can't. You're just a mean bastard that disrespects her and the things she loves. Can you blame her?" Lucas was bold in his words. He didn't fear Mickey, not because of the injuries, but because of Mickey's lack of aggression. He seemed to want to talk.

"She hates me because of what I've done." The boy shifted uncomfortably. "Don't pretend you're ignorant. I know you know." Mickey raised his fingers to his nose and touched it gently. It was swelling.

"Know what? I don't have any idea what you're talking about," Lucas said forcefully. He was tired of the stress Mickey had caused him and now the confusing conversation was making him mad. He had no clue what the boy was trying to say to him.

"Come on Lucas, she tells you everything. Everything! You're like her best friend. You're like one of her girlfriends. I see the whispers and laughter. Don't play stupid. Why do you think I can't play football this year?" Mickey turned and glared at Lucas. For a moment he was afraid that Mickey might strike at him. He considered stopping the truck just in case the fight resumed. It didn't.

"She tells me a lot, but not everything..." Lucas face hurt as he spoke.

Mickey pushed himself up in the seat and stared blankly out of the windshield. She began to speak softly.

"Randy Peeper. Me and Randy Peeper. She told you, I know she did. She said she was going to tell you. She said it would give you something to fight back with if I ever tried to hurt you." Mickey cradled his head again and leaned forward.

"Peeper?" Lucas was confused and shocked. Bits of the puzzle began to complete themselves in his mind. He knew what Mickey was saying, but didn't know how to respond. The conclusion was becoming clearer. He was uncertain how to reply.

"What happened with you and Peeper?" he finally asked. His eyes were fixed on the road ahead. He couldn't look at Mickey.

Mickey continued resting his head on the dashboard. "The truth? Sure, I'll tell you the truth. I'm sure Heather lied to make it worse than it was." He paused for a moment and stared into the darkness. "I was drunk at a Dark Bridge kegger last spring, you know, over break. Peeper was there. We knew he liked boys more than girls and we started giving him a tough time, pushing him around. He seemed to like it, you know." Lucas slowed the truck down a little so he could hear.

"Anyway, he wandered off into the woods and I followed him. I was going to kick his sissy ass. When I found him he was real scared like. I knocked him down a couple of times. He knew I was going to bust him up." Mickey quit talking.

"Then what happened?" Lucas looked over at Mickey, his face was resting in his hands.

"He told me he would *do* me if I didn't hurt him. It was just him and me you know. Nobody was around. So I let him. Right there under the bridge. I still slapped him hard when we was done, so the guys wouldn't think anything weird had happened. I was pissed and confused. Drunk I guess." Mickey was mumbling. "When I hit him, he was still on his knees. He started crying, you know, like a little kid. I told him to tell no one." Mickey looked like he was going to cry himself. "I shouldn't have hit him."

"That's why you were put off the team? For making it with Peeper? Who else knew?" Lucas was no longer angry. The agony on Mickey's face was not coming from his outward wounds but from someplace deep inside. Lucas felt sorry for him. Mickey had been hiding behind his macho image. The tarnish he must feel, the shame, would cripple him at school, were it known.

"Nobody else knew. Peeper started threatening me at school saying he was going to tell the coach what we did and that I was just like him...unless I started seeing him. I couldn't take that. He even came by my house one night and asked me to be with him, you know." Mickey wiped at his eyes forcefully. There was anger. "Can you imagine that!? I thought about all kinds of things I should do. I thought about killing him and stuff. I finally told the coach myself."

"What? You told the coach?" Lucas said. He could not believe what he was hearing. Coach Merrick was a former Marine in Korea. Sunnyside worshipped him for the discipline he instilled in his athletes and the various state records they had set over the past fifteen years. Mickey was Merrick's pride and prize.

"Yeah, I did. I told him. He slammed me against the wall and cursed me. Called me a queer and threatened to tell my dad. I begged him not to. He finally calmed down and said he couldn't trust me around the guys anymore and that I should collect my stuff and not come back to the team. I really wanted to kill Randy after that. I thought about killing myself, too." Mickey began crying, his shoulders shaking.

"And Heather knew all this?" Lucas said in a quiet voice.

"Yeah, I told her a few weeks ago. She said she understood, but I don't think she did. She kept looking at me different and talking to me different. All she seemed to talk about was you and how smart and talented you were. I wanted to show her that I was still a man, that I was just drunk, but she wouldn't let me touch her, you know. I just went crazy after that. I'm not a fag. I'm not."

They drove in silence again. The lights of Sunnyside were clear as they dropped below the smelter smog. Lucas looked at his watch. It was almost eleven o'clock.

Lucas didn't know what to say. He didn't know whether to ask questions or remain mute. He continued to stare out into the darkness. It was silent in the cab again.

"I don't need the hospital. Just take me home," Mickey finally said. He was still crying, though he tried to force a normal voice.

"You might need stitches. You need to have a doctor see it." Lucas' throat was dry. He felt a tightness in his chest and a sadness he couldn't understand.

Mickey pulled the towel from the back of his head. The cloth was soaked through with blood and his hair was a dark brown mess. There seemed to be no more bleeding.

"No. I'm fine. If I need stitches, I'll have my old man take me in the morning." The truck pulled onto the city street. Lucas was thankful for the smooth sound of pavement. He steered down Maki Avenue towards Mickey's neighborhood.

"You gonna tell everybody about me and Peeper? I'm not a fag," Mickey said, still not making any eye contact. Lucas could hear the hidden pleas in Mickey's voice. He knew that the pain and alcohol had loosened Mickey's lips.

"No. I won't," Lucas replied, trying to sound mature and nonplussed. "It was a mistake. A stupid drunken mistake. What you do with it and what you learn from it are up to you. If you want people to know, you tell them. I don't care really. I'm just sorry that it happened, but you deserve it. You've been such a bastard to me my entire life I truly don't want to get involved. Just put this stuff behind you. Stay away from me and Scabby and Heather. I don't want to be your friend, but I don't want to be afraid of you anymore."

"You won't have to be. I'm dropping out of school at the end of the semester. My grades have turned to hell and I can't do sports. My father wants me to go underground."

"Come on Mickey, you've only got a few more months. Why quit?" Lucas said. He was surprised by his own earnestness.

"I don't have Heather. I don't have anything anymore." Mickey's voice was weak.

Lucas pulled to the front of Mickey's house and let him out. Mickey staggered up the steps and quickly opened the door. The house was dark. In a moment Lucas saw Mickey's bedroom light come on. He made a u-turn in the street and headed towards his own home.

CHAPTER 20

The temples on Lucas' forehead pounded with the pulse of his heart, each one tugging a headache from somewhere deep inside his brain. The alcohol in his blood, wearing thin, did little to mask the pain of the bruises on his cheeks and the rising agony on the inside of his lower lip. His tongue slid over the soft broken flesh. There was still a taste of blood.

Lucas checked his watch with the cab light. Although only 11:30pm, he felt like the night had already passed and that morning would soon be erasing the eastern horizon. This morning seemed days ago, the sequence of events and their intensity crushed around him. His pickup truck was warm and relatively quiet. The smelter smoke had lifted, blown east by a strong breeze. He could see the fire still burning far up on the mountain near Flat Top, as well a several sets of car lights weaving down the logging road toward Sunnyside.

He was exhausted from the battle with Mickey and the boy's secret drunken revelation. He wondered and worried that Mickey might become vengeful upon realizing that Lucas held a new card in their lifelong confrontations. An athlete fallen into depravity was bad enough, but the way in which he fell could destroy him in the community's vision. Lucas puzzled on why nobody else knew of the encounter and why such a hot topic could have missed the gossip lines at the school. Randy Peeper was a loud mouth and braggart, and although never totally open with his sexual preferences, didn't hide from the limelight either. Under duress and desire from and for Mickey, Lucas supposed, Randy must have maintained his silence. Lucas would have to keep his as well. Some things aren't worth dying for.

The fight with his lust on the mountain and the lurking embarrassment of intimately touching Rita tangled with the guilt and confusion surrounding his need for Heather and her likely reaction to the revelation of the night's events. This too would need to be capped with candor. He committed to calling her when he got home. Unsure of what to say, he would feign fatigue and get her to talk about her day. He now wished he had maintained his wits at the party and kept his hands to himself. Rita would need, actually deserved, assurance and respect from him. On Monday he would speak to her, take her aside and talk out what had transpired between them.

Lucas' stomach was becoming unsettled. Rolling the window down he drew fresh air into the cab. The streets were empty and most porch lights were off. Swerving, he missed a fast running cat as it dashed from beneath a parked Volkswagen. Driving past his own home, he looked up at Heather's bedroom window. The lights were still on. He knew she was studying or reading. Instead of pulling into his driveway he continued on and drove back toward the heart of Sunnyside.

With each mental replay the image of Scabby attacking Mickey grew bigger and exaggerated. Scabby could have killed Mickey with the club in his hand, Lucas reasoned, and were it not for some self control, that would have been the outcome. The look in Scabby's eyes, the lack of emotion in his face, the rigid stance, were all new. Throughout the years of their friendship, Scabby had cowered or run from confrontation, but this time he was embracing, aggressive and sure. Even frightening. Lucas was uncertain whether he liked what he saw in his friend. The very thing he had told Scabby he needed had played out, but the actions were far different than Lucas had imagined. At least Scabby was relenting in his anger at Lucas and seemed to have forgiven him. This was the only positive thing that had happened today.

The whorehouses and bars appeared vibrant as Lucas wove through uptown. A couple of staggering miners clung to one another as they stumbled into the alley near the Powder Rooms, the oldest and most well known brothel. The Powder Rooms were shielded from the main street by a small drive-up bank building. Russell had pulled Lucas into this very alley and coerced him into the waiting room of the Powder. The *Butt Huts*, Russell had called the whorehouses. It was an appropriate name, Lucas thought with a smile.

The headache was in full hammer swing as Lucas drove across the river and into downtown. He needed to eat and wanted aspirin. Jingling the keys hanging from his ignition, he found the one for the back door to the Shop & Save. It would be easier to stop by the store and retrieve some food than to scrounge his mother's pantry at home. Georgie had railed several times about the box boys entering the store after hours, but Lucas knew he was trusted and that his IOU from the cash register would suffice payment and pacify Georgie.

The alley behind the S&S was still unlit as it had been the previous evening. Stray light from a street lamp at the end of the alley provided barely enough to see. Pulling up to the garbage Dumpster, Lucas parked next to the back door and turned off his motor. The night air cut at his throat. He zipped his jacket completely to his neck and walked towards the locked metal door.

"Ouch," he said as he dropped the keys onto the concrete sidewalk. His fingers were numb and his hands sore from the fight. Looking at his knuckles, he saw they were stained with dried blood. Staring at the front of his jacket, he saw streaks and spots of blood. His shoes had speckles on them too. His stomach churned again.

The door opened on well oiled hinges. The backroom of the store was dark save for a light near the time clock. Lucas closed the door and walked across the floor and into the store proper. Energy efficiency was in force, a challenge from the government to ease a supposed shortage of electricity, thus only four florescent lights illuminated the entire floor area of the S&S. A humming and rattling sound echoed through the aisles as the refrigeration units turned on and off.

Lucas rounded up a bottle of aspirin, a can of cola, a bag of doughnuts, barbecued chips and a roll of breath mints. He tallied the cost on one of the cash registers, pulled the receipt, wrote a note on it and carried it to Georgie's office. As he neared the office he was surprised to see the door opened slightly and a slice of light spilling out onto a nearby bread display case. He heard a voice. Cursing.

"I don't give a damn, they'll find out and take us down with them. What do you mean he tried to help? The slime went out of his way to screw me before he screwed his family, the mine and the union." The voice was familiar and obviously speaking on the telephone. Lucas stepped closer. There was anger and urgency in the speaker's voice.

"You better get in here and start cleaning this mess up if you don't want to sit your butt in lock up at Deer Lodge for the next ten years." There was a pause.

"Yeah, well they can search wherever the hell they want and trust me brother, all paths lead to me and you. Get in here and bury this trash. Burn it. I don't care, but do it now. I'm going to his house before anybody else connects the dots." The speaker slammed down the receiver.

Lucas stood in the dark just beyond the door. He could see an arm and hand digging through an open drawer. His heart stopped as he held his breath. The hand found what it was looking for. Lucas watched as it retrieved a revolver from the depths of the desk, spun the chamber and checked for ammunition. The light snapped off. Lucas jumped behind the display case and crouched. Ernie Shaggal strode into the aisle and closed the office door behind him.

"Rotten bastard," Ernie cursed. He fumbled with the front glass door to the store, opened it, stepped outside and let it close. It locked automatically with a metallic click. Lucas stayed hidden for several minutes before he peered around the case. Ernie was sitting in his car, warming it. Many more minutes passed before the car pulled away. Lucas entered the office, placed the receipt on Georgie's desk and ran to the back of the store. He wanted out of there before Ernie returned. Lucas placed his small grocery sack in the back of his truck as he unlocked his door.

"Hey kid, got any booze in that bag?"

Lucas spun around at the sound of a voice behind him. A shadow stood between the store wall and the Dumpster.

"Who's there?" Lucas called out nervously. The figure moved towards him and stepped into the stray light.

"Just an old broad looking for a date." Dolly Young stumbled slightly as she walked towards Lucas. He recognized her as a store customer and knew her reputation as an old prostitute. What filtered light touched her face favored it by rendering her wrinkles unnoticeable. In the dismal pall she looked younger, but the croaking of her voice betrayed any pretense of youthfulness. She was holding a beer bottle in her hand and flicking a half burned cigarette with the other. Wrapped in a heavy fur coat, she looked like a starving bear forging for refuse. Dolly halted her stride and pointed to a power meter on the brick wall of the store.

"Is this the switch?" she said, her voice was thick with intoxication, her expression inquisitive. Dolly apparently thought the alley was dark because some one had forgotten to turn the lights on. Forgoing an answer, she redirected her attention to Lucas. "Gimme a look in that sack. I know you got something to drink in there."

"No ma'am, I don't have any thing to drink." He began to open his truck door hoping to extricate himself from the alley and be gone from the drunken woman.

"Yeah, but you got store keys and can get something, can't you sugar?" Dolly smiled and sounded sickly sweet as she spoke. She tripped again and almost fell against Lucas. He stepped back and instinctively reached towards her to prevent a further fall.

"No. I'd get in trouble." He tried to slip behind the steering wheel, Dolly pushed the door, prohibiting him from climbing into the cab. Lucas felt frightened for an instant before realizing the woman was not a threat, really.

"Then maybe you can just gimme a ride uptown? That you can do, right? My butt is freezing." She ran a hand up her backside. Her long coat was unbuttoned and Lucas could see that she was wearing a short black dress. Her legs were clothed in dark nylons ending in black strapped high heels. Dolly leaned toward him. Her breath crossed Lucas' nose. It was tainted with alcohol and tobacco. He was immediately offended and thought about cursing her and driving away as fast as he could. The thought of her freezing to death behind the grocery store gave him reason to pause. Even she didn't deserve that.

"What are you doing here anyway?" he said, looking up and down the alley. He hoped that his question would not encourage her to be any more bold. As soon as he spoke he could tell that Dolly was relieved. He supposed he had been duped by her.

Dolly began laughing, her throat sounded phlegm-filled, "Performing a political favor or two…" She lifted her foot to her hand and tried adjusting the strap. The imbalance from the alcohol toppled her and she fell backwards against the fender. Catching herself, she began laughing even heartier, the deep chuckles turning into cigarette coughing. Lucas hoped she wouldn't pull up something and spit it out in front of him. She had dropped her beer bottle, which didn't break, but clattered loudly enough. It rolled towards a sewer grate opening and stopped. Elbows planted on the fender, Dolly's knees wobbled and she struggled to stand upright.

Lucas thought about Ernie moments ago and the anger in his voice. Dolly insinuated that she had been with him. But why?.

"Ernie drop you off?" he said to her. Dolly was again standing and adjusting her skirt which had crept up a bit too high, exposing her panties.

"Kicked me out is more like it, the louse. So how about the ride?" She sounded disinterested in conversation about Ernie. Rather, her tone was pleading. Lucas noticed she had started to shiver.

"Fine," Lucas said indignantly, "Just get in. I don't want your cigarette in there though."

Dolly snuffed the butt out on his tire, flipped it into the trash bin, then clung to the hood of the pickup as she walked around its front. Lucas sat down in the cab, reached across and unlocked the passenger door. An old car slowed as it drove near the end of the alley. Dolly waved and stumbled. The car increased in speed and disappeared. She slid into the seat next to him and kicked the remnants of empty beer on the floorboard.

"Hey, thought you didn't have any booze?" she said. The gargled laughter returned. So did her tainted breath

"They're empty," Lucas said flatly. He turned the key and started the engine. The defrost fan came to life and began cleaning the mist from the windshield.

"This one ain't," Dolly said, picking a full beer off the floor. She opened it and sprayed beer onto the passenger window. Droplets flecked the fur on her coat. They glimmered slightly. The stale smell of her perfume circulated in the cab. Lucas rolled down his window. This was almost worse than Scabby.

"I need to get home. Where do you want me to take you?" he asked as the truck pulled out of the alley. Another old car crept by. One headlamp was broken and the other light was very dim.

"Turn the heat on, sugar, please. Just take me to the union hall." Dolly pulled her coat closed and wrapped her arms around her chest. Beer spilled from the open can unnoticed by her onto the seat. Lucas tried to ignore it, but his disdain was beginning to show through his expressions.

"I can't take you there," he said. Lucas looked at his watch again. The alcohol was wearing off, the anxiety and frustration with Rita was become less intense, he was becoming very tired.

"You afraid the guy's will think you lost your cherry to an old hooker?" she laughed. She tugged at the collar of her coat and smoothed it with her fingers.

"No. They hate me and my father." Lucas looked around outside of the truck thankful that nobody had yet seen him with the drunken woman.

"Your daddy? Who's that?" She continued wiping at her coat and began primping her hair.

"Jonathan Kaari, the mine manager," he said with a touch of authority and pride. He realized he had spoken quite loud.

Dolly chuckled again and said with wonder, "The company king's baby is taking me for a drive. Hell those boys will hate me too, cutie."

Lucas began to detest the situation he was in and was certain that he hated Dolly. A life in Sunnyside was bad enough he reasoned, but taking money for intercourse and accepting the life beyond the bedridden years in the same small town had to be horrible. The woman had no self respect. She was still gossiped about and pointed at by the women in the city. Her name was synonymous with any sexual slur. He wondered how many divorces she was responsible for. She was the antithesis of the goodness he believed in concerning woman. Whatever his ideal feminine image was, he was certain she was the opposite.

"Just tell me where you want to go, please. I'm going to be in trouble if I don't get home." Dolly seemed unconcerned over his potential problems.

"Fine, just take me to the Tall Pine trailer park then." Her words were sloppy and slurred. She was finished with her makeover and was sipping loudly on her beer. Lucas shifted the truck into reverse and backed down the alleyway.

"Tall Pine? That's over near the county line. I can't drive there this late at night," he said.

"What, you want to put me back out in the cold, little boy? I'll give you a tip when we get there. You are rather cute," Dolly purred, then sputtered a laugh again.

Lucas thought about stopping and kicking her out. His anger and frustration over the evening's events had a focal point. He wanted to vent at her. She was a perfect target, yet something inside of him held his tongue in check.

"Forget it, just stay over there, drink your beer and don't talk to me. I'll take you to your trailer." The rancor in his voice, if noticeable, was ignored by his passenger. Instead she turned on his radio. The impulse to push her hand away and turn off the receiver was also squelched by his self-control. He surrendered himself to the half hour drive. The sooner he got her home the sooner he could get back to his house and phone Heather. Hopefully she would still be awake. The local AM radio station, static filled as it was, filled the cab with country music. He loathed it, but let it play.

"Russell your brother?" Dolly finally said after the song ended and a commercial for a local motorcycle shop began to play.

"Maybe. Why?" Lucas said, curious that she would know his brother. Certainly Russell would not intimately know this woman.

"Me and him are just friends. See him at the union hall all the time. He's just as gorgeous as you." Dolly reached over and tried to pinch his cheek. His head pulled away towards the window as his hand intercepted hers. She snapped it back to her lap and smirked.

"Them boys like him even though your daddy is a big shot," she said.

"Everybody likes him."

"Billy didn't like him much," she replied. She sounded a bit distant.

"What do you know about that?" Lucas asked. He turned onto the interstate highway and began to accelerate. Just off the freeway he could see the tall smelter stack and his blinking lights. A large semi truck drove towards them in the opposite lane, its high beam lights on high. Lucas squinted and cursed the driver. Dolly turned the radio off.

"Me and Billy were friends too, you know, good friends." She was slurring again as she stared out of the window. "We worked together for all them years. He was a good man." Her voice trailed off as if overtaken by a memory.

"He beat my brother and his daughter this morning. He was human garbage," Lucas said angrily. Dolly turned sharply towards him and pointed at his face.

"Don't you say that. You don't know what he was made of." She was mad. Lucas had touched a feeling that even she seemed surprised to find.

"He hurt my family. He hurt everybody that knew him. Blowing his brains out was a cowardly thing to do."

"All he wanted was to do right by the miners. He hurt, too. Deep inside." Dolly lowered her hand but continued piercing him with a glare.

"Seems he just wanted what was best for him," Lucas said. He looked at his speedometer. The needle read sixty-five.

"He got me my job and kept me in it. There aren't too many places a person like me can go when we are, you know, finished working." She had retreated a little from her rigid stance and returned to her beer. The can empty, she dropped it to the floor.

"As long as there was something in it for him, I'm sure he'd help anybody," Lucas said.

"All men are like that. Even you, sugar."

"What do you mean? I don't want anything from anybody."

"Oh, a dreamer, I see. You have a lot to learn about being a man. You ain't never goin' to make much of yourself if you can't accept what you are made of. You are a male and trapped."

"What makes you think you know so much?"

"Because, I thought I knew everything when I was your age too. Men would tell me they loved me if I showed them my love first. After awhile you realize that it's all about what you can get, not what you can give. Don't matter if the gent is sixteen or sixty. Its always the same."

"That's why you became...." He hesitated on his next word.

"A whore?" Dolly laughed again. "You can say it. It's not that bad of a word. Whores are honest. Most other woman ain't, though they are all whores in one fashion or another. I've always been an honest woman, never pretending to love somebody so I can be safe and secure."

"Honest. Right. Honest enough to work for Billy. What'd that cost him?" Disgust was evident in his voice.

"Me and Billy had an understanding. It's always about getting not giving," she continued. Dolly leaned over again and began feeling around on the floor for another drink.

"So you got a job and a retirement? Billy got what? Sex?"

"It worked out for both of us."

"He was married and had kids. Didn't that mean anything to you?" Lucas kept glancing at the woman, hating her more each time she spoke.

"It meant everything. I never had to worry that he'd lie to me. We both knew how it all went together. I didn't want anything but money. He didn't want anything but relief."

"God. You're sick." The words almost spat from his mouth.

"Sick? Sugar, you are just beginning to get into the world. In a few years, you'll wish you could get out of it. Having somebody to hold when *you* want them, having somebody to take care of you without some guilty commitment, that's the ideal world. I had that."

"So, now you turn to Ernie to pick up the slack? That was a fast move."

"Ernie. He wants power and position not an old prostitute." Lucas could hear the anger mounting in her voice as well. Up ahead he saw the exit to Tall Pine creek. He flipped the turn signal on.

"You said you were with him...I thought..."

"Of course you did. Your dirty little mind had me naked in the back of his Caddy pleasing his fatness. So sorry to disappoint. Billy made sure that Ernie was my retirement."

"What?" Lucas said, confused.

"I have all of Billy's secrets," Dolly said. "Every last one of them."

CHAPTER 21

Frozen mud ruts held the truck tires firmly as Lucas navigated the final hundred yards to Dolly's trailer house. She hissed at him when he referred to the dwelling as a trailer, preferring, she said, to call it mobile home. Despite the choice of words the home was nothing more than seven hundred square feet of aluminum and wood complete with wheels propped up on cinder blocks. Tall Pine creek ran behind the shack, replete with mining taint like its sister tributaries.

"Ain't you going to see a lady to the door?" Dolly asked, her voice still thick with cigarettes and booze.

"I'd rather not," Lucas replied curtly.

"For God's sake," Dolly said, "I don't bite... at least not that hard." She began her throaty chuckle again. Lucas faked a smile and remained in his seat. The only light shining was from his myopic headlamps.

"I'll watch to make sure you get in alright, but I've really got to go. My folks would have my head if they knew I was out here. Especially with you..." His voice trailed as he carefully chose his words. He was tired of trying to offend the woman. She seemed beyond it anyway.

"Twenty years ago you'd have beat me inside and I'd of had your face turning blue, sweetheart."

Dolly opened the passenger door. Cold air blasted into the cab. Lucas saw mist on his breath immediately. He reached over and turned the defrost fan on high, pumping hot air against the windshield. Dolly faced him.

"You're a good kid. Not many left in this town." Her voice was softer and carried a sense of sadness. "Thanks," she said.

Dolly stepped into the night and closed the door. Lucas watched as she slid her left hand along the fender and steadied herself. He felt sorry for her. Imagining her life in this valley, ending up on some dead end swamp, in a trailer park, regaling in hustling beers and cigarettes. She was like an old has-been actress, existing on memories, ignoring reality. Her decisions brought her here, he thought, and the consequences she was living were hers. Even this idea did not alleviate the emptiness he was feeling for her.

In the headlights, he saw her clearly for the first time this evening. Her fur coat, fake obviously, was matted, probably from spilled beers. The cloth was frayed and had become shabby. The back of her legs, still strong, actually youthful, were the only things that seemed redeeming about the old prostitute. He smiled briefly. Of course they were attractive, she'd spent most of her time on her back.

In an instant she was gone, fallen into one of the frozen ruts. Without a thought, Lucas opened his door and rushed to her. Dolly was twisted on the ground, lying on her hip, her arm twisted, the contents of her purse tossed before her.

"Are you alright?" He was shouting to her as he knelt. Her hair hung in stringy strands around her face. "Talk to me..." he said. Slipping his hands under her armpits, he tried to lift her. Through her coat he could feel the absence of muscle in her arms. She cried out as he tried to lift.

"It hurts," she said. There was pain in the air.

"Where? Where does it hurt."

"My wrist... it hurts..." Lucas looked at her face. Tears slid down her cheeks. Ink black smudges from her mascara traced over her skin. He lifted again, this time gently, surprised at how light she was, he helped her to stand. The front of her dark nylons had torn below one knee, gravel and blood speckles clung to the material. Her foot had lost one of its shoes.

Lucas steadied her with one hand and stooped, retrieving the purse items; cigarettes, a lighter, folded papers, coin purse, lipstick, keys, a small pistol with a white pearl handgrip. He gathered the items to his chest and helped her walk toward the two wooden steps to her trailer door.

"I'm so sorry. I should have helped you to the house in the first place. Sorry." Lucas felt awful. Dolly was still hobbling. Sniffling, she held onto his arm.

"Which key is it?" He asked as he started sorting through them.

"Door is never locked," she said, "Got nothing worth taking."

He tried the knob and tugged. The metal door popped open, sticking slightly at the top. Two long-haired cats scattered upon seeing a stranger. He let Dolly step inside first. The interior was hot. A small Franklin stove stood in the corner of the tiny living room. A fire, long burning, heated the house beyond comfort. Low wattage bulbs glowed in two small lamps, each shade covered with light red scarves. The shag carpet, long ago cleaned, reflected back the light making the room a wash of dark orange, shades of red and dark blues. There was a scent of lilacs and baby powder in the air. Lucas felt queasy for a moment; this reminded him too much of the waiting room at the whorehouse. He closed the door behind him, sealing off the cold night air. Dropping the spilled items on the floor he helped her across the room.

"Let me see your wrist," he said.

Dolly sat on the edge of an old velvet covered couch that took up most of the living room space. A small table top ironing board and iron covered the breakfast counter that separated the kitchen and living room. Lucas dropped to his knees near her and held her hand. Her fingers were extremely cold. He examined them closely, turning her hand, looking for abrasions. The nails on her fingers were dark brown and very long. He wondered if the nails were even real. There was a small cut on the outside, near the wrist bone. Dolly winced when he touched near the wound.

"I think it is sprained is all," he finally said releasing her hand. "Do you have an ice pack?" Lucas glanced at her. Her head was wobbling slightly.

"It's ok, honey, I'll take care of it." She reached her good hand towards his head and pushed his hair back from his face. The gesture was tender and natural.

"You could use some help too," she said. There was still a slur in her voice.

Lucas had forgotten about his own appearance. Dolly had been oblivious earlier to his bruised condition, but now in the soft light, she must see that he had been injured. He wondered how he must look through her drunken eyes. The cockiness in him was gone, replaced by sensitivity and concern. Dolly had dropped her tough woman attitude. In this lost place, the two of them sat in silence, hurt by the world and by themselves. He was ashamed for how he had treated her earlier and for the thoughts he had had.

"You sit. You need to get some ice on your wrist and hand."

Dolly instructed him to look beneath her bathroom sink for an ice bag and some bandages. Lucas helped her take off her coat and eased her feet up onto the couch. She favored her injured hand. He laid it gently on her stomach.

In the bathroom, Lucas was again confronted by the cats who raced into the back bedroom. The shower curtain was transparent. Dozens of unlit candles filled every open space. Bottles of lotions and perfumes lined one shelf above the sink. The entire house was immaculate. Old and rundown, Dolly still took good care of it. He realized that the place looked ready for a nocturnal rendezvous.

He turned on the sink light and checked his look in the mirror. Swelling had caused his right eye to become puffy. His lower lip protruded slightly, the outside purple and red. Crusty blood caked his nostrils.

Lucas washed his face and hands. Dolly was talking, actually mumbling, to him from the living room. He feigned understanding of what she was saying, acknowledging her on occasion. He found the pack and first aid items and returned to the fallen woman.

"Let me clean your knee for you," he said. Looking at the wound, he saw the abrasion wasn't serious. It had bled slightly. Dirty, it needed to be cleaned. The stockings were clipped to a hidden undergarment. There was a hint of embarrassment in his voice. He returned to the bathroom and retrieved a warm wet cloth.

"I need to take these nylons off," Dolly said. "You'll need to turn your back." Her voice was clearer than it had been all evening. Lucas turned around and faced the closed trailer door.

"I think this is the first time in years that I asked a young man to close his eyes while I got undressed." Her laugh returned as she talked. Lucas heard her rustling behind him. He thought about where he was and what had transpired over the past hour. He had gone from contempt to pity to compassion.

"Finished. You can turn around," she said.

Lucas half expected to find her totally disrobed but wasn't disappointed when he found that she had returned to her reclined position, the hosiery tossed into a mangled black heap near the couch.

He dabbed at the wound, dried it and covered it with a clean bandage. The wrist, now swelling, was cleaned gently. Dolly shuddered once, but didn't utter a sound. He packed the bag with ice from the freezer and wrapped it all loosely with a kitchen towel. He gave her two aspirin and returned to the bathroom to finish cleaning himself. Dolly had fallen asleep by the time he stepped back into her living room.

The kitchen wall clock said two. Momentary panic hit him. He knew that Heather was asleep. He wanted, no needed, to talk to her. His mind was clearer despite his bruises. The alcohol had worn off. He thought about calling her from here, but realized the explanation of his whereabouts would have had to be a lie and lying to her was not how he wanted to pepper their conversation.

Checking Dolly one last time, he covered her legs with a shawl from her bedroom. Reaching for the door, he saw the items from her purse still strewn on the floor. He thought about leaving them, but the tidiness of the living room was

Scott R. Baillie

disrupted by them. Better he should put them on the kitchen table and let her wake up without the nuisance.

The folded papers were too bulky to put back. They were out of place in her otherwise uncluttered purse. She had obviously planned for a night out. Why would she have several sheets of paper with her? He felt some guilt as he unfolded them. Leaning toward one of the lamps he could see they were photocopies. It was a handwritten letter. The first words startled him, *"Dear Congressman Temple"*, they said, *"We will strike as planned..."* He read quickly, fearing Dolly might awaken and catch him. The letter was precise and demanding. It was signed by Billy Murphy.

CHAPTER 22

Heather's bedroom light was on when Lucas rolled into the driveway. He had to walk from his truck and navigate between the two houses to see for sure. It was almost three o'clock Sunday morning. He cursed the hour under his breath. The young woman would be angry, rightly, if he called this late and was certainly not going to be happy with him when he did speak to her. One night prior they had shared the beginnings of romance, unearthing new feelings for one another. She would be wondering what he was thinking, why he didn't call. She would want to know about Russell, whether Lori was ok. There would have been dozens of questions, each one needing an answer, each one germinating more concerns. These questions went beyond just their friendship. She cared about the people involved, she loved them and deserved to know. This must be the reason she was still awake, he reasoned. He turned and stumbled over a frozen stubble of long dead grass, swearing audibly this time.

Lucas had expected to see his brother's truck parked in its usual spot when he got home, but the driveway was empty, washed by the pale light of the corner street lamp. He supposed that Russell was with Lori, comforting her verbally and probably physically. He didn't imagine they were on another drug and drink binge. Thinking about it, he wondered why Lori would indulge in those abuses knowing she was pregnant. In the reaches of his spirit, he wondered if she really was expecting a child. He shook the notion off and walked towards the basement door. It was unlocked.

The house was dark and drafty. Over fifty years old, the home had been remodeled recently, but the leaded windows, prized by his mother, were left intact, providing no insulation. Several debates had raged between his parents during the upgrade. Mom usually persevered through tears or a cold shoulder. He wondered why his father argued with her at all, he would give in eventually. His mother seemed less happy with her victories these days. Lucas vowed he would never marry anybody who coerced with emotions. His father had laughed and hugged him when he told him this. Lucas didn't understand the gesture but his father said someday he would, that he would learn how to 'dance'. It was an interesting concept, but he didn't want to know any more.

Finding his way to the living room, he turned up the thermostat and walked to the kitchen. The refrigerator was covered with a maze of pictures and drawings. Lucas stopped and examined them. His mother coveted the photos and finger paintings more than any of her other possessions. There were sketches of trees and cars, notes of love on holidays, Cub Scout awards, perfect papers and albums worth of photographs. Some of them had been displayed here for over fifteen years. A black and white Polaroid snapshot caught his attention. Clamped by a sunflower shaped magnet, it held an instant of life from twelve years earlier.

Lucas leaned in and squinted. He had seen the picture so many times that he never noticed it anymore. Sitting on the front porch of his home, some random summer day in 1962, were a little girl and little boy eating sugar sandwiches and drinking grape juice. He thought he looked goofy, a buzz haircut and big ears, but

Heather, her hair in braids, was like a cherub without wings. Their clothes were wet from running through the lawn sprinkler he figured. Seated behind them, a bit blurred, was Heather's mother.

Lucas lifted the photo from its makeshift easel and moved it closer to his face. The likeness to Heather was amazing. Mrs. McKenzie was beautiful. She couldn't have been thirty years old at the time he thought. Leaning forward, elbow on knee, she was resting her chin on her hand. A half eaten Popsicle poked from her fingers. The look of peace and love on her face as she watched the two children was unmistakable. He stood for a few more moments and absorbed the images, then returned it to the fridge.

The house was empty. In the dark, the normal robustness of family, the sense that those you loved were near, was absent. It felt strange to Lucas, this absence of life. So much had transpired over the last two days, so many things had occurred that needed to be talked about with his parents. *Needed* to be talked about, but almost certainly he would succumb to silence and offer only the kind of questions and explanations that pacified instead of unified. He would have to explain his bruises for sure. His dad would be mad and his mom disappointed. They might try to ground him, but he would convince them that he was an adult and needed no such guidance. They would give in, they always did, content that their words would shape his values and correct his behavior. He smirked at the thought. Russell would drop his bomb somewhere, sometime, leaving an emotional wake that would dominate the home and dramatically change the family's future. He wanted his moments and confessions to come before Russell's. He even thought about speaking to his mother about Heather, not the previous evening's events, but his heartsick desire for her. His father would not understand, but his mother was always open to her sons. She had lived and loved a lot for this family, and at least would give Lucas some kind word or nudging direction. She would never be the same after his brother shared his latest news. He began to miss who she was and wondered what she would be like after the revelation.

Russell had always charged the home with energy, some good, most bad. During his teen years, Russell kept the tension hot between their parents, dividing them on almost every domestic topic. Lucas had begun to hate him for the tears he brought to their mother. He told his mother once that he wished that Russell would just run away or die. That statement had grounded him to his room for a week and cost him his allowance for a month. His mother, despite her pain, told him that he was to never say anything like that about his brother. At that point he understood that his mother accepted her children for what they were, and that she loved them in spite of their actions. It took him time to stop despising Russell.

Lucas carried the foodstuffs he had purchased secretly at the S&S into his bedroom. Peering out of his curtains he could see the light diffusing through Heather's window. It too was shielded by closed blinds. Was she awake, he wondered, or simply sleeping with a book on her chest, drawn to slumber by what she had read. Did she fall asleep thinking about him? How did she feel now that a day had passed? Was she mad because he had not called? Did she know he had gone to the keg party? And the unimaginable, did Rita call her before he had a chance? That thought scared him.

He visited the bathroom, checked his wounds again, and resigned that he would have to tell the truth to anybody that asked how he got them. The school gossip mavens would distort the events. Better to set the record straight in advance. This truth would be hard for Heather to accept, but she was already angry with Mickey. He would tell her that Mickey had disclosed his secret to him and how the fight had actually put an end, at least for now, to the battle that had lived with the boys for years. Maybe she would understand. She knew both boys well and had an insight into the dispute. He reasoned that she would have to accept what occurred.

The night before had been mystical and was becoming surreal. Just like the fight tonight, it had its foundation laid years before. Growing steadily towards a mighty moment of emotion. The distant outcome would not be any more predictable, but it had served as a significant point of turning. Lucas actually felt relieved that the fight had taken place without Heather present. Maybe God had set the stage for this to happen. Mickey was in a different place with both him and Heather. Jealous, Mickey might try to unnerve him, but with the knowledge that Lucas knew of the interlude with Peeper, he would most likely keep some distance. Maybe Mickey told him for that reason. Maybe Mickey knew deep inside that he needed to give up something to make him stop tormenting him and Scabby, something he seemed unable to do on his own. Weird as that seemed, Lucas was grateful that he knew. He promised himself that he wouldn't tell anyone.

He continued wondering why Mickey would divulge such a dark issue to him. Years before, Lucas had been encouraged by a cousin to touch him in a manner not too dissimilar. His cousin had reciprocated. They stopped themselves before much happened, sensing they were involved in something that both would regret. Lucas remembered the shame he had later felt at his own excitement. He had questioned himself for a time, realizing as he got older that sometimes the body reacts where the mind wouldn't normally. His cousin and he never talked about it and never broached one another again. He would keep this interlude to himself forever. He would never tell Heather about his cousin. At least he didn't think he would any time soon. In a way, he understood Mickey's predicament.

Lucas sat on the edge of his twin bed and turned on his stereo. Normally he would listen through headphones, but an empty house invited loud music. Russell used to have a bedroom right next to Lucas, but had been vanquished to the basement because of his blaring music. This late at night the only station worth a listen broadcast from Missoula and favored pre-programmed rock and roll. No disc jockeys, just some recorded guy from New York or Los Angeles announcing the songs and artist. On other nights when he was alone, he would dance and fake sing to the music pretending he was the star and songwriter. He knew he didn't have a voice, which kept the dream intact. Scabby could pull the voice off, but he was far from rock poster fodder.

Lucas removed his clothes and piled them next to the bed. Picking at the lint between his toes, he massaged his feet. He would shower in the morning and wash his laundry, erasing the blood, booze and stale smoke. His mother's nose was keen enough that people would talk about it from time to time. No sense in giving her cause for concern.

Lucas stood up and turned off the overhead light and returned to his bed. The room was illuminated by a desk lamp perched on a night stand. In the low light he looked down at his naked body. Unlike his grandfather, dad and brother he had little hair on his chest and stomach. A feathery line of fine hair ran below his navel to the thick hair of his pelvis. Never athletic, he nonetheless had no fat that he could see; no serious muscle either, which was discouraging. Maybe a few sit-ups and push-ups would be helpful, he thought. Tensing his stomach he checked for ripples. None. He slowly traced his hands down his chest, ribs and abdomen and stared at the ceiling. His thoughts returned to Heather.

The music was shattered by the ringing of the phone in the hallway, causing him to jump and knock his potato chips onto the floor. Racing from the bed, he ground some of them into the carpet. Groping in the dim light towards the clattering he cursed his parents for not allowing him to have his own telephone. The compromise was a long handset phone cord that almost reached to his bed. Fear grabbed him as he imagined his parents in a wreck, his brother hurt, or worse.

"Hello?" he said, faking a sleepy voice.

"Are you ok?" It was Heather speaking. She sounded tired.

"Are you? What are you doing up so late?" He attempted to sound cheerful and in control.

"My dad isn't home yet. I'm starting to worry. He usually calls if he is going to be late."

"He's probably working a double. There were lots of cars at the mine parking lot when I drove by." Lucas strengthened his voice. Hearing Heather eased his panic, but brought a new disorder to his thinking. All the pending questions were there. He knew she would pick a few from the list. He decided to take charge of the conversation before she could steer it towards trouble.

"I'm sorry I didn't call this afternoon," he said. He surprised himself with the softness in his voice. It sounded fake to him, not the way he normally spoke to her.

"I'm sorry you didn't either. Are you ok?" she asked.

"Ok? Yeah, why? Don't I sound ok?" Maybe she heard the insincerity.

"Not really. You sound different is all. I was worrying about you, too."

They discussed Lori and Russell, the strike, Billy Murphy and other tough subjects, but seemed to avoid the obvious question and concern; them. He thought about telling her of Billy's letter to the Congressman, but divulging that would betray his evening and expose his drinking. He would tell her, but not now.

Several times Lucas almost interjected his thoughts about her into their dialogue. He rehearsed the first sentence that would lead to his profession of love, as she spoke. Each time he found the nerve he couldn't find the voice. Finally she pushed the conversation the wrong way.

"Are you alright with us? I mean about Friday night?" Heather was searching for the right words too, Lucas could sense it. "Where are you with me...?" she finally said. She was clearly nervous.

The moment arrived suddenly. The fatigue, the worry, the stress were heavy on Lucas. The next words might change the direction of the foundling relationship. Suddenly his courage shrank. He would wait.

"I'm naked," he said.

"What?"

"I'm naked. I'm standing in the hallway, naked."

She began to giggle. He relished its sound.

"What's so funny? You can't see me. Can't be that humorous." He puffed out his chest and spun the long phone cord slowly in the air like a cowboy preparing to rope a calf.

"It's just that the last thing I ever think about is whether you have clothes on or not when I'm speaking to you on the phone." She paused and asked suspiciously, "Are you naked often when we speak?"

"Nope. This is the first time."

"The last time, too perhaps?" she said. There was still a grin in her voice.

"I hope not," he replied. The words escaped before he could halt them. He stopped fidgeting and stood still.

A long silence filled the phone line.

"I hope not too," she said softly. There was warmth in her words.

Lucas pressed his back against the cool wall and slid to a crouching position, the heels of his feet pressing against his buttocks. The bones in his knees made a popping sound.

"I can't say it all over the phone, Heather," he said, "I need to see you and talk to you when I can look into your eyes, read your face, feel all my senses." He thought he sounded too mushy and was ready to explain. He lay on the carpet and crossed his legs.

"Me too. Come with me to church and we can take a walk afterwards. I need to see you."

"Church? Um, sure, church…" He didn't want to go, but he wanted to be with her. He agreed to see her in a few hours. He hoped he wouldn't smell like beer.

He almost said 'I love you' before they bid goodnight. Hanging up, he sat for several minutes in the dimness of the hall. He could hear the furnace fan turning on and off, forcing hot air into the cool house. He was already too warm.

Walking back to his room, wide-awake, he turned his stereo down. Across the courtyard, between the houses, he saw that Heather had turned off her light. Slipping on a pair of briefs he climbed back on his bed. On the headboard sat his music notebook, filled with poems and verses. He'd asked his mother to not read it. She was prone to spontaneous bedroom cleaning. Russell said it was because she was looking for dirty magazines and generally snooping. For a time he would hide a hair between pages of the notebook and check at night to see if it was still there. If the book had been tampered with, the hair would be missing. It was always intact.

He thought about copying one of his poems down and giving it to Heather as a gift on their walk tomorrow, an introduction to the words that would follow. Searching, he found ballads and cryptic notes. Nothing seemed to fit the occasion he was planning, even though he recognized much of the writing as something inspired by the young woman. Scabby knew many of these were about Heather, but he pretended not to know or care. The songs were there too, carefully penned in Scabby's eloquent hand. Nothing seemed to fit. He decided to write something that would capture her and his feelings. Something that would never be read by Scabby, a sonnet or a love letter, a testament to his emotions. He removed a blank sheet and began to write.

The words came quickly, filling every line on the page. Reading them he saw they were not so much an ode to love as they were a snippet of the time he had with her on the porch swing. He wrote them again, in a clearer hand on crisper paper. Tethered with a letter, he would give them both to her. In his mind he saw her reading them, understanding him, absorbing the feelings that he couldn't speak, etching them into her heart. The writings would be hers to keep, to revisit and recapture all that he felt for and about her. Life ahead together was unknown, but this small tribute to a golden moment would stand as a reference for both of them.

He read the poem out loud:

"A Season of You"

The night ended too soon,
our secret silence stolen
by autumnal leaves
dryly flying across our path.

Finger shadows
from barren branches
paint webs
on your chilled hands
as they rest
on the stubbled warmth of my face.

Fluttered by a whispered moon
your infinite eyes,
your soul windows,
follow mine as they close
to meet a wintered kiss.
It is spring again.

If love is worth waiting for
then I shall hold onto my
dreams until the stars fade
into the bleak of night.

If love is worth waiting for
then I shall wait in my sleep
until the heaven's cease
and dreams disappear.

If love is worth waiting for,
then an eternity of patience
will be worth you,

my emptiness will only
be a short memory,
and I won't be alone
anymore.

The phrases finished, he stared, confused, and considered shredding them. He felt the familiar touch of self-doubt rising in him. Too much and she might withdraw. Too much and she might laugh. His father had once told him that committing something to writing committed it forever. Better to say it and let it be gone than to pen it for the world. But this was different, he *wanted* her to read it and he didn't care, at least in this moment, if the world did know. Whatever her reaction, he would travel the lengths necessary to show her his heart.

He finished the letter by six o'clock and placed them both in a sealed envelope. He would give them to her today. Nothing would stop him.

Mrs. Nellie would be proud.

CHAPTER 23

Catholic's seem to have all the fun, Lucas thought. The local priest, Father McElroy, was known to gamble, shoot pool, drink scotch, hunt and fly fish. The Father's only drawback must be the hands-off policy concerning woman. Why, he thought, would God make you give up women to prove your love for Him? The job couldn't pay that well.

Heather was raised in the Catholic church and spent several evenings a week listening, learning or teaching at St. Rachel's. Her mother had been immovable in her resolve that the McKenzie kids would follow the Saints, honor the Pope, abide by the Holy days and live by the Word of God. Heather actually seemed to enjoy going and told him that church was fun for her. She would take every opportunity to invite him along on outings, never pressing hard, but Lucas couldn't help feel that she was worried about his immortality. He used to tease her about the Pope and fish dinners on Friday. Mickey's involvement at St. Rachel's made Lucas worry more about his mortality and sank his decision on not attending Mass or any other related function. Besides, he detested St. Rachel's since it appeared to have been the spawning ground of Heather and Mickey's ill fated love.

Scabby and his family were members of St. Rachel's and seemed to be an outreach for the congregation. Many Sunday mornings Lucas would see the Cipher vehicle drive by piled with people heading to Mass. Lucas knew the Cipher kid's clothing came from compassionate church members as hand-me-downs. Delmer Cipher was even working as a sanctuary custodian at St. Rachel's to earn extra money.

Lucas' parents were members of a non-denominational church, the Grace of God. He liked the services for their informality and the youth group was lively. Mrs. Kaari was active enough in the fellowship, yet told Lucas that he would need to find his own relationship with God. She would help, she said, by encouraging and educating, but never forcing. She told him that each person had to have their own reckoning, whatever that meant. Russell never really attended, but Lucas would try to sit through services or Sunday school at least once a month. This pleased his mother and satiated any concerns she had about his soul. His father seemed disinterested in the whole matter and would only mumble something about the NFL when asked if he would attend services.

The two hours of sleep earlier this morning only made Lucas feel awful and look worse. The bruises on his face couldn't be hidden. Much of his face was numb and the ridge of his nose was certainly swollen. Lucas considered covering the marks with some of his mother's makeup, but discarded that idea almost as swiftly at it had formed. Tenderly, he touched his mouth. The lips were not quite as lumpy as they were last evening, but had a dark purple hue to them. Moving his head side to side with his hand, he peered intensely at his reflection in the bathroom mirror. He looked like the devil. A grin crossed his mouth as he envisioned himself walking into St. Rachel's and having the priest try to perform an exorcism on him.

Showering, he overdressed in a suit, hoping that the serious Sunday attire would take away from his otherwise hardened look. Placing the sealed envelope with the poem and letter into his interior breast pocket, he smoothed the front of the coat and adjusted his tie.

He walked next door to the McKenzie's. The morning air was crisp and lightly tainted.

"Lucas Aaron, oh my God, what happened to you?" The shocked look on Heather's face almost caused him to turn and run home. Instead, he reached for her. She stepped into his arms. Her little brother and sister, Vernon Junior and Katie, upon hearing Lucas, ran into the living-room and abruptly stopped and stood stone still, staring.

"Mickey and I made up," he said, trying to be funny. Before she could start with the questions, he drove straight to the story and explained the fight scenario. Heather listened, still wearing the wide-eyed expression. She didn't interrupt, waiting for him to finish.

"Daddy didn't come home last night. I tried calling the guard shack at the mine and nobody answered. I'm worried," she said. Lucas was surprised she didn't start asking him questions about the fight.

"He's just working. I'm sure he's fine." Lucas touched her cheek with the back of his fingers. Heather pressed slightly against them.

"How can you be certain? He always calls if he is working over or going to be late." Heather's tone was emphatic. She stepped away from him and slipped her arms into a sweater.

"Maybe the phones went out. There were a bunch of guys at the gate. Maybe one of those drunks cut the line. You never know." His words were intentionally light.

"That's the point. We don't know."

Lucas lost his thoughts, realizing he too was becoming worried. He hadn't heard from Russell either.

"Let's just go to church. We can come back home and call the guardhouse. They'll know if anything has happened," Lucas said, glancing at the two youngest McKenzie children. They still hadn't spoken but appeared nervous about the conversation. Lucas knelt and held open his arms. The children ran to him, knocking him down. He could hear Heather's giggle as he wrestled on the carpet.

The six block walk to St. Rachel's was all up hill. Lucas became aware of the stiffness in his legs as they began the final incline. His back and shoulders felt bruised. The conversation felt strained as unspoken words drifted between them. Maybe she didn't care about the fight.

The cool October air staved off a worse headache, but Lucas could feel the lingering effects of the alcohol toxins. Though he had peppered his breath with mouthwash and was currently chewing gum, the acrid taste on his tongue served as enough evidence that his body was not yet through processing the prior night's abuse.

"Is Mickey ok?" Heather asked.

The question seemed out of place. Lucas felt an initial spike in anger at the mention of the boy's name. Given his unkempt and bruised condition he fancied the idea that Heather would not mix her thoughts between the two boys, rather choosing by way of her heart to focus on him instead of her errant ex-boyfriend. Reasoning that it was her good nature and not some deep attempt to pacify a lingering affection for Mickey, he decided to make light of the question and answer simply.

"Yes. He's ok." That was enough Lucas reasoned. Any more words concerning Mickey and he would reveal his negative nature. He didn't want to slander the fellow, especially on the way to church.

Heather slipped her hand into the crook of his elbow. It felt odd, out of place, too grown up, to be walking this close to one another, dressed up. His suit made him feel and look responsible and mature, but the bruised broken skin, dark spirit and lust filled mind were only lurking beneath this disguise. Sitting through a sermon, hearing a celibate pontificate the virtues of a pure heart, mind and body would only add to the contrast and make him feel worse instead of better.

"Let's sit in the balcony, please," Lucas said, slowing a bit and turning toward her. She made no attempt to speak and only nodded. She slipped her hand into his, intertwining their fingers. Warmth spread across his chest, and for the first time in two days, he relaxed a little. Any Mickey malice abated.

St. Rachel's towered ahead. Lucas lifted his head and looked up at the golden spire and crucifix. The church was an early landmark of the mining town. Italians and Irishmen had built it. Both factions focused on Mary, but each side was rigid in their tastes, the Italian Catholics grand and overstated, the Irish bland and thrifty. St. Rachel's was pompous and bleak crafted together. The cross he was looking towards had been lifted to the spire in the late 1890's. It was covered in pure gold, donated by a backsliding businessman from Helena who had wished to buy God's favor. Story had it that he actually arranged for the cross to be stolen several year's later when his corporate dealings went bad. The cross was eventually returned after a smelting craftsman refused to reclaim the gold. For over eighty years it had stood high above the silver mining town, drawing attention on rare sunny days.

Several dozen people cluttered the long stairway to the entrance of the church. Lucas waved back at many of them who recognized him from the Shop & Save. Two fat middle-aged women with over-teased and over-dried hair leaned towards one another as they whispered conspiratorially, glancing at him and Heather.

"Everybody loves you, Lucas." The voice belonged to Katie McKenzie. Lucas looked down at the five year old, her beautiful smile exaggerated by a missing front tooth. He bent over and lifted her into his arms, her white-tighted legs intuitively straddling his right hip. A light scent of fresh shampoo wafted from her hair.

"I wish that were true," he said. The little girl clung to his neck as they walked up the final few steps. Heather smiled knowingly at him, catching the subtleties of his comment. Vernon Junior disappeared into a crowd of grade school boys, promising as he went to behave and find Heather when church was over.

The balcony was sparse of people. Heather pulled Lucas to the front railing and pew. Katie sat between them and immediately began to fidget. From this perch, Lucas could see the rest of the congregation, the din of their voices rode over the ominous notes echoing from the church's pipe organ. Below, the pews were divided into two rows, separated by an aisle of red carpet, which extended the length of the entire church. Lucas looked at the candles on the altar, the cloaked choir seated to one side of the lectern, a huge Jesus hung from a staff, naked, save for a cloth covering his groin. Painted blood covered his crown, cheeks and chest. The agony on the statue's face was overdone Lucas thought. The redness of the carpet runner looked like blood running from the base of the cross out into the sanctuary.

"They're divided again," he said looking at the colorfully dressed people below.

"What?" Heather replied, interrupted from some lost thoughts.

"The congregation. Look, the union families are all on the left and the company families are on the right." He pointed his finger. As he glanced about he could see the nattering and sideways glances exchanged between the two sides, mostly from the woman. "Can't they leave that outside?"

"Why pretend? That's who and what they are. It's hard to leave something outside that is so much a part of you. It'd be like denying the color of your eyes or skin," Heather said.

Lucas watched for another moment. Scabby's mother and some of her brood were sitting in the second row pews. No one sat near them. Scabby was seated in the back of the choir.

The organ music stopped, causing the choir to neatly rise. Catching the next note from the musician, the choir began the first hymn. The rest of the gathered stood and began singing. Below, Father McElroy and a robed entourage strolled down the aisle toward the podium. The musical dirge continued until Father McElroy began speaking. Self conscious, non-Catholic, Lucas tried his best to follow Heather through the crossing and kneeling and Hail Mary's. For her part, Heather gracefully ignored him when he faltered. Finally, the good Father began speaking a lesson. Katie crawled into Heather's lap allowing Lucas to sit a bit closer and follow along in Heather's hymnal and Bible. He felt Heather's fingers find his own.

McElroy droned. Lucas felt light-headed and wanted to puke. The Good Father was waving his arms in circles trying to make a point. The gathered seemed as still as a painting, overcome, he supposed, by the tempo of the service, and the bitter disdain for their pew neighbors.

"...but if thine eye be evil, thy whole body shall be full of darkness. If therefore the light that is in thee be darkness, how great is that darkness...!" McElroy was quoting from Matthew. The phrase stuck in Lucas' ears. He followed the passage as Heather's finger glided over the words. It seemed the Father was speaking directly to and about him. He thought about the people beneath him, himself, this town, and the evil that even a boy lives with and sees and accepts. Sitting in this solemn place, passing judgment, aching from his abuses, yearning for the flesh of others, Lucas could only sense emptiness and a bleak sense of nothingness inside. But it didn't seem dark, only vast. In an instant he wanted to cry. He tried to clear the bulge in his throat with a cough.

"Lucas?" Heather said, apparently aware that he was uncomfortable.

"I'm fine. Really." He was curt and tried not to look towards her, afraid she could see the discomfort resident behind his eyes. Nellie's words of love were not too distant in his thoughts either. The letter, crumpled inside of his jacket, begged to be released. He slipped his hand inside the pocket and checked it, withdrew it, folded it and slipped it between his legs.

"I have something for you. I need you to read it. Its…" His words trailed as he became distracted. A member of the church's leadership was walking down the aisle toward Father McElroy, determined to interrupt the sermon. McElroy had fumbled a few words then stopped speaking waiting for his patron. The man approached the altar and whispered to the Father, who leaned forward and balanced slightly on one leg, his robes swinging outward.

The man walked hurriedly back down the aisle. The sanctuary was completely devoid of sound or movement. The priest walked back to his microphone, the expression on his face was puzzling, not surprised, not serene, but obviously searching for words.

"In a few moments, the Bull Run Mining Company is going to begin blowing their emergency siren. We'll hear it and wonder why. Apparently a situation exists that necessitates vacating the tunnels. It is also not known if anybody is in danger. This is preliminary. I've been asked to inform you and ask that you return home after the service and listen to the local radio station. I have been assured that we will all be kept informed. At this point, there seem to be no serious problems. These are just precautions. Any mine rescue team members are asked to report immediately to the portal."

A vocal stir moved through the attendees. Lucas watched as people tilted and turned and chattered. There was an immediate and full sense of fear. Father McElroy nodded his head toward the choir signaling them to start the next hymn. Several of the men from both sides of the aisle made quick exits from their seats. Some of the younger ones kissed their wives.

Heather's mouth was wide open and her eyes unblinking. Katie was leaning her chin over the railing watching the activity below, unaware of the circumstances. She dropped a tissue. Lucas watched it weave side to side and float onto the bonnet of an elderly woman sitting directly beneath them.

"Daddy is down there," she said. Lucas fought the excitement in his chest and breath.

"Russell is too. We need to go," he said. He was anxious. His thoughts stumbled over one another, forming chaos.

"No. I don't want to scare the kids. We'll do what the Father says and go home and wait." Heather's voice was hushed enough to cause Katie to turn around. Heather smiled at her and ran her hands through the youngster's braids. The act was forced. Katie seemed to sense that.

A prayer was started for those who might be in danger and those who would seek to help them. The Father had no script this time. Lucas listened to the plea and was surprised at the warmth of it. Bowing his head he saw the folded envelope peeking up from his lap. He slipped it into this pants pocket.

The baleful sound of a muted siren filled the church. The steeple bells began to chime. Lucas continued praying on his own.

CHAPTER 24

Russell felt the air rushing past him and Delmer as they crested the corner to the K Drift. Ripples rolled on the water in the waste ditch, caused by the furious wind.

"I'm tellin' you Russell, this here's bad. We shouldn't go back none further."

"Man, what could cause things to switch like that? I talked to one of the engineers below and he said that the fans were off. This is like a giant vacuum."

They stopped the manchee at the last air door. In spite of the high humidity, Russell was actually feeling a bit chilled. The wind and moisture cooled him. He ripped off his blood soaked and torn T-shirt, tossing it into the waste ditch. The pain in his shoulder was abating slightly. Mud and grease coated his arms and flat stomach.

"What are you waiting for? Pull the air door switch so we can check this out," Russell shouted. His words were lost in the whistling noise around the air door. He looked over at the nipper. Delmer was visibly nervous. His hand was raised above his head resting on the air door lever.

"I don't smell no sewage or lye," Delmer shouted back.

"Your point?" Russell said as loud as he could.

"When I get to this here door, I smell that stuff. Lye makes my eyes tear up sometime. Maybe we should call above and tell them something is up. Or go find Freddy."

"Fine. I'll do it." Russell stood up before Delmer could react and pushed the hydraulic lever. The air door began to hiss, its hinges groaning as it began to swing open. As the dual doors parted, Russell could feel an intensity in the velocity of the air coursing around them. Opened, the wind was flowing fast enough to knock Delmer's hard hat off his head. His lantern cord kept it from blowing away. Delmer retrieved it and pressed it back firmly onto his head.

"Only one time I seen something like this. Forest fire back home in the Dakotas. Pulls air from everywhere."

"Fire? You think this is a fire? If this is a draft from a fire, there'd have to be a hell of a lot of wood making this. There'd have to be pretty good ventilation. Thought you said this was sealed off."

"It was. By wood." Delmer and Russell stared at one another for a long moment.

"If this is a fire, we'd be dead by now, wouldn't we?" Russell said.

"Not if the fumes is going the other way."

"Where could they go? There's nothing back there."

"Boy, there's miles of tunnels in them old workings. Fire wants to go up, but with all them stopes and such, the ventilation could take it anywhere."

"We need to see where this stuff is so they know what they're dealing with."

"Don't get off the manchee. If we see anything we need to get out of there as fast as we can," Delmer said.

The train moved slowly forward.

"Sewer pit is about 100 yards around the corner. Bulkhead is just beyond that."

Russell stood and shined his miner's lamp over Delmer's shoulder. The sound of the air door diminished as the train rounded a corner. Russell could see no signs of fire, although the wind was still fierce. As they neared the sewage pit he could see dozens of garbage cans, some with lids open, others sealed, sitting on a long wooden platform. Beyond them several toilet seats were piled near a water hose and scrub brush. A wooden pallet was braced on the opposite side of the tunnel, piled high with unopened bags of lye. The actual pit was further behind the garbage cans. A hoist hooked to the top of the tunnel provided a means to dump the contents into a cavern below. Russell felt awful that somebody would actually have to perform this job.

"Them lights is still on over my staging area," Delmer said pointing toward the sewer pit. "Mean's we still got power and such."

"Got a phone back here?"

"Nope. Nobody figures I need anything like that. Don't think nobody cares. Ain't no one ever come back here except me."

"Stop the manchee. I'm going to walk to the bulkhead. The tracks might be out."

"Don't think that's wise. If we gotta go, we gotta go fast," Delmer said.

"You just wait here. If I'm not back in two minutes, come with the damn train."

"Ain't making no sense to me."

Russell jumped from the manchee and began walking. He turned and looked at Delmer who was still trying to convince him to stay and be careful.

"Get back on here, boy. I'm tellin' you you're making trouble for yourself."

Russell ignored him and kept walking. Delmer began following him with the manchee.

"Nipper, you don't have to come. Just stay put."

"Ain't goin' to let you get hurt. Just get on." There was resignation in Delmer's voice.

Russell jumped back onto the manchee as Delmer inched it along the tracks. The cart attached to the motor shifted loudly, several of the barrels slid sideways.

"Them old rails don't look good," Delmer said. "If this train slips between them, we ain't got no way to put it back on."

The tracks groaned. Russell felt the motor bounce. Delmer increased the speed of the engine. A loud metallic clanging sound shot from the train wheels.

"Dammit. See? We almost fell between them rails."

"We didn't though, did we? You're a good driver. Just keep going."

Russell saw it first, the tube of fire 100 yards ahead. It looked like the bright end of a cigar at first. The bulkhead was gone, crumbled into a pile of burning timbers, but the tunnel was now open. Russell could see the flames and coals running off into the distance. They were intense. He thought we was looking into hell. He could feel the radiant heat. A low roaring sound masked the noise from the fast moving air.

"Dear God, Delmer...."

"We gotta get outta here right now. If that air current changes we're goners."

"I'm with you," Russell said.

Delmer reversed the polarity on the electric motor and thrust the vehicle into reverse. The wheels spun quickly and found their traction. Pushing the timber cart was difficult on good tracks, Russell thought, but this might be a problem.

Behind them Russell could hear timbers falling, giving in to the fire. Looking back, he felt a stab of panic.

Delmer increased the power to the motor. The sewer pit was coming into view, when the timber cart, still laden with full barrels of feces, bounced from the track. Flipping sideways and against the side of the tunnel, the manchee was jackknifed, tossing both miners into the waste ditch. Russell's shoulder shouted with pain as the earlier wound split open.

Delmer lay partially straddled on one of the toppled barrels. Russell could see some of the contents oozing into the ditch.

"Get up, dammit, before you drown in that stuff," he shouted to Delmer.

Delmer struggled to his feet, sweeping sewage from his pants legs. The lens on his miner's lamp was cracked, causing the bulb to flicker.

"We gotta get this motor back on the track," Russell said, his voice ripe with fear.

"Ain't got no time. We need to get outta here." Delmer began walking down the drift back toward the sewer pit. Russell winced as he pulled himself over the wreckage. He whiffed a scent of the stale human excrement and lye, and realized that the wind was still strong and drawing the odor, thankfully, away from them.

Delmer's miner's lamp went dark.

"This ain't good," he said flatly. Russell shone his lamp towards Delmer who had stopped walking.

"None of this is," Russell replied. "You'll have to walk behind me. Keep your eyes focused on where my light falls."

Shining his lamp on the slimy rusted train tracks, Russell took the lead and began walking quickly. His boots slipped with almost every step. Delmer walked a pace behind him, stumbling every few strides. Within a few minutes they were at the lit sewer pit.

"You get hurt back there at all?" Russell asked, looking at Delmer.

"Push my bad arm out of whack is all," Delmer replied, rubbing his elbow. "Don't matter though, it don't work good no how." Russell noticed a lengthy scar on Delmer's forearm. He knew it was a reminder of his strike breaking years before.

"We're screwed, Nipper. We don't know where the smoke and fumes are going. If we head back to the main shaft, we may just be walking into a gas chamber if it is circulating back up from the lower workings."

"It's the only place where we'll find a phone or a way out. We need to let them boys topside know what's goin' on down here. 'Sides, they're more of these out there." Delmer touched the self-rescuer hanging from his belt. Russell looked at it and immediately regretted not taking one earlier in the shift when Delmer had suggested it.

"I doubt that'll do much good. You can't live long using that thing anyway."

"Moment or two of extra breath might make all the difference, boy," Delmer said.

"As bad as that fire is? No way," Russell said, "I remember the safety classes." The higher the concentration of carbon monoxide, the shorter the life span of that damn rescuer, and the shorter your life will be. Probably be better to die from the monoxide than choke to death using that thing."

"I'll take any chance I got."

Russell looked again at the self-rescuer and knew that Delmer was right.

"We better get a move on," Delmer said.

"Here, Nipper, you take the lamp and the lead. You know your way outta here better. I'll stay close behind. Just don't fall and break this light."

Quickly Russell undid his miner's belt and slipped the battery from the lantern from its clasp. Delmer clamped the lamp to his hard hat.

"Better water up before we get goin'," Delmer said, reaching for a water hose.

"I'm not drinking that nasty stuff. That water is awful."

"Boy, we'll be sweatin' so bad so soon, you'll probably drink from the waste ditch. I suggest you stomach as much of this as you can."

Delmer placed his lips near the end of the dirty hose and began drinking. Russell saw him gag several times as he drank. Coughing, Delmer finished and handed the running hose to him.

The first sip was hideous. Tainted with the flavor of rust, the water was warm, almost hot. As he filled his stomach, the urge to vomit returned to him. Still he drank. Finished, he spat out as much of the remaining fluid that he could.

"I hope that doesn't kill me," he said.

"Well, it'd be better then getting fried or choked. Right?" Delmer replied, a simple smile filling his face. Russell grinned back.

"Sure. Some choices, eh? Lead the way," Russell said, pointing down the pitch black tunnel. Delmer strode hurriedly onto the tracks, his boots sloshing and grinding against the railroad ties. The air was still moving furiously past them as they hurried down the track.

The air doors were no longer hissing. Apparently the air lines were down, the compressors most likely shut off by unaware repairmen.

"We need to close these behind us," Delmer said.

"Why?"

"Cut down the fuel to the fire. Air is fuel. Anything we can do to slow it down could help us."

"We don't know if it'll help or hurt Delmer. Let's just go."

Delmer ignored Russell, instead he began pushing against one of the steel doors, attempting to close it. Russell could see the strain on his face. The door wouldn't yield. Delmer grunted regardless and pushed to no avail.

"It isn't working, Nipper. You're just wearing yourself out. Let's go."

"No!" Delmer's gentle demeanor changed quickly. "I worked in this here tunnel long enough to know that no air ever gets back there. I don't give a mind about where the smoke goes, I just know that it don't need no help getting there. Now help me close this door!" Delmer's eyes were wide open and angry. Russell thought about talking back, but something in Delmer's passion made him move to the steel door. Together they placed their shoulders against the steel and pressed. Still the door would not move.

"This thing was made to open and shut with the help of the compressor. Look. Those steel arms at the top of the doors are hooked to that valve. Maybe if we just unhooked the arms, we could swing the doors shut. Only problem is, the arms are three feet above our heads." Russell was speaking and pointing. Delmer shone the lamp onto the steel arms and rods attached to the air doors.

"Get on my shoulders," Delmer said.

"And do what?"

"Pull them pins out. Here use my wrench." Delmer pulled a ten inch pipe wrench from a makeshift holster on his belt.

"Oh yeah, every miners mandatory tool. A ten inch pipe wrench," Russell said. "Only thing I ever used that damn thing for was to hammer spikes with."

"Well, its sure good enough for that. Just bang them pins as hard as you can."

Delmer knelt to the ground. Russell stepped over him and straddled the back of his neck, the crotch of his miner's pants resting on Delmer's shoulders.

"I'm getting horny," Russell teased, "Why don't you turn around and stay there for a minute."

"I would, boy, but you'd never go back to women," Delmer replied. Both men laughed. Delmer stood quickly, almost knocking Russell backwards. Rising toward the top of the drift, Russell was surprised at the older man's strength.

"How'd the hell did you get so strong?" Russell said.

"Ain't nothin'. Only difference between you and a barrel full of crap is about fifteen pounds." Again both of them laughed.

The heat was becoming unbearable. Delmer shone the light from the sole lamp onto the arms of the air door. Russell began hammering at a cotter pin clasping the iron arm to the air valve. Several blows missed, causing him to slam his knuckles into the pin itself. Blood began to cover his fingers.

"Not working, Delmer," he shouted.

"Just keep poundin' away. You'll get it," Delmer said.

Several minutes passed. Russell could feel Delmer begin to shake under his weight. Slowly the pin began to unseat itself.

"It's loosening a bit," he said, looking down.

"Hurry, boy, I don't know how much longer I can keep you up there." Delmer's voice was quivering.

The pin finally popped up and toppled to the ground, bouncing off of Delmer's hard hat.

"Now the other one!"

The heat was too much, Russell could feel sweat rolling down his back, trickling passed his tailbone. His stomach churned. The light Delmer was shining suddenly dropped away.

"Ah, damn," Delmer shouted. Russell could feel the nipper begin to stagger. Glancing toward the ground he could see the lamp swinging from its power cord.

"Don't break that damn thing or we are dead for sure," Russell hollered.

Delmer fumbled at the power cord, pulling the lamp back towards his chest.

"It ain't broke. Just slipped is all. I'm fixin' to drop you. Better hurry." There was very little breath in him.

The second pin popped and dropped. At the same instant, Delmer's legs gave way sending Russell forward. He landed on his feet. Shadows from the lamp cast about his legs.

"You ok?" he asked, turning around.

"Yeah, outta breath and strength is all. Lets see if we can close them doors."

Energy spent, Russell joined Delmer at the steel doors again and pressed. The pain in his chest and shoulders was almost unbelievable. The door moved slowly.

"Push, push," Delmer groaned as he heaved his weight against the metal. The great doors began to close. Russell braced his feet against the side of the drift and placed his back against the plates. The doors yielded. The closer the two doors drew to one another, the louder the sound of rushing air. Finally, they connected. The volume of passing air dropped appreciably, whistling loudly through the minute openings around the door's hinges. The two miners looked at each other, satisfied with their feat.

"Let's get to the shaft collar," Delmer said, moving quickly again down the drift. Russell marveled at the man's stamina and determination. It inspired new energy. He set off after him. It was at least a half a mile to the main shaft station.

The Nipper was ten feet ahead when Russell saw him slip, stumble slightly, catch himself, then fall face first onto the tracks. Delmer's boot had snagged an errant boulder lying in the track. The miner's lamp, their only light source didn't even flicker. It went out immediately. Russell shouted to Delmer. There was no response, only the sound of water trickling in the waste ditch. The darkness was total, dense and complete.

CHAPTER 25

His dirty sneakers peeked out from under the pristine white robe. The deep red of the collar sash was twisted and wrinkled. Lucas saw Scabby walking toward him and Heather, pushing through the church crowd gathering loudly again on the steps of St. Rachel's. Even at a distance, the contrast in his friend's appearance was quite noticeable.

"Daddy is underground," was all Scabby said. The look on his face was solemn. Lucas was surprised at the lack of emotion. He noticed that the boy's hair was well washed and combed, a Sunday morning tribute to God, he thought.

"Russell and Mr. McKenzie are too," Lucas said. Heather was gathering her sister and brother and hadn't seen or heard Scabby.

"Momma wants to go to the mine and see what's going on. Where's your parents?"

"Not back from Helena yet."

"You ok, I mean from last night?" Scabby said, referring to Lucas' bruises.

"I hurt. I think my dad will lose it over this one. I'm going to tell him everything."

"Even about you and Heather?"

"No."

"You going to tell Heather about Rita?"

"No."

"You tell her about how you feel about her yet?"

"No, Scabby, its only been a few hours since all that happened. Now we got this 'thing' going on at the mine. I can't just dump heart and soul on her right now. It'll confuse her; hell, it'll confuse me. Besides, I think that'd be a bit selfish."

Several women standing close by heard Lucas raise his voice and curse. He looked at them and mouthed the word 'sorry'.

"Look, I'm going to take Heather home. You want to come along?"

"No. Momma is upset. I need to be there with her. I'll come down to your house after we go to the mine gatehouse."

"I hope your dad is ok," Lucas said. Scabby began to walk away, stopped and turned around.

"He is," Scabby said assuredly, "I know he is. Russell too."

Heather returned to Lucas' side, holding the hands of her siblings.

"Father McElroy said there might be a fire burning underground. I just overheard him telling one of the choir members."

"Why didn't he say so in church?"

"I think he just heard that himself. He also said there are a lot of people gathered at the mine gates. I'm scared, Lucas. Should we go there?"

"Let's go home, like you said, and see what the radio says. My parents should be home soon and my dad will know what to do."

The walk home was far faster than the walk to church. Lucas was feeling fear, but no more pain from his fight or lack of sleep. The aching in his heart to share his feelings with Heather was very strong, making him anxious.

As the four of them walked, even the two youngest seemed focused on getting to their house. No words were exchanged.

Lucas looked at the barren branches of the trees along his street. A cold wind had begun to blow, tossing the dried leaves into whirlwind spirals. Dark clouds had moved in from the west, heavy with moisture. He was sure snow would fall before the day was over. The temperature had dropped since earlier in the morning.

"Can you talk to me for a minute?" he asked as they walked onto the front porch of the McKenzie house. Heather released her brother and sister who opened the door and ran into the living room. The screen door closed with a hiss behind them.

"Daddy is dead, isn't he?" Heather's voice quaked slightly at her own question. Lucas could see that she wasn't seeking an answer, only assurance that her thought was untrue.

"Don't even think that," he said, unsure of how to respond. Tears began to run down her cheeks as she bit into her bottom lip. Instinctively, Lucas stepped toward her and met her outreached arms. She buried her face into his chest as he wrapped her tightly about the back. Her sides shivered as she cried. Holding her, he felt his own fears for Russell reach his heart. "It'll be fine, I promise," he said, kissing the top of her head.

The sound of tires grinding gravel broke the quiet. Car doors slammed in the driveway behind his house. Listening, Lucas could hear his mother and father talking and laughing. He felt like staying where he was, putting off the news that would break whatever joy they were living.

"I need to go," he said, "I'll come over in a few minutes." Heather stepped back, and looked at him. A rush, a quickening of his pulse, rose as he met her eyes. Leaning forward, he gently touched her face with his fingertips and kissed her lightly on the lips. She pressed, naturally, into him, deepening the kiss. For a long moment they held tight, heads resting on the other's shoulder. Lucas opened the door for her, turned and ran to the side of the house to greet his parents.

"Dear God, what happened to your face?" The words were his mother's, spoken before Lucas could make a single utterance. She was immediately poking his bruises and searching his eyes for an answer. He decided to tell the truth.

"I got into a fight with Mickey Whitehead," he said, eyes downcast. He could feel the tension quickly growing around them. The mention of Mickey made his wounds suddenly hurt.

"Where?" she said, placing her hands on her hips. The surprise and disdain in her voice was unmistakable.

Lucas hesitated for a moment, considering a lie, fumbling, he finally said, "At a party."

The phrase was a bit slow and suspicious. His father, jacket slung over one hand, suitcase clasped in the other, raised his eyebrows. Slightly taller than Lucas, he looked down upon him. Lucas tried to avoid his gaze but couldn't. His dad's eyes could wound and pierce quite easily. He felt their sudden pain. His father's eyes could say more than most men's words.

A gust of wind ruffled the collar of his mother's coat. She turned it up completely to block the cold air.

"A party? Give me a break, Lucas!" His father's tone was terse and whining. He watched the knuckles of his father's hand squeezing the handle of the suitcase, rolling it back and forth.

Oh God, here it comes, he thought.

"We leave you alone and you go to a party and get into a fight? What the hell is wrong with you? You're seventeen years old and can't be trusted! Unbelievable." His father had now joined the conversation at full voice and anger.

"Dad, it wasn't like that," he interrupted, "The fight had been going on for years. It finally turned physical." He tried to sound even, assured, mature; however, he felt himself shrinking, falling back into childlike shame, backing away, fearing the loss of his father's approval. He was seven years old again.

"Where was the party? Whose house?" Jonathan was almost barking, demanding. He paced side to side then stopped. Inside the house, a phone was ringing.

"That doesn't matter," Lucas said dryly. He realized his tone was antagonistic. He regretted the statement.

"Doesn't matter!? Don't challenge me. Where?" His father was very rigid and bristling.

"Outside," Lucas said defiantly with some resignation. "Flat Top. The party was at Flat Top." He watched his father's expressions. They changed quickly. He saw concern, ire, anger, and frustration criss-cross his face.

"A keg party? For the love of God...did you get drunk? That's it, isn't it? You go to a party, get drunk and get into trouble..." His father was beginning to rage. Lucas could see dark red creeping into his complexion. He himself was becoming scared. His father had never struck him, beyond a juvenile spanking, but the tone and lather of his father's voice and words were extreme, more so than any other time he had been chastised.

"No sir... I mean, yes, but it isn't like that." Lucas was becoming confused, frustrated, frightened with each sentence. He wanted to run, run back to Heather.

"I don't care what *its* like!" His father paused for a long moment, apparently in frenetic thought, "Give me the keys to your truck," he finally said.

Jonathan's hand was open, palm up.

"What?" Lucas said, certain of his father's words and meaning but feigning ignorance. He looked at his mother imploringly, turning back to his father. The hand was still open, inches from his face.

"You heard me, Lucas. The keys. Give them to me, God damn it. You're not deaf. You'll not drive until you are out of my house and on your own. I'm not having you turn into your brother!" The last words were like sniper bullets, fired rapidly, with direct force and attention, hitting their mark with extreme accuracy.

"My brother?" Lucas was shocked and confused at his father's insinuation. "Dad, no, I'm telling you, there's more." He struggled for words, caught off guard, he said, "I'm not doing anything like Russell." He felt awkward, defending himself as if his brother were a criminal.

"You're not? Hell, all *he* does is drink and fight. How are *you* not being like him? Next thing you know its drugs, hookers and jail for you." Another long pause, hand still open. "Now give me the keys!"

133

Lucas knew this was the final demand. He pushed his hands deep in his pockets, protecting his key ring. A car drove slowly by the driveway. Scabby's face peered from the back window. It didn't stop.

"Jonathan, let's take this inside…" Amanda said, reaching for her husband. Jonathan pushed at her hands as she tried to touch him, as she tried to calm the situation.

"No. He can hand me his keys," he said turning on his wife, "Don't protect him. This will be finished here. I don't need to know any more than what I already have seen and heard. I'm not living through this nightmare again."

"Jonathan…." Amanda's voice was pleading.

"I'm not giving you my keys! You're going to listen to me!" Lucas was shouting, almost screaming through fiery tears. Jonathan sat his suitcase down on the sidewalk, dropped his jacket and stepped towards Lucas.

"You'll give them to me, or I'll take them. Don't think you are too big or…"

"No! Its Russell…. Its about Russell…"

"Your brother? You're blaming him for your actions? I don't believe this…" Jonathan had a hold of Lucas' arm. He could feel his father's firm grip and made no effort to pull away.

"No! He's underground. There's been a fire or something. They're evacuating the mine." There was sudden silence. Lucas could feel his heart beating rapidly.

Jonathan released his arm and waited a moment. His eyes darting back and forth as he looked at Lucas.

"Mr. McKenzie is down there too. Scabby's dad and others."

The anger in his father's face disappeared into a drawn expression. He spoke no more but quickly stepped around Lucas and ran into the house, leaving the basement door open behind him. Lucas looked at his mother. Her face was ashen. She was staring at him, tense, rigid. A solitary snowflake glided onto his cheek, melting, blending quickly with his tears.

"I'm sorry Mom, I'm sorry," Lucas was gagging as he tried to speak, coughing, trying to hold back, trying not to cry, but failing. "Why does he hate me…?"

Amanda embraced him, pulling his head to her shoulder. His sobbing shook them both.

"He doesn't hate you…." she soothed. Her hand stroked the back of his head.

"He hates me *and* Russell…" Lucas croaked stubbornly.

His mother continued holding him, remaining silent, as he slowly calmed.

She finally spoke, almost with a whisper, "He hates what this town does to young people. That's all. He'd do anything to stop this place from devouring either of you."

They stood for several more minutes. Inside the house, Lucas could hear his father on the telephone, speaking loudly, with authority. Comforted, he felt the anger and fear slipping aside. Balance was returning; his father was taking charge, his mother was protecting.

"Mom…", Lucas said, as he let himself from her arms. He leaned his shoulders against the side of the house. Pulling his dress shirtsleeve down over his wrist, he wiped his eyes and nose.

"Yes?" she answered, holding his free hand as she adjusted his tie with her other. Stray flakes of snow drifted around them. He watched her, marveled at the minuteness of her fingers, and the serene effect that being near her had on him. She was attentive, tough and tender.

"I'm in love with Heather," he said, his voice hoarse.

Amanda stopped primping and gently took the lapels of his dress coat, tracing their threads with her thumbs. Looking into her eyes, Lucas felt relieved that he had spoken the words.

"I know," she said with a small ripple of a smile, "You have been for a very long time."

He thought for a moment, concerned that she misunderstood, worried that she was appeasing him.

"No, I mean, I'm in love with her; with all my heart. Not like when we were children. This is real." He could feel himself becoming anxious, hoping that she would not downplay what he felt. He examined her face. She was looking at him, intently. He could feel the warmth of her gaze. The corners of her eyes were becoming moist as they welled with tears.

She took his hands into hers and said, "Then you need to go to her right now, be with her. She needs the certainty and strength of that love."

He turned to leave. Stopping, he reached into his pocket, retrieved his car keys and extended them to her. Looking at his hand, she closed his fingers around them and shook her head. He pulled his mother close and kissed her cheek.

"Lucas…"

"Yes?" he said.

"Her love for you may be far different than you expect."

He paused for a moment collecting her meaning then said, "It may be far better, perhaps." He watched as she covered her mouth with the fingertips of one hand, cradling her elbow with the other.

"Just know that love is sometimes selfish in its intent," she said. Turning, she walked into the basement door and closed it quietly.

Lucas stood for a moment feeling the emotions dribble into the distance enclaves of his heart. The snowflakes were beginning to collect briefly on the ground before dissolving. White and clean, they yielded to the barren soil and dead grass before disappearing. Soon, he thought, the ugliness around him would give way to the full force of winter. A frozen pristine beauty would, for a season, cover the bleak and lifeless.

Slowly he unlatched the gate and walked to the steps of the McKenzie's back deck. The stairway was coated with snow.

CHAPTER 26

"What are you doing?" The voice belonged to one of the newer officers on the Silver Bow County police force. Ernie lifted his head from the filing cabinet, striking it on the still open top drawer. Pain shot through his skull as he cursed.

He was ransacking Billy Murphy's home office. At first he had been careful to return papers and books to their original places, preserving them for the widow. Unsure of what he was looking for, he was certain he would find it.

As he dug and dredged, his frustration grew. Now he was tossing folders and envelopes on the floor. Later, he could cover himself. This interruption was an inconvenience. Ernie could feel rings of sticky sweat under his armpits. His brow was moist as well

"Aimel!" Ernie said, faking a smile as he spoke. He had approved the hiring of the handsome young man, Aimel Merrick, less than three months ago. He had grown up in Sunnyside, returning home to work after a few years as an MP in the Army. His father coached at the high school. Clutching his pulsing scalp, Ernie extended his right hand to the young officer.

The cop was tentative as he returned the handshake. He asked again, "What are you doing here, Ernie?"

"This?", he stammered, gesturing towards the clutter, "I'm looking for Billy's personal papers, his Will and such. His wife asked me. She is in no shape to search for it. The poor guy, he was pretty disorganized. I'd be surprised if he even had one. Did find his life insurance papers though." He lied to the officer as he gestured again toward the papers on the floor. "I might ask, what are you doing here?" Ernie knew the best tactic when confronted is to ask questions instead of answering.

"Sheriff said this is a crime scene. One of us has to watch the place. New guy equals least desired jobs. You know how that works." The young officer was relaxing, which in turn slowed Ernie's apprehension.

"You'll be in charge some day, son," Ernie said, gently slapping the cop's shoulder, "I'm sure you're doing fine."

"Would you like me to help you?" Aimel asked, stepping toward the open filing cabinet.

"No, that's just fine. I'm done. Been through everything already. I think we'll need to check the bank and see if he had a safe deposit box. You are very thoughtful though." Ernie wanted the man to leave so he could continue his digging. Instead, he closed the filing drawers. "I'll come back later and tidy this up. I'm so torn up about Billy's suicide, I just got a little frustrated. He was like family. I don't want his wife to see this mess. Please don't say anything." He walked past the policeman and turned off the office light. Officer Aimel followed him to the entry hallway.

"I won't," Aimel said. "It's very kind of you to step in at a time like this. I know how busy you are. The world could stand a few more people like you."

Ernie knew a brown noser when he heard one. He smiled to himself. Perhaps he would make this boy Sheriff someday. The current one was costing him a small fortune. *Keep it up*, he thought. They walked to the squad car together.

"Looks like snow," Ernie said, glancing up at the noon sky. A small misty cloud formed in front of his face as he spoke.

"Hope not. If it freezes, I get to work the fender benders too. Another job for the 'newbie'." The policeman was sounding warm and familiar. Ernie was beginning to like him. Aimel pulled a notebook from his breast pocket and glanced at his watch. "What time did you say you got here?" he asked.

Ernie was puzzled, "What? Why do you ask?"

"Nothing really. We just keep track of everything. You know, in case there are any questions later on. Doesn't really mean much of anything." Aimel was smiling sweetly, unblinking, at Ernie.

"Eleven thirty, I think. Half hour or so ago..." Ernie lied again. He had been in the house most of the morning. Aimel scribbled on the notepad and dropped it back into his pocket.

Aimel opened the door to his car, the police radio was immediately alive, squelching static. "Oh, where did you park? I don't see your car," he asked.

"In the alley. Actually in Billy's garage. I didn't want to block the alley way." Ernie was becoming annoyed. He was purposeful in hiding his car in the garage. The extra effort was wasted.

"I see," Aimel paused. "If you come back later, can you just park in front?"

"Sure," Ernie said. He was disgusted, his affections gone. Aimel stepped into the police car and closed the door. Ernie watched as he picked up the microphone and began speaking. He wanted to stand by and hear what Aimel said, instead he took a few steps towards the garage.

"Commissioner?" It was Aimel again. Ernie turned around, smiled, and looked back toward the police cruiser. The officer had a startling expression on his face.

"Aimel?" Ernie said feigning concern.

"That was our dispatcher. The Bull Run Mine is on fire. They've ordered an evacuation." Before he had finished speaking, Aimel had ignited the car's engine and turned on his emergency lights. In the distance, the mine's warning siren began its fateful howling. Gravel sprung from the vehicle's tires as the young policeman raced away. Ernie stood and watched as the car sped off. He strolled back to the main entrance of the house.

Ernie said aloud to no one, "The dead fool." He rubbed the back of his head. It was still throbbing.

137

CHAPTER 27

Russell spoke Delmer's name again. He could hear the scraping of the man's boots as they shifted back and forth. The darkness squeezed at him.

"Delmer, speak to me." He crawled toward the shuffling sound. Finding Delmer's boots, he felt the man trying to move. He was obviously still face down on the train tracks.

In the absence of light, Russell could sense terror rising up inside of himself. Rising to his knees, he rolled the older man onto his back. Leaning as close as he could to Delmer's face, he struggled to make even the slightest visual contact. He could feel the man's rancid breath just an inch away, but could not see a thing.

He removed his gloves and gently touched about Delmer's head. He found his miner's hat, still attached to the broken lamp, lying just near his ear.

"Can you talk? Speak to me. We need to get out of here."

Delmer was moaning slightly. Russell tapped at the his cheeks, trying to revive him. The heat and moist density of the moving air was making him feel claustrophobic. Delmer groaned loudly and moved his arms towards his face. Russell felt for Delmer's hands and grabbed his wrist.

"Delmer...Delmer, you knocked yourself out," he spoke, hoping his fallen friend could hear him. Delmer sounded like he was growling, low and deep. Russell began groping through Delmer's pockets. He could not recall whether the man smoked, if he did perhaps there would be some matches. None were found.

Delmer began to mumble. Russell's stomach was heaving.

"Sorry, boy..."

"It's ok. Can you tell if you're bleeding?" Russell asked. Delmer didn't answer, instead, he began to try to sit up.

"We're screwed here, nipper. That was our only light." He was sensing panic.

Delmer spoke, "We ain't screwed yet. The shaft collar is in only one direction. Can't get lost. We just need to crawl along them tracks to it." His voice was sounding stronger. "I banged my head a good one," he said.

Russell was still holding Delmer's wrist. He let it go when he felt him raising it to his forehead.

"Don't think I broke nothin'. Feels like blood though. Can't tell." Delmer's voice sounded stronger.

"We crawl that far," Russell said, "and we'll be dead before we get to the shaft. Let's try to walk it. You know the way. Tap your foot along the rail. I'll hold onto the safety ring of your miner's belt. If you start to fall, I'll be able to grab you."

"See, I told you earlier you was a bright boy. Use that brain for a livin' when we get outta here, ok?"

"Sure Delmer." He admired the man's optimism.

Russell helped him stand. Delmer was unsteady and tentative with the first few steps. Gripping the large metal o-ring on the back of Delmer's webbed mining belt was awkward. Russell slipped two fingers through it and held tight.

"Makes you appreciate seein', don't it?" Delmer said.

"Scares me that the last thing I may have ever seen was your ugly face," Russell replied.

Delmer chuckled. He had found a stride moving along the tracks. Standing between the rails, Russell could hear Delmer's boot tap the left track, slide, then stop, followed by his right boot. It reminded him of a wedding procession march. The only music was their labored breathing and the trickling metal laden water in the nearby ditch. They moved in unison. Russell trusting Delmer to lead the way, Delmer trusting him to catch him should he fall.

"I was thinkin'," Delmer said, "There's a manchee motor barn up by the collar. We could take one of them lights from the manchee and splice it to our miner's lamp batteries. Should be enough light and juice for us to see. If they ain't shut down the skip, we won't need much light on the way out."

"What do you mean if they 'ain't shut down the skip'? They wouldn't close down the hoists. Nobody knows about the fire yet."

"They might. We don't know that. I'm just sayin' if they ain't."

"What do we do if they have?"

"Don't make no worry for yourself when you don't need none. We only have this problem right now, gettin' to the shaft collar. Just think of one thing at a time. It'll make your life easier. That's what I always do. Just deal with what I got, and don't think much about what I ain't got."

"That's deep, Delmer." Russell was being sarcastic.

"It's true ain't it? Think about it. If all you got is a mind full of 'what ifs' you ain't never goin' to have a pleasure for the 'what is'. Worryin' bout stuff is what makes old men ornery and old women mean."

"I think if you worry, it'll prevent things from happening. It can make you be more cautious," Russell said with assurance.

"Nah, now where'd you get that idea? I was thinkin' you was brighter than that." Delmer was sounding weary and stopped walking.

Russell felt a bit put upon by the last comment and said, "When I think about things, you know bad things, I try to steer away from them."

"That'll make your life miserable, boy."

"What do you mean by that?" Russell said. He felt indignant and insulted. His life after all must be better than Delmer Cipher's, he thought.

"Simple. If you try to avoid all the bad things that come your way, you might miss the good that will come out of it. Every bad thing in my life that ever happened to me has made stuff better."

"That's impossible. If that was the case, we'd all want bad stuff to come our way so that we could have better lives."

"We'll, there you go, you're thinkin' the right way now," Delmer said.

Russell was confused. He remained silent for a long while, listening to the slippery grinding of their boots. Delmer occasionally stumbled, hesitated or tripped, but didn't fall. The ground beneath them was becoming less slimy. Russell reasoned it was because there was a slight uphill turn in the tunnel. The smell of the air was rich with mildew and a scent of dirt.

"I don't see it, no pun intended, about bad stuff bringing on good stuff."

"Well, tell me something bad that's happened to you and I'll tell you the good that you probably didn't see."

Russell thought for a moment then said, "Well, my grandmother died a long slow death from cancer. It was awful. My family suffered along with her."

"She went to Heaven, that's a good thing."

"That is a cop-out, Delmer. It was ultimately good for her to quit suffering, but it was bad for our family to see it."

"But we ain't talkin' about the bad for your grandma. She's at peace. That is good. But what about the results of all that cryin' and hurtin'? What do you see that came after that?"

Russell thought for a moment, "Anger. Emptiness. I don't see any good."

"What about closeness? Your kin came together and loved on one another. You got closer in a lot of ways to everybody. What about your baby brother? How'd you feel goin' through that with him?"

"I was in my teens. I think he was like twelve then."

"And…?"

"Well he was close to her, just like I was. I guess we cried a lot together after she died. Don't know how that makes me feel about him. Don't think it was much different."

"Had to be. You don't cry with somebody about somebody unless you love them. See, it showed the bond between you. It showed that you are family. Cryin' is one of them gifts a lot of folks don't think is useful."

"Lucas has always been a crier," Russell said, "Mom babied him a lot. Still does." For an instant his brother's face almost seemed to float in front of him in the darkness. There was a stirring in his heart.

"He just cries 'cause he's honest. Honest people cry a lot."

"I've needed to watch over him because of it sometimes. People picked on him, the scrawny kid."

"That's why God made older brothers."

"Yeah," Russell laughed a little. The thought touched his heart.

"Your grandma's death brought you to tears, honest tears. I'm sure you looked at your brother differently."

"Maybe. I know I didn't want to lose anybody else in my family."

"See? That's a good thing. Death brought you closer to your kin."

They walked along for several more minutes. The rhythm of their gait was perfect. If people could see them, Russell thought, they might think they were slow figure skating. It seemed like they were making good time. In back of his mind Russell could feel the sequestered fear of their situation. He tried to focus on the walk and nothing else. Delmer was correct, taking a single problem at a time would help tremendously.

"Delmer?" Russell finally said.

"Boy?"

"Do you think we are going to die down here? I mean that fire and those gasses could be going anywhere."

"For sure they could. But we know they are behind us, not ahead of us. We just need to figure out how to stay that a way. Me for one, I don't plan on dyin', but if it comes, then there'll be good in there somewhere."

"Are you afraid of dying?"

"Nope. I don't necessarily want to die, least ways not right now. But dyin' is just a instant in our lives. We'll have a whole lot more time bein' dead then we do alive. I think that there are good things after death, I mean why would it be so much longer than life, right? But for me, I want to make the minutes I got here good."

"You have an interesting way of looking at things," Russell said.

"Maybe. I just know that knowing death is there for sure, that lots of folks have done it, well it can't be all that bad. We all got to do it sometime."

"So why do you think we are alive in the first place?"

"Lots of reasons, but mostly to be kind to each other. See, I think there is a God, and he just wants us to practice lovin' people, so when I see Him we'll be good at it."

Russell grinned. Listening to the nipper, in the dark, it was hard not to focus on what he was saying. The words were simple and sensible and held some truth. Maybe that's why he could do it, live such a lowly life and seem to be so content. He followed the words through the darkness.

Delmer asked to stop for a moment to relieve himself. Russell thought it was funny when he had been asked to turn his back. *Modesty in absolute darkness, go figure*, he thought. As they continued their journey, his mind turned to Lori and the battle with her father. There would need to be a reckoning with him. Russell thought about surprising Billy and cracking a couple of ribs. He fantasized about it and the jubilation he would feel. His anger was more focused on the disrespect that Billy seemed to have for him and Lori. Russell felt no shame in him concerning her, just tense bitterness about her father's perspective. He knew that Billy thought his daughter was a tramp and that he, Russell, had helped make her that way. The thought began to sour as he realized that Billy was the father of the girl he loved, and that ultimately, he would have to find peace with the man.

Another thought crossed his mind, one that he often had and always avoided. Maybe he didn't really love Lori, at least not in the way that he should or that she wanted. Maybe the sex, dangerous, somewhat risky and forbidden, was the tether that held them together. Their interludes were always loud and full of energy. Playing with this idea, he sorted through conversations he had had with her. He had held off any commitment, long term anyway, each time she had pressed. A 'permanent' relationship she had called it. That sounded fatal. Why couldn't they enjoy the here and now? Each time she addressed it, the subject would bring about a fight, then a resounding reconciliation in the sack. Each time they fought, their lovemaking seemed to get better and more intense. He figured they would probably end up killing each other between the sheets someday. If he got out of here, he would try to be better towards her he resolved. He'd talk about their relationship, honestly. Something good might come of this situation.

"See it?" Delmer's voice was excited as it broke Russell's thoughts.

"What? All I see is dark. Which I can't see at all. You know what I mean."

"There. Way down that way. Straight ahead."

Russell knew that Delmer was pointing. He could tell his arms were moving. Squinting, he could make out an extremely faint yellow glow.

"It's the station at the collar. We got only a bit to go," Delmer said.

"Yeah, well don't run to it!"

"Just hang on, somewhere between here and there, we gotta cross the ore dump. We fall in there, they'll find us in an ore car on the next level sometime next year."

"You be careful. If you fall I'll most likely let you go down there by yourself."

The pace quickened a bit. Russell felt a shade of excitement. At least the odds were better if they could see where they were. The fire raging behind them was still drawing air and they were not overcome with monoxide.

A foul smell suddenly filled the tunnel.

"Hey, what is that? Smells like natural gas."

"Stench-warning. You never been part of no fire drill underground?" Delmer said.

"Stench-warning? Nope."

"When they need to clear the mine they pump that crappy smell into the main compressor lines and vent hoses. When you smell it, you get outta here."

"Smells like skunks and Propane. It's making me sick."

"Ain't suppose to smell like lilacs. Made to get your attention. Works don't it?"

"Then somebody knows about the fire."

"Yup. Means that somewhere, someway they got word somethin' is wrong."

"This is a good thing then. Right?"

"Suppose so. Just mean they know there's danger. Doesn't mean they know what is goin' on." Russell could tell Delmer was acting more concerned.

"Tell me what you're thinking," Russell said.

"Well, the fire is back there, right? We're up here. Smoke and gas is goin' up, I suppose. Stench is coming down, least it should."

"Your point?"

"If the smoke is goin' up, the stench is coming down, the gasses could be crawling through the back part of the upper workings."

"So?"

"Or they could be venting out of the main line into the mine, which means, we could ride up the shaft, get on the train and die on our way to the portal."

"That's great Delmer. I thought you said that we weren't suppose to deal in 'what ifs'."

"Boy, this ain't a 'what if', it's a 'maybe'. We just moved onto our next problem is all."

Russell felt the toe of his boot clip a spike or rock. He started to stumble forward pushing Delmer, losing his grip as he went. He lost his balance and tripped over the rail. Reaching out with his hands, he expected to find the wall of the tunnel. It wasn't there, instead he met with open space.

Time seemed to slow. Waving his arms blindly in front of him he tumbled off the rails and began to free fall. He could hear Delmer's voice. There was no sense of direction, though he thought momentarily that he was upside down. He heard his own voice cursing as he felt his body lose contact with solid ground. The ore dump had found him.

His shoulder struck the end of one of the protruding railroad ties that blocked the edge of the pit, causing him to tumble. Russell's body landed on its side, feet slightly forward, throwing him into a somersault. The ore pit was full of gravel, slush and broken boulders. He rolled toward the bottom and stopped, unhurt. He heard Delmer shouting his name.

"Damn," was all he could say. Ground ore and gravel filled the back of his pants. He could feel grit between his buttocks. His hard hat was missing. His boots too were filled with busted bits of fine rock. "This is great," he muttered.

"Pit must be full!" he heard Delmer shout.

"Almost to the top," Russell said, spitting bits of sand from his mouth. He could taste blood where he had bitten the inside of his cheek.

"Just be careful. Feel your way around to the edge. Pit may just be plugged. You move too hard or fast, you might loosen that stuff up and fall down the rest of the way for sure."

Russell swept the corners of his eyes with his bare fingers. Sand covered his face. Gently he slogged his boots toward the back of the ore pit. He felt the wall and inched toward the sound of Delmer's voice.

"There's a ladder over near the side. Just keep movin' toward my voice," Delmer reassured. Russell could sense from the change in direction of the sound, that Delmer was standing near the top of the ladder. "I'm gonna come down to the bottom of the ladder. I'm just gonna keep talkin' to you."

Delmer began to recite the Pledge of Allegiance. Russell shifted his weight slowly. Beneath him, he could hear the sifting of ore.

"It's plugged is all. I can feel the ore move a little when I press down."

"You gotta just keep headin' this way," Delmer said, "It'll hold true, if you do."

Russell crept along, feeling an occasional large, unbroken rock. He moved at a tentative pace, pressing his back against the side of the ore pocket. Delmer was now reciting Humpty Dumpty.

"I find no humor in that one, Delmer," he said. The genuine levity in Delmer's voice gave him some comfort. He could sense he was only a few short feet from the ladder.

"My hand is hangin' down. Sweep your arm in the air and see if you can find it." Delmer was directly above him. The last rung of the ladder was a few feet above Russell's head.

"I can't find it. I think you are too high up. You got anything you can lower down to me?"

"Just my shirt. It won't hold you though, boy. You're gonna have to jump up and see if you can grab the last rung."

"Oh no. If I do that, I could loosen all this ore. I can't risk that."

"You can't risk just sittin' there neither. You're gonna have to give it one shot. Just jump with all you got."

Russell stood with his neck and head facing upward, though he could see nothing.

"The ladder is made of wood two by fours. It's big. You just gotta find the faith – yeah, and the last rung."

Russell shifted his feet back and forth. He found a large boulder and pressed it down into the gravel.

"I made a small, solid stand with a rock. I can jump off of that."

"That's that brain I was speakin' about earlier," Delmer said.

Russell positioned himself under what he perceived to be the center of the ladder.

"How far down do you think I am?"

"Not more than three feet, boy. Most likely only a couple feet from where I was hangin' my arm down. I'm gonna keep it hangin' there."

"Ok. Here goes."

Russell considered swinging his arms back and forth for momentum. He chose to try a standing jump, rather than risk shaking the ground. He bent his knees slightly, pulled his hands into fists, brought them up behind his waist, swung them fast forward and thrust his legs upward.

The boulder platform under him shifted as his feet lifted off. He felt his body rising. The tips of his fingers connected with the slippery wood of the lower rung and could find no immediate solid hold. He struggled for a moment to hold on. Suspended, he hung motionless, feeling the full weight of his gravity drawing him into the earth. Beneath him he could hear the sudden roar of the blocked ore pocket giving way. His hands slipped from the rung. He began to fall. Delmer's glove grasped at his wrist, connecting quickly, pinching hard. Russell spun slightly and grasped at Delmer. He felt like a doll hanging from a child's hand.

"Don't move, boy. Just hold still." Delmer's voice was straining. Russell could barely hear him over the echoing avalanche beneath him. Heeding the demand, he stopped kicking his feet.

"I'm barely holding on, but I'm gonna pull you up. You gotta find the last rung."

Russell felt himself lifting upward slowly. Delmer's gloved hand held firm. Russell found the last ladder step and quickly released one hand. The added assistance and offset of weight allowed Delmer to pull him up faster. In an instant, he was holding the ladder securely with both arms.

"Can you climb now?" Delmer asked.

Russell wasn't injured from the fall. He had landed on fairly crushed ground. Aside from the pain in his shoulder and strained muscles in his back, he felt confident enough to make it the rest of the way up the ladder.

"I'm fine. Thanks Delmer."

"Thank God, boy, not me."

They quickly climbed from the ore pit and found their place again on the track.

"That sucked," Russell said, shaking grit and gravel down his pants leg, "When we get out of here, I am never going back into any mine again."

"See? Something good just may come out of this. I told you that every bad thing brings a good thing." In the darkness, Russell could hear Delmer's smile.

"Shut up, Delmer," he said tilting his head backwards, chuckling, "Just shut up." Together, they walked quickly toward the light.

CHAPTER 28

Lucas hesitated before knocking on the kitchen door of the McKenzie house. Through the misted window he could see Heather speaking animatedly into the black handset of the telephone. The gesturing of her free arm accented her anxious speech. Standing to the side, Vernon Junior and Katie watched her gyrate, their faces holding hints of fear and curiosity. Muted by the solid door, the words she spoke were unclear, yet each syllable carried power. Lucas tapped gently on the glass. Oblivious to the knock, Heather continued speaking, her back to the door. As Katie looked toward the rapping sound, her face visually lightened. Lucas stepped into the kitchen.

"When will you know something...?" Heather said into the phone. Lucas could see she was fighting back tears, her eyes pressed shut. Hearing the door close, she turned towards Lucas. Her expression did not change. Katie ran to him and clutched at his hand. Heather continued asking the same question repeatedly.

"Daddy is gone," Katie said, looking up at Lucas. "We can't find him."

"He's working, is all. He'll be home soon." Kneeling, Lucas picked up the little girl. Her arms encircled his neck, her legs quickly straddling his left hip. Heather hung up the phone, her frustration causing her to cradle the handset with a loud clunk.

"They know he is underground, but they don't know where. They don't know anything or won't tell me anything," Heather said. There was anger in her voice, peppered with intense fear.

The room became silent. Lucas looked at the three McKenzies, each staring at him, unblinking, waiting for some word, some solace, some explanation that would ease their fear. He desired the same thing. But at this moment he was the one being turned to.

"My dad is home. He'll start making sense of things," Lucas said. The only strength he could find in himself was the assurance that his father could fix things. Throughout his life his dad was the solid ground for the family. He was the fixer, the mender, the peace maker, the authority. Perhaps his name would help here as well.

Heather walked towards Lucas. Gently, he sat Katie on the kitchen counter, her little fingers remaining tightly interlocked around his neck. He tugged at her wrists and unclenched them. The little girl gripped his fingers, finally releasing them when he touched her cheek. Heather reached for him also. He wrapped his arms around her shoulders and pulled her head to his chest. Her hands rested palm down on his collar bones. Lucas could hear the envelope in his pocket crinkle slightly.

"Why don't you kids go watch TV," Lucas said. Both children looked at him and didn't move. Softening his voice, he said, "It'll be alright. We'll find your daddy. Now go on." Katie turned around on the counter and dropped to the kitchen floor. The children walked into the living room. Lucas heard the television snap to life. Football cheers filled the air. Immediately the kids started arguing.

"They don't understand what's happening yet," Heather said, her cheek resting on his lapel. Lucas lightly kissed the top of her head, drawing the scent of her fresh hair into him.

"We don't either. Its best if we just stay as positive as we can." He continued holding her, his chin perched on her head. Words escaped him. Holding her, binding her with his arms, pressing her into his body, he felt his own fear abating. He drew strength from their unity and the love that blistered his heart.

"What if he's dead, Lucas?" Heather's words were halting, unsure. Lucas understood the possibility of Mr. McKenzie's death, and Russell's. There were other men underground as well, their families must be all pondering the same issue, clinging to the same concern. He didn't have an answer for her.

Squeezing her, he wanted to speak of his love. He wanted to push her back gently and reach into his pocket and hand her the poem and letter and let her read it while he watched. He fantasized about her eyes gliding back and forth over each line, phrase and sentence, absorbing their meaning. In his mind, he saw her begin to smile, her tears pooling near her nose. The moment she stopped reading, she would set the letter down and rush back into his arms, her simple words of the acceptance of his love and her return of the same would weld their hearts together. Life from that moment would be full and complete. Their future together would unfold the mysteries of passion, romance, love making. They would leave Sunnyside far behind, see the world together, explore its meanings, grow closer with every second, consume one another until there was no division, no distinction between them, only the love. He slipped his hands to her waist and locked his fingers. She was crying.

"We'll find a way...", Lucas said, "If he is gone...." His voice was soothing. "But we can't speak darkness over this. He could very well be safe."

Heather released herself from his embrace and walked to the kitchen table. A box of Kleenex sat next to a vase of fake silk flowers. She dabbed at her eyes and nose with one of the tissues. Her back turned, Lucas withdrew the packet from his breast pocket and held it in his fingers. It was creased, wrinkled from being twisted in his coat. He had neatly written her name on the outside, each letter carefully penned.

"What's that?" Heather's voice interrupted his thoughts. He looked up at her and hesitated. She was gently blowing her nose, her eyes a bit distracted, yet questioning. From the living room the sound of television channels being searched filled the house.

"Um," he fumbled for words, "It's a letter for my father. Something for work... I forgot to give it to him." He folded the envelope and placed it in his back pocket. She seemed to accept his answer and continued drying her eyes.

The kitchen telephone rang again. Heather asked Lucas to answer it.

"Hello?" he said into the receiver.

"This is Scabby Cipher. Lucas? Is that you?"

"Yeah, its me. I'm just checking on Heather. Hear anything about what's going on at the mine?"

"Yeah, your dad said you were over there," Scabby paused, Lucas could hear fatigue in his friend's voice. "Me and Momma went to the mine offices. It was crazy. The union is still trying to put up a picket line. Them union guys said there ain't no problem, that the company is just trying fake a fire or something so that there won't be no strike."

"My God, you're joking."

"The company said that they think there are over sixty men underground. Some guys came out, but they didn't know nothin'. All kinds of cops are up there too. Couple of the union guys wouldn't let people into the mine yard."

"Bastards," Lucas said. His own words surprised him. He looked over at Heather. She had sat down at the table and was staring vacantly at him.

"Georgie and Ernie Shaggal were up there also. Momma said they told her Congressman Temple was coming down this afternoon from Helena, you know, to help things out."

The mention of the Congressman's name triggered Lucas' memory from the previous evening when he read the note at Dolly's house.

"The Congressman is coming here? What the hell can he do? This is kind of fast don't you think?" Dozens of questions began to fill his mind. He fingered the loops of the phone cord.

"Somethin' else interesting, too. They had Lori Murphy. She was in Georgie's car with Adam Shaggal. They said that she was going out to the lake to be with her momma."

"She needs to be around here. She can't go out there. Russell...." Lucas stopped speaking. Scabby didn't know about her pregnancy. "Look, I'll come and get you. We need to go find Lori and bring her to my parent's house."

"Why?"

"I'll tell you later. Your mom going to be ok without you for a bit?"

"I think so. My uncle and his family is here."

Lucas hung up the phone. A puzzled look covered Heather's face. He told her of the dialogue then said, "This whole thing is weird. I don't mean just about the fire or whatever it is. I'm going to get Lori and bring her to my house. I think you should go next door, too."

Heather argued briefly with him about staying close to her own phone. She tried to convince him to stay with her as well, "I need you Lucas; we need you," she said. Vernon Junior and Katie had returned to the kitchen and were sitting with Heather.

"I promise. I'll be back as soon as I can." He walked across the room, leaned forward and lightly kissed each of them. Turning at the kitchen door, he looked back at the three huddled at the table. They looked so small. Gently he closed the door behind himself and ran down the steps.

"Lucas dropped something," Katie said, slipping to the floor near Heather's feet. She picked up the sealed envelope and handed it to her sister. Heather frowned as she read her name.

147

CHAPTER 29

The shaft collar station was still well lit, though the humidity, floating like a suffocating blanket, ringed the lights with smudged halos. Able to see and discern his surroundings, Russell was feeling safer, yet his sides and head hurt. Each footstep was rubbed by grains of gravel in his boots. The emergency stench smell was overpowering, causing both Russell and Delmer to cough and hack.

Ten feet ahead of Russell, Delmer's shadow cast back into the tunnel from the base of his legs and disappeared, melding with the darkness. Russell walked slightly to one side of the tracks, while Delmer chose the other. It was no longer necessary to find their way by sliding their feet along the inside of the rails. The final fifty yards went quickly.

The collar station was empty. Hissing sounds seethed from a poorly sealed air line overhead. An electrical hum resounded from the tunnel beyond the station.

"This stench stuff will kill us if the smoke and gas doesn't," Russell said, spitting as much mucous from his throat and mouth as possible. Reaching for a water hose, he rinsed his body, stuffing the hose in the rear of his trousers, flushing grit out his pant legs. The water was warm, but still cooler than the air around them.

"Don't try to think none about it," Delmer said. "Suppose they know the smell ain't good for you."

Delmer rinsed himself off when Russell finished.

"Try the shaft phone over there, and I'll tug the emergency signal on the skip. Hopefully they'll know somebody is way down here," Delmer said, his voice sputtering through a mouthful of water.

Russell opened a wooden box attached to the side of the drift near the shaft. The telephone inside was black, old, scratched and smeared with streaks of dirt, grease and bits of sand. There were no dials or buttons on the phone. As Russell picked it up he could hear the squall in the ear piece, signaling the hoistman. If there was a need, the hoistman could patch the call to the surface. Russell listened as the phone continued its deep buzzing. Nobody answered. He cradled the phone to his shoulder and looked towards Delmer who was standing near the main shaft, the safety gate open, tugging on the skip's signal cord.

"Nine tugs in a row and they'll know there's someone on this here level," Delmer said. He continued intermittent sequences of tugs.

"Nobody is answering the hoist room phone," Russell said.

"Just stay on that phone. They may be talkin' to somebody else. Might be a lot of folks tryin' to get their attention," Delmer said.

Russell cradled the phone with his neck and continued to wipe grit from his naked chest with his bare hand. The phone continued its squawking. After several minutes he hung up the receiver. The stench smell was becoming stronger.

"No answer, Delmer," he said. Russell had lost all tonality in his voice. He felt exhausted. He was bleeding again from his chest.

Delmer leaned into the shaft, gripping the safety gate and craned his neck upward.

"I see them lights way up there at the different levels. Ain't no sign of the skip or nothin'. Air is blowing up the shaft."

"Yeah, so?"

"Means that wherever that poison back there is goin', it ain't goin' below, least not yet." Delmer stepped away from the shaft and walked back to Russell.

"So what do we do?" Russell asked.

Delmer moved toward a wooden bench at the back of the collar station and removed his miner's belt and sat down.

"Boy, it means we can sit here and hope for help, or we can go below and see if we can find others."

"Go lower? That's nuts. We need to get out of here."

"The hoistman is most likely dead. Means that them gasses got him. If we go up, they'll get us too." Delmer placed his elbows on his knees and leaned forward, wiping his face with his hands.

"Yeah, or he had the sense to get the hell out of the mine."

"Them hoistmen got oxygen masks like firemen. In an emergency, they can stay a lot longer than anybody. They ain't goin' to leave if they know there's people below that need to get out. I suspect that whoever runs this hoist is sitting at his controls, dead. Them gasses sneaked up on him."

Russell thought for a moment about Delmer's comment. He shuddered.

"Gimme your lamp battery," Delmer said. Extracting a small knife from his pants pocket, he began cutting the wires off of his own miner's lamp. Russell unhooked his battery and handed it to Delmer.

"We can make us a light, but we need to get the headlamp off of the motor back in the manchee barn. Can you find your way back there and drive that motor out here?" Delmer asked, pointing down an adjacent tunnel toward the electrical humming.

Russell looked beyond the station into the dark. The manchee barn was eighty or ninety yards straight ahead.

"Sure," he said with limited confidence.

"Better take one of them," Delmer said.

Russell turned around. Delmer pointed toward the cabinet. Labeled in green were the words, 'Safety First'.

"There's them self rescuers in there. If you feel your head gettin' light, put one of them on right away. You won't have but a second. If you wait, you'll be dead."

Russell opened the cabinet. Inside were a first aid kit, several bottles of aspirin, an assortment of inflatable splints and a chart demonstrating CPR. In pencil on the back of the cabinet door a latent artist had drawn a graphic cartoon of a couple copulating. *Just like cavemen,* Russell thought. He saw several pencil-scrawled epithets condemning various managers and miners. Moving a folded army blanket, he found ten self-rescuers stacked on the middle shelf. Grasping one, he turned again and began walking toward the manchee motor barn, slipping the rescuer onto a tab of his miner's belt.

The droning sound of the recharging batteries became louder the closer he moved towards the motor barn. Though the air was ripe with stench, Russell could smell the electrical vapors wafting from the powered-up motors. Lungs aching, he wondered whether he would be able to breathe successfully on his own if he ever made it to the surface. Violent nausea overcame him, forcing him to vomit onto the tracks.

"Damn it," he cursed aloud, wiping his mouth.

A long cable snaked from an enormous charging unit to a coupling on the manchee battery. Russell pulled the cable loose and climbed onto the operators perch. Engaging power, he sped the manchee down the tracks, back towards Delmer. The ride lasted less than twenty seconds.

At the shaft collar Delmer was filling a burlap bag with the remaining self-rescuers. Russell slowed the manchee and crept it into the middle of the station, stopping within inches of Delmer.

"Why take those rescuers Delmer? We'd die long before we ever got through our second one."

"They ain't for us, boy. They's for anybody else we find."

"Oh…"

Russell stepped from the manchee. Together he and Delmer removed the headlight from the iron motor. Strapping their two miner's lamp batteries together, Delmer bound them with white first aid tape, then wrapped them with a piece of wool cut from the army blanket, creating a sling. Russell held the headlight, balanced on his knees, as Delmer spliced the battery power wires together and twisted them to the lamp. The headlight illuminated the ground by Russell's feet.

"Let there be light," Russell said, smiling at Delmer.

"And there was light," Delmer replied.

Delmer placed the wool sling over Russell's good shoulder. The headlamp hung to the middle of Russell's chest, "You need to carry this. Anytime we are in a good lit area, disconnect them wires. We need to conserve what battery power we got." Delmer walked toward the open safety gate at the shaft.

"You'll need to go down first," he said, turning his head toward Russell.

"Down the main shaft? No way. Let's go back down through my stope."

"Ain't time for that. Fresh air is comin' up through here. The ladders along the sides are good. It'll be faster."

"Yeah, a faster fall. Delmer, it's a least two thousand feet to the bottom of the shaft from here."

"Boy, you wouldn't even have a chance to scream. Just be careful." Delmer motioned toward the open gate.

Russell adjusted his belt. The wool sling on his shoulder wasn't heavy, but the pain of his injuries were aggravated by the additional pressure. He stepped to the edge of the shaft. Grasping the safety gate, he leaned forward and looked down the shaft. Rings of diffused light from the lower stations glimmered. A strong steady wind blew up over his face, cooling him. Shining his large light around the inside of the shaft, he could feel the heat from the burning bulb. A wooden ladder ran vertically three feet from the shaft opening. Moving his light up and down the ladder, he could see that the rungs were slimy with mud. Water trickled down the sides of the wood. Bolted on opposing sides of the shaft were single steel train tracks, guides, Russell supposed, to keep the skip from swinging freely in the shaft.

"The ladder is going to be slicker than cat crap on linoleum, Delmer," Russell said as he pulled his work gloves onto this hands.

"Just gonna have to be extra on guard. Tie this to the safety ring on the back of your belt." Russell looked at Delmer's outstretched hand. He was holding a length of bright yellow plastic rope. "I'll hook the other end to my safety ring. Least ways if one of us slips, the other can try and hold on."

"Right. Hold on as we bounce together off the sides of the shaft on our way to a splattered demise at the bottom." Russell tied a sailor's knot through his safety ring and passed the other end to Delmer.

"'Til death do us part, eh boy?" Delmer grinned and chuckled.

Stepping into the shaft, Russell felt a tickling in his stomach. The back of his neck tensed as he grasped the wooden rung in front of him. Slipping his foot to the next lower step, he added his weight and felt the firmness. The lamp swung slightly as he shifted from side to side.

"I think its pretty solid," he said.

Delmer peered over the edge of the collar. He was adjusting the safety rope and tying the bag of self-rescuers to his miner's belt. Russell looked down again.

"Should be solid. It's the service route for the shaft," Delmer said, "We got about eight feet of rope between us. Just move steady if you can. Don't want too much slack."

Russell moved down two rungs. Delmer stepped onto the ladder above him.

"Only two hundred and fifty rungs to the next level, boy," Delmer shouted. Russell continued to slowly slip his foot to the next rung. The boards were slimey, but the rough hide of his gloves seemed to provide enough friction to hold him firm.

Neither of them spoke as they moved in unison down the shaft. An occasional spray of water would splash onto them, dripping from somewhere in the shaft above. The only sound, beyond their breathing and boot slips was escaping air from poorly sealed pipes.

The headlight slung from Russell's shoulder was becoming hot. Each strike against his bare flesh was like a wasp bite. He stopped climbing.

"Hold up, I'm turning this lantern off. I can see the collar on 4200 below," Russell said. Delmer stopped moving. Twisting one of the wires loose, the lamp went dark. Russell waited a moment, adjusting to the dark. He slid his foot to the next rung.

"Lookin' like there ain't gonna be no strike," Delmer said. Russell tipped his head upward. He could see Delmer silhouetted by the ambient light from the 3700 level. He figured they were at the halfway point between levels. A stone, loosened by the trickling water, bounced off his back.

"Might not have a mine to strike against," Russell replied. They continued their descent, not speaking, focusing instead on the ladder.

It started as an awareness at first, not a sound. Most likely it was the vibration echoing through the solid rock or possibly the shaft's steel tracks.

"Delmer, you feel that?" Russell said, stopping. He placed his hand on the rail closest to him.

"I don't feel nothin'," Delmer said.

"Shhh. Listen."

Both men silenced themselves again. The vibration was there somewhere, in the stone, in the air, in the ladder, in the steel rail. It seemed intermittent.

Russell reconnected the power to the lamp and turned the beam upward. The walls of the shaft were shiny with trickling water.

The vibration was becoming more intense. Russell continued to pan the light, shining it as far up the shaft as he could.

"Dear God, boy, the skip is coming down the shaft. We need to get off this ladder," Delmer shouted.

Russell flashed the lamp around and down the shaft.

"There's no place to get out of the way," Russell hollered back.

The vibration intensified blending with the emerging sound of metal hitting metal. A rumbling began to fill the air around them.

"Squeeze behind the ladder, boy," Delmer screamed.

"I can't, there's not enough room." Russell shone the lamp around the shaft again, its beam frantically searching for safety. Delmer was quickly untying the yellow safety line. Tall and lanky, he began working his body into the small space behind the ladder.

The vibration was now gone, replaced fully by the sound of clanging metal.

The yellow rope, disconnected from Delmer, flopped about Russell, still tethered by one end to his belt. He moved the lamp beam up and down the opposite wall of the shaft.

"Hurry boy!" Delmer was barely audible over the sound roaring from above.

Twelve feet across the shaft, behind the air and water lines, Russell saw a crevice. Shadows danced around the pipes, distorting his visual perception. It might be big enough. Maybe.

Spinning around, turning his back to the rungs, Russell grasped the ladder with both hands and leaned forward. The lamp swung from his shoulder, casting light across the expanse. Glancing down, the shaft looked like a hungry monster, ready to devour unwitting miners.

"God help me," he screamed as he jumped across the dark expanse of the shaft. The lamp slipped from his shoulder sling and swung wildly from its power tether. Russell's chest hit the vertical pipes first. His arms, wide open, instinctively tried to wrap around them. His legs slammed against the air line as his hands fought for a grip. It felt like the skip was almost upon him. The world was now darkness, vibration, stench, pain and fear.

He slid a few feet down the pipes before his grip held. The battery sling and lantern stayed with him, though the lamp was now extinguished. Russell twisted his arms and legs around the backside of the pipes tearing the flesh from his back against the coarse wall of rocks. The pipes pressed against his chest. Their coolness contrasting with his flaming skin.

The skip hammered loudly against the steel rails as it plunged less than a foot away from him. Its steel frame and doors banging, shaking and roaring like a deadly dragon. Sparks spit from its side where its guide wheels met the steel rails. It plummeted down into the dark depths, taking its sound and anger with it. Looking down the shaft, Russell could see the spray of sparks twinkling and getting smaller and more minute. The sound became a vibration, the vibration became silence.

He clung to the pipes, breathing violently, "Delmer! Are you there?" he shouted.

From somewhere in the dark above him he heard movement.

"Thank God boy, you're alive," Delmer hollered back. His voice was shrill and fear filled.

"I did," Russell said in an almost whisper, "I did…" He could hear Delmer moving down the ladder across from him.

Pressing his knees and legs against the pipes, Russell pinned his back against the shaft wall and pulled the lamp cord up to his chest. Removing a glove he felt for the loose wire and reattached it to the headlight. The shaft became illuminated. He shone the light onto Delmer.

"You ok?" Russell asked.

Raising his hand to shield his eye from the light Delmer replied, "Yup," and turned his full body toward Russell, hooking a rung with the elbow of his bad arm. A dozen feet separated them.

"You've got a guardian angel holding onto you down here, you know that?" Delmer said.

"I don't believe in angels."

"Got to be the only way a big boy like you can float across this shaft in the dark and not die, don't you think? God must like you."

"If He likes me, why is He trying to kill me?"

"He's protecting you. It's the devil that wants us dead," Delmer replied.

"We're in hell as it is."

"Then you best make your peace with God."

Russell and Delmer clung to their respective perches in silence. Russell's panic, adrenaline and fear began dissipating slightly. A black greasy skip cable, five inches in diameter, swayed in the middle of the shaft, dropping to the dark depths. It abruptly stopped and bowed slightly.

"That skip was empty," Delmer finally said, "Weren't nobody on it. It was in a free fall. Think it hit the bottom or got stuck down there somewhere."

"Must mean somebody is up above in the hoist room, right?" Russell said, trying to sound upbeat.

"Could mean that nobody was there to set the brake."

Russell adjusted himself against the pipes. He tried to ignore the searing agony of his back.

"That angel better still be around here. I don't think that I've got the strength to jump back over there," Russell said as he spun the lamp around the interior of the shaft.

"You lean in and I'll lean in and grab hands. You'll just have to let go of them pipes and you'll swing right to this here ladder. Wrap the rope around your wrist and I'll do the same once our hands connect. It'll be easy."

"Why not," Russell said with resignation.

Slithering from behind the pipes, Russell found footing and grasped the smaller of the two tubes. Weaving the yellow safety rope around his wrist and hand he left enough for Delmer to do the same.

Leaning into the shaft he said, "Hurry Delmer, I can't do this for more than a few seconds.

Delmer dropped down one rung and leaned toward the shaft center and reached out for Russell. Enough light emanated from the makeshift lantern that Russell could see there was still a foot of distance between their two hands. Flipping the end of the yellow rope to Delmer, he watched as the man quickly rolled his wrist to secure it. He knew Delmer was holding onto the ladder with his bad arm.

"Just jump gently," Delmer said, "You'll swing right over here."

"I'll probably break your bum arm."

"Nope. Bone can't break twice in the same place."

Russell counted to three, released his hand from the air line and pushed against the pipes with his feet. His body dropped forward. Delmer instantly pulled back on the tether between them. Again, Russell impacted the ladder with his full body weight and found firm holds without frightened fumbling.

"Told you them angels are still here," Delmer said.

"The only angel here is you, nipper."

CHAPTER 30

"I keep getting this feeling that something isn't right," Lucas said. Scabby had just closed the passenger door of the Toyota. He was wearing the same clothes as he had earlier in church. The tires slipped sideways in the ruts of Cipher's driveway, causing the truck to bounce hard. Lucas pressed hard on the gas, spinning mud and gravel onto the porch steps.

"This here whole fire thing ain't right," Scabby replied. His mouth was a bit full of unchewed food, causing his words to mute. He forced a large swallow.

"No, Scabby, that's not what I mean. Billy's suicide, the fire, the letter in Dolly's purse..." Lucas' voice trailed off. He realized he hadn't told Scabby about the trip to Dolly's trailer the night before.

"Dolly? The old whore?" Scabby asked. He was turned toward Lucas and wearing a puzzled expression. Lucas noticed that Scabby's hair was still neatly combed, and his glasses appeared to have just been cleaned.

"Yeah, I gave her a ride home last night. She was behind the S & S. Ernie had just kicked her out of his car. He showed up there later too," Lucas said. He gave Scabby the details of Ernie's phone call and Dolly spilling her purse.

"You're for sure that the letter was one from Billy to the Congressman?" Scabby said.

"Well, it was signed Billy. The writing was in longhand. It was a copy not the original. It said he was going to be sure the mine wasn't producing. Maybe he knew about the fire."

"Why'd he go and kill himself then?"

"Guilt? Who knows. Billy has been a mess since Dale got shot hunting. Lots of people say it was Billy's fault. We need to get that letter from Dolly. Maybe she even knows what's going on," Lucas said.

Steering sharply to the right, Lucas bounced the truck onto the paved road leading back to Sunnyside.

"Then what's all this gotta do with Ernie and his phone call?"

"I don't know, but everything and everybody seem to be overlapping," Lucas said. He bit hard onto his bottom lip, chewing it slightly.

"Maybe we should just tell your father or something."

"No, he's got too much to think about right now," Lucas said. His thoughts moved quickly to his brother. He wondered if Russell was still alive.

Snow was still speckling the ground and melting almost on impact now. Lucas looked at the surrounding mountains, just a hundred or so feet up, the bushes and barren rock were covered in white. The cab of the truck was becoming warm. He turned the heater down a notch and lowered his window an inch. Scabby dropped his a little as well.

Driving past the mine parking lot, Lucas saw several dozen people standing under umbrellas and a makeshift canvas canopy. He spotted his father talking with several of the union members. The local radio station's brightly marked van was parked to one side. He noticed 'Blaine the Brain', the station's only disk jockey, leaning against the vehicle. The DJ was fiddling with an antiquated microphone.

"Suppose the world's going to hear about this pretty soon," Lucas said.

"It's a shame, too," Scabby replied, "The world doesn't seem to care much for us as it is."

"Death makes great press, Scabby."

"Yeah, death makes great press," Scabby said, "But we ain't sure if nobody's dead yet."

Lucas stopped momentarily to allow a woman and her two children to cross the road. He scanned the crowd, recognizing most of the faces. They were all customers of the Shop and Save.

"Yesterday, these guys were wanting to beat me up because of Dad. Now look at them. They're all over him wanting his help." Lucas moved his truck slowly around several cars parked haphazardly in the street. He followed the road to the interstate highway and drove up the on-ramp.

"Is Heather doin' fine?" Scabby asked, breaking the silence.

"She's frightened. Worried. Just like us," Lucas replied.

"You tell her about your feelings yet?"

"No. I wrote her a letter and poem explaining that, but I couldn't give it to her. Not with the way things are, not knowing whether Mr. McKenzie is ok," Lucas said. He tapped his fingers on his jacket, reassuring himself that the letter was still with him. It wasn't.

Leaning to one side, he frantically searched his pants pockets and the sport jacket.

"Damn it. It's missing," he said with exasperation.

"Where did you put it," Scabby asked.

"If I knew where I put it, I wouldn't be looking for it would I?" Lucas snapped. "Damn it. It must have fallen out at her house or in her yard. If she reads that without me there…no…no…no…."

"If she finds it and reads it at least she'll know," Scabby said, trying to soothe his friend. It wasn't helping.

"She'll think I changed my mind. She saw me with the envelope," he said. "If somebody else finds it, it could ruin everything."

Lucas clicked on his turn signal and exited the freeway. In ten minutes they would be at Dolly's trailer.

"You need to ask her when you see her," Scabby said.

"I can't. If she didn't find it, then I'd have to explain everything. If she did read it, I'd have to explain everything, too. But if I don't ask and she doesn't say anything, then I can hopefully find the letter and not have to deal with it."

"Oh," Scabby said. Lucas knew his friend didn't understand.

The Tall Pine Trailer Park sign was topped with an inch of snow. Many of the letters were peeling or missing. At the bottom of the sign Lucas read, 'No dogs allowed in ark'. He smiled at the implication of Noah leaving dogs behind.

The park was close to the river and in a small valley, making the air cooler than that in town. Lucas tried to remember which trailer belonged to Dolly. Everything looked different in the daylight.

"I think it was at the end of the road," Lucas said after driving up and down two lanes. The homes in the court were basically the same. Dirty white aluminum, turquoise trim and broken wooden steps leading to small porches with rusted out barbecue cookers. Almost every home had toys or plastic tricycles littering their dead lawns. There was no sign of anybody. Lucas reasoned that everyone was either at the mine or listening for details on their radios.

"This is it," Lucas said, "I remember her house being one of the smallest." He steered his pickup into the small driveway and stopped.

"How you goin' to get the letter from her?" Scabby asked.

"I guess just tell her I saw it last night and that I want to know what she knows," he replied.

"She ain't gonna tell you nothin'. Why should she?"

"She trusts me," Lucas said.

"Oh," said Scabby.

Lucas rapped gently on the metal door to Dolly's home. He could hear the faint drone of the television.

"I think she is probably still asleep on the couch," he said. He knocked a little harder. No answer.

"She ain't here, Luke, let's go back into town. I'm getting' cold," Scabby said.

"Don't call me Luke." He glared long enough to make his point. "Look, I'm sure she's in there."

Lucas banged the door with his fist, shaking the frame. Still nobody. He tested the doorknob. It was unlocked. A slight twist and the door opened a crack.

"Dolly? Are you in there? Its Lucas Kaari," he shouted. There was no response. Lucas pulled the door open and stepped inside.

"I ain't goin' in there. That's trespassing if she ain't home," Scabby said.

"I'm just going to look and see if her purse is still here. That's where I put the letter. Just stay here and watch for anybody."

Lucas closed the door behind himself. Dolly was not on the couch and there was no sign of her. He felt the television. It was hot and had obviously been on for some time. The room had the same fragrance as before. The blanket he had placed on her when she passed out, was on the floor. He scanned the room for her purse. It was no longer on the table.

He moved into the kitchen and glanced on the counters. They were empty except for a drinking glass with a smudge of red on its rim. Walking slowly, the floor creaked under the soles of his shoes. The hallway, bathroom and her bedroom were just ahead. A cat litter box stank in the corner of the kitchen.

"Dolly? Are you there?" The stillness in the trailer was making him nervous. He could feel the hair on his arms stand up. He moved quietly down the hall. The bathroom appeared untouched from the night before. Looking up, he saw that her bedroom door was closed. It had been open last night. Maybe she got up from the couch, got a drink of water, walked to her bed and went to sleep. He tapped with his fingertips on her bedroom door.

"Dolly?" he said in a low voice, "Its Lucas." Silence remained. He touched the doorknob and moved it. The door opened a bit. He peered through the crack. The soft red light in her room tainted the color of everything. Opening the door further he began to step inside. A sudden movement on the bed startled him. It came towards him in a rush. Lucas jumped backwards. Dolly's cat zipped between his legs and darted to the other end of the house. His heart pounded with adrenaline fury.

"Damn cat," he muttered. He opened the door the rest of the way. Dolly was lying face down on the floor.

"Dolly," Lucas said in a loud voice. She didn't move. Fumbling near the door frame, he found the overhead light switch and turned it on. The room became illuminated. A large dark pool of blood saturated the carpeting around Dolly's head and spread to the wall and under her bed.

"Oh no, Dolly!" He could feel his stomach turning, a frigid sweat washed over his chest. The back of her skull was split open. Next to her knees he saw a clothes iron, its tip smeared with hair and blood.

Lucas turned and ran down the short hallway and into the bathroom. The contents of his stomach filled the commode. He began coughing and held onto the toilet seat.

"Luke, you all right?" It was Scabby. "I heard the noise. Why you pukin'?"

Lucas looked up at his friend. "She's dead," he said, pointing a finger in the direction of the bedroom. Scabby appeared shocked. He looked around quickly then disappeared down the hall. Footsteps pounded back toward the bathroom.

"Oh God, she's more than dead, she's murdered," Scabby said. Lucas rose to his knees and wiped his mouth with a hand full of toilet paper. He spat several times into the toilet then flushed it. The sour smell of his own vomit began to make him queasy again.

"We need to get them cops," Scabby said, handing Lucas a wad of tissue from a box on the sink.

"No, we can't," Lucas said. "They'll think it was me. I was the last one she was with last night. Her purse is even gone." Lucas reached for Scabby's outstretched hand, fetched the wadded paper and started wiping the puke from his chin and lips. Scabby stepped into the narrow hall way outside the bathroom and turned back toward Lucas.

"Nobody saw you with her right?" Scabby said. The electric furnace clicked on, startling both boys. Warm air began rushing from a vent on the floor near the bathtub.

"Some car drove by when she was getting into the truck. Whoever it was, she recognized. Soon as they find out she's dead they'll tell the police about seeing her at the S & S alley and some small truck. I'm screwed." Lucas pulled toilet paper from the dispenser and mopped his forehead. Finished, he dropped the tissues into the toilet and flushed it.

"We ain't just goin' to leave her are we?" Scabby asked. Lucas looked up at Scabby and read the fear in his friend's face. It was a reflection of his own.

"We'll leave and hope nobody saw us drive in here. We can call the police from town and let them sort it out," Lucas said. The thought of leaving a dead body behind and the lie and denial ahead pushed his heart into his stomach.

"I'm not likin' this that much," Scabby said, scanning up and down the hallway.

"I know," Lucas answered. Laying his hands on the edge of the bathtub, he lifted himself to his feet. Dizziness fluttered into his head as he steadied himself. He pushed Scabby gently on the shoulder as he walked by him into the hallway. Scabby stepped aside and followed Lucas down the hall to the living room.

Lucas opened the outside door a crack and peered out. It was calm and very quiet. He motioned for Scabby to follow him as he walked down the stairs. Scabby complied and quietly closed the trailer door behind him. Quickly they ran to Lucas' truck and climbed into the cab.

Driving slowly, Lucas exited the rear of the Tall Pine Trailer Park. He prayed that no one saw him and Scabby coming or going. Neither of them spoke until the city limits of Sunnyside. The sky was dark gray. The windshield was fogged. Lucas hesitated turning the heater on. His guts were still tender and the added heat could make him retch again.

"You think maybe Ernie did it?" Scabby asked, breaking the long silence. Lucas took his eyes from the road for an instant and glanced in his direction. Scabby's glasses had slipped to the end of his nose. He made no effort to adjust them. The inside of the lenses were misted like the windshield.

"I don't know. Why? Anybody could have done it," Lucas said.

"He was the second to last person that saw her. Maybe she stole that letter from him and he went to get it. Could have happened that way," Scabby replied.

Lucas turned his eyes back to the highway before them. The truck bounced gently as it hit a small asphalt patch used to fix a minor pothole. He swerved too late to avoid an untouched hole filled with icy water. The rear of the truck dropped into the opening and clattered loudly, the tailgate popping open. He cursed under his breath.

Lucas thought for a moment then said, "We need to find out more about what Billy was up to." It was becoming dark. Lucas clicked the headlights on.

"Where we goin'?" Scabby asked, wiping the side window with his bare hand.

"To the union hall," Lucas said. He almost whispered the phrase, unsure of Scabby's reaction. The bruises on his face were throbbing. His throat was feeling raw from the acidity of vomit. He swallowed hard, hoping to relieve some of the soreness, to no avail. His mouth tasted rank.

"But the union hall will most likely be locked and closed up after dark. Everybody is up at the mine," Scabby said. He pulled the glasses from his face and began rubbing the lenses with the corner of his shirt cuff, his face in full squint as he tried to see what he was doing.

"I know," Lucas said, guiding his truck down the exit ramp as bits of frozen rain began to chatter against the windshield, "That's what I'm hoping for."

CHAPTER 31

Big Hand Lake was festooned with small whitecaps, driven by a western breeze. Ernie thought they looked like they weren't moving, though the wind was rocking metal chimes hanging outside near the dock. At this distance he could hear their tinkling. The fir trees across the small bay were flocked in snow, fluffing themselves up the steep mountain. He turned his back to the picture window and continued speaking to his brother.

"Georgie, all those credit memo's with Billy's name on them are a pointing finger aimed at me. I told you not to keep an audit trail on that bastard." Ernie scratched the side of his leg, walked to his desk and sat down and stared at Georgie sitting on the brown leather couch across the room. The polished log walls reflected the flames from the fireplace. Ernie settled himself into his wheeled office chair. It groaned as it accepted his body weight.

"I know. But the books were always out of balance. I figured that someday I would slip Billy enough money to make it look like he paid the bill himself," Georgie said. The man was fidgeting as he spoke. Ernie stared hard at him, purposely not blinking, keeping his eyes as wide as possible.

"Sheesh, I slipped him enough dough over the past few years to feed half the damn county." Ernie was becoming angry, not so much at his brother but at himself. The money was not a big deal, really, but he wanted his brother to feel some remorse and guilt. For most of their lives, he had lied to and pushed his younger brother around, never sure whether Georgie realized it or not. If he did, he didn't seem to mind all that much.

"The rest of the books are pretty clean," Georgie assured.

"Clean? Heck, the Shop & Save is the dirtiest damn business in town. Christ Georgie, how would we explain all the cash flow? You think the IRS is going to overlook the fact that the inventory and income don't quite fit? Come on, what would you tell them? That we charged ten times as much for the items that we did sell?" Ernie's voice was exaggerated, just like his expression. He continued to fix his gaze on Georgie. He smiled to himself as his brother shifted side to side, almost unnoticeable, but certainly caving into the ranting. *Guilt is a fine tool*, Ernie thought.

"I didn't think giving Billy credit and food would get us in trouble." Georgie got up and walked to the window where Ernie had been standing. He slipped his hands into the back pockets of his polyester pants. His store apron was still looped and tied around his waste. Ernie felt annoyed that Georgie had stepped out of his glaring gaze.

"You shouldn't have been giving him groceries and stuff anyway. See the problem now is everybody is going to want to know why Billy blew his brains out. The cops are picking over his house pretty good. Estate lawyers and executors are going to want to see his bank statements. All kinds of things. If a court case comes out of this, all of his financial transactions will be discoverable. People are going to want to know where he got all his money. They'll trace some of it to you, then come straight to me. I've got so much going out to so many, this whole county would end up in jail." Ernie leaned back in his chair and laced his fingers behind his head. The chair creaked again.

"Did you get any of his records when you were at his house?" Georgie said.

"Yeah, some. But that new cop kid came in and messed things up. It don't look like he kept much stuff at his house anyway. His old lady said he paid all the bills and she has no idea about any of his records. Mostly, he dealt in cash, she said," Ernie rattled a fart as he spoke. Georgie turned around and looked at him, raising an eyebrow.

There was a knock at the study door. Ernie heard coughing, muted by the wood.

"Come in," Ernie growled. Fumbling with a polished wood box on his desk, he withdrew a cigar and bit off the tip of it.

Adam Shaggal stepped into the room, wiping his mouth with a handkerchief.

"What is it, son?" Georgie asked, his voice sounded soft, less tense.

"Um, I just wanted to let you know that Mrs. Murphy is finally asleep upstairs. Her son and daughter are sleeping as well. She took some of them sleeping pills you gave her. Lori is out in the guesthouse. She refused to come in and see any of her family. She wants to go into Sunnyside and find out what is happening at the mine." Adam stood, almost at attention, in front of Ernie's desk. Ernie shoved the entire cigar into his mouth, closed his lips around it, and withdrew it. The rolled tobacco leaves were moist with his spit.

"Keep an eye on her," Ernie said, "We don't need anybody going back into town yet." Ernie slid a match against the wall, bringing an immediate flame. Puffing his cheeks, he drew the cigar to life. A cloud of smoke circled his head as he shook out the remaining flame of the match. With his fingertips, he flicked the wooden stick across the room toward the fireplace. It bounced off of the hearth and dropped to the floor. Georgie walked over, bent down, fetched the match and tossed it into the fire's flames.

"Yes, sir," Adam said, "I'll stay out there with her." Ernie puffed on his cigar again, harder this time. He didn't like the buried enthusiasm in his nephew's voice.

"And Adam," Ernie said, "Keep your hands off that girl. We have enough trouble as it is." Georgie nodded his head at his son, agreeing with his brother.

"Sure, Uncle Ernie. Don't worry. I'll just have some beers and watch TV. I had her before and she wasn't that good anyway," Adam said. Ernie couldn't miss the macho bravado in the young man's voice. It made him grin, exposing his teeth that were now gripping the stogie. Adam turned and left the room, closing the door behind. The sound of the front door shutting followed an instant later.

"So what are you going to do now?" Georgie asked, as he walked back to the couch and reseated himself. The leather sputtered against the rear of his pants.

"I suppose I'll go back into town and dig through his desk and locker at the union hall. What time is it anyway?" Ernie began digging at his ear canal with a new wooden matchstick. The end of his cigar was white with ash. He flicked it into a coffee cup on the corner of the desk. A bit of tobacco clung to the inside corner of his mouth. He pursed his lips and gently spit it to the floor.

"Its four-thirty. It'll be dark in an hour," Georgie answered. His left wrist was turned upward exposing the face of his watch. Ernie had remarked that wearing the watch backwards like that made Georgie look sissified. Georgie told him that it protected the watch's crystal face.

"It'll take that long to drive in." Ernie stood up. His chair squealed and groaned. Walking to the den door, he pulled his jacket from a deer antler coat rack attached to the wall. His smoke followed him in a wispy swirl.

Georgie stood too and stretched a bit. Ernie heard him yawning.

"You want this?" Georgie said in a hushed voice.

Ernie slipped his arms into his jacket and turned back towards his brother. Georgie pulled his hand from his apron pocket. He was holding a pistol.

"What for?" Ernie asked, surprised.

"Just in case…." Georgie said.

Ernie stood silent for a moment, then said, "Sure. Just in case."

CHAPTER 32

Russell couldn't feel his arms. They were cold, which seemed impossible in this heat. He could see them. He could make them work. He could wiggle his fingers. They gripped the shaft ladder, but it was like he was watching somebody else's hands.

"I think I really screwed up something, Delmer. My upper body has no feeling to it. Maybe I've torn some muscles or something real bad." Rolling his shoulder, he felt sharp, almost bone splintered pain.

"You feel numb?" Delmer said as if reading Russell's mind.

"Yup," Russell replied.

"It's most likely the heat. We'll sit a spell at the station. You'll feel some better," Delmer said.

Russell stepped onto the collar station at the 4200 level. The safety gate had swung wide open. The area was well lit. Delmer joined him. Together they walked to the benches on the far side of the station. A large wooden cabinet, used by the mining engineers, butted up to the benches. A padlock hung from a hasp, securing the cabinet's contents from pilfering miners. Delmer fumbled with the lock, tugging several times as if hoping that it would open.

Russell sat, picked at his ripped flesh, digging out pieces of grainy gravel. Every fiber in his body throbbed or ached. The air was moist and stagnant. He could smell mildewed wood.

"Where's Freddy do you suppose?" Russell said, watching Delmer.

"Most likely back in one of them drifts. He's gotta know somethin' is goin' on. We all been down here almost two whole shifts back to back. We best be movin' on though," Delmer said. Russell watched as the man adjusted his pants and miner's belt. Delmer pulled his pipe wrench from its holster and began beating on the padlock. He missed several times and scarred the painted wood.

"Where?" Russell shouted over the hammering, clanking sound.

"As far from here as we can get. You ever been up the old east spur?" Delmer asked, his words spoken in halts between each swing of the pipe wrench. The lock bounced with each strike, but didn't yield.

"A little way. They store timber and dynamite, blasting powder and stuff back there. I get stuff for my stope from there. That's just a dead end drift, isn't it?" Russell said. Delmer was lifting the wrench over his head and slamming the lock with hard even strokes. The noise echoed across the empty collar station.

"Not always," Delmer said. The locked uncoupled. Another hard swing and Delmer knocked it off it's hasp. He was covered in sweat. His chest heaved as he drew deep breaths. He returned his wrench to its holster, planted his hands on his hips and circled his lips with his tongue, wetting them.

"What do you mean, not always?" Russell asked as he stood up and walked over to Delmer.

"It used to run back to the bottom of the old upper workings," Delmer replied, wheezing the word. He was rolling his wrist and opening and closing his hand.

"Say that again?" Russell rubbed his own arm as he spoke. The muscles were beginning to tighten. Feeling was returning to his fingers and hands.

"What I mean is, that there area got mined out a long time back, just like the area where we seen the fire. Only difference is, these workin's ain't connected to them other workin's."

"What good is it going to do us getting back there?" Russell said.

"Some of the old miners I used to work with when I was a new kid down here said that area was some of the cooler ground in the mine. Used to be a place where they'd go hide out from the foreman. They said fresh air came down from an old exploration shaft," Delmer replied.

"You think that there is a surface opening back there?" Russell said. He rolled his shoulders again and started to shake his hands and fingers. The station lights flickered slightly. Both he and Delmer looked up at the light tubes above them.

"Not sure. I think it is possible that the old entrance to the upper workings might be back that a way. Got no idea for sure." Delmer stood up and adjusted the burlap bag he had been carrying.

"Even if we could get back there, we couldn't get out," Russell reasoned.

"No, but if there is fresh air, we can sit and wait. We just need to mark a trail for them to find us. Like that one right there." Delmer pointed to an arrow spray painted on the side of the drift, apparently drawn some time ago by the mining engineers.

Russell bent forward hoping to usurp some of the agony along his backbone. His butt muscles and calves seared with pain. The hamstrings in his legs felt ready to snap.

"Boy, you look like hell," Delmer said with a hidden laugh. "Your own daddy wouldn't know who you are." Russell looked up at him. He thought about telling Delmer how awful he too looked.

"My father has never known who I am," Russell replied instead.

Delmer gave him a puzzled look then pulled open the storage locker and began rummaging through it, knocking some of the contents to the ground. The overhead lights dimmed again.

"Here's one," Delmer said. Russell had no idea what the man was referring to. He looked at him. Delmer was holding a can of orange spray paint. He began briskly shaking it as he walked back toward the shaft. The marble inside the can clattered as it mixed the paint contents. Delmer tested it by blasting some into the air. He then sprayed the date and time on the rock wall near the safety gate. Beneath that he drew an arrow with a crook to it, indicating the direction they were headed.

"Let's get," Delmer said jogging the short distance back to Russell. His boots made sloshing sounds. Russell gathered his few belongings, pulled at the waistband of his trousers, then slung the bag with the self-rescuers over his shoulder.

Together they walked down the side drift, Russell shining their lamp on the center of the tracks, occasionally checking the rib of the tunnel for additional spray painted arrows. He found none. At a switch in the track they stopped.

"See the direction that switch is flipped? Means that any train back here went that way," Delmer said. Russell nodded his head in agreement. They continued walking, the hum of the rechargers growing louder.

The motor barn was empty. The lights over head flickered with the groaning rhythm of the charger.

"Somebody took the main motor out of here. Went back beyond us. We need to keep walking that way. It's the way we is headin' anyways," Delmer said.

Russell shone the lamp down the tunnel. He saw nothing but track and pipes.

"How far back are we going?" Russell asked. The light from the lamp dimmed a bit. Russell jiggled on of the battery cords bringing the intensity back.

"To the very end. Mile maybe," Delmer answered. Both men stared into the far darkness of the drift.

"Great," Russell said, "A little more exercise to round out the day."

"Don't complain. Least you're still walkin'." Delmer said. He patted Russell on the back of his head.

"Feels like a death march," Russell replied. They continued walking.

The drift slowly curved to the left. At each crossing or intersection, they checked for the direction of the track switch and followed it. Delmer painted a large arrow each time they took a turn.

"We have to go this way, not that way," Delmer said. They had stopped at a large open crossing. He was staring at the track switch. His good arm was extended and pointing into the darkness. The air and water lines near his head hissed. "Bulkhead and old workings are up there a ways." Delmer nodded toward the tunnel.

"But Freddy must be down there. We need to find him first," Russell said pointing into the opposite tunnel and darkness.

"We don't know how much longer them little batteries are goin' keep that light goin'. If we waste too much time we'll die in the dark. I ain't that interested in playin' hide and seek with Freddy Whitehead."

Russell heard disdain in Delmer's voice.

"Look, I know that Freddy hurt you when you crossed the picket line. Everybody knows that. But if he has the train motor back there and his lamp battery has even a little juice, it'll increase our chances of getting out of here. Freddy knows this mine as well as you do. Maybe there's something back there we don't know about. We need to find him."

Delmer rubbed the crook of his bad arm and quietly said, "The man never once asked my forgiveness. He never said he was sorry. I don't expect his kind would. But the man hurt my family. His selfishness made my babies go hungry 'cause I couldn't work - nowhere. I had to beg for food and money. My wife and kids knew it. They depended on me and all I could do was to plead with folks. Because of him, I was no longer a man, still don't feel like one. I became like a disease, like I had the plague. People stayed away from me. Each day I have to ask God to stop me from bustin' out after Freddy and them union boys. My broken bones healed somewhat. My memories and shame never have," Delmer stared at the ground as he finished speaking.

Russell searched for something to say, some wisdom to give Delmer. Hearing the hurt and pain in Delmer's voice made his own agony and suffering seem meaningless. Russell placed his hand on Delmer's shoulder.

"You're more of a man than anybody I've ever met, Delmer," he said softly, "Maybe God is giving you a chance to feel whole again. It's what you pray for, right?"

Delmer lifted his head and looked at Russell. He stood staring for a long moment.

"Ain't it funny, boy," Delmer finally said.

"Funny what, Delmer?" Russell asked.

"Funny how God talks to us." He touched Russell's forearm with his glove, tapped it a couple of times and stepped around him. "We'll go back there aways," he said, "Maybe Freddy will see the light comin'."

CHAPTER 33

Heather motioned for Lucas and Scabby to enter the kitchen. She was on the telephone again, her free hand pushing fingers through her thick hair. Colored wax crayons were scattered on the kitchen table along with a variety of coloring books. The room smelled of fresh cooking and bleach. The sounds of children arguing filtered down from upstairs.

"That was your mother, Lucas. She is at your dad's office. He just went underground with a rescue team," Heather said. Her voice was even and steady. "They don't know where the fire is." She walked to the sink and began scrubbing dishes. Lucas noticed she made no attempt at eye contact.

He stared at her back then looked at Scabby. The tension in the air was obvious and growing. Behind a door on the far side of the kitchen, the washing machine and dryer rattled and splashed. Water from the kitchen faucet rushed with a whooshing sound. Dishes banged against one another as Heather fished around them in search of forks and spoons, hidden in the soapy water. Her auburn hair was tangled and free, swaying gently down her back.

She must have read the letter, Lucas thought. His chest surged and he felt a quickening of his pulse. He wanted to ask her directly, but this moment was awkward. Maybe this was his answer, he thought, maybe she couldn't bring herself to tell him she didn't want him. Maybe.

"I think I'll go say hello to them kids," Scabby said, gesturing with his thumb in the direction of the living room. He raised his eyebrows at Lucas as he walked from the room. Lucas nodded at him in thanks.

Standing behind Heather, Lucas placed his hands on her shoulders. They were rigid as steel. He tried to massage them. She shrugged a bit and continued briskly rubbing a sponge on a pan. He dropped his hands to her hips, feeling their gentle curve and the hip bones themselves. She made no attempt to move them, but continued her cleaning. He could feel the forced distance. His mind cried out to him, wanting to wrap his arms around her waist, maybe kiss the side of her neck, nuzzle his face in her hair. Smell her, taste her lips, make the day disappear, if even for a second.

"Talk to me," he said, stepping back from her. "Tell me what's going on." His voice wavered slightly, still tender and hoarse from the earlier retching.

Heather plunged her hands into the dishwater, withdrew them, pulled a dishtowel from a drawer near her waist and began drying her hands. She stared out the window as she began speaking.

"What's going on? My mother is dead, Lucas. She should be here, not me. Daddy is lost in that mine, probably dead too, but I'm the one that has to deal with it. I'm the one that has to wonder and worry about the kids. I'm the one that has to give up whatever life I have so that everybody is comfortable. She died and doesn't have to live with this. Instead, I have to take her place."

The kitchen became silent. Heather's hands were on the sink edge, her head and face tilted toward the kitchen window. Lucas backed up to the counter and stuffed his thumbs into his pockets.

Heather turned around and faced him. There was a rigidity in her movement, almost threatening. Lucas remained still. He examined her, looking for a trace of hope in her eyes, waiting for words that might speak away the pain inside of him. But her face was anything but serene. Still beautiful, it was drained of color and life, her green eyes the only contrasting color, though they too seemed without spark.

Withdrawing the folded envelope from her back pocket, she held it up near her tear stained face. She crinkled it, squeezing it into her fist.

"I can't open this. I can't read what's in here. I already know what it says. I've seen it on your face a thousand times. I heard it in your voice, in your laughter, in your whispers. It is in everything you do. As real as this is, as genuine as we both might feel, this life is now a prison for me. You can't get trapped by that. I won't let you. I can't read this. I can't see or believe in a future that can never be." Her voice was rising with fear and anger. "You are my best friend, Lucas, and I love you... I love you more than I could ever hope to love somebody. But don't make me dream any more..."

Her words became choked beneath her tears. She dropped the letter to the floor. Lucas walked to her, bent down and retrieved it. The seal was unbroken. Taking her hand into his, he gently placed the envelope on her palm, smoothing it out.

"Keep this," he said gently, "What's in here is a gift of my heart to yours. When tomorrow looks brighter, when these days have passed, then you can open this. When you are ready, then read this. I will be waiting for you. For always."

She closed her hands around the letter. He leaned forward and kissed her gently on the cheek and held her close to him. The tension lifted as her body softened against his. Heather closed her eyes and kissed back at him. Her lips trembled as they met his. His mouth slowly explored the warmth of hers. Then he withdrew, pushing his passion back into the pit of his gut.

"Until that time," he said softly, "I'm here, however you need me to be." Heather pulled her head back slightly. His eyes met hers. She closed them again and lay her cheek against his chest.

Scabby returned to the kitchen, stumbling against one of the kitchen chairs and fell forward onto his hands. Several crayons rolled off the table onto the vinyl floor. Lucas and Heather glanced at him, their moment broken by the sudden noise.

"It's getting dark. We need to go," Scabby said, scrambling to his feet. His sneaker snapped one of crayons, creating a short red streak.

"Go where?" Heather asked. She looked from Scabby back to Lucas.

Lucas considered telling her about Dolly and the Billy note, instead he said, "To find Scabby's mom and see if she has heard anything else. And to see if we can locate Lori."

Heather nodded at him. "Then you better leave," she said.

Lucas kissed her again and walked to the kitchen door. Scabby followed him. Turning back towards her Lucas paused then said, "I love you."

"I know...," she said, her voice whispered with resolve.

Scabby opened the kitchen door and walked onto the deck. Lucas was directly behind him. It was dark in the alley. The street lights shown.

Heather stood in the doorway, silhouetted by the soft kitchen light, her face indistinguishable from the rest of her body. Slowly she shut the door.

"You ok, Luke?" Scabby asked.

"Yeah, I'm alright," Lucas said when they reached the bottom step, "She didn't read the letter."

Scabby was looking at him with a curious expression on his face.

Lucas continued, "She told me that she loved me before I had a chance to say anything to her." The gravel under their shoes crunched as they walked. There were no other sounds.

"Oh," Scabby said.

Lucas knew he didn't understand. How could he? Scabby lived through Lucas, heard Lucas' words, but couldn't feel his heart and hurts. Lucas suddenly felt sorry for his friend. Scabby looked very small. Lucas placed his arm across Scabby's shoulders and gave him a small squeeze as they moved across the space between the houses.

They walked to Lucas' house and entered the basement living room. The house was silent and cold. Lucas was seized by a wave of sorrow when he looked toward his brother's bedroom.

"Call the police and tell them to go to Dolly's trailer. Speak slow, try to change your voice, then hang up," Lucas said pointing to a telephone next to the couch.

"I don't know if I can," Scabby said.

"You can. Your voice is your gift. You're a great actor, pretend. You can do it," Lucas said. Scabby walked across the room and touched the phone. He glanced back at Lucas looking for reassurance. Lucas nodded his head.

Scabby picked up the receiver, dialed the police station and delivered the message in a feminine falsetto voice, with just a hint of a southern accent. Gone were the slang and twisted phrases of his normal banter.

Lucas was surprised and watched him as he spoke. There was a grace, a lilt, a confidence in how Scabby delivered the news to the police.

"God, you sounded just like girl," Lucas said when Scabby finished, "Amazing." Scabby grinned at him, his face briefly turning red.

"I just watch a lot of television is all," he said, "Speakin' of which…" Scabby reached over and turned on the black and white television sitting on the coffee table in front of them. He found the six o'clock news channel from Missoula. The lead story was from Sunnyside, Montana.

A somber gray haired reporter stood with a microphone near the gate of the Bull Run mine parking lot. Behind him a crowd moved slowly about, blurred together in a mass of blue and white colors.

"We don't know exactly how many miners were working at the time of the discovery of the fire, but estimates are as high as one hundred. On a normal weekend that number could be less than twenty. With an impending strike, workers were apparently trying to earn some additional pay. Strikes in this area have been known to go on for over a year."

"Congressman Temple is said to be en route to Sunnyside, apparently to offer any help and assurances that he can. He had already planned to attend a meeting tomorrow with mine owners and the labor union to hopefully avert the strike."

169

Scott R. Baillie

The reporter continued to drone, giving no more details than the boys already had. Scabby turned off the television, the dimming picture tube crackled with discharging static.

"I have a screwdriver and flashlight in my truck. Let's leave the vehicle here and walk to the union hall," Lucas said. He opened the basement door and let Scabby out first. He turned the lights off as he exited. Bits of sleet began peppering his hair and face. In the distance, coming from the direction of town, Lucas heard the shrill siren sound of a police car or ambulance echoing off the mountains.

Lucas paused for a moment, exhaled deeply from his lungs and watched his breath turn into a small foggy cloud. He looked up at Cemetery Hill. Two of the crosses were dark. The center one emanated in yellow, smudged behind a light cover of fog.

CHAPTER 34

Delmer saw the motor train light first. It was dim, not from a lack of battery power, but because it was quite a distance away. Russell had to squint to see it, but its small dot appearance far down the drift brought a jump to his heart. He began circling his lamp light around the sides, top and bottom of the drift, hoping to signal whomever was running the motor. There was no sign of activity or motion, so they continued to trudge, albeit faster, toward the dim light.

"I don't think anybody saw our light," Russell said.

"Maybe," Delmer replied, "Though they could be off in a side drift down there sittin'. We need to hurry whatever we do."

The motor light became stronger and brighter as they walked. Fifty feet out the lamp was very bright, illuminating the tracks. Russell had to keep his eyes focused on the train ties, and avoided looking directly at the lamp, it was so bright.

Russell touched the side of the heavy motor battery. It was warm as if it had just been run, though there was no sign of any body else near it. Above them a ladder ran up and into the darkness. Russell shone his lamp upward. He could see nobody.

"Freddy must have tried to climb up and out," Russell said.

"That don't make much sense should you ask me," Delmer replied. "Look here," he said pointing to the floor of the motor's cab. Russell leaned over and saw several opened lunch pails. Wrappers, napkins and other remnants lay about.

"You think maybe there are others?" Russell said. Delmer was sifting through the litter.

"Think so. Look at the names on the pails. *Chrome, Little Squeaky, Picker, Grunts, Dingleberry, Pee Pee* and *Shotglass.* All them guys worked the level below, 'cept *Chrome Dome* Freddy."

Russell dug through the lunch boxes. He realized he was starving and hadn't eaten since yesterday. The miner's nicknames were well known to him. Staring at them in white enamel paint on the black metal lunch pails, he realized that he didn't know the real first names of any of them.

"Maybe we should go up after them," Russell said, "Maybe this is a way out that Freddy knows about."

"I don't think so. We climb up there, we most likely are climbin' into carbon monoxide."

"Then wait here. I'm going to go up a ways and see what I can find."

"You're injured boy. You climb up there, you most likely are gonna die. We only have one light and not enough battery juice to make it for more than another hour or two anyway."

Russell picked up the lantern batteries and lamp and said, "We need to see." He climbed onto the top of the motor battery and pulled himself up onto the ladder rungs. Delmer scrambled behind.

"Dang it boy, you got a stubborn streak," Delmer said.

The ladder was fairly dry and sturdy. Fresh clods of dirt were on most the rungs.

"They aren't that far ahead of us," Russell said.

Delmer didn't answer, but continued climbing up beneath Russell.

"Just hurry, every second counts. Don't be stoppin' and talkin'," Delmer said.

Every fifty or so feet, the ladders ended at a small platform and shifted to the opposite side of the narrow upward shaft. This prevented rocks from falling too freely or too far. Russell craned his neck backwards and stared up. They must have climbed a couple of hundred feet in very few minutes.

"There is no air movement here, Delmer," Russell said.

"Noticed that," Delmer replied, "That could be a good thing. Least if the poisoned air is up above, it ain't be pushed down on us."

"Look!" Russell had stopped and was pointing. He was still looking upward. Two stations up he saw a miners lamp light. It was hanging over the edge of one of the little platforms.

"That don't look too good. Why would they leave a lamp there?" Delmer said.

"I'll go up and see," Russell said.

"Boy, you may just be climbing into death. Use one of them self-rescuers. Get up there and get that lamp and battery. Hurry."

Russell untied the bag swinging from his belt and pulled out one of the miner's self rescuers. The metal was cold in his hands, its square hard cased aluminum shape was slightly bigger than his fist. He snapped open the top and pulled the breather and straps from inside.

Inserting the mouthpiece into his lips, he clamped his teeth around it and created a seal. Drawing air through his mouth and through the rescuer seemed easy enough, though the air seemed warm. A nose plug clamp hung from the same strap. Russell placed it to his nostrils and squeezed, sealing off any potential leaks. He felt as if he were suffocating. Delmer tapped Russell's boot.

"Breath slow, not hard. That thing will change monoxide to dioxide. That'll kill you, too. Just get up there and get back. You hear?"

Russell nodded his head and began climbing again. The air coming through the rescuer was getting hot. The mouthpiece was making him drool.

Fifty feet above, the lamp hung very still into the center of the raise. Russell turned off his makeshift lamp by unscrewing the exposed wires. The huge light went black. Enough illumination came from the lamp up above.

Five feet below the lamp Russell stopped and looked up. His chest jumped. A hand and arm were hanging from the platform as well. The thought of suffocating seemed very real. He considered climbing quickly back down the ladder into the known pure air. He looked again at the arm. It wasn't moving. He climbed the rest of the way to the platform.

Seizing the free hanging lamp, Russell swung it around. A miner lay face down on the little stage with his back toward him. The air was hot and moist. Russell knelt and reached for the shoulders of the downed man. He hesitated, moving the lantern light towards the man's head. It was Freddy. He was wearing a self rescuer. He was unconscious, but still breathing.

Russell shook Freddy, hard. He wanted to shout out the man's name, but feared for the poisonous air around him. He pressed hard on Freddy's arm again. The man stirred and fumbled with his hand to his mouth. Russell stopped him before he withdrew the rescuer. Freddy rolled onto his back and looked up at Russell. The small lamp between them illuminated the confined area. Freddy pulled his rescuer from his mouth before Russell could stop him.

"You can talk, just don't inhale," Freddy said. He inserted the rescuer back into his mouth and drew a breath. Russell stared down his nose at the self rescuer hanging from his mouth. The elastic straps were pinching behind his ears. Pulling the mouthpiece away from his teeth and face he said, "What happened to you and the others?"

"The heat got me, I think. I got dizzy. Could have been monoxide, too. I put this on after they left. The others told me to..." Freddy ran out of breath and jammed his rescuer back into his mouth, drawing deep rapid breaths.

"Can you climb down?" Russell said, pulling the rescuer from his mouth.

Freddy nodded yes.

Russell helped his boss to his feet and shuffled around him allowing him to proceed first. He adjusted Freddy's lantern and clamped it back to the man's hard hat.

Russell breathed with the rescuer again, cleared it and said, "Climb down quickly. Delmer is about two hundred feet below. I'm going up to see about the others...."

Freddy shook his head back and forth, signifying the word 'no'.

Russell nodded up and down and began climbing again. He glanced back at Freddy. He had already disappeared. Russell hoped that the man had not fallen.

The heavy lamp swinging from the tether around his neck began to flicker and dim. Russell stopped and fumbled with the wires. Still the light did not brighten. It was running out of power. He stood for a moment on another small staging area and thought about climbing back down. At this point, he was going to be in the dark in several minutes anyway. If he climbed up, he reasoned, he may find somebody else. If he didn't, he could simply climb down, an easy direction to follow. Freddy had a strong lamp. The three of them could use it to light the way. Russell continued climbing. His lamp was growing dimmer.

The ladder ended in a wide open stope. The stope had been mined out and filled with water and sand. The water had long ago drained off, leaving the ground as gray and solid as concrete.

Directly above him, another ladder started and disappeared into the dark. Russell looked around the stope. It branched off into three directions. He tried to see if any footprints had been left on the gray ground. The faint light he was carrying gave everything a tint and obscured any and all clues. He dropped to his hands and knees at the ladder and put his face very close to the ground. Small clods of brown dirt and grit smeared the concrete. Footprints.

Russell followed the boot tracks for a few feet and determined that they went down the furthest left opening in the stope. He decided to rush in that direction and see if there were any signs of the other miners.

The self rescuer was so hot he thought his gums were cracking. He had been warned that the rescuer would get heated, but that it was better to live with burnt lips than to be dead. He strode quickly down the small drift. Turning a corner the tunnel opened into a smaller stope. The room was bright with lights. The five miners were lying in various contortions on the ground. They were all dead. None of them had opened their self rescuers.

Fear tore at his guts. He wanted to scream. Seeing the twisted bodies of men that he knew, that he joked with, who teased him, who cursed him and helped him earn a living, all quiet and lifeless, was distant, something he couldn't feel or sense or touch, only see. The shadows painted from their lamps, poised and pointed in five different directions added to the eerie silence. He didn't move. He couldn't. He felt himself slowly spinning, falling, and twisting. His lamp, the makeshift lantern of batteries and a train light flickered and winked out. He dropped to his knees, unwillingly, the super heated air from the rescuer blistering his lips, lungs and tongue though he could not feel it.

Face against the concrete, Russell looked across the stope, the intertwined shadows wavered and shimmered. From their blurred grasp his mother walked towards him, younger, prettier than he had ever seen her. At first he was frightened, he knew where he was and she shouldn't be there, then she coolly touched his face with a cold damp cloth. He relaxed as she hummed a quiet song.

A noise, joyful and alive, pierced the stope as Lucas rode his bike near the back wall, balancing on the rear wheel. He was laughing and calling to Russell, telling him to get up and come play.

The cavern became simultaneously washed with the brilliant warmth of summer, the clean of winter and the fragrance of spring. It was like a new season.

A gentle kiss found his neck. A single finger slid his hair behind his ear as Lori lay down next to him and pulled his body into her arms. He smiled and reached for her. His hands melted into the smoothness of her skin, blending with her, until he could no longer see her, only sense her and feel her passion in every cell, every fiber, every thought.

He slowly closed his eyes. He heard music, giggling, singing.

Another sound, the voice of his father, warm and wonderful whispered into his ear, "*Everything is fine. You're safe,*" he said over and over, "*Daddy's here.*"

With each word the pain in his back, chest, legs and soul seeped from his body into the ground beneath him, disappearing into the dark rock.

CHAPTER 35

"I feel like a criminal, Scabby," Lucas said as the two boys walked the alleyways toward the Mineral Worker's union hall. They crossed a street and stepped onto the railroad bed. The tracks wound around behind the hall. There were no overhead lights along the way, only the diffused shadows from the city streets on the other side of the old buildings and warehouses lining the train tracks. Lucas and Scabby had played many times on these tracks as children and knew the route quite well. They led to Scabby's home to the east and west to the city park and town swimming pool. The tracks left the valley and touched the rest of the world.

"Yeah, well you are, really," Scabby replied after some thought, "You trespassed. You didn't report a crime you found. You're gonna break into a building. You didn't…"

"I get your point," Lucas snapped. Scabby quit speaking. The city streets were empty. The frozen rain had turned again to large wet snowflakes, though nothing was sticking to the ground yet. Scabby's sneakers, a bit too big for his feet, squished loud enough to caused an echo off of the old railroad warehouse to their left. He wasn't wearing socks either.

"Aren't your feet getting cold?" Lucas asked.

Scabby looked at him and shook his head, "No, not really. They are wet most of the time, so I don't think that I notice whether they are cold or not."

Lucas grimaced a little at the thought of Scabby's clammy feet. He remembered how the boy was ridiculed for wearing black socks, the only socks he owned, during PE class in the eighth grade. Lucas' mom had given Scabby several pairs of socks that Russell had outgrown or that Lucas never wore. Scabby had in turn given them to his little brothers.

"I don't want to go to jail, Luke," Scabby said. His voice was pleading and a bit childish.

"You won't. You can wait outside the union hall and keep a look out. I shouldn't be in there very long."

"What are you gonna be lookin' for anyway?" Scabby asked.

"I don't know. I'm not sure what I'll find," Lucas replied.

"You don't smell no smelter smoke do you?" Scabby said. Lucas looked again at him. Scabby's nose was sniffing the air like a mutt. His glasses were sprinkled with specks of water from melting snowflakes.

"No. They must have shut everything down. At least the union boys got their wish. No production."

"You think lots of guys are dead underground, right?" Scabby asked.

"I don't know that either. I hope not. My dad has worked on the rescue teams for years and he says that the miners are all trained on what to do if there is a fire and stuff," Lucas answered. His mind wandered back to his brother, Russell.

"I don't want Daddy to be dead. Your brother, neither," Scabby said. "I don't think I can take care of my family any better than Daddy."

"Let's just pray that they are ok. Ok?" Lucas said.

Scabby stopped. "Should we hold hands?" he said, looking at Lucas.

175

"What?" Lucas was puzzled. He stopped walking as well. The question baffled him. Scabby had his hand extended toward Lucas.

"Hold hands? Are you crazy? I'm not holding your hand," Lucas said.

"You said we should pray. We hold hands at church when we pray. Lets pray right now."

Lucas looked at his friend. The innocence of the question, the simple expression of faith and the sincerity on his face moved him. He hesitated, then stepped towards Scabby, taking his hand in his.

For a moment Lucas felt awkward, as if holding another boy's hand was a shameful event. Scabby's fingers were ice cold and rough.

Scabby bowed his head and closed his eyes. Lucas looked up and down the train tracks. The silence hung thick and dark, it was as if they were the last living members of the human species left on the earth. The wind whistled flakes of snow around them.

Lucas watched as Scabby whispered a prayer, crossing himself with his free hand. Bowing his head, he closed his eyes, and joined his friend. He had never prayed much except at church or when his family met on holidays to eat. Then it was usually some rote poem of thanks. Standing here in the damp sloppy weather, alone with Scabby, the least respected kid in school, he began to feel empty, sorrow-filled, frightened.

He began to whisper to God.

The world became still.

Lucas prayed for his brother, his parents, Heather, Heather's father, her brother and sister. He prayed for the miners and the union members and the people of the town. He began to pray for Scabby. The prayer was of thanks. It was a prayer reaching for forgiveness, for being ashamed of his friend, for having pride and arrogance around the boy. He opened his eyes and looked at his short dirty friend. Scabby was still intent in prayer, uttering his silent plea. Lucas looked at their hands, intertwined, Scabby's fingers were stubby, his palm fatter.

Scabby finished praying and lifted his face toward the sky. His cheeks were glistening with tears. He crossed himself again. Lucas stepped in front of Scabby and wrapped his arms around him, freeing their hands, hugging him, embracing him as tightly as he could, patting him on the back. Scabby's arm encircled Lucas' rib cage.

"I'm never going to call you Scabby again," he said. "You have an angel's name and a saint's heart. Thank you for being my friend, Gabriel."

Scabby stepped back, releasing himself from Lucas' arms.

"I don't know when the last time anybody called me by my real name. If you call me Gabriel, maybe everybody else will too," he said. His voice cracked, his eyes glistened, black, with wonder. He wiped his nose with his sleeves and pushed his glasses up the ridge of his nose. They looked at one another for several moments. Words were not necessary. They didn't always have to speak to know the other's thoughts.

"Let's go. The union hall is just ahead," Lucas said, "You lead and I'll follow."

Gabriel turned to the west, the wind pushing at his face. The smokestack of the smelter blinked in slow cadence near the horizon. Lucas listened to the first squishy steps of the boy's sneakers, then fell in behind him.

CHAPTER 36

The Mineral Workers Union Hall's parking lot was empty, save for one old station wagon with a flat tire. Gabriel and Lucas ran from the shadows of the alleyway and squatted near the rear of the vehicle. The city streets in front of the building were empty and wet. In the distance, to the west, the smoke stack lights winked.

"That back bathroom window is open a crack," Gabriel said, "Maybe we can climb through there." Lucas looked where Gabriel pointed. It was actually a vent window for the bathroom behind the union's business office. Although the structure was only one story tall, the window was closer to the roof than to the ground.

"One of us can, maybe, can climb in there. One of us being me that is. I don't want to hurt your feelings, but I don't think you are thin enough to squeeze through there. Follow me." Gabriel looked down his chest and sucked in his stomach. Lucas ran to the backside of the building, his friend sloshing behind him. They stopped beneath the partially opened window.

With his back against the wall, hugging the shadows, Lucas felt like he was escaping from a prison. At any moment a spotlight would strike him, followed by sirens and a volley of bullets. His heart was fluttering and the mist on his breath almost obscured his head.

"You want I should boost you up there?" Gabriel asked. Lucas looked at his friend then back up to the window. It was only a foot above them and seemed to open out with a small crank. Lucas turned and faced the wall, pressing his body against the cold bricks. He pointed his face back up towards the window. The glass in the window was the unbreakable kind with chicken wire mesh running through it.

"I don't know. There is a bar that moves the window in and out," Lucas said. "I don't know if we can get it opened far enough."

Gabriel interlocked his fingers and said, "Step in here and I can lift you up." Lucas stared at the boy's hands, they were shaking from the cold. He feared placing his cold wet shoe onto Gabriel's palms.

"You sure you can do this? You look cold." Lucas did a half-turn to face Gabriel. Melting snow dripped from the eaves of the building and splashed on the ground behind him. Gabriel was standing in a puddle of ice water.

"I ain't cold. Scared is what it is," Gabriel said.

"You're going to get frostbite," Lucas said as he placed the toe of his shoe into the cupped hands. He pushed his hand down on Gabriel's shoulder and started to step up when he felt his body being lifted swiftly. He marveled for an instant at his friend's strength. Lucas' head was immediately level with the open window. Tugging on the frame, the window opened a few inches more, then stopped. Lucas cocked his head sideways and looked into the bathroom. It was dark, but he could make out the window crank and support arms. He reached in and twisted the crank a couple of turns. The window moved out a bit more.

"I don't think I can get in there. Even I'm too big," he hush spoke to Gabriel.

"Just try. Pull yourself through. Think small," Gabriel said. There was a sound of straining in his voice.

"Think small? What are you talking about?" Lucas said, looking down at Gabriel.

"Just try to make yourself really small. It'll work. It's all in your head. Mind over matter," Gabriel replied. Lucas smirked at the insidious thought.

Gabriel began to wobble slightly as he shifted his body to shore up the weight he was holding. Lucas gripped at the window frame and pulled, lifting some of the burden from Gabriel.

"Am I too heavy?" Lucas asked.

"Not right now."

"Don't drop me."

"Don't stay there talking so much and I won't. Just try to pull yourself in."

Lucas stuck his head, neck and shoulders under the open window. He felt around the edges of the interior and found the side walls. He tried to pull himself up, but his lower back and hips became wedged between the window and the lower part of the window frame.

"I'm stuck," he said. Gabriel had let go of Lucas' feet. His legs wiggled freely in the air. Lucas imagined the police would have a very easy time apprehending him for breaking and entering. Most likely they'd find him hanging dead, his rear-end frozen, stuck in the window.

"Think smaller," Gabriel said.

"Think smaller," Lucas mumbled under his breath. The weight of his body at his hips was beginning to hurt. He was straining to keep his balance, knowing that he could slip backwards. Closing his eyes, he pulled hard again against the frame. He felt Gabriel's hands on the heels of his shoes, pushing. He slid past his groin into the bathroom, his arms pushing him up. Half his body was in the room, the other half was hanging outside. A cold draft blew up his back where his shirt had pulled from his pants.

"Your butt crack is showing," Gabriel whispered loudly.

"Ouch," Lucas moaned. The pressure on his lower back was tremendous. All of his weight was balanced on his hands and groin. His manhood was being crushed. He could care less about his exposed rear end. Wiggling his feet, he kicked himself even further into the room. The air temperature inside was warm.

"You in yet?" Gabriel said.

"Do I look in?"

"No."

Lucas' eyes adjusted to the dark of the small room. Below him he could make out the outlines of a toilet, sink and garbage can. To his left he saw a shelf, loaded with extra toilet paper, cleaning products and pornographic magazines. The air smelled a bit like pine and loaded diapers. Grabbing the shelf with his left hand, he tested its ability to hold his weight. It seemed strong enough. Silently he counted to three and used all his energy to drag himself up and onto the window ledge. His knees and shins scraped past the window and onto the window frame. He was perched inside the bathroom. The cold air outside was wafting down the back of his jeans. He reached behind himself, grasped his belt and yanked his waistband up to his hips.

For a moment he rested, then the shelf collapsed, causing his weight to shift. Wildly he grasped into the air, instinctively seeking a handhold. The cleansers, bottles and rolls of paper clattered to the tile floor of the lavatory. Lucas tumbled with them.

He wasn't hurt. He had landed on the garbage can, which had turned out to be a large plastic variety full of used paper towels. The noise of the collapsing shelf was more frightening than the fall.

"You alright?" The excited voice of Gabriel carried from the outside.

"Shhh...yes, I'm fine," Lucas said. Fumbling in his jacket pocket, he found his flashlight. "Stand guard out there. I'll come out the side entrance when I'm done," he whispered to Gabriel. He received no response and assumed that his friend had already moved away from the window.

Shaking the light, he brought it to full intensity and shone it about the room. The interior door to the office was opened slightly. Lucas could see the outline of an emergency exit sign. It's light cast enough illumination into the room that he could easily see. He stood up, adjusted his coat and pants and walked into Billy's office. A low hum buzzed from a small refrigerator near the largest of the two desks in the office. Across the room, a large upright storage cabinet stood. Near it, a row of filing cabinets, wedged side by side, pressed against the back wall.

Lucas crossed over to the nearest desk. An ashtray, filled with butts, sat on the edge. Half full coffee cups and a dozen strewn pencils covered its surface. He panned his flashlight around the desktop. Stepping around it, he sat in its chair and opened the desk drawer. This had obviously been Dolly's desk. Several women's magazines were jammed in the back of the drawer along with a tube of petroleum jelly. He scanned their headlines. Each one touted some secret to bigger breasts, better sex or confessions of prohibited passions.

Rummaging in the side drawers he found a bottle of vodka, file folders containing receipts for union dues and other business related correspondence. A plump folder with phone bills overflowed. Lucas picked it up and stared at some of the numbers. The most recent bill was several papers long. He folded one of the pages and placed it into his coat pocket and returned the folder to its previous place.

Billy's desk was set at an angle to Dolly's. Lucas walked over and sat down. Billy's chair squeaked loudly. Lucas heard himself shushing the chair as if the thing would quiet down.

The drawers to Billy's desk yielded nothing out of the ordinary. The desktop was virtually empty. A brass holder for pens and pencils, etched with the union's name, sat next to the black telephone. A picture of Billy with his kids in a motor boat, they seemed very young, stood framed on the opposing side of the desk. A large blotter with huge calendar numbers and scribbled phone notes covered most of the rest of the desktop.

He began to feel frustrated. Nothing seemed extraordinary here. This break-in was a waste of time. His heart began to sink. Standing, he moved the light across the surface of the desk one last time. The corner of a paper peaked from under the blotter. Lucas tugged at it. Lifting up the blotter, he shone his light underneath. He squinted, puzzled at what he was seeing. It was a map. A blueprinted map, perhaps three foot by three foot wide. Pushing the blotter aside he exposed the entire drawing. The map was precise, engineered in straight lines with detailed letters and angles.

Lucas shone his flashlight across the top of the paper, 'The Bull Run Mining Company, 1943 – Upper K Workings' was stenciled in blue. He returned his light to the center of the map. All of the detail was done in blue, but in the diffused light he could see that lines of black had been added, traced over the original etchings. He followed them with his light. Cryptic directions in small hand printing speckled the paper. They were done in ink, freehand, scribing a route from a central shaft to a distant one. Pulling the map closer to his face, he looked hard at the end of the black line. The color had changed. He was staring at a large red circled X at the bottom of a shaft.

The room suddenly lit up as the overhead lights snapped on. Lucas, startled, bounced back in the chair. The ballast in the lights buzzed loudly. One of the fluorescent tubes flickered, making a strobe effect.

"What the hell are you doing here?" Ernie Shaggal's body filled the doorway, his voice boomed across the room. The man was angry.

Lucas struggled for words. He could find none. He looked back at the map, then up at Ernie. He considered charging at the man, trying to get past him and make his way out of the front of the union hall, but Ernie knew him and would certainly make trouble, especially if he was responsible for all that was transpiring.

"You did it didn't you, Commissioner?" he said. Ernie had not moved and still blocked the door. Lucas tried to glare at Ernie, hoping that he might intimidate the older man. It did not seem to have an effect.

"Did what?" Ernie said sarcastically, "I'm calling the cops you little punk. Don't move. I'm going to toss your can in jail." Ernie stepped towards Dolly's desk and reached for the phone. Obedient to adults since he was a small child, Lucas struggled with disobeying Ernie.

"You started the mine fire, or had Billy do it, didn't you? You wanted the mine shut down." Lucas was still seated. He could feel his heart in his mouth. The back of his throat was dry. Pissing Ernie off might not be a good idea, but if the Commissioner had anything to do with the fire and thought that Lucas had found out, maybe he could have some leverage.

Ernie stopped dialing the phone and sat the receiver back into its cradle. His back was turned slightly toward Lucas. The nub of a cigar clung to the side of his mouth. Lucas couldn't tell if it was lit or not.

"I have no idea what you are talking about, kid," Ernie said, again with sarcasm. "What are you looking at?" He started walking towards Lucas. Jumping back, Lucas pulled the map to his chest and picked a letter opener off the desk.

"Billy started the fire for you didn't he? I heard you last night on the phone at the S&S. I saw you with Dolly. I talked to her. You killed her. I know what's going on." Ernie stepped closer. The man's eyes were piercing in anger. Lucas moved away from him backing against the wall.

"You don't have any idea what you are saying, you little bastard. Give me that paper." Ernie was turning red. His cheeks had small broken veins in them that were actually a deep violet color. He was wheezing around his cigar, partially breathing through his nose. The fat man's face was sweating, he was seething and still blocking Lucas' exit.

Lucas stared hard at Ernie and waved the letter opener in a threatening manner. Ernie's expression changed to a sinister grin.

"You gonna try and take a poke at me with that you wimp? Here, try this." Ernie reached into his pocket and pulled out the revolver Georgie had given him earlier. He pointed it at Lucas. "Now put that pathetic knife down and give me that damn map. I'm tired of screwing around here."

Lucas stared at the open end of the barrel. Ernie was no longer smiling. Dropping the opener, it bounced off the desk and onto the floor with a metallic clatter. Lucas placed the map on the desk and stepped backwards.

A noise broke the strained silence. Lucas and Ernie both looked toward the office door at the same time. Gabriel stood in the entrance, squinting into the light.

"Run, Gabriel," Lucas shouted as he jumped onto the desk and threw himself at Ernie. Gabriel dropped forward to the floor instead of fleeing. The pistol fired as it dislodged from the Commissioner's hand and tumbled to the ground. Ernie tripped backwards and fell near the storage locker. Lucas crawled across the floor toward the gun. He felt Ernie grab his ankles and begin pulling him backwards. Lucas' shoe slipped off. Ernie clung to his sock.

Gabriel belly crawled across the room, retrieved and slid the gun to Lucas. Rolling onto his back, Lucas cocked the hammer on the revolver and pointed it at Ernie. The Commissioner, leaning forward on his knees, released him and dropped his hands to his sides. The stogey was still clenched in his teeth.

"Shoot me, you little bastard," Ernie said, opening his arms exposing his broad chest. Huge sweat rings soaked his shirt. Lucas scooted across the floor on his back and pulled himself to his feet, keeping the gun pointed at Ernie.

"I'm not afraid to shoot you," Lucas said, lying. He felt the fear rising in him again. "Get up and get in that chair." Lucas motioned the gun at Billy's desk. Ernie grunted as he lifted himself to his feet, using the corner of the desk for balance. Lucas heard the bones in Ernie's back and knees pop. Ernie walked to Billy's chair and sat down. The map lay before him. He stared at it, then looked up at Lucas.

"You think I set Billy up? To start the fire? Come on, kid, I'm a lot of things, but that is a stretch even for me." Ernie stuck his fingers into the pencil holder and pulled out a matchstick, struck it on the corner of the desk and ignited his cigar.

Gabriel walked over to Lucas and said, "Should I call the police?"

"Not yet. I want to hear what Ernie has to say." Lucas moved closer to Commissioner, keeping the pistol even with the man's head. Gabriel stayed right next to him.

"Yeah, I think you did," Lucas said, "I think you are behind a lot of things. You suck the people of this town for everything they have, steal their dreams, their money. Anything you want, you take."

"It's always about money. No matter who you are, kid. Don't forget that. Hell, you make it sound like a bad thing." Ernie folded his arms across his chest and leaned back in the chair. Stray cigar ashes dropped onto the collar of his shirt.

"You still didn't answer me. Did you put Billy up to setting the fire?" The fear was slipping inside of him as he spoke. Ernie did not appear to be very threatening.

"No."

"I don't believe you."

"You don't have proof either. All you have is a story of breaking into the union hall. I can take this map and show it to the cops and tell them Billy was behind it." Ernie spoke nonchalantly and stopped looking at Lucas.

Ernie tipped the chair forward, picked up the map and stared at it. Lucas struggled for his next move, his next words. Ernie placed the map back down on the desk. He stood up and walked towards Lucas and Gabriel. Both boys stepped backward. Lucas extended the gun straight out from his shoulders. Ernie was now less than five feet away.

"Think about it, kid. You shoot me, you go to jail. I walk out of here, you go to jail. Either way, you're fresh meat. The juvenile folks at the courthouse will get to know you. Nobody screws with me, but I can assure you, those nasty teen thugs in the State lock up will certainly be screwing you. They like pretty boys." Ernie extended his hand, "Give me the gun and I'll let you leave. This will be the end of it."

"I can't let you get away with this," Lucas said. He could feel hot tears filling his eyes.

"I told you, punk, I did nothing. To be honest, I'm as shocked as you are. Billy pulled some stuff on me and I intend to find out who helped him. Give me the gun. This is the last time I ask." Ernie was two feet away. The barrel of the revolver was pointed directly at his chest. Lucas looked at his hands encircling the grip and trigger. They were shaking. Ernie took the barrel into his own hand and raised it to his face. Lucas applied pressure to the pistol grip and trigger.

"Come on! Shoot! It's your last chance to be a big man," Ernie said as he moved his nose tip to the end of the gun barrel. Lucas could smell the hot smoke from the cigar.

Lucas and Gabriel stood shoulder to shoulder looking at the Commissioner. Lucas released the revolver and dropped his hands to his sides.

"I hope this doesn't mean you won't vote for me," Ernie said as he turned the gun back around and pointed it at the boys. "I changed my mind. I think we'll all take a ride in my car. Please lead the way." Ernie waved the gun toward to office door.

"You said you'd let us go," Gabriel said.

"Sometimes, you gotta lie to get what you need or want," Ernie replied.

Gabriel walked ahead of Lucas. Behind them, Lucas could hear Ernie breathing and wheezing. As they exited the office, Ernie turned off the light switch and closed the door.

The interior of the union hall was large and empty. The clicking of Ernie's hard soled shoes echoed across the open space. Gabriel stopped at the partially opened side door.

"My car is right outside. Let's not be too hasty. You two will get in through the driver's door. Skinny there can drive." Ernie stopped speaking abruptly.

"Damn," he said, pausing again, "Shorty, go back and get that map." Ernie had pointed the gun at Gabriel and nodded back toward Billy's office. "Hurry up."

Gabriel ran back to the office and reappeared almost instantly, the map fluttering in his hands. He handed it to Ernie then walked back over to Lucas.

"You don't say much do you kid?" Ernie said to Gabriel.

"Got nothin' to say really."

"You're in as much trouble as your pal here, you know that right? Course you didn't break in, but I'm sure that the judge will understand when I tell him what really happened. You were standing watch, weren't you?"

"Yes, sir."

"That's what I thought. Not much of a good scout though. You didn't see me walk right in here." Ernie tilted the gun barrel downward and scratched at his groin.

"I was peeing."

"Peeing?" Ernie began laughing. Lucas looked over at Gabriel.

"Peeing?" Lucas whispered. Gabriel shrugged his shoulders.

"I saw the side door open when I stepped around the building. I just assumed that you came over and unlocked it," Gabriel said. Ernie motioned for them to continue walking.

Gabriel pushed the door completely open. Cold air blushed their cheeks as they crossed the parking lot. It was snowing again. Ernie's car was behind the building.

"Drop it!" A voice shouted from the shadows just beyond the front of the Cadillac. Ernie spun in the direction of the words. Gabriel and Lucas, seeing the distraction, bolted down the alley. A shot was fired. Then another. Lucas thought that Ernie was firing at them. The boy's continued to run and dropped behind the disabled station wagon.

Looking over the car hood, Lucas saw Ernie scrambling at the door of his car. Another shot rang. Lucas saw the white gunpowder flash coming from the bushes. Somebody was shooting at the Commissioner. Ernie fired back at the shadows, pulled the car door open and started the engine. His tires spun backwards on the asphalt. Sliding sideways, he swung the car around and shot out into the street and veered down toward the freeway.

Aimel Merrick, the policeman, ran from the shadows, crouched and fired one more shot at the speeding car. Lucas and Gabriel stayed hidden. Officer Merrick stood up and turned down the alley, pistol still drawn.

"Come out here boys. If you have any weapons, you better drop them."

"What should we do, Lucas," Gabriel said.

"Lucas? You never call me Lucas."

"I know," he said. Gabriel was smiling.

Raising their hands in the air, both stood and walked around the car. Aimel recognized them both and holstered his gun.

"Mr. Kaari what are you doing? Put your hands down." Lucas complied and lowered them.

"We, I, us… we think that Ernie started the fire at the Bull Run Mine. We think he put Billy Murphy up to it. Show him the map." Lucas nudged Gabriel's arm with his elbow. Gabriel withdrew the map from the inside of his jacket where he had stashed it during their run.

Explaining the circumstances leading up to their break-in of the union hall, Lucas detailed his conclusions.

"Let's go back inside," Aimel said, leading the boys to the side door of the union hall. Lucas was surprised that nobody seemed to have noticed the abbreviated gun battle.

"I wonder why nobody called for help or reported what just happened," Lucas said.

"Everyone is at the mine or in their homes listening to the radio. Its very late as well. I just happened to have seen the light come on in the hall and saw Ernie's car. He was acting odd earlier at Billy's house. I figured something was going on. Then I heard a muffled shot."

Inside the hall, Aimel phoned the County Sheriff's office and reported the gunfire exchange with Ernie. Lucas listened as the officer spoke. Not once did he mention Lucas or Gabriel.

"How come you didn't say anything about us?" Lucas asked.

"Don't worry. I will. I've just learned that you can't really trust anybody that is elected in this county. Ernie seems to be their best friend. I'm not sure if I believe your conclusions, but I don't want to jeopardize you either. You better call your folks though." Aimel handed Lucas the telephone.

Lucas dialed his house and spoke to his mother. He didn't tell her about the union hall or Ernie, only saying that he would be bringing Gabriel home later.

She had been worried, she said, about him, that his father would be going back underground with the rescue team and wanted to see him before he left. Lucas didn't like the idea that his dad wanted to see him. It might be the last time.

"Does Dad have to go back underground? Can't he send some other guys? He's more valuable above ground right?"

"Lucas," his mother said softly.

"Yes?" Lucas replied.

"Your father wants to find your brother and bring him home."

They hung up the phone. Aimel looked at Lucas. He had been studying the map.

"I used to work the mines with Russell, right?" Aimel said.

"I remember something like that. Why?" Lucas replied.

"Look at this map. This trail, this dark line, leads back into a sealed off area. Nobody worked back there for years. And look at this. Here is Billy's handwriting on this phone message. Here, on the map, these direction notes, it is different. It isn't his."

"Could be Ernie's."

"Maybe. But doubtful. If Ernie put somebody up to this, he wouldn't want his fingers anywhere on it."

"You don't trust him either do you?"

"No. Not really. One of the reasons I became a policeman here was to see if I could clean up some of the dirty stuff in this town. Each time I find something bad, I find Ernie. Or at least a telltale sign of him."

"If he didn't do it or know about it, then who did it?"

"That is a good question. You boys go home. I'm taking this map to the rescue station at the mine. If this is where the fire is, they need to know. Your breaking in here might actually have been a good thing."

"What about Ernie," Lucas said.

"Ernie? Screw him," Aimel answered as he patted Lucas' shoulder. Gabriel stuck his thumbs into the waistband of his pants and shifted slightly causing his shoes to squish.

Aimel walked them out of the union hall and pulled the door closed. Lucas and Gabriel watched him speed away towards the mine in his police car.

The boys began their walk back down the train tracks. As the fear and momentum of the past hour ebbed, Lucas' mind began to focus. He was no longer shaking. The cold air on his face felt good. The bruises from the weekend didn't seem to hurt as bad. He drew big breaths, filling his chest and exhaling clouds of fog.

"I seen a map like that before," Gabriel said.

"What?" Lucas replied with surprise. He stopped and turned towards his friend. Across town on the cemetery hill he could see the glow of the crosses.

"Yeah. I seen it a long time ago. Daddy got one from the mine engineers. I used to ask him all the time where the Suck Tunnel up on Cemetery Hill went. I guess he started to really wonder, too."

"Where did it go?" Lucas asked as he tucked his cold hands under the armpits of his coat. His elbow was throbbing where he hit it during his fall at the union hall.

"Down in them old workings on the other side. It used to be a fresh air shaft."

CHAPTER 37

Delmer felt a few grains of sand rattle off his rain slicker. Looking up the ladder, he could see the outline of a solitary miner, a hundred or so feet up, descending.

In the darkness he had prayed for Russell. The young man was like a bull, he thought, strong and stubborn. Any other man would have died during the previous few hours, but somehow Russell kept finding it in himself to move on. There was a desire for life in him, a challenge to beat the devil.

Delmer had never really known Russell, at least not very well. Certainly his son and Russell's little brother were friends, which usually was the only topic of conversation between them. A lot of the other miners didn't seem to like Russell that much, given his status as a company man's son, but Delmer knew what it was like to be despised for no reason. The darkness of these mines seemed to create a similar darkness in the hearts of the men that worked here.

"Boy? Is that you?" Delmer shouted up the raise. The miner was about twenty feet up.

"No, it ain't. Its Freddy." The voice was garbled.

Delmer squinted as several grains of sand and mud bounced off his face. Freddy's boots stepped onto the last wooden rung. Delmer extended his hand to the miner and helped him jump to the tracks.

"Where's the boy?" Delmer asked. His concern was evident, his voice a bit higher pitched than usual. Freddy turned around and faced him. There was a tremendous amount of sweat rolling from his brow, beneath his miner's hat. Freddy's cheeks and chin were covered with dirt and mud. In his teeth, he clenched a self rescuer although he was freely breathing around its mouthpiece. Delmer felt the muscles in his chest tighten. He looked up the raise again and stared into the darkness.

"He went up to the stope. That's where the other boys headed," Freddy said. There was no air pressure behind his words. The miner was apparently exhausted. Delmer became concerned that the man might have a heart attack. Freddy was not doing well at all. The pallor of his skin was ghostly white. Delmer had seen heat stroke victims change the same color before they collapsed.

"Why'd you let him go, Freddy? It weren't a good idea. That boy was almost dead when he started climbin' up there."

"I didn't let him do anything, nipper. He found me collapsed and sent me down here. He shouldn't have gone up, but I couldn't stop him. Damn fool."

"Climbing out of here wasn't that great of an idea, if you ask me," Delmer said. "Them workings are still tied to the main mine. That boy knew better. I told him myself. I should go up and find him. Gimme your lamp," Delmer said, reaching for Freddy's lantern.

"No," Freddy said, "The boy is dead, just like them other kids. No sense in you climbing to your death, too. We need to get out of here. Together. I can't make it by myself."

Delmer stared hard at Freddy. The pain and torment he had suffered for the past decade could all be traced back to this man.

And now here he sits, almost dead, asking for help, on the slight chance he might live. Maybe he left Russell up there and took off to save his own hide. Men do cowardly things when faced with death, he thought.

Ten years ago he had killed a part of Delmer, the peace of mind that a man needs to enjoy life. Delmer didn't choose the lot he had been handed, but he had tried to make a good life for his wife and kids. But Freddy, in his bravado and his blind union pride, had turned Delmer's life upside down. Delmer cleaned up other people's sewage because he didn't have good enough hands to be a miner any more. Freddy went on to be a big shot, primarily because he stood so firm against men that differ with the union.

If Delmer hated anyone, it was Freddy. He knew it was sinful to pray for another man's death, but he had done it anyway, figuring that God would exact some revenge for him. After all, didn't he follow God and try to do the right things? God should owe him one, right?

"I should just sit here and watch you die," Delmer finally said. Sitting down on the train motor, he removed his gloves and picked up a water bottle that sat on the driver's seat. Freddy walked to the side of the motor and leaned against the battery.

"You'll die too, then," Freddy said. He wheezed as he spoke. Reaching his hand toward Delmer, he motioned for a sip of water. Delmer passed him the water jug. Freddy tipped his head back and drank.

"It's ok to die. If you are ready. I've been ready for a long time," Delmer said. His assurance at the acceptance of his mortality was real. His faith that there existed a better life beyond here had been the sole factor in his ability to step forward into each new day. His concern for his wife and children and their need of him kept him alive, kept him working in these dank tunnels.

"If you have been so ready, then why would you come back here and try to find me and the others? It wasn't for Russell's sake. It had to be for yours. Maybe you thought we'd all get out of here alive together, instead of dying in the dark."

"I come back here because the boy wanted to save you," Delmer said.

"Then give the boy his dying wish, Delmer," Freddy replied. His eyes were fixed and hard. Delmer could feel the contempt the man still had for him.

"I'd trade places with that boy, if I could," Delmer said. "At least there'd be joy for both of us. I don't want to save you, you don't deserve it."

Freddy pushed himself away from the motor and stood in front of Delmer.

"I don't," he said. Freddy wiped his nose with his gloved hand and adjusted his miner's hat. He had stopped sweating and seemed to be recovering a bit. His breathing was almost normal. "I don't deserve your help. You're right. I should be dead up there in that stope and that young man should be here trying to get out of this God awful place. But that ain't how it is. I'm here right now and so are you. We don't know why it's us. Why, Delmer, why do any of us go through the things we do?"

"You broke me bad, years ago," Delmer said. "I didn't do nothin' to you and yours. But you chose to hurt me and doin' that you hurt my entire family. It ain't fair that I should be the one that has to get you out of here alive."

"You scabbed. You crossed the line. What was I supposed to do? If I hadn't done something, who knows who else would have broke the strike." Freddy was shouting, the sweat began to reappear on his forehead.

Delmer jumped to the ground from the motor and stood face to face with Freddy.

"Don't you get it? It is about having a choice or no choice," Delmer said. "I had my reasons for crossing the line. They had nothing to do with you. Yet you chose to make it a personal matter. This is just a job, it ain't anything more. Because one man needs to eat doesn't mean that another man needs to decide that he can't. This world is bad enough without men creating situations that don't mean nothing."

"It was the principle of the matter," Freddy said defiantly.

"Principle? It's prejudice. Hating one man for his thoughts, for who he is and what he does is nothin' more. You hatin' me because of what I done has no principles. It's just evil and you are an evil man."

Freddy stood for a long time looking at Delmer.

"Then I'm sorry Delmer. Is that what you want to hear? I'm sorry," Freddy said.

"I don't need no apology. Ain't no apology gonna change neither of us, or anything what has happened," Delmer replied.

"Probably not. But what we do from here on out will change us both, don't you think?" Freddy said.

Delmer turned his back to Freddy and stared down the pitch black drift. His shadow cast off into the dark. He turned slowly around and stepped toward Freddy, who was leaning against the motor again.

"Lets get on the motor and find our way back to the old workings. I think I can find a fresh air shaft. We'll probably die there, but at least we might have a better chance," Delmer said.

Freddy extended his hand to Delmer, slowly. There was relief and resignation in the gesture. Delmer looked at the hand and clutched it in his own. He shook it gently, withdrew his grip and stepped onto the motor's cab. Freddy walked to the front and sat on the battery. Looking up the raise one last time, Delmer whispered a final goodbye to Russell.

The wheels of the motor spun several times before they found traction. Sparks cast from them onto the sides of the drift. The engine's light pierced the dark as they sped down the tracks.

CHAPTER 38

Heather and her little brother and sister were sitting in the living room at Lucas' house. Walking in the front door, Lucas heard Heather's voice and the clamor of her young siblings arguing. Gabriel walked in behind him and closed the door. From the hallway, he could see into the family room. His mother sat with Heather on the couch and the two children were on the floor fussing over a jig saw puzzle.

"Where's Dad?" Lucas asked as he walked onto the carpeted floor. His mother looked up at him. Heather, her face flushed from recent tears, smiled weakly at him. He stepped over the fragments of puzzle and sat next to her.

"Your father returned to the mine. He couldn't wait," Heather said.

"Couldn't wait? It was only a half hour…." Lucas felt panicked.

"He said to call him at his office if you got in during the next few minutes. He said he was sorry."

"Any more news?" he said.

"No. Nothing."

Lucas removed his coat and dropped it onto the arm of the couch. The house was too warm.

The phone rang. Lucas jumped at the sound and hurried into the dining room and lifted the phone from its cradle. The smell of stew cooking touched his nose.

"Hello," he said.

"Lucas?" He immediately recognized his father's voice

"Dad, I need to see you before you go underground. Scabby, I mean Gabriel, and I found something. A map. Officer Aimel has it. There's lots to tell."

"He is here son. He showed me and told me about the union hall." There was a strain in his father's voice, unusual for even the tenseness of this moment. Lucas thought for a moment that his father was hurt and angry with him. The image of him breaking into a building must be too much like the issues he had had with Russell. He felt sorry for a moment that he had done it.

"Son, you need to bring Heather up here," his father said.

"What? Why?" Lucas asked. The concern in his father's voice meant only one thing and his request to have Heather brought to him confirmed his fear.

"Just bring her up to the main office by the portal. Your mother can stay with the little ones. I'll be here waiting for you." His father didn't even say goodbye, but abruptly disconnected the phone.

Lucas hung up and walked back into the living room. Heather was leaning her head into Mrs. Kaari's shoulder. Lucas sat next to his mother and looked over at Heather. Her eyes had been closed but were slowly opening. He fixed his gaze on her face. She was beautiful, even through the strain and the emotion. Their eyes met. He knew that Heather was reading his thoughts. Tears began to fill the bottom of her eyelids.

"Dad wants us to come to his office, Heather." His mother turned toward him. The questioning look on her face, full of fear and uncertainty, crushed him. Gabriel walked over and knelt down with the children. He began placing pieces into the puzzle.

Heather reached for Lucas' hand. His fingers met hers. Mrs. Kaari placed her arms around their shoulders and pulled them toward her chest. All three of their heads touched.

"I'll get your coat," Mrs. Kaari said to Heather. She stood up and walked toward the hallway. Heather wiped the trailing tears from her cheekbones. Her brother and sister, oblivious to her fear, played with Gabriel, who was being as distracting as possible with them.

Lucas slipped his arm around Heather's shoulder and held her close. Mrs. Kaari returned and handed Heather her jacket, the same one she had worn to the cemetery. Lucas lightly kissed Heather and stood up, offering her open coat sleeve to her.

"We are going to take a ride. You want to come along, Gabriel?" Lucas said, trying to sound nonchalant, hoping that the kids wouldn't ask questions. Gabriel glanced up at him and nodded.

"You kids finish this puzzle before I get back, ok?" Gabriel said to the children. They giggled an affirmative. Gabriel stood up and walked toward the hallway.

Mrs. Kaari hugged Heather again and helped her zip her jacket. Lucas took her hand and led her to the front door. Gabriel was already outside looking up at the evening sky. His breath was misty and there were tears on his cheeks, too.

The drive through town, usually short, usually familiar, seemed far different than before. Seated between Gabriel and Lucas, Heather held on firmly to Lucas' hand, even as he shifted gears. The town looked different, deserted, vacant and lifeless. There were no other cars, no one walking. It was as if the city had stopped existing. Lucas looked at the uptown buildings and bars. Some had lights on, but no patrons could be seen through their windows. Even the alley to the whorehouse was empty, though a solitary red light shone from an upstairs window.

The Mineral Hotel, the last vestige of the prosperous founding days of the city, was crumbling. Lucas had never noticed how bad the place really looked. It had a sense of decay and death around it, even though it was the likely conception place of Lori and Russell's baby. The baby nobody knew about yet. Maybe the baby nobody would want.

Rain mixed with snow began to fall hard onto the windshield. The windows of the truck began to fog. Lucas turned on the defrost fan and dropped his hand into Heather's lap. She encircled his fingers with her hands. They were as cold as the air outside.

The mine yard was crammed with cars, news crews, miners, and dozens of other people. Lucas recognized many of the faces as he drove by. Some of them he had seen earlier at church, some came into the store, others were familiar, images from his past, that just seemed to have always been part of his memory. There were no pickets or signs of the strikers. All the anger seemed to have turned to sorrow. The crowd was moving very slowly. Lucas didn't even see one beer.

Some of the reserved parking spots near the main office were still open. Some of them were filled with the cars of the more important mine people, others had TV crew vehicles. Lucas found one marked Kaari and parked in it. His father must have walked to the mine.

The mine office sat directly in front of the main portal to the Bull Run. Normally, somebody driving up to the office could see the mine opening. Over the

191

years, the company had made the opening very gothic looking, with ornate wording etched into concrete. When he was a child, Lucas used to stare at the lettering and sound out each letter. One of the first words he learned to spell was 'bull'. The portal was totally obscured by a huge gathering of people. The railroad tracks created a natural partition in the crowd. Every head was turned, looking into the mouth of the mine.

Lucas, Heather and Gabriel stepped from the truck into the night air. Heavy snow flakes began to clump into their hair. Lucas brushed away a few flakes, then turned his attention to the crowd. Silently they walked to the main office door. A security person greeted them.

"Lucas, your father is upstairs. He said for you three to go on up," the watchman said. There was a telling tone to the man's voice. He looked at Heather in an odd way, first with concern, then as if he thought his mind would betray him, he looked away. Opening the door, he let the three teens walk past him.

The interior of the office was warm and dry. The side windows of the entrance looked directly onto the portal tracks and the crowd. Lucas led the way and climbed the stairs to his father's office, a trip he had made a thousand times since he was a little boy. The room at the top of the stairwell was wide open. Drafting tables, adding machines, computer consoles with ticker tape and various office supplies were scattered haphazardly across the interior. Mr. Kaari's office was to the rear. His window looked straight down at the portal of the mine.

Several men were huddled around one of the drafting tables. All of them were wearing miner's hats and had slickers that said 'Mine Rescue' on them. The safety engineer was pointing to some scattered drawings. Several of the miners were arguing with one another, although Lucas could not make out what they were saying.

He held Heather's hand firmly. She was shaking. Gabriel had taken her other hand. Together they walked into Mr. Kaari's office.

Officer Aimel Merrick sat in a chair next to Jonathan Kaari's desk. Mr. Kaari was on the telephone, his back to the door. The phone had no dial on it. Instead it was labeled 'Hoist Room'.

Jonathan apparently saw the reflection of his son and companions in the darkened window. He turned around and nodded to them. Aimel had the map Lucas and Gabriel had found earlier. Several new lines had been drawn onto it. Aimel was wearing a mine rescue slicker as well. Jonathan hung up the phone and walked around the desk. Without speaking, he embraced Heather and held her to his chest. Lucas released her hand as did Gabriel. Mr. Kaari had known Heather since the moment she was born and had treated her like the daughter he never had. He always acted a bit nervous around her. But now there was a deliberate certainty to him.

"They found your father, honey. He's dead. He was sitting with three other men eating lunch and apparently was overcome by carbon monoxide. He didn't even know what happened. I'm so sorry." Jonathan's face was drawn. Lucas could see no life in his father's eyes, only fatigue and emptiness.

Lucas was shocked. Heather didn't move. Her eyes were tightly closed as she gripped Mr. Kaari's shirt. Aimel stood up and walked over to her and began to rub her back. The room felt hot, damp, close. Gabriel shifted from one foot to the other, nervously. The fate of his father could very well be declared next.

"We'll do whatever we can to help you," Jonathan said. He buried his cheek into the girl's hair. Lucas watched as Heather began to shake. First her shoulder, then her full body.

"Lucas," Heather said, "Please, Lucas…" She began to cry. Turning from Mr. Kaari she stumbled towards Lucas. Embracing her, she collapsed into his arms, the weight of her body, pulling him forward. From the depths of her soul, she began to wail. Lucas held her as tightly as he could. The shrill sound of her cries, the rendering of her heart, the pressure and the sorrow rose from inside her and filled his ears.

He didn't know what to say, or whether he should say anything. His love for her was not just about passion. He loved her on a very simple level. They were bonded as children, raised as siblings, reared to respect and love their families. He knew her, knew her desires, her wants, her needs. He respected her. But most of all, she was his friend. Maybe his best friend. In this moment fraught with all the agony a child will ever know, the tragic death of a parent, he knew that he was her connection to life. The one that she would need the most, the one that she would adhere to. Where she no longer had strength, he would need to be her support. He would need to lead her, take whatever steps were necessary to see that she was safe. She would have done the same for him.

He kissed her forehead and brushed the hair from her face. His own heart, surrendering to her pain, broke. His throat choked and a flood of hot tears washed his face and ran into her hair. The room felt awkward. The pain of the moment, witnessed by those who themselves feared the death of the ones they loved.

Several of the men from the outer office had gathered at the door. Lucas knew each one of them could very well feel the same loss. Seeing her fall, her world imploding, may just be the beginning for them all. He held her, with all his strength. He tried not to cry much, not to add to her burden, but he could not contain himself.

Vernon McKenzie was a good man, a great father and center of his daughter's world. Now he was gone. She was left with the remnants of a family that had seen its soul disappear when Mrs. McKenzie died. All that remained was Heather and the lives of the two little children. All that remained was the foundation of family and friends. Lucas felt a part of both of these things.

"Where is he," she finally said. Her words were so muted, uttered under her breath and with a raspy throat, that they almost could not be heard. She lifted her head from Lucas' chest and looked back towards Mr. Kaari. She cleared her throat and asked again.

"They are bringing him out. His body…he will be downstairs in a few minutes."

"I want to see him," she said.

"Ok," Jonathan answered.

"What about the others?" she asked. "Who are they? Who did he die with?"

"A couple of his apprentices and a track repairman. Looks like they might have been playing poker, too." Jonathan was deliberate in not naming the other dead miners. Heather smiled for an instant.

"Playing poker? He said gambling was a sin," she chuckled a little as she spoke, drawing breath through her nose, catching her tears. Her face returned to a sadden pinch as she began to well up. Lucas found a tissue in his coat pocket and offered it to her. Gabriel walked over to Mr. Kaari.

"What about my daddy? Any word on him?" Gabriel asked. His vocal tone was strong, bracing.

"No. We aren't sure where he is," Jonathan answered, gripping Gabriel's shoulder.

"I think I know where he is," Gabriel said.

Jonathan looked at him and furled his eyebrows.

"You think you know where he was working? Did he say something?"

"No. Nothing like that. I just think I know what he would do in an emergency like this. Come and look at this map."

Gabriel walked over to the maps scattered on Jonathan's desk. He slid his fingers over the drawings and moved them to the furthest left edge of the paper.

"Daddy has a map like this, see. When I was little, he told me that if he ever wanted to sneak home he could climb out the Suck Tunnel up behind Cemetery Hill. I knew he was joking, but he used to say it a lot."

"Suck Tunnel?" Jonathan said.

"Well, that's what we called it. Daddy said that it was an old ventilation shaft or something. When me and Lucas were little, we used to go up there and throw leaves into it. It was like a vacuum. Didn't know where they went. Daddy said that a long time ago, it was used for underground air or something."

Jonathan left the room and returned with several other maps. They were larger than the one in front of Aimel and Gabriel.

"This map is from the original drawings done when the old workings were first cut. Where is this Suck Tunnel?"

Gabriel traced his finger again across the surface of the map. The lines were faded, but some of the above ground geography was listed.

"I don't see no cemetery on here," Gabriel said.

"No. You wouldn't. The cemetery probably came in about the time those tunnels were cut. Could this be it?" Mr. Kaari pointed to a thin line that ran down a good portion of the map.

"Maybe. Is that back behind the cemetery?"

Jonathan retrieved another map from the exterior office. Several of the rescue workers were gathered around the maps as Mr. Kaari laid them out.

"It looks like it is behind Brown's Point. That is the original name of cemetery hill. Supposedly this area was sand filled. There really shouldn't be any access back there. But you said there was air being drawn into it?"

"Yes sir."

Jonathan turned to the senior safety officer.

"Take a crew, a truck, rescue equipment and rappelling gear up to Brown's Point. I don't want you going deep, just go back and see what you can find. If this is true, if the air is being drawn back there, we might just find some of those guys alive."

The mine safety men rushed from the office. Lucas could hear their heavy boots echoing down the steps.

The Hoist Room phone rang. Mr. Kaari picked it up, had a brief conversation consisting of two words, 'yes' and 'ok'. He hung up.

"We need to go downstairs. They'll be there in a minute," he said. Mr. Kaari picked up his rain slicker and turned towards Lucas. He walked over to him and hugged him.

"Son, I need to go find your brother. Just know one thing," Jonathan said.

"Yes," Lucas answered.

"You are my world. My sons, my family. You mean everything to me. Don't forget it, ok?" He pulled Lucas' head to his chest, placed his hand on the side of his cheek and kissed him on his crown. He could hear his father's heartbeat.

Lucas knew how hard those words were for his father to say. Tough and insensitive to most of the issues in life, his dad was never open in his affections. He often spoke in the third person, 'we love you', 'we all care', but rarely said how he felt. He remembered as a little boy that his father used to kiss him goodnight, every night. He never said anything when he kissed his sons. Words weren't really needed. He couldn't remember the last time his father had kissed him. He hugged his father tightly around the ribs.

"Be careful, Dad," he said. "I love you." Jonathan kissed Lucas' head again.

Mr. Kaari was already wearing his mining boots. The self contained breathing apparatus he would use was sitting in the security office downstairs. He had folded the maps and placed them in his rain slicker.

The crowd outside near the portal had grown larger. Word apparently had spread that some bodies had been found. Mr. Kaari stepped out of the door first. Several flash bulbs blinked quickly and a dozen people began speaking at once. Mr. Kaari answered several of them, then pushed through the crowd, followed by Lucas, Heather and Gabriel.

The snow flakes were drier now and beginning to stick on the ground. Lucas held Heather close, protecting her from the wind and snow. The crowd was silent. A few stray camera flashes hit them.

Standing a dozen feet from the portal, Lucas watched how the crowd parted when his father came near. His stature, his presence, his command of the mine yard was obvious. Lucas had never thought of his father as a leader, but here, at this time, he was truly the one in charge.

Peering into the dark of the tunnel, Lucas could see the far distant sparks of the overhead trolley line that controlled the main line motors. A signal light above the portal turned red signifying that a train was heading their way. The crowd became absolutely still. On the opposite side of the train tracks, a TV crew from Missoula had focused their camera down toward the portal as well. Lucas could heard the snowflakes as they hit the ground. Wind pushed through the overhead power lines and made almost inaudible whistling sounds.

"Amazing Grace…How sweet the sound…that saved a wretch like me…."

A voice began singing, floating through the darkness and sorrow. It was a beautiful tenor, full of power and strength. The crowd shifted toward the sound. It was coming from directly behind Lucas. He turned. Gabriel was standing, his hands folded, face turned skyward, singing. He had removed his glasses.

"I once was lost…but now am found…was blind…but now…I see…."

Some people in the crowd began to sing with him. Gabriel raised his hands toward the sky and continued. A serene look covered him. Flakes of snow feathered his hair.

Lucas looked back down toward the portal. The flashes from the overhead line were closer and he could feel the ground vibrating. Metallic squeals from the motor's wheels echoed from the tunnel. The train was getting closer.

The sound of the hymn became loud, louder than the approaching engine. The gathering was now a choir, singing praises of hope. Lucas began to sing, so did Heather. The TV crew moved their camera from the mine opening and focused it on Gabriel. The power of his song brought an energy to the crowd. The silent agony of the moment was broken. Gabriel continued to sing, his eyes tightly closed, his hands reaching out to Heaven.

The train rumbled out of the mine portal and began to slow. First the engine, then a couple of man carriers, then the flatbed of some timber trucks. The first of the fallen rested on the timber trucks.

The dead were not even covered in body bags. There hadn't been time. The singing continued. It was as if the entire crowd was focused on the hymn and not the tragedy. Heather gripped Lucas' hand. Lucas held onto his father's. Together they walked to the last of the timber trucks. A huge body lay prone there. The body was far bigger than the rest. Lucas knew it was Vernon. The train stopped.

Lucas released his father's hand and walked with Heather to the side of the train. Vernon's face was a bit smudged, just like all miners. His open lunch pail was between his knees and his rain slicker was draped over him, as if to protect him from the cold. Heather stepped onto the timber truck. Two men who had ridden with the body, climbed down and removed their rescue masks and hard hats, pulling them to their chests in respect. The snow was beginning to stick to Vernon's cold skin. Heather reached out and brushed the flakes away, wiping the grime from her father's cheekbones.

Lucas climbed onto the car with her and drew his arm around her waist. Several people on the other side of the tracks were crying, their sobs muffled by the singing. Lucas stared at Heather. The tears he expected were not there. Flecks of snow and droplets of water peppered her face, but she was not crying. Her expression was one of compassion and peace. He puzzled for a moment, slipped his hand from around her and found her fingers. She moved them towards her face and looked at their hands, then gazed into his eyes.

"He ate his dessert first," she said, "I told him that wasn't right. But I knew he did it anyway. Sometimes he'd bring his pail home and the sandwich would have two bites out of it, but the dessert would be gone." She began to smile a little. The chilled air passed around her face, moving a stray wisp of hair into her eyes. Her little finger gently tucked the hair behind her ear.

Lucas looked at the open lunch pail. A sandwich, cellophane covered, lay squashed on one side of the metal container. A Twinkie wrapper peeked out from under his coffee Thermos. Heather reached and closed the lunch pail, latched it and handed it to Lucas. Leaning over she kissed her father's cheek and pulled his rain jacket up over his head.

The night became silent again. The voices had died down. Lucas looked at the crowd. Many of the heads were bowed, some people were crying, others were watching him and Heather.

Nellie Montgomery stood at the very front of the group. She was gazing at him and Heather. Lucas found comfort in her presence. Looking at her, short height, gray hair, bundled in several coats and caps, she radiated, stood out from the rest. He wiggled a finger at her. She slowly waved back at him, just like she did from her kitchen window each time he left her house. Folding her hands, her head slowly bowed and she closed her eyes.

Heather found Lucas' hand again and turned to him. She hugged his neck and whispered into his ear.

"I'll bet he's dancing with Momma in Heaven right now," she said. "It was the one thing she said she would do, whenever she saw any of us again."

They embraced for several more minutes. Heather's reaction, her change of emotion, upon seeing her father, had surprised him. Inside somewhere she was finding strength. Even these last words were of hope. Maybe in the din of death, a small light can radiate enough to guide even the most sorrow-filled heart.

The people parted as he and Heather walked back to the office door. Gabriel was talking to the newsmen. A large crowd had gathered around him, many of them were taking pictures. Lucas could hear him talking about God and his father, Delmer.

Looking over his shoulder, he saw that Nellie was gone. A solitary glove lay on the ground where she had been standing. Lucas released Heather's hand and ran to retrieve it. Heather turned around. He picked up the glove and scanned the crowd for Nellie. Not finding her, he returned to Heather's side and slipped the glove into the handle of the lunch pail.

Jonathan Kaari drove slowly by them on a motor headed toward the portal. Five other rescue workers were with him. Lucas and Heather watched as the men donned their self-contained rescuers. The sparks from the overhead trolley flashed, startling Lucas. He could smell the ozone from the electricity. His father nodded towards him. The train inched its way slowly into the mouth of the mountain.

CHAPTER 39

Several women encircled Heather, embracing her as Lucas walked her into the lobby of the mine office. Simple words of sympathy spilled from their solemn lips. Repetitious. Words cannot describe the agony of the heart, he thought. These people, sickened by the loss of life, hanging onto some somber hope that perhaps their loved ones were still clinging to life somewhere, deep in the massive mountain, awaiting rescue, found in themselves the need to touch Heather, extend their warmth, knowing too that they may need a human touch.

Heather finally began to cry. Lucas held her close to his chest. Feeble hands from the women stroked at her hair, rubbed her back. The ferocity of her wailing rose in tempo and timbre, echoing from the walls. She released all of her anguish, filling the hearts of those around her, including him, with grief, sympathy, longing and sorrow. He began to cry with her. Her pain, retching and no longer contained, overpowered his own. He felt her suffering enclose his. Hers became his.

The women in the room yielded their emotions at the sight of the young girl, beautiful, intelligent, orphaned, alone in the world, left to care for her siblings, broken beyond agony. A small hand slipped onto his. Weathered, speckled, it coupled Lucas and Heather's fingers. The touch was warm and familiar. It brought some comfort and peace. Lucas, sobbing, blinked at his tears and followed the hand. It was Nellie's.

"Greater is He that is in you, child, then is in this world," Nellie whispered to Heather. "You can turn to His strength. He knows your suffering. Just let it all go." Nellie cradled Heather's arm, and stroked her face. Heather's cries softened, lowered in their intensity. She turned from Lucas and looked at the frail, old woman.

"Your Daddy loves you," Nellie continued, "He doesn't want you to suffer. You are the most precious thing in this world to him." Lucas stepped away from Heather, relinquishing his hold on her. Heather, taller than Nellie, leaned into her, placed her head on the woman's shoulder and continued weeping. Nellie closed her eyes and held Heather. The room quieted as Heather quieted. Some of the gloom dissipated.

Lucas continued to shudder, convulsing on choked tears. Two of the greatest loves of his life stood before him. One consoling, one collapsing. His love for them, flush in his heart, was clearer than he had ever imagined. Love was real now. He could see it. Touch it. It was a tangible thing, not just the inkling thoughts of a child. This love, this pure, unconditional love, didn't move him. It became him. All passion, all desire, all yearning, warmth and empathy, combined could not rival what he was feeling.

"Lucas, I'll take this child with me. She'll be safe. You need to find the girl, the lost little girl. She may need you more than this one." Lucas looked at Nellie as she spoke. He knew she meant Lori Murphy.

Heather's cries were almost silent as Nellie continued coddling her.

"I'll find her, Mrs. Nellie," Lucas said. Nellie must know his brother is dead, he thought. Somehow, she must have sensed it. Looking at his hand, he saw Vernon's lunch pail, swinging from his finger tips. Tucked into the handle was a small wet glove. He slowly pulled it loose and handed it to Nellie. Her gentle fingers clutched it. A solitary tear washed from the corner of her eye, sliding over her wrinkled skin, to the middle of her cheek. With his thumb, Lucas gently wiped it away and rubbed it between his fingers.

Turning, he ran from the building and into the frozen night. People stepped aside as he slipped and stumbled towards his truck.

CHAPTER 40

Gabriel was leaning against the side of Lucas' pickup. Perched actually, against the passenger front fender. Lucas didn't see him at first. He had kept his eyes cast toward the ground, partially to obscure his face from the crowd, hiding his tears, and to prevent himself from falling in the snow that stood a half inch high on the parking lot.

"I really felt His presence, Lucas," Gabriel said. Lucas, startled by his friend's voice, looked up. Gabriel was staring into the darkness, looking up at the hillside. His shoulders were covered with snow. His glasses, speckled with water drops, had slipped to the end of his nose.

"His who?" Lucas said. He knew what Gabriel was talking about, but didn't know how to respond.

"God's. I could feel Him. He was there when I was singing." Gabriel slipped from the fender and onto the ground. He walked over to Lucas, who was leaning against the truck's tailgate. Lucas watched as he approached him. There was an assurance in the way he talked. He even looked taller.

"It was remarkable," Lucas said. "I've never heard you sing like that before."

"I never even knew I was singing," Gabriel said. Their eyes had not connected yet. Lucas was unsure of what to say next. Uncomfortable in spiritual situations, he did not feel like having a God talk right now. Gabriel was still craning his head toward the mountains.

"I don't think Daddy is dead, neither."

Lucas began to feel a little discomfort. Gabriel sounded drifty, almost blissful. Given the moment and the sphere of death around them, he assumed that his friend was in some state of denial.

"I need you to come find Lori with me," Lucas said. Gabriel didn't respond. His dazed expression carried an almost bemused look about it. Had this been some other moment, Lucas might have thought that the boy was high. Across the parking lot, Lucas could hear people shouting, arguing with the rescue workers.

"Did you hear me?" Lucas asked. There was no response. Lucas walked over to Gabriel and grabbed his shoulders. He tightened his fingers, digging into the boy's coat.

"Look, I need you. Your help. Its great you had some spiritual awakening, but I'm not convinced anybody is alive down there. If you want to turn priest on me, I'll go by myself," Lucas said. He was almost yelling.

Gabriel shook his head abruptly. His eyes opened widely. With his finger he slid his glasses up his nose and looked at Lucas. For a moment Lucas thought he had hurt Gabriel's feelings. The words were harsh and angry.

"No. I'll go with you. I need to go with you," he said. The normal tone of voice had returned. "Where are we going?"

"To Ernie's lake place. It's the only place I can think of."

"If we go out there and Ernie is there, he'll kill us. He's a murderer anyway," Gabriel said.

"If he's there, we'll just have to sneak up and snatch her away. She needs to come here. If my brother is…." Lucas' voice trailed off, "…If Russell doesn't make it, she'll have nobody. She needs to be here."

"Well, we've done enough already today. One more stupid thing ain't gonna hurt." Gabriel was himself again.

The boys climbed into the truck and closed the doors. Lucas fired up the ignition and turned on the windshield wipers. Snow flipped back and forth and splashed to the ground on either side of the vehicle. Lucas whiffed Gabriel's telltale sour scent. He rolled the window down an inch.

The streets of Sunnyside were snow covered. Only one set of car tracks broke the surface of the blanket of white. The streetlights, glowing brightly, reflected back from the ground, giving the city an eerie, peaceful feel. Heading towards the highway, Lucas passed the union hall. The parking lot was empty. The building was dark. The bathroom window was still open.

Gabriel turned on the local AM radio station. Music had been replaced by a voice-over from 'Blaine the Brain' stationed at the mine portal. The boys drove and listened. So far twenty-two bodies had been found and accounted for the mine. It was estimated that over eighty men were still missing. The reporter read the names of the dead, at least those whose relatives had been contacted.

As the boys listened, Lucas recognized every name. They were the fathers, brothers, cousins, uncles, children and friends of the community. There were company men listed, union men named. The announcer was direct and spoke without emotion. Outside the truck, snow was becoming furious. Large flakes, blowing sideways, obscured the road. The mountains, pinching together on either side of the highway gleamed with a ghostly white pallor. Normally, a day like this, the first true snowfall, would cause joy and celebration in the hearts of schoolboys. The first snowmen of the season would be built, snowball fights would be fought, sleds would be waxed and tested if the snow was deep and solid enough. But not tonight. Tonight the snow was a nuisance. An ecological reminder that the weather had a mind of its own, that nature did what it wanted when it wanted, to whomever it wanted.

As Lucas drove he thought about Russell and his father. The fate of both unknown. The fear that he had seen both for the last time tore at his chest. He fought back a scream.

All we are in life are the words we say, he thought. Telling somebody of your love for them, your anger with them, your thoughts about them, can change things. It can make situations worse, or it can make them better. Words can be wasted, but precious few ever have the impact that we really want.

As he drove he remembered the last words he shared with his brother. They were an interchange of love of sorts. Russell offering advice, Lucas offering the assurance that only brothers can really share.

They had fought many times in their life together. Argued about toys, friends, money, girls. There had been a few black eyes and several long periods where the love of one another had been replaced by a feeling as near to hate as Lucas could conjure. But as time tallied, the disposition between them would wane. There never seemed to be a defining moment when everything went back to normal. But it always did. Here, alone in his thoughts, he wished he had told his brother more about how he felt. He wanted to tell Russell to leave Sunnyside, to leave the girl who was destroying him, to run from the family that was always hanging on for the next dilemma that Russell would cause. Those thoughts and feelings were beginning to haunt him. Maybe Russell had done all of those things. Perhaps he was gone now, away from all the hurt he caused, the frustrations that lived inside of him. But this absence and loss would greatly overshadow any and all of the ire and pain that his actions and decisions had created.

Lucas became aware again of his tears. In the darkness of the cab, illuminated only by the greenish light from the dashboard, he felt cut off from life. Heather had changed, in a flash. Gone was the schoolgirl, destined for a grand life in college and career. She was now a parent. The hopes and dreams and aspirations of her life were snuffed. He knew her sense of responsibility would keep her in Sunnyside. She would raise the children. Provide for them. See that they had their start in life and forego, at least for now, the destiny that had beckoned her since childhood.

Maybe she would tire of life and settle for an existence in town. She was beautiful, a true prize for any man. Perhaps one would find her heart and keep her there, to exist and die, an obscure soul in a lost town. The world might never know her and it should. The greater sin, other than trapping such a bright life in such a troubled town, is the loss of something great to all men. She might have changed the world, done something with it.

The thoughts crushed at him. He would stay in Sunnyside too, to be with her. He would live at home, help her, guide her, comfort her. Seek a life, any kind of life, with her. Leaving Sunnyside and Heather would be the same as losing Russell. He would stay, watch out for Russell's baby, love it too, and see that it would have every opportunity to succeed where Russell had failed.

The life garnered from this experience, this disaster, might not be the one he had dreamed of, but maybe his destiny was simple after all. To live in love with Heather, however she would have him, to protect what was left of his brother. To complete his heart, he needed this, needed them. Nellie said that the best thing in this world is a friend, a friend who would die for another. She said that dying did not mean a physical death. It meant a sacrifice of life for another. He would give up the life he wanted to better the life of these two others. He would die to himself so that others would be blessed.

The truck suddenly spun sideways, losing some control. Ice, hidden by the crust of snow, surprised the truck's tires. Reflexes, honed from months of winter driving, took over as Lucas turned the wheel in the direction of the truck's skid and accelerated slightly. The truck straightened. He heard Gabriel sigh.

"We're almost there," Lucas said. The road had twisted around the lake in bends and turns. The final quarter mile was fairly straight. No other cars had traveled this route since the snowfall began.

"We should park on the side of the road and walk down to his cabin," Gabriel said.

"There is a flashlight under the seat," Lucas said. Gabriel leaned over and fumbled with his hand, searching for the light. He grunted as he stooped.

"Found it," he said. Flicking the switch, the lamp flickered and died.

"Oh no, its dead," Lucas said.

Gabriel slammed the device against his hand several times and flipped the switch on and off. Aside from a dull glow, there was no worthwhile or usable light.

"We'll just have to trust our night vision," Lucas said.

Lucas slowed the truck.

"It's around here somewhere," Lucas said. "I was out here last summer at our store picnic." He continued driving.

"There. See the sign. Shaggal's Sanctuary. That's it ain't it?" Gabriel said.

Lucas stopped the truck and turned off the lights. The road leading down to the cabin was almost a quarter mile long. Even at this distance he could see the mellow lights from the house. Lucas parked the truck on the opposite side of the two lane and stepped out onto the ground. Gabriel did the same, closing and locking his door behind him. The snowflakes were falling less frantically, though they were still accumulating. Mist floated from Lucas' breath onto the night air. It was cold. He could actually hear the snowflakes as they hit the ground and touched the trees. The night was silent other than that.

Gabriel walked over to Lucas' side.

"So what are we gonna do? Just walk up and say, 'Is Lori here?'" Gabriel said.

"If Ernie is there, that might not be such a good idea. Maybe Georgie is down there. We can just tell him that we need to take Lori back to town."

"But her mom is there too, I suspect. They was all together earlier," Gabriel said.

The boys stood side by side and surveyed the woods. Neither moved. It was apparent to Lucas that there really was nothing else he could do other than approach the house and ask for the girl.

"Let's just go and see what happens," he said.

"Yeah, let's just go," Gabriel repeated.

Lucas' sneakers were cold and soaked. He could hear the slopping sound of Gabriel's shoes as they squished through the snow. Looking back, Lucas saw their footprints, pressed into the white ground. There was no way they could hide their clandestine march to the house.

The boys walked down the narrow road, shrouded on either side by stories tall pine trees, their boughs just beginning to collect the nighttime snowfall. It was beautiful and peaceful, Lucas thought. And desperately cold.

On the edge of the broad driveway, they stopped and surveyed their surroundings. A Jeep Wagoneer stood parked by the front of the main cabin. A soft light shone from an upstairs window. Downstairs, a light peeked from deep inside the house, near the lakeside. Lucas remembered that the living room was on the far end of the house. Smoke floated from the chimney, smelling the air with charcoal scent.

"That's Georgie's car," Lucas said, pointing at the Jeep. "It's pretty late. Maybe everybody is sleeping."

"Yeah, maybe," Gabriel said. They stood quiet for another moment. Lucas looked toward the guesthouse. Softly glowing lights washed from the windows. He could hear the muted sounds of music.

"Let's go look in the guesthouse window," Gabriel said. "I think somebody's over in there."

Lucas nodded his approval and followed his friend as he walked along the wooded edge of the driveway. The ground between the two buildings was undisturbed. There had been no foot traffic since the snow had begun to fall.

The guesthouse, made of logs, was fairly small, a one story affair. The main and only door was one step up from a little covered porch. Lucas remembered that the entrance led immediately into a kitchenette. The front of the house faced the lake and was all glass. The window closest to them looked into the kitchen and over into the living room.

Lucas followed Gabriel, who was now trotting like a spy, hunched over, fingers splayed, looking over his shoulders, turning his head from side to side. Lucas almost laughed. Gabriel planted his back against the log siding, but left of the kitchen window. He was too short to see in.

Lucas ran to his friend's side. The music, loud and methodic, pulsed against the walls. It sounded like *Steppenwolf*. The ground beneath their feet sloped down and away from them toward the lake.

"Move over. I'm going to see if I can peek in," Lucas said. "Keep an eye on the door to the main house. Let me know if you see anything." Gabriel nodded and stepped aside, allowing Lucas access to the window. Grasping the lower window ledge, Lucas pulled himself up and onto his toes. His eyes barely made it high enough to see in. His heart stopped.

Adam Shaggal was sitting astride Lori Murphy on the couch. She was struggling with him. With one hand he held her wrists as she flailed and covered her mouth with the other. His shirt was unbuttoned as well as his belt. His fly was completely open. Beer cans littered the top of a coffee table. Lori's blouse and bra were torn aside, her bare breasts exposed. Adam was raping her.

Lucas dropped back to the ground and jumped around Gabriel without speaking. Grasping the doorknob, he twisted it, flinging the door open in one quick motion. The music was suddenly much louder. The room smelled of marijuana. Lucas ran through the kitchen and into the small living room. Adam, surprised by the flurry of activity, spun toward Lucas and cursed.

Lucas stumbled on a rag rug in the kitchen and fell forward, catching himself on the entrance to the living room. Blindly he lunged in Adam's direction.

"No! Lucas! He has a gun!" Lori was screaming, her mouth free from the gag of Adam's hand. A loud shot exploded into the air. Lucas dropped to the floor near a rocking chair and rolled aside.

"Lucas mucus! Great to see you. Get up!" Adam was slurring and yelling at the same time. Lucas looked toward the couch. Adam was sitting on Lori's stomach, holding her in place. "Get in here too, you faggoty maggot," Adam said, nodding at the kitchen.

Lucas looked over his shoulder. Gabriel was standing near the refrigerator, his hands held high like some robbed stage coach driver. He walked slowly over to Lucas.

Lori had quit struggling but was pushing at Adam's hip.

Lucas looked at the pistol in Adam's hand. It was small and had a pearl handle. It was the same gun he had seen in Dolly's purse.

"Get over near the wall, boys," Adam said.

"What's this all about," Lucas said, staggering to his feet. He used the rocking chair to pull himself up.

"What do you mean? Lori here likes it rough. She wants to be slapped around a bit, before a good romp. Don't ya, honey?" Adam, still pointing the gun at Lucas, reached over and squeezed Lori's breast. She cursed and slapped at his hand.

Gabriel was standing next to Lucas. His hands still held high.

"That's Dolly's pistol, isn't it Adam?" Lucas said.

Adam, raised his eyebrows and smiled at Lucas.

"What do you know about that old whore? Did you get some from her? You finally lost your virginity, didn't you?" Adam was grinning. "Shame on you!" There was a wild redness to Adam's eyes.

"I know that she's dead. I know that's her gun," Lucas said.

Adam's smile washed from his face. He stood up and walked to the end of the couch.

"You don't know squat, sweet pea," Adam said. Lori sat up and pulled the torn remnants of her blouse together, covering her exposed flesh.

Lucas stared at the pistol. The smell of burnt gunpowder wafted passed his nostrils.

"Why'd you do it, Adam?" Lucas said, "Why'd you kill her?"

Adam pointed the gun at Lori and motioned it toward Lucas.

"Get your slutty self over there with those other girls, you tart," he said. Lori, opened her eyes wide and stood up. Adam motioned the gun again. She didn't move. He pulled back the hammer. "Get over there. Or I'll shoot you in the knockers, I swear it." Lori shuffled around the beer-can-laden table and stood near Lucas. Lucas took her arm into his hand.

Adam zipped his fly, tucked his shirttails into his pants and leaned over toward the coffee table, plucking a dead joint from an ashtray. Placing it to his lips, he fidgeted through his shirt pockets and found a lighter. He lit it, puffed quickly, held the smoke and exhaled.

"She killed Billy. That's why."

"What do you mean she killed Billy. Billy killed himself."

"Billy died because the old prostitute was going to go to his wife. He fired her flabby butt and said they were done screwing. But she knew a lot of stuff she shouldn't. So she had to die."

"Billy set the fire, didn't he?"

"You are so cute sometimes, Lucas. Damn, you just warm my heart. Billy set the fire...right." Adam shook his head and smirked as he spoke. His sarcasm was thick.

"Then who did Adam?"

"Billy loved this town and those miners. He'd never ever had done anything to hurt any of them. All he wanted was a compromise. But ain't nobody in this town ever heard of that side of it. No. Guys like your old man think they can run and control everything. They end up screwing everyone. No, Billy never set no fire."

Adam took a deep drag on the joint, held the smoke, exhaled loudly and said, "I did."

Lucas was stunned.

"Why? You had no cause. No reason." Lucas voice was shrill. He was terrified.

"I didn't? Really? You, again, don't know anything. Billy and me set it up. He and me used to work together when I went underground. When Uncle Ernie began helping him out, well, things got a bit different for him. See, Ernie thinks that he doesn't need to compromise either. He just keeps on buying people. Guess he figured that Billy was strong enough to get them union boys to do anything. But Uncle was wrong. If there'd been a strike, we Shaggal's would have lost everything. Ol' Billy couldn't stop the strike neither. So we came up with the fire."

"You figured you'd kill everybody? That'd solve all the problems?"

"We didn't figure on killing nobody. A little smoke should have shut the place down for months. The company would have had to pay the workers and eventually they would have given up on the place. Congress would have investigated, the EPA would have come around. It'd been a long time before ore was brought out of that hole. Ernie would just buy up what was left, break the union, and never have to worry about worker problems again."

"But people are dead, Adam."

"Well, that is unfortunate. Guess there's going to have to be three more as far as I can tell." Adam stood up and stepped toward his captives.

"What you're saying is delusion, pure delusion," Lucas said. "Ernie had to know about all this stuff. He knows everything."

"He would have known. If it had all come down like it was supposed to, I'd have told him. You see, Uncle doesn't have anybody to pass all this on to. He ain't gonna give it to my dad. Once he saw what I did for him, how I helped, he'd finally see that I was just like him. I could handle his business. Take care of stuff just like he does. That would be his legacy, and mine."

"Your only legacy is going to be the first man executed by the State of Montana in years. Put the gun down, Adam." Lucas turned toward the kitchen. The voice was coming from just outside, in the dark. Officer Aimel stepped into the kitchen, his gun drawn, pointed at Adam's head.

Adam spun toward Aimel and fired. Several other gunshots followed. Adam's chest splattered into a frenzy of red, his blood splashing against the couch. Stumbling backwards, Adam fired one more shot, this time into the floor. His back against the wall, he began to slump, sliding to the floor. Neither Lucas, Gabriel or Lori had a chance to move. Lori began to scream.

Aimel walked over to Adam's body, his revolver still pointed at him. Kicking the pistol from Adam's hand, the policeman stooped.

"It hurts," Adam said. Slowly his head tilted backwards against the wall. His eyes, open, stared toward the ceiling.

Gabriel held Lori in his arms trying to calm her. Lucas walked over to Aimel, who had holstered his gun. The officer was feeling Adam's neck.

"How'd you know to come out here?" Lucas said.

"Because this is the craziest thing you could do. Its something your brother would have done."

Aimel stood up and put his arm around Lucas' shoulder. They stood looking at Adam. The blood from his chest trickled onto the hardwood floor.

"Oh God! Adam! Adam!" Georgie Shaggal ran into the room followed by Mrs. Murphy. Aimel grabbed Georgie as he tried to embrace his dead son, pulling him back to his feet.

"I'm sorry Georgie. Leave him," Aimel said. Georgie feebly struggled with the policeman.

"You'll have to come with me, Georgie. I've got to arrest you for embezzlement, bribery and fraud. Ernie is already at the county jail," Aimel said.

Georgie began raging at Aimel, cursing him. Aimel pulled Georgie's arm behind his back and pressed him against the wall.

"Calm down, Georgie. I'm sorry. I'm so sorry. But you've got to come with me."

Lori's mother, Vivian, was holding her daughter, cradling her as they cried. Gabriel held them both. The younger Murphy children stood to the side of the room in shock.

"What about that, Aimel," Lucas said pointing at Adam's pants. Protruding from the side pocket was a folded piece of paper. Aimel handcuffed Georgie and sat him on the couch. Retrieving the letter, Aimel unfolded the parchment. It was the letter addressed to Congressman Temple, written in Billy's hand.

"Go back into town, Lucas. Find your family. We'll sort through this later. You going to be alright?"

"Yes. But Lori needs to come with me. She needs to be with my family."

"Then take Georgie's Jeep. I'm sure he won't mind. He won't need it, will you Georgie? Here, I took the keys from the ignition in case somebody tried to get away."

Aimel dropped the keys into Lucas' hands.

"Thanks Aimel. He could have killed you," Lucas said.

"He tried. You better hurry. I'm sure your mother needs you," Aimel patted Lucas' shoulder.

"Scabby, you better drive Lucas' truck," Aimel said.

"His name is Gabriel," Lucas interjected.

Aimel smiled at Lucas and nodded.

"Drive careful, Gabriel," he said.

Lucas helped Lori and her family into Georgie's Jeep. Lucas took off his jacket and wrapped it around Lori, covering her from the cold.

CHAPTER 41

The snow had stopped falling as Lucas pulled the vehicle onto the main road. Gabriel flashed the lights of Lucas' pickup and proceeded to follow them into town. The drive was slow because of the snow on the roads. Lucas listened as Lori talked to her mother. The unity and bond of mother and daughter must be strong, he thought. The words exchanged were of forgiveness and love. Still, Lori did not disclose her pregnancy. He felt he should say something, but didn't. With all he had been through, the situation for Lori was worse. She knew Russell was missing. Her world was changing, but losing him could destroy it for her.

At the mine yard entrance, Lucas saw dozens of flashing lights. The crowd had grown considerably. He looked at the clock on the Jeep's dashboard. It read eleven-thirty. Ambulances from as far away as Missoula had come to Sunnyside. Not to give comfort, but to aid as hearses. Carriers of dead miners. The radio said that a morgue had been set up at the junior high cafeteria. Relatives were asked to go to the gymnasium and await word of their loved ones. Still, it seemed, almost everybody was here.

Lucas simply stopped the Jeep in the middle of the road. Barricades had been erected to form a driveway for the makeshift hearses. Walking slowly toward the crowd, the Murphy family in tow, Lucas saw floodlights and camera crews bathing a man, impeccably dressed, in harsh white light and adoration. He recognized him as Congressman Temple. The politician was speaking.

"With every bit of power and authority at my command, I will see that this community is served and comforted by the people of this country. This tragedy, this disaster, proves again, that corporate greed overlooks and undermines the safety of workers. The very substance of our lives is played with carelessly, recklessly, by these out of State concerns, so bent on raping our resources, exporting their profits and leaving us, the good people of Montana and the hard working citizens of this town, with nothing but death and despair. I will call on OSHA, the EPA, the IRS and any other agency who can thoroughly and completely scrutinize The Bull Run Mining Company. We will find out what happened here. We will get to the truth. We will seek to bring those who are responsible to social and financial justice."

The Congressman had the crowd in a swoon. Several of the families gathered began shouting support for the politician's directives. As he watched the eloquent man manipulate the grieving crowd he remembered the sheet of paper he had taken from the union hall and folded into his coat pocket. The Congressman was now taking questions from the crowd and reporters. Lucas stepped to Lori, who was surrounded by her family, shivering in the cold.

"Lori, see if there is anything in my coat pocket," he said. Lori, broken momentarily from her sorrow, nodded at him and slid her hand into the jacket pocket. She extracted a crunched piece of paper and handed it to him.

In the dim light, Lucas unfolded the paper and squinted at it. It was Billy's phone bill from the union hall. Looking again at the Congressman, Lucas began to feel anxious. He glanced back at the paper then at the reporters. Questions were peppering the air and the Congressman, with all the graciousness and concern he could muster, waxed poetic answers. Lucas pushed his way through the crowd. Feeling a tug on his shirt, he turned. Gabriel was behind him.

"I got your truck stuck, sorry," he said.

"That's ok," Lucas said. He continued his march to the front of the crowd.

Gabriel glided along with him. The shadow he had always been. Only this time, Lucas welcomed his presence, was comforted and strengthened by it.

"Sir, I have a question," Lucas shouted. Nobody looked at him. The Congressman continued chatting with the reporters.

"Mr. Temple. A question. I have a question," Lucas hollered again. The Congressman stopped and looked in his direction. He stood about twenty feet away. Several of the Congressman's lieutenants eyed Lucas with a level of suspicion.

"Yes, son. You have a question. First, what is your name?"

"Kaari, sir. Lucas Kaari."

"Jonathan Kaari's son?"

"Yes sir. My brother is missing in the mine."

"Yes, I know. Your father is very brave, looking for him," the Congressman turned back to the cameras. "Mr. Kaari is probably the only company man worth saving at this point." He turned back to Lucas and Gabriel.

"What is the question, son?"

"What is your phone number?"

The Congressman seemed as if he was going to answer, drawing in breath, then stopping. A quizzical look crossed his face.

"What? I don't understand your question?" Some people in the crowd chuckled. The reporters, momentarily focusing on Lucas, swung their cameras back to the Congressman.

"Your office phone number. What is it?" Lucas said. His voice was very certain and very calm.

"Why would you need my phone number? If you need to contact me to talk, ask one of my aides and they can arrange it. Any other questions?" The Congressman turned back to the reporters.

Lucas began to recite a series of numbers, loudly.

The Congressman looked back at him.

"What is the problem, young man?"

"Is that your phone number, sir?" Lucas asked.

"Yes. I believe so. You seem to have it there. Why would you ask me for it if you already know it."

"Because, sir. There are dozens of calls to your office from Billy Murphy's private line at the union hall. It's on this bill." The crowd began to mumble. The Congressman, shifted slightly on the makeshift platform and stared at Lucas.

"Is there a point to this, Mr. Kaari?" the Congressman asked.

"Well, I think so, sir. Why would you be talking so much to Billy. I mean, isn't that odd?"

"I knew Mr. Murphy, certainly, but that doesn't mean anything. What are you trying to say?"

"I'm saying Mr. Temple, that Adam Shaggal admitted to starting the mine fire and that Billy knew about it. I think that you knew about it, too. Wouldn't it make sense to create a strike or shut the mine down so you can come down here and make yourself look good by solving a problem you helped create?"

The crowd began to murmur. Loudly. The reporters evenly spread their cameras between Lucas and the politician.

"That is nonsense, young man," the Congressman said. The anger in his voice was obvious.

"Billy kept a journal." The voice was Vivian Murphy's. "He has it locked in his gun cabinet," she said. Reporters surrounded Vivian. Others peppered the Congressman with questions. Clearing his way, the Congressman's aides pressed through the crowd toward his courtesy car. Lights and cameras followed him.

Lucas looked around him. Hundreds of eyes stared at him in frightened disbelief. A city police officer kept the crowd back as Lucas answered the press questions and detailed the events with Dolly, Billy, Ernie and Adam.

A rescue miner, filthy with mud and grit approached Lucas.

"You're needed at the portal. Your mother is there. A train is coming out," the man said.

Slowly, people stepped away opening a path, a channel for Lucas and Gabriel. They walked toward the building, Lori and her mother with them. On the office steps, Lucas saw his mother, Heather, her brother and sister. Bundled next to them, in her scarves and coats, Mrs. Nellie was smiling.

CHAPTER 42

Lucas' mother had been crying. Seriously crying. He hesitated to ask her whether she had heard anything about Russell, for fear that her words would end hope for his brother. She was holding Heather's hand, fingers intertwined with hers. Even in the pale glow from the parking lot lights, Heather was radiant in her beauty, the pain on her face could barely touch her perfection.

Heather reached for Lucas as he climbed the steps. Gabriel embraced Lucas' mother, who held him close and began to weep.

"The phone lines to the hoist room are dead. Nobody knows what's going on down there anymore. Nobody has heard from your father," Heather said as she held Lucas. Nellie was kneeling, talking gently to Heather's little brother and sister. They too had been crying, apparently informed that their father was gone. Nellie was reciting a children's poem to them.

"How many men have they brought out?" Lucas asked. Heather's eyes, swollen from her anguish, closed.

"Almost seventy," she said.

"That's almost everybody, isn't it. That's almost all of them that were down there."

"They don't know for sure, who was working. Some of the ones they thought had gone underground were either out hunting or down in the bars. No one knows the exact number," she said.

The ground began to rumble and vibrate. The heads of those gathered turned back to face the mine portal. A train, sparking in the distance, was approaching.

"Its been this way all night," Lucas' mother said. "The train comes out every hour or so. It's so hopeless."

"The only time there is no more hope is when we are in Heaven, love," Nellie said. She had finished her tale to the children and was standing next to Mrs. Kaari. "Then we don't need any hope, because all of our hopes have been realized."

Mrs. Murphy squeezed Nellie's shoulder and kissed the top of her head. Together they stood watching the approaching train.

Lucas continued holding Heather's hand in his. Gabriel had stepped into the mine office and was using the telephone. Lucas could hear him crying and talking to his mother.

The man-train was louder. The rumbling was a hail of metallic screaming and iron clanging. The headlight of the train motor shone on the crowd. Several men rode on top of the flat motor battery. The timber trucks held the familiar shadows of the dead.

Lucas searched the covered faces of the men on the motor, hoping to find his father. Breaking from Heather, he ran to the motor coach. Miners began removing their rescue masks and hard hats. One by one they revealed themselves.

"Have you seen my father?" Lucas asked one of the men.

"He's in the coach," the miner said, pointing to the train car immediately behind the engine. Lucas ran to the side of the car. Several miners were huddled around a body that was slumped backwards. An oxygen mask covered the man's face. He stared hard. Miner's lamps flashed around the interior of the man coach. On the back of one of the yellow rain slickers he saw the words, 'J. Kaari'.

"Dad," he shouted. The miner turned around and pulled the rescue mask from his face. Lucas ran around the side of the train, climbed between the cars and raced to the seat where Jonathan was sitting. His father stepped from inside the coach and grabbed Lucas, pulling him into his chest. The yellow slicker was wet. His dad smelled like oil and sweat. Other men climbed from their seats and stepped around Lucas and his father. None of them walked away.

Jonathan Kaari kissed his son, placed his hands on Lucas' shoulders and looked at him. Lucas stared at his father. Tears poured down his dad's cheeks.

"Dad...Russell...." Lucas' voice quivered into silence. His father began to shake. A grin, then a smile broadened across his face. Lucas gazed at his father again. He had never seen him cry before.

"Help me with your brother, son," Jonathan said, nodding toward the train. Lucas leaned forward and looked into the coach. The miner with the oxygen mask sat slumped against the seat wall. His eyes were partially opened.

"Russell," Lucas shouted. Climbing into the coach, he pulled the oxygen mask from his brother's face. "Russell!" he shouted again.

Russell lifted his head away from the wall and looked at Lucas. His face was swollen and dirty. Cuts and scrapes seemed to crisscross every part of his exposed flesh.

"Baby brother..." Russell whispered, his voice hoarse and dry. He began to cough. Russell placed his hand behind Lucas' head and pulled him towards his face. "Baby brother...." Russell said again.

Lucas held his brother, cradled his face. Hot, stinging tears flooded his cheeks. Russell embraced him, squeezed him and began crying as well. Lucas' mouth fell open. From his stomach he felt the shuddering, shaking cry. He began to bawl. Russell continued to hold him, pulling him tighter and tighter.

"I love you," Lucas said, gagging over his sobs.

"I love you too, baby brother, I love you too..."

They stayed embraced for several moments. Lucas didn't want to let go. Couldn't let go. He didn't want to let Russell leave his sight, didn't want to stop touching him. He wanted them to be little boys again, running through the dandelion fields up the river. He wanted to go back to the days when wrestling in the front yard was the delight of the day. Lucas clutched his brother, feeling his life, his breath. He inhaled his scent. He kept repeating Russell's name. He treasured the name, speaking it as if it were holy.

Hands reached in and began tugging gently at Lucas' shirt and belt. Still he gripped his brother. He felt blind, unable to see or think or feel anything but his love for his brother. Russell wouldn't release him either.

"Come on, son, he needs a doctor. He'll be ok," Jonathan loosened Lucas' fingers and pulled him from the coach. Lucas struggled to hang on, almost fighting his father.

Paramedics lifted Russell from the train and placed him on a backboard and stretcher. A cervical collar encircled his neck. Mrs. Kaari leaned over him, kissing him fiercely on the cheeks, crying in hysterics. Russell reached for her, kissed her, and began sobbing again.

"I'm sorry, Mom, I'm so sorry," he said. His voice barely audible. Reporters clicked away at the embrace, filming the reunion of the once thought dead and the living. On the fringe of the crowd, Lori Murphy stood with her mother. She too was weeping. The medical attendants pushed the stretcher towards a waiting ambulance. A cheer began rising from the crowd. Russell weakly raised his hand and waved. Cameras flashed, filling the wintered sky with little lightening bolts. The cheer became a roar.

Lucas ran to Lori, grasped her hand and fought through the crowd to the ambulance. The doors were being closed.

"You've got to let her see him," Lucas said to the medics.

"Sorry, son, he needs to get to the hospital."

Lori was shaking, tears washed her face.

"This is his wife," Lucas lied, pushing Lori at the medic.

"Sorry, ma'am. Yes, go ahead, get in with him."

Lori climbed into the ambulance and knelt next to Russell. Lucas watched as she gently kissed him. Russell's arms wrapped around her back and pulled her onto his chest. The ambulance attendant closed the door, pounded twice on the fender with his fist. A siren pitch blasted into the air, startling those gathered. The car began to slowly inch through the crowd. Lucas ran after it, keeping his eyes fixed on the figures through the van's windows.

He stood alone in the crowd, the dark of night cloaking him and his sobs. Jonathan walked to him and stood at his side. Lucas felt his father's arm slide across his shoulders.

"How did you find him, Dad? How come he lived and so many others died?"

"Because he's smart, strong, and blessed. He's just like you, son."

Together, they walked back through the crowd to the office steps. Heather and Mrs. Kaari were inside with Gabriel and Nellie. There was laughter and smiles. On all but Gabriel's face. Jonathan walked over to Gabriel and sat in a chair next to him.

"Your father saved Russell's life," he said. "He wouldn't have made it out without your dad. Delmer is a hero."

"But he's dead, ain't he? If he's a hero, how come he didn't come out just now?"

"He could still be alive. Russell told me that your dad was trying to get to the old vent shaft. Just like you said. We couldn't find him, but we think he headed that way. We think he had Freddy Whitehead with him."

Lucas watched as Gabriel absorbed his father's words.

"Do you think he could make it to the vent shaft?" Gabriel said.

"If anybody, any miner, could do it, it would be your father. I'm going to the Suck Tunnel right now. There is a crew there already. We can pray that he made it."

Jonathan stood and walked to his wife. He embraced her, cried with her, kissed her and embraced her again. The dirt from his clothes smudged her face and dampened her dress.

"He was unconscious when we found him. I thought he was dead. Everybody else around him was," Lucas heard his father say. "Another minute or so and we would have lost our boy. He had pulled himself into a low corner of the stope, pushed sand up into a wall around him and opened one of the air lines. It was enough to keep him going just a little longer." Both parents began weeping again.

Lucas walked over to Gabriel who was still sitting next to the phone.

"Lets go to the Suck Tunnel with my dad and wait...and pray...." Lucas said. Gabriel looked up at him and nodded.

"Do you think he made it, Lucas?" Gabriel asked.

"I think so. Yes. I think so."

The phone rang on the desk next to Gabriel. Jonathan picked up the receiver and spoke into it. He hung up and faced his son and his friend.

"Some of the rescue men at the vent shaft think they can see lights at the bottom. They aren't sure. I need to get up there." Jonathan ran towards the office door.

"Get in my truck, boys." Gabriel and Lucas ran after Jonathan as he pushed through crowd.

Jonathan's truck, a huge banged up four door Ford, owned by The Bull Run Mining Company, spun on the icy ground as it backed from its parking spot.

"Dad. Stop. Wait." Lucas said. He opened the passenger door and jumped to the ground.

"What is it," Jonathan said, watching his son dash into the crowd. In an instant he returned with another boy. A boy with a bandaged head, wearing a stocking cap.

"Dad, this is Mickey Whitehead," Lucas said. Mickey climbed into the truck behind Jonathan. Lucas sat next to him.

The truck sped out of the parking lot. A news van chased after them.

CHAPTER 43

Lucas gripped the arm rest and held on tightly to the edge of the bench seat. The truck had very little suspension and every pothole, every dip in the road, bounced him, hard, almost to the cab ceiling.

Mickey Whitehead was mute, saying only a cursory 'thanks' when Lucas asked him to come to the Suck Tunnel. Sitting next to him, a day after their death match, seeing him grieve the possible loss of his father, turned Lucas' heart and emotions from bitterness to empathy. He too had lived through the waiting and fear, not knowing whether a dear one was dead. He knew the thoughts Mickey was fostering, the guilt over not speaking well of and to his father, the turmoil over his misdeeds and how they would be perceived by those he loved and maybe lost.

The bandage on Mickey's head was rather large. Bigger than Lucas thought it should be.

"Did you go to the emergency room and get stitches?" Lucas asked, "I mean that looks pretty nasty."

Mickey faced him and grimaced. Lucas knew that the boy's mind was anywhere but on his wounds. Mickey gingerly touched the tail of the bandage peeping from under his stocking cap. He said, "No. No, I did this myself. The bleeding stopped but I just wanted to keep the wound clean and dry."

"I'm really sorry for what has happened. I mean not just for this weekend, but for all the years. It seems like such a waste," Lucas said. His words felt like a confession. He had hated Mickey for so long that any other thought or emotion concerning the boy was new to him. Mickey's drunken rambling, his liaison with Randy Peeper, now a shared secret, and the boy's loss of the girl he had loved for so long was a cement, a bond, between them.

Lucas would never tell anybody, not even Gabriel, about Mickey's dilemma, his mistake, or his misgivings. Mickey was living in a hell that he had created. His plastic armor had melted, his bravado had failed him, his weakness had overpowered him. Sitting in the back of this dirty truck, in the incubation of winter, driving to a destination that held maybe more misery for Mickey, was enough. Enough justice for all of Mickey's injustices.

Lucas did not treasure this outcome. He had prayed for Mickey's pain, wished for it many times. Conspired to cause it. And here it was, real, demented, and awful. Instead of release and relief, Lucas felt empty and shame. Mickey was just a boy, like him. Trying to make sense of a life in a town shut off from the real world. What and who they are, and who and what they would become was changing with each moment.

Jocks and geniuses. Studs and slugs. Victors and victims. These were images, really, not who they were. Lucas felt a hate and anger frothing in his chest. This town, these people, their whims, their narrow vision and thoughts, crafted their children into little monster shadows of themselves. The kids in this valley were victims of the convoluted frustrations of their ancestors. Every ideal, every impression, every positive or negative detail that made up their substance, their personalities, was a reflection of their ancestors misfortunes or fate.

But that isn't who we really are, Lucas thought. We can't be the repetition of these lost soul's lives. We were born unique, then molded to be mad, to be cynical. We learn to hate, to judge, to condemn. But why? Why should one man's son hate another's simply because of age-old rivalry? The world is really too small, life is certainly too short, to corrupt the thoughts and dreams of the young simply to continue the cycle of hate and anger.

He felt like a captive. The youth of this town, this county, were prisoners. Inmates to all the failed dreams, the lost loves, the angst, the cynicism, the selfishness of their fathers. Yet, the prisoners didn't know they were trapped. They had never been afforded a free thought or given a choice.

Those that made it out of Sunnyside usually stayed away. Nobody famous came from here, at least famous for good. The world drained life from Sunnyside, pillaged it, blighted it's mountains, poisoned its streams, strangled it's air, broke the backs of its citizens, to enjoy the plunder of silver, to make their lives rich, whole and wonderful. But no one from this town had seen or tasted of such a life. It was flashed on the televisions or printed in magazine gloss. Yet those images, the details of external, unique and interesting lives, were nothing more than adult fairy tales. And now, this disaster, this leveling of life in the valley, would take away many of the wishes for a new tomorrow. It would end the struggle for a better life, a brighter future. Life as it had been known here would only become darker, harder, sadder. But maybe not. Maybe this carnage would break the dark hearts of the city so bad that the prejudices and hatred would become a memory. Perhaps this death would be the beginning of new life.

"Mickey. Where's your mother?" Lucas asked, breaking from his thoughts.

"Drunk. On the couch. Like she is every weekend," he mumbled.

"I'm sorry," Lucas said. He reached across the truck seat and tentatively squeezed Mickey's shoulder. Mickey looked at him, a little surprised, and patted Lucas' hand.

"Heather's father was a great man," Mickey said. "I'm going to miss him a lot. She was his world. Just like she is…was mine."

Lucas felt a sting from the words. Not a damaging pain, but a tint of jealousy. He knew that Mickey loved her. Maybe loved her as much as he did.

"She'll make it work, somehow. She is strong and smart," Lucas said.

"She is…" Mickey concurred. He turned his head and looked out the window. Lucas felt uncomfortable. His emotions concerning Heather were being capped by his fear and frustration over the deaths.

"I love her, you know. With all my heart," Lucas said. He paused, waiting for Mickey's reaction, expecting him to turn back, to sneer. But he didn't. Instead, he kept focused on some dark point beyond the truck. "And she loves me," Lucas finished.

Mickey inhaled a heavy breath. Lucas saw his exhale fog the window. Still Mickey did not turn back. Slowly the boy's head began to nod.

"I know she does. She loves you more than she ever loved me. I protected her body, her image, but you protected all the things that are good and right about her. You protected her soul," Mickey said. "You gave her a safe place to be herself. Doing that, being that, kept her from becoming like the rest of us."

"The rest of you?" Lucas asked.

"The lifers, Lucas. The lifers," Mickey said. "I know you are different, just like Scabby. Somehow you got brains and desire and are so positive about yourself. A place like this can't keep you. Doesn't want you. Just as much as you don't want it." Mickey turned his face toward Lucas. "Heather is like that, too. She was free, once. She would have gone the first moment she could. But this valley didn't want her to go. I didn't want her to go. Now she can't. Who she was died with her father in the mine today. Can't you see that?" Mickey's face was wet. He was crying.

"Then if you love her Mickey, you need to help her find that freedom. Someday. I'm going to. Whatever it takes. I'm going to help her find a way out of here."

The boys looked at each other. Mickey continued weeping. Lucas squeezed his shoulder again, reassuring him.

Heather was indeed a captive. What Mickey said about her dying in the mine was true. Where could she go? How could she leave? He knew that the fire inside her, the life, the spark, was covered. It would be hidden, perhaps forever. Maybe this was the greatest tragedy of them all.

The crosses on Cemetery Hill were all lit. Lucas' father shifted the truck into a low gear and began the climb up the snow covered road. Gabriel remained silent and very still. Lucas could feel his friend's suffering and fear.

Around the backside of the cemetery, the road dropped and wove through a grove of pine trees. Lucas could see floodlights and a dozen trucks, headlights blazing, clustered around the opening to the Suck Tunnel. Bushes had been beaten back or torn loose, exposing the opening in the mountain.

Jonathan parked his truck, left the engine running, sprang from the cab and ran to a standing group of yellow rain-slickered men. Lucas, Mickey and Gabriel walked slowly, slipping in the muddy tire tracks and approached the opening to the ventilation shaft.

"One of the crew has rappelled down the shaft. He's at least a quarter mile down," one of the team members told Jonathan. "The rope has gone slack. We don't know if that means he fell or disconnected or what. We don't dare pull the rope up."

"Then send somebody else down there. Get the power company up here with one of their cable spool trucks. We'll lower a rescue basket and see what we can find." Jonathan barked orders and men scrambled. The television truck sloshed up behind them. The TV crew spewed forth with their cameras blazing. Despite rapid fire questions, no one answered them.

Lucas watched as Mickey walked towards Gabriel. The two boys stood side by side, neither one looking at the other. Lucas approached and stopped a few feet behind them.

"I'm sorry, Scabby," Mickey said. "I'm sorry about your father."

"The name's Gabriel."

"What?"

"Gabriel. Don't call me Scabby. Scabby is gone. Dead."

"I'm sorry, Gabriel."

"I'm sorry about your father too," Gabriel said. "I'm sorry about a lot of things." There was a tense tenderness in his voice.

217

Mickey stood, staring at the shaft opening. Lucas could feel unspoken words between them. He wanted to step forward, to prod the words, but held back.

"You've got very little to be sorry for," Mickey said.

"But I do, Mickey, I really do. I'm sorry for not standing up to you years ago. I'm sorry for letting you make me run in fear. I'm sorry for letting you control me, my emotions, my social life. I'm sorry for allowing you to use me to make yourself stronger," Gabriel stepped forward and turned toward Mickey.

"I helped make you what you are, Mickey. It was wrong for me to do that. If I had stood some ground, made some noise, instead of shake each time you walked into a room, then maybe you would have become a better person. And I'm sorry I tried to kill you this weekend. I would have. I wanted to."

"You should have," Mickey said, sullenly.

"No. If I had, I would have become you. That would have been the worst punishment I could imagine," Gabriel said.

Mickey and Gabriel stood in silence for a very long time. The sound of generators and CB radios cluttered the cold night air. Lucas moved forward and joined the two boys. The television crew shone their lights and cameras on the trio. Lucas ignored them.

Several men entered the tunnel, garbed in their rescue uniforms and tanks. The Montana Utilities truck arrived. A huge spool of cable on a rotating drum filled the back of the big vehicle. Other trucks were moved as the utility vehicle backed up to the vent opening. The reporters, joined by other news media, gathered on one side, filming, hoping for a scoop. Jonathan Kaari stooped and entered the ventilation tunnel.

"Mickey," Gabriel said, "I want your daddy to be alright. You don't need no more pain. I think you've hurt worse than any of us."

Mickey looked at Gabriel. A sincere, empty look filled his eyes and face.

"Thanks," he said. Gabriel nodded and smiled a small smile.

It was past midnight, Monday morning. The snow clouds had disappeared, replaced by barely twinkling stars and high drifting vapor clouds. Steam and mist rose from the workers gathered at the tunnel. Somebody announced that they had found no more bodies at the main mine. They said that the rescue teams had all returned to the surface. The President of the United States had called the Governor and had ordered the Secretary of the Interior to report to Sunnyside to help with the situation and lend his support. Congressman Temple had been called back to Washington, D.C.

Midnight turned into one o'clock. The utility winch unwound slowly for over an hour, until very little cable was left on the spool. Nobody entered or left the vent tunnel. A tired silence fell over the crowd. Many town's people found their way up the Cemetery Hill and waited. For what, they did not know. There was only hope and praying. The lights from the crosses cast shadows across the headstones on the hill above. Those shadows mingled with the shadows of the waiting citizens, creating a black and gray quilt.

Two o'clock came. Lucas' feet were freezing. He was shivering. Looking at the ground, he saw that Gabriel's sneakers, caked with mud, had become frozen. Gabriel was vibrating from the bone chilling air.

Three o'clock. Officer Aimel Merrick joined Lucas, Gabriel and Mickey.

"Ernie and Georgie confessed to giving kickbacks and payoffs to the union. Ernie even said he knew of the Congressman's involvement with Billy. He thinks that Billy was trying to win favor with Temple in order to get some national union office. We found Billy's journal. It didn't say much, but had records of his cash deposits and some notes about Dolly and Temple. Enough though. It'll help," Aimel said.

"But what about Adam?" Lucas said.

"Its hard to prove whether Adam set the fire or not. I mean, I heard him say he did. We might not ever know. We searched his apartment. Lots of drugs. Lots of vulgar snapshots of his many teeny bopper girlfriends. The guy was sick and insane, I think. But there is no proof, so far, that Georgie or Ernie had anything to do with the fire."

Four o'clock. Lucas' mother, Heather and Gabriel's family joined them. Nellie had remained at Heather's, keeping watch over the younger children. Lori was at the hospital with Russell.

A sudden noise emanated from the utility truck. The spool and winch began to retrieve the long extended cable. Lucas looked around at the crowd. During the past two hours, hundreds of people had converged on the mountain. Men, women and children spilled up the hillsides, standing among bushes, trees and grave markers. The cable slowly wound around the spool, moving exhaustingly slow. The generator on the winch sputtered and growled as it took on weight.

Heather stepped between Mickey and Lucas, slipping her gloved hands into each of theirs. She squeezed Lucas' fingers, knowingly, tenderly. He knew she was only comforting Mickey, but loving him. He tightened his grip on her hand, signaling her his returned love.

Five-thirty. The cable spool stopped and the generator engine became silent. An anticipation, already thick, heightened. Lucas' mother held Gabriel's mom. Gabriel clung to his mother's arm. Miner's lamps could be seen bouncing and blinking inside the tunnel. Jonathan Kaari emerged. Camera bulbs flashed, filling the night sky like fireworks. The reporters moved back. The utility truck pulled away from the opening.

Just inside the mouth of the tunnel, a dozen miners walked slowly, inching towards fresh air. Several men, clad in self contained rescuers, emerged. From his vantage point, Lucas could not discern the faces of any of the men. Suddenly the crowd closed in on the opening. Screams and crying erupted. Lucas pulled Heather and Mickey down the slight slope toward the vent mouth. Too many people blocked his view. Lucas pushed, pulled and fought toward the front. Gabriel was beside him, Mickey on the other.

They broke to the front and stood on the periphery of the crowd. On the ground, strapped to a stretcher, lay a large man, covered in rain slickers, attended by medics. It was Freddy Whitehead.

Mickey slung his way through the remaining people and dropped to his knees. Freddy's eyes were closed. Mickey grabbed his father's hand. Lucas watched in pain and sorrow as Mickey began wailing, his eyes closed, face towards heaven. Slowly, Freddy's free hand lifted from the stretcher and touched Mickey's cheek.

The boy opened his eyes, and stared down at his father. Freddy's eyes too were open. He was smiling. Mickey lay across his father's chest, shaking, sputtering in tears. The crowd was crying with him.

Gabriel and Lucas anxiously scanned the men at the portal, looking for Delmer. Together they pressed toward the opening. Three lights remained several feet inside the tunnel. Slowly they moved forward. Jonathan Kaari stepped back into the mountain, disappeared into the dark and joined the lights. Lucas ran his arm around Gabriel's shoulder. Heather found Gabriel's hand and held it to her chest.

First a rescue worker emerged, carrying a handful of lantern batteries. Then another came forward, holding water jugs and lunch pails. The three friends clung to one another. Lucas could feel his breath holding, waiting. Gabriel was shaking, though not from the cold. Lucas saw sweat on his friend's brow. Heather was kissing Gabriel's fingers and pressing his hand to her face.

Jonathan stepped into the glare of the floodlights, his arm around Delmer Cipher. The crowd exploded into a cheer. Raising its collective voice in relief and thanks. Delmer squinted and covered his eyes, protecting them from the harsh glare. He feebly waved with his crooked arm to the gathering that surrounded him.

"Daddy," Gabriel cried, breaking loose from Lucas and Heather's grip. He ran the short distance to his father, slipping in the thick mud, almost falling. Delmer stepped forward into his son's arms. Gabriel scooped him, lifting him from the ground. The cheers became louder and louder. Applause exploded into the chilly morning air. The Cipher family enveloped their loved one, covering him in kisses.

Heather and Lucas held hands again and walked over to Jonathan. Reporters had stopped asking him questions and were focused on Delmer. An ambulance gathered Delmer and Freddy and slowly wound through the crowd, which turned and followed it in its slow procession down the cemetery hill.

Lucas' mother Amanda joined them. Jonathan was weary, worn, dirty. His yellow slicker was torn and brown streaked. Mrs. Kaari kissed him, held him.

Lucas approached his father. Jonathan, seeing him, smiled broadly and drew him into his arms with his mother.

"Russell?" Jonathan asked, hesitating, as if expecting sorrow in this moment of joy.

"He's fine. He's got some broken ribs. A lot of stitches. His lungs are damaged. He'll never be able to work underground again. But he is going to make it," Amanda replied. Jonathan held his family again. Lucas pressed his face to his father's, the stubble of the man's beard grated against his cheek.

"There's one thing, though," Amanda said tentatively, stepping back far enough to see Jonathan's face. She paused, breathing deeply. "He's going to be a father."

Lucas also stepped away from his dad and gave him space and time to react. Jonathan's eyes examined Amanda's, sweeping up and down, side to side. A brilliant smile spread across his father's lips. Mrs. Kaari leaned into her husband, pulling her head to his chest. His father closed his eyes, and lay his cheek on the top of his wife's head.

Lucas turned back to Heather. She was standing in the shadows, a small outline against the backdrop of crosses and diffused floodlights. She looked very small and very alone. Walking to her, he saw that pain was back on her face. The sorrow, the reality had returned.

"I love you," he said as he embraced her, "I love you so very much." The sweet smell of her skin filled his mind. He poured his heart onto her, forced his spirit to try and touch hers. In the shade of the crosses, in the light of love, in the early morning, he kissed her, with passion, devoid of lust.

Heather kissed back, intimately, with the same emotion, freely.

"And, I love you," she said, "I have always loved you."

Seven o'clock. The sky in the east was becoming light. Behind them, one by one, the crosses darkened. They walked slowly down the hill, returning to Sunnyside. A new day had dawned.

CHAPTER 44

Late May 1975 – Sunnyside, Montana

Lucas' bedroom seemed so small, when once it was a universe to him. A place of toy soldier battlefields, space ship rides, Indian attacks. His dreams were born here, his desires and passions emerged from his heart when he read under the blankets with a flashlight. The tears his mother shed as she sat on the edge of his bed with him, were not so much of sorrow, but of joy. The joy that her youngest son was stepping out, starting his own life, finding his own way. Bittersweet, she had called them. She said she didn't want to surrender her baby, not quite yet, to the world. But she told him she had to let him go. They had cried together, joined by his father.

Still, a new baby was due any day now. Russell and Lori, wed last Christmas Day, lived in the basement, and were planning their own life away from Sunnyside. The College of Education had accepted Russell for the fall semester. He wanted to become a coach. He would be leaving then, taking his new little family with him.

Lucas had watched his mother pack his clothes, carefully folding each shirt, holding some to her nose, breathing deeply, then tucking them into his suitcase. He would miss her, miss all of them. His promises to return for vacations and holidays were empty lies, yet he championed them, being the dutiful son. But he did not want to come back to Sunnyside. Ever. Since the fire, his association with the town, the valley, the people, was only feigned happiness. He had seen all the darkness he wanted to see. Experienced all the suffering, confusion, frustration, and emptiness he could handle. At least for now. He wanted to purge this life from his heart, cherish only the good memories of Heather, Russell and Gabriel.

The Bull Run Mining Company had survived, only recently rekindling the smelter and quietly tainting the air. Workers were working again. The cold pall of the fall and winter had driven the community depression even deeper. There was very little joy.

The school year had been a robotic walk of classes and recitations. Last week's graduation was a non-event, except for Heather's valedictorian speech, which ended in a standing ovation.

Nobody talked much about the deaths or their hurt. Some families had moved on. Others, without income, had weathered the year, dependent on charity and the government. Ernie and Georgie were in prison. Aimel was the new sheriff, the youngest ever in Montana history as far as anybody could recall. The Honorable Congressman Temple was under criminal investigation.

Sunnyside was sinking into the past. It was becoming a memory. The old hates had disappeared, replaced by a shared sorrow. Death had made all men equal. Equal for the first time in a century.

The press had been kind to the community and especially to Lucas. Raising an awareness of the problems, the pollution, the greed and the emotional filth. Lucas could feel the change coming a little at a time. The town of his boyhood wouldn't be here much longer, he supposed. Even his father had talked of retiring early and moving.

Gabriel and Lucas had received accolades for their daring and involvement in the traumatic events. Millions of people had seen the news footage of Gabriel's hymn at the mine portal. Letters had come from around the world, praising him for his faith. A Christian record company had even approached Gabriel about doing some work with them. He left yesterday for Nashville. That was a little dream that was becoming a big reality for his friend.

The Cipher family was moving to the Dakotas. Delmer had a job as a safety inspector in a non union mine. Lucas didn't see much of Gabriel, except during school classes. The boy had changed. His looks, demeanor, confidence had all sharpened. They didn't drift apart as much as they drew closer to their families. Lucas couldn't remember anybody calling him Scabby anymore.

Mickey had quit school at the beginning of the new year and was working on the surface crew at the mine. They had shared a pizza one night at Papa's not too long ago, but never spoke about their past or Mickey's secret. Freddy still punched him around, he had told Lucas.

The Bull Run Mining Company had given Lucas a full ride college scholarship to any university of his choice. Nellie Montgomery had matched it, provided he attend the same school her husband had graduated from in Georgia. He accepted her challenge and was moving to the southeast at the end of summer to study English. He had spent the day with her, yesterday, planting bulbs in her gardens. She gave him a bouquet of dried flowers when he left.

Lucas carried his last bags down the steps and out the basement door of the house. He secured the rest of his belonging into the back of his pickup truck. A local dealership had offered him a new car, but he had turned it down, asking that the money be given to the children of the deceased miners.

Lucas looked at his house. His mother and father were framed in an upstairs window, waving to him. This was home, regardless of all.

Glancing toward the McKenzie house, his heart fluttered momentarily, anxious about Heather, hurting for her father.

This Memorial Day weekend, the first true weekend of summer, was brilliantly bathed in sunlight. The sky, dazzling blue, hurt his eyes. He needed to be in Yellowstone Park by Wednesday to start his summer job. The Interior Department had arranged it for him. He was going to be a tour guide and host. He had one final stop to make before he left the valley, before he put this chapter of life behind him.

The State of Montana had erected a tribute, on the edge of town, to the miners that had died that fall afternoon in The Bull Run fire. A bronze miner, lunch pail in hand, walking with his children, an eternal light positioned in his hard hat, stood over a granite ledger. The names of the dead, chiseled, like the letters on a tombstone, pronounced a lasting memory to those that had given their most precious gift.

Heather was waiting for him at the statue. As he pulled his pickup to a stop, he saw the soft touch of the sun mix with her auburn hair, highlighting it. She glowed. A halo radiated around her. She was reading the names, etching letters with a delicate finger.

She turned and smiled at him. Her legs were already tan from working in her yard. There was a naturalness to her, a wholesome spirituality. He watched as she glided towards him. He had loved her through the worst part this winter, through the dark wrenching pain of her loss. Not only the loss of her father, but the finality of her childhood, the ceased dreams, the unfulfilled wishes.

They could have easily become lovers. She wanted the assurance, the intimacy, and said as much. So did he. But he felt the draw of her body stronger than the draw of her heart. Yielding to her would only hurt her further. He knew he had to leave Sunnyside. He had to leave her. His life, his future, was far beyond these beautiful mountains, still laden with snowy peaks. She would have consumed him, not of her own maliciousness or wants, but because of his absolute need of her. All that he craved, all that he desired, in a woman, in a relationship, fell to her. If it was love, true love, between them, then tainting it too early could destroy them both.

He kissed her and cried his good-byes. With every fiber of his soul he wanted to stay. To cherish her, to marry her, to hold their babies and live forever in her arms. But he needed to find who and what he really was.

"Come with me," he had begged. "My mother and father can help with your brother and sister. Come with me, please." He had asked this many times of her. She said she wanted to leave, to be free, but held back, keeping the promise to her mother to raise her siblings.

"But I can't," she would say. "I'll wait. Come back to me someday. Time should only make this love stronger."

Holding her this last time in the light of a beautiful fresh spring afternoon, he felt incomplete. No words could clarify his feelings for her. Heather kissed him again and again, wetting his cheeks with her tears. He finally released her, brushing his own tears from his eyes.

The steps to his truck were heavy. This was the end. His childhood would stop the moment he turned the key and left her standing alone. But he persevered.

Sitting in his truck, he looked in the rearview mirror one last time at the little girl from next door. Her head was hung forward, hair cascading enough to hide her face and shaking shoulders. In her hands she held a familiar letter and envelope. She raised her eyes and looked towards him. Peace was on her, glistening in her eyes. He slowly released the clutch and drove away, moving toward tomorrow and a new life.

Lucas stopped a mile down the road. His sobbing, uncontrollable, impaired his driving. Climbing from his truck, he looked back again at his hometown. The trio of silent white crosses, reflecting the light from above, stood as silent centurions over the city and the dead. Their long shadows, touching the fresh graves collected about them.

The darkness of the winter had been invaded slowly by the emerging spring. Snow and cold held on long into late April. The freshness that claims the Montana mountains stayed hidden, clenched beneath a cap of sooty ice. May melted into green buds and swollen rivers. The sun, championed by the western breezes, pushed the acrid cloud away from the valley and burned brightness into the lives shattered by the darkness of death and life.

Lucas felt he was seeing the sun for the first time. The radiance illuminated him. For a moment he felt eternal, lifted beyond himself into a newness he had never touched. He was free, free of the guilt that hampered his childhood and pushed him inward, making him a shaded waif fearful of shadows. Its power loosened him from the bondage of his youth, the insecurities of his destiny, the devastation of his broken heart and the isolation from a troubled world.

Lucas staggered momentarily in the light. His chest was seized for an instant by a joy that he would go beyond this place and time. An awareness and energy filtered through his blood and his mind. Life had changed, not just for him, but for a community. Yet this place and time marked itself eternally upon each essence of family. Radical as death is, life seems to always emerge from its maw. Those tainted by tragic absence are left to grow beyond their ruin and seemingly mortal soul wounds into new creatures. The sun exposes darkness and claims those things it helped create.

He suddenly felt calm, relieved. A warmth spread through his heart, his mind, his soul. His spirit was released. Into the fresh mountain air he soared, rising above the pain, the sorrow, the loss.

Looking at the center cross prominent and proud, he knew that no matter the darkness, no matter the sin, no matter the hatred fostered by men, despite the efforts of the selfish, despite death, despite corruption, one element is certain, one thing is instrumental. Darkness is ferreted out by light. Goodness will always overcome evil.

We are born of the light. Changed by it. Saved by it. In this life, in this world, it takes only simple faith and an understanding of one truth – there is no place in heaven or on earth, in spirit or in flesh, where the sun won't shine.

Scott R. Baillie

About the Author:

While still in his teens, Scott R. Baillie worked underground in some of the most dangerous mines in Idaho. His experiences as a hard rock miner shaped who he was and who he became. Before his twenty-first birthday he'd promoted stadium rock concerts for the biggest bands in the country. By his thirties his insights into business and technology placed him in the middle of the Internet revolution, influencing the very heart of companies redefining the world of commerce. Today, as a writer and producer, he continues to rely on and write about the lessons, values and wisdom drawn from his life in a mining town. He is currently working on his third novel, producing a television series and writing a screenplay based on the struggles of Chinese laborers in the Idaho mining camps of the late 1800s. Scott and his wife Kathleen live in the Seattle suburbs with their five cats.

For more on Scott and his writing, visit www.scottbaillie.com.

CPSIA information can be obtained at www.ICGtesting.com
Printed in the USA
BVOW07s2320270814

364532BV00001B/53/A